BOSS I LOVE TO HATE

MIA KAYLA

MAM BOOKS LLC

Copyright © 2019 by Mia Kayla
All rights reserved.

Visit my website at http://www.authormiakayla.com
Cover Designer: Jersey Girl Designs,
http://www.jerseygirl-designs.com
Editor: Jovana Shirley, Unforeseen Editing, www.unforeseenediting.com
Proofreader: Mitzi Carroll
http://www.facebook.com/MitziCarrollEditor

No part of this book may be reproduced or transmitted in any form or by any means, electronic or mechanical, including photocopying, recording, or by any information storage and retrieval system without the written permission of the author, except for the use of brief quotations in a book review.

This book is a work of fiction. Names, characters, places, and incidents either are products of the author's imagination or are used fictitiously. Any resemblance to actual persons, living or dead, events, or locales is entirely coincidental.
ISBN-13: 978-0-9996757-3-1

 Created with Vellum

*To my Daddy, whose birthday is today.
"A father holds his daughter's hand for a short while, but he holds her heart forever." – Unknown*

CHAPTER 1

SONIA

"Her boobs can't possibly be real."

My best friend, Ava, always tried to make me feel better. Too bad I knew she was lying. Lying through her teeth.

With my forefinger, I pushed my glasses farther up my nose and leaned closer to the computer screen, so close that I nearly went cross-eyed. The scent of coffee hit me directly in the nostrils. The sound of paper spat out of the printer. The chatter of my coworkers rang loudly behind me. But I ignored it all and concentrated on my computer screen—her—my replacement. Jeff's replacement for me.

"She's not that pretty," Ava continued.

I scrolled through my ex-boyfriend's Facebook feed again, fixated on their endless pictures together, laughing, hugging, smiling, eating. And her ... I couldn't get over her. The replacement was beautiful, her body built like those mannequins at the store, tall and perfectly proportional. Blonde hair. Blue eyes. High cheekbones contoured like those stupid tutorials Ava always watched on YouTube.

"I hate her." Venom dripped from my tone. Not only because she was beautiful, but also because she had him.

Already tired of looking at my computer screen, I leaned back against my chair and straightened my pens, separated by color in their cup-like containers.

"I'm telling you, she's not that ..." She coughed. "But do you think her boobs are real?"

"They can't be." My eyes level with the screen. "Who has a perfect face, body, and boobs, too?"

Why must life be so unfair?

"Sonia!"

I jerked back at the sound of my boss's voice and knocked over my coffee in the process, causing me to jump back and drop the phone. "Damn it!"

Liquid spilled everywhere—on the desk, on my keyboard, on my skirt.

Fisting a handful of Kleenex from my tissue box, I cleaned up my desk. The light-brown liquid soaked the tissues. I grabbed more, repeated the process, patted my damp skirt down, and glared at his office door.

I had ordered his breakfast, picked up his dry cleaning, and gone over his schedule for today. *What the hell did he want now? Couldn't I get some peace for five freaking minutes?*

I reached for the phone dangling off my desk and placed it to my ear. "Gotta go, Ava. The crass hole is beckoning."

She sighed overly loud. "Tall, dark, and oh-so fine. Give my love to your BILF."

Boss I'd Like to—yeah, right.

How about Boss I'd Like to Kill?

"I'll tell the BILK you said hello. Bye." I reached for my iPad, adjusted my glasses, and skittered to his office, my two-inch turquoise Mary Janes clicking against the black marble floor. After I pulled down my plaid knee-length skirt, I entered his fishbowl office.

Floor-to-ceiling windows outlined every single wall. His eyes focused on the screen in front of him, his backdrop was worthy of a picture frame—the Chicago skyline.

Brad Sebastian Brisken had the face of a Hollywood heartthrob, the jawline of a *GQ* model, and the body of someone who lived at the gym all the time. His suit was always perfectly pressed, and the lines in his sleek slacks always hugged his firm thighs. There was never a dark strand of hair out of place. He looked like a Greek god—tall, fit, and fine.

"Took you long enough."

"Sorry, was on the phone with my mom." *Jerkface.* I didn't sound sorry.

And this was how our two-year working relationship had been going. Him being a jerk, me snapping back or blatantly not caring.

Who cared if Brad was a millionaire? Who cared that he was seriously one good-looking, fine specimen of a man with his chestnut hair and dark brown eyes? Every woman fawned over him. Every male wanted to be him.

Me? Sometimes, he drove me to the point of insanity where I wanted to wrap my arms around his neck and choke hold him, WWE-style, until he turned blue.

After working for him for over two years, there was one thing I had come to realize: good looks and all the money in the world did not make up for his jerk-like attitude.

He motioned to the chair in front of his desk, and I sat down. And, as I swiped at my iPad, his phone rang.

"Hey, Jimmy." He leaned back on his chair, resting his ankle on the opposite knee, and with a flick of his hand, he waved me off as though I were a fly on his shoulder.

I stood, about-faced, and was almost to my desk when he called out to me as though he had a permanent megaphone attached to his mouth, "Sonia!"

I pivoted and walked back into his office. When I sat down, his phone rang. He picked it up, and with a flick of his hand, he waved me off—*again*.

"Yeah, yeah. But did you get the tickets?" His boisterous laughter grated on my nerves. He swiveled in his chair and faced his floor-to-ceiling windows, his back toward me.

This guy!

I glared at him, stomped back to my desk, and was about to sit down when he called out again.

For the love of all that is holy.

My eyes fell shut, and I inhaled deeply. I took out my essential oils and rubbed one at my temples and my wrists. Lavender was supposed to alleviate stress, and I debated on dumping the whole bottle on myself to speed up the process.

Breathe. Or go postal and lose your job.

I counted backwards and walked into his office at a normal pace, purposely taking my time.

"Did you spill coffee on yourself?" He lifted a perfect eyebrow and eyed the brown stain on the front of my skirt. "That's a first."

Of course, it was a freaking first. I prided myself on being organized and neat, and I was—before stalking Jeff and his new girlfriend. Seeing them together and being so in love had officially screwed with my head.

Brad's head ducked back to his computer screen where he tapped away. "Dry cleaning is on the couch. Where're my other clothes?"

I peered over at the far corner of the room where a pile

of pants, suit jackets, and shirts were stuffed into an overflowing bag.

"Last week's dry cleaning is in your closet." That was the first thing I had told him when I saw him this morning.

Maybe I needed to slip him some of that earwax solution, leave it on his desk with a little courtesy note.

"I've also made reservations at Alessi's Restaurant for your date tonight."

He lifted his head from the screen. "I said Carlucci."

"You said Alessi." My eyes widened, and I double-blinked. I'd chased this reservation down for the past few weeks and called every day to check if there was a cancellation. I'd finally snagged a reservation yesterday. *Is this man serious?*

"I'm pretty sure I didn't."

This coming from the guy who couldn't read his schedule. Despite that I kept it organized, yesterday, he had met with the wrong Mr. Wilson.

Boss, really quick, can I borrow your desk because it's closer than mine so I can bang my head against it?

"Did you book the hotel?"

"Yes." I clenched my teeth in a tight smile and ground my molars. "I also ordered flowers, and they will be delivered to your table."

I'd basically set the plans for him to get laid tonight. Who knew what poor soul he had his sights on?

I had tried to warn off the countless interns and account officers who walked through Brisken Printing Corporation, but they still wanted him. Brad threw them one look, and they were all a forgone without-a-job conclusion.

Because canoodling between the sheets with the boss could turn the most professional women into the jealous and crazy stalker types, which usually ended up with them quitting and heading to the back of the unemployment line.

"What kind of flowers did you buy?" He leaned back on his chair and steepled his fingers by his lips.

"Roses, the kind I always order."

"I want to change it up this time. Order me some peenees."

My brow wrinkled, and I leaned in, clutching the iPad against my chest. "What?"

"Peenees. Remember, I told you about them the other day. The front desk had an arrangement of peenees."

My boss loved to hear himself talk, and I was on the receiving end of that one-way dialogue, but I filtered out all things not work-related, and that didn't require my attention.

What the hell is he even saying?

"What kind of flowers?"

"*Peenees*," he drawled out the word as though elongating the E would make me understand him. He sounded like he was saying penises.

Why will I have to order that? Isn't she going to get that later?

He almost looked annoyed, so I made him repeat it again.

"Sorry, what was that again?"

I bit my lip and schooled my features. If he was going to make my life hell, I could at least have a little laugh of my own.

"Peenees." His voice was softer this time as though he were unsure. "Oh, for shit's sake, come here."

He began typing on his keyboard, and when I approached behind his desk, I expected to see a bunch of penises on his screen, but he typed *peenees* flowers in his search engine, and peonies came up.

Like a smart-ass, I pointed to the screen. "There's an O there. It's pronounced as pee-O-nees."

He visibly frowned. "Real funny," he deadpanned. "Do I look like a florist to you? Just add those flowers to the order."

"Okay, will do." I smirked, stepping around his desk.

He waved a hand, dismissing me. "Thanks. Wish me luck tonight."

Brad didn't need luck. He'd get laid, and he'd lose interest. It was his MO. And I'd hear about it all the next day because he was a sharer—but only to me, it seemed.

"Make sure you pick up my lunch at Klypso," he added.

"Already ordered. Is that it?" I lifted an eyebrow.

The sounds of him typing on his keyboard echoed through the room.

"Yeah." He didn't even lift his head from the computer.

He was in fine form today. I tried not to roll my eyes as I slowly shut the door and made my way back to my desk.

This is just a job, I reminded myself.

Charles—his brother, the CEO of Brisken Printing Corp.—and Mason—his younger brother and the VP of finance—had hired me over two years prior. They had interviewed me, and I had been told that the job had two main functions. One: keep Brad's schedule organized and on track. And two: do not sleep with him. It was two requirements that I had to adhere to.

Before me, Brad had gone through six secretaries within six-months. But his inability to keep it professional and their inability to say no were affecting their work, and his schedule was disorganized. It didn't help that some of those secretaries had gone on a warpath when Brad decided to move on. And he always moved on.

He changed women like he changed the channel—quick and wanting to know if there was something better.

I had been in a serious relationship with Jeff, so that number two rule was a no-brainer. It would not happen. Following rules was built into my DNA, and organization was one of my strong points.

And, although super fine, Brad was not my type.

I was kinda geeky. I embraced the romantic nerd in me. I loved playing Pokémon Go, I read a dangerous amount of romance novels, and I was the biggest Harry Potter Head.

I couldn't exactly picture Brad watching a marathon of everything on the Hallmark Channel or all seven Harry Potter flicks.

Brad tended to like the girls with the A, B, Cs—ass, boobs, and curves.

And I was five-two, petite, and flat-chested with dark brown hair and glasses because I couldn't function without them.

It was a match made in secretary-boss heaven. Purely platonic.

No secretary in the whole Chicagoland area made as much as I did. Seriously. I was overpaid but under-laid, which was fine by me. And it was worth it. My friends who had full-time jobs worked a part-time job to make ends meet. Me? I had a one-bedroom condo in walking distance from work in downtown Chicago, and I could only afford it because of my job. Every year, I got a substantial raise and a bonus. It was as if they were increasing my pay exponentially every year I continued to keep my legs closed.

The Brisken brothers paid their employees well, and keeping my panties on meant it would stay like that.

Brad

Maybe Charles was right. I was already tired of the dating game.

Looking at myself in the hotel bathroom mirror, I ran one hand through the top of my dark hair and let out a tired sigh. Tired dark brown eyes stared back at me.

My younger brother, Mason, was in a five-year-long relationship with the epitome of a gold-digging she-devil. When I thought of their relationship, it only confirmed what I never wanted in one of my own.

But my older brother lived in romantic bliss with his second wife, reminding me again how a good relationship should be. Seeing Charles and Becky together changed my mind about relationships.

I wanted what they had and what my parents had—a real relationship with someone I could connect with.

"Come back to bed, baby," Olivia cooed when I stepped from the bathroom. Her tone increased in pitch, the way women tried to sound cute but weren't.

I toweled off my wet hair and body, slipped on my black pants, and worked to button my shirt. I stared at her long and hard, trying to force a connection between us, but it simply wasn't there. "I'm sorry. I have to go. Early morning meeting."

She'd seemed prettier earlier, but maybe that was because I'd been drinking.

That wasn't true. I hadn't had too much to drink. I had purposely remembered to pace myself.

I averted my gaze, disappointment seeping deep into my skin. I had known this night would come. I was hoping it wouldn't, but it had with the previous girls I dated. Like clockwork, after sex, I lost interest. Not because the sex was bad. It was good, as all orgasms were, but that closeness I had been hoping for—that familiarity—wasn't there.

This was our sixth date. I'd thought dragging it on would be sweeter, and we'd have more of a connection, but I guessed not.

It wasn't only Olivia's red hair and deep brown eyes that had caught my attention; it was also her sharp wit and intelligent, investment banker self. Now, her red hair had lost its sparkle, and her brown eyes, which had once seemed endless and deep, were now shallow. I'd spent time getting to know her, wanting to know her, yet something else was missing.

She pulled the sheets to cover her breasts and sat up straighter on the bed. "Are you really doing this right now, Brad?" Her once-strong tone turned whiny.

This was the part I hated, but honesty was better than leading her on.

"I really do have to get to work early." I walked closer to the bed and sat at the edge, finishing off the last button. "You are welcome to stay till the morning. Breakfast will be delivered." I took in her tousled red hair, her once-piercing brown eyes ... but there was nothing. No spark. No sudden urge to kiss her. Only an unbearable itch underneath my skin to get up, leave, and shower again at home.

"You're not going to call me." Her tone was resolute, soft, her high-pitched, trying-to-be-cute voice gone.

This was better than the previous psycho woman who had destroyed the hotel room when I left, but it still sucked.

I sighed resolutely, trying to add some feeling into it. "You're way too good for me, Olivia. I'm too busy, I would never pay you any attention, and I'm an asshole."

All of this was true, but really, she wasn't the right girl

for me. Maybe I was looking for something that didn't exist. My parents had been married thirty-five years, and when my father had met my mother, he said he had known. It was in the way she'd made him laugh. He'd just known that she was it for him. I knew Olivia wasn't it. And the woman before her hadn't been it and the woman before that.

Will I eventually find someone I want to be with? What if it isn't in the cards for me—to have what Charles or my parents had?

My gut clenched at the thought.

She leaned into me and rested her head on my shoulder, and I resisted the urge to cringe.

"But, if you change your mind, you will call me, right?"

"Of course." I forced an even smoothness in my tone, knowing I wouldn't, and I kissed her forehead one last time before standing up to leave. Relief flooded me once I was out of the hotel.

I hopped into my Aston Martin and headed home to the suburbs. I didn't want to sleep alone tonight, not at my condo in the city. That wasn't where I called home anyway.

As I drove and the city lights disappeared behind me, my shoulders slumped. I should've felt energized. Olivia was a freak in the bedroom, but all I felt was fatigue in my bones and an undeniable desire to knock out on my bed. All this work when dating—the wining and dining and the sex—was tiring. I didn't mind the sex, but it seemed as though I were on the hamster wheel of dating. I'd pick a girl, repeat the cycle, and hope that it was different this time, that I'd like a girl long enough to keep her. But finding *her* hasn't happened yet and round and round the cycle I went.

I hated when my brothers were right, and they were; I was already tired of the game.

I waved at the guard at our palatial estate to open the

gates and drove up the winding road to the mansion that my parents had built and expanded over the years.

Thinking of not having them here anymore always sent an ache to my chest, an unbearable tightness in my lungs. It was almost four years ago, and it seemed as though tragedy had hit us one after the other during that time.

Charles's wife, Natalie, had died when giving birth, leaving him to raise two girls by himself. And my parents asked Charles to move in so they could help with their grandchildren. Charles was an absolute wreck during that time, unable to go to work or properly care for the girls. It was one of the hardest times we'd gone through; we were all afraid he wouldn't break out of his depression.

And, just when life had gotten back to normal, a drunk driver had taken my parents' lives. It had gutted us, and we'd never been the same since.

But family was of the utmost importance, so we all tried. Mason and I had moved in to help Charles raise the kids. Though Mason and I had our places in the city, we were sleeping in our Barrington suburban house we'd grown up in because family always came first in the Brisken household.

As I entered our house and stepped into the silence, an agonizing sadness took over me. I took the stairs two at a time and slowly opened Sarah's door. I could see the moonlight shine a light over my niece's small twelve-year-old frame, and I released a soft sigh, knowing she was safe.

Next, I tiptoed into Mary's room. The night-light on the wall illuminated her room in a faint amber glow. The princess decals on her walls smiled down on my sweet niece. I walked closer and took in her petite features, the way she hugged the elephant that I had given to her when she was three, and the way she slept with her mouth slightly ajar. *Damn precious.* I kissed the top of her head and brushed the back of my hand against her cheek.

Dads weren't supposed to play favorites, but no one ever said anything about uncles.

∽

Sonia

I lifted my head from the iPad screen, already seated in front of the BILK's desk.

"Did you get that?" Brad paced the length of his office, talking while I typed, the Chicago skyline his backdrop.

Of course, I'd gotten it. I wasn't an idiot, nor did he speak a foreign language. I typed faster than he spoke and had a typing accuracy of ninety-nine percent. I simply smiled.

Grinding my molars, I gritted out, "No, I didn't. If you can speak a little slower."

I lifted an eyebrow, looking at him as though he were an idiot, and he merely laughed.

If he had woken up on the wrong side of the bed this morning, I had fallen off the bed and woken up under it. I had been up stalking the replacement until midnight last night, and obsessed was an understatement. Now, I was sleepy and cranky, and three cups of coffee were not helping my foul mood.

"There is never a dull moment with you, Sonia." He shook his head, amused. "You're in fine form this morning."

Me? ME!

I smiled often, but it wasn't because I was happy or amused or even slightly entertained. I smiled because, in my head, I was ticking off ways I would secretly torture him if he weren't my boss. *Pull out his nose hairs with tweezers.*

Put itching powder in his dry cleaning. Or spit in his morning coffee, lunch, or afternoon snack. Or better yet, delete all his e-mails and pretend that it was a virus.

And that was why I smiled. It was that or throw this damn iPad against his beautiful face.

I bit my tongue. *Don't say a thing.*

I reminded myself again, *This job is easy and they pay well and I like living on my own and not with my five siblings back at home so I can handle his rude 'tude this morning.*

"Why does it look like you have a bad case of stomach issues?" He smirked, entertained, and I so badly wanted to punch that cocky smile off his face.

"What?" My smile faltered, and I gave him that look, the look that didn't hide a thing, the look that I was irritated beyond the highest mountain, the tallest skyscraper. I wasn't in the mood, so it was especially hard to fake it today. And, after seeing booby girl kissing Jeff on his Facebook feed, I didn't have enough room in my patience jar for any more of Brad's rudeness. "I'm fine."

"Did you get everything?"

"Yes," I snapped.

He accepted my attitude with another smirk.

Asshole.

"All right then, read it back to me."

My hands clutched the iPad harder within my fingertips, so tightly that I could have cracked the screen. I read back his schedule for the day, down to every last detail, knowing that I had captured every word, capitalizing the beginning of every sentence and ending with the right punctuation.

I should transcribe for a living. Given how fast I typed and my accuracy level, I'd rock at that job.

I had written down what was necessary, about Titan Printing company—a business they were looking to acquire—but ignored his regular topics off point, like how the CEO of one of our clients was a pompous ass or how the CFO of the same company was having an affair. Worst yet, he'd had to mention his horrendous date last night, his disappointment in not liking her as much as he'd thought he did. *Honestly, how does that concern me?*

Do men usually gossip this much? I hadn't known him to talk this much to other people, or maybe he was only like this toward me.

The phone buzzed in my side pocket, and when Brad turned toward his floor-to-ceiling windows overlooking the city, I swiped at my screen, reading back the text: **Jeff is invited to the wedding**.

It was Ava.

What?

An intense ringing initiated in my ears.

I blinked, staring at the screen, reading it over and over.

How does that make any sense?

My face scrunched at the cell. Then, I read it four, five, six times, as though reading it multiple times would change the text. Nope. Still the same.

There was only one wedding that she could be talking about. It was the only wedding that Ava and I were in together as readers of passages from the Bible and the only wedding that I had been invited to this year.

My stomach dropped and kept on going. I gripped my center as though I would throw up my breakfast on Brad's black marble office floor.

I quickly typed back: **What? How did you find out?**

I pushed my glasses farther up my nose and peered up at Brad, who continued to babble. For once, I was grateful he liked to hear himself talk.

Because I couldn't wait, I sent another text: **How?**

When Ava didn't respond, I typed another slew of question marks to fill the next line.

Ava: Carrie told me. She's going to tell you herself. But I wanted to tell you first so you wouldn't be surprised.

I shook my head and lifted a hand to the ceiling as if asking the heavens above what was happening.

Ava was the gossip queen of the universe. This time, I was glad that the gossip queen was closer to me than she was to Carrie. *Why would Carrie do that to me?* She knew how brokenhearted I had been for months over our breakup.

Ava kept typing, little dots popping on my phone, and then she stopped. I was waiting for words. Reasons as to why Carrie would betray me.

I held my breath the whole time I was waiting, seconds ticking by. Good gosh, this woman needed to be more direct, even in her texts.

Ava: Tim wanted to invite him. He and Jeff have become good friends.

So? was my response.

I lifted my head to the ceiling, feeling my face brighten with heat that rose from my cheeks to my ears to my hairline. If I were a cartoon character, smoke would be steaming from my scalp.

What happened to girl code? Friendship? I'd known Carrie since college. *Where is the loyalty in choosing to invite Jeff to the wedding instead of taking my feelings into consideration?* I thought Tim was my friend, too. They needed to pick a side, and right now, they had chosen the wrong damn side.

I gripped the phone, feeling it form an indentation within my palm. I wanted to throw it out the window—or better yet, ram it up Replacement's hoo-ha so Jeff would find something extra special when he was up there.

Gah!

Ava: Don't be mad. They're friends, too.

I didn't care. They had only met Jeff through me. This was beyond messed up. Carrie "wore the pants" in that relationship. Nothing got past her. *Why didn't she tell Tim no?* My stomach churned, and I blinked, staring at Ava's last text, thinking of what I needed to do to get out of the wedding.

The buzzing in my ears intensified. Then, the worst possible scenario filtered into my brain.

Wait!

Me: Does he get a plus one???

Waiting.

Waiting.

Waiting.

I bit my pinkie nail, my leg bouncing as I held my breath. The dots on my phone blinked, indicating she was typing, and then she stopped again.

Damn it!

Seconds ticked by.

I glanced up, and Brad was still babbling.

Then, one word popped on my phone that made the world around me stop dead, followed by my heart.

Ava: Yes.

All I could see was the one word on my screen as

though it were a flashing neon light. All I could hear was the pounding in my ears, loud and deafening. All I could feel was the tightness in my chest, making it difficult to breathe.

No. No. No. This is too soon. I wouldn't be able to deal with seeing them together.

"Sonia!"

I dropped my phone, and it fell to the ground in a big clatter.

"Is there something more important on your phone than your job here?"

I heard what Brad said but not really.

He gets a plus-one.

He's bringing my replacement.

Typically, I never cried. I was built like a man. Internally and somewhat externally as well with my lanky, unshapely body. But, this time, I wanted to cry, and it would not happen in front of my boss.

"Sonia?" He took a step toward me.

Immediately, I stood, embarrassed that I had gotten caught on the phone and fuming beyond belief that my friends had betrayed me and, more than that, devastated at the realization that I would see Jeff and his new girlfriend—the Replacement—in almost three weeks, at one of my supposed best friend's weddings.

"Sorry, I need to use the ladies' room." I averted my eyes, taking the iPad with me. Then, I walked stiffly toward the door, not looking back.

CHAPTER 2

BRAD

Meetings went by in a flash, and I had secured two new clients to add to our portfolio. Before I knew it, I was out the door and in my Aston Martin, driving home. Win-win on my part. Like there was any doubt. I was damn good at my job.

Being the VP of acquisition at our printing company, sales and acquisitions were my strong suit. Maybe not numbers, maybe not financials, and not even being tactful in real life, but selling a client on our product or acquiring a new company to merge with ours was where I excelled. It was where I thrived and got my natural high. I could seal the deal and sell practically anything to anybody. I could sell condoms to nuns if I wanted to. Not to be cocky, but it was true.

I left the city skyscrapers behind me, heading home to the suburbs.

The car phone beeped, indicating an incoming call.

"Charles calling," the automated woman on the receiver announced.

"Big brother!" I smiled. "How is the honeymoon going?

And, anyway, what the hell are you doing, calling me from Jamaica?" It was only day four of their almost-month-long honeymoon.

"Hi." Charles's voice was rushed and nervous and nothing like my typical older brother. "I just wanted to check on the girls."

"I'm not home yet. Did you try the house or Annie's or Sarah's cell?"

Sarah, my twelve-year-old niece, had had a cell phone at eight. It was what the cool kids did. Annie was the sitter, the hired no-help.

Charles and Becky didn't want to burden Mason and me, so they'd hired a sitter. The worst sitter. The sitter they'd found via an overpriced and overrated agency. Watching my nieces wasn't a burden. They couldn't be a burden if I wanted to do it. My nieces were my joy outside of work, my vacation in the everyday grind of things.

The babysitter. Did I trust her? Nope. Not when the first thing she'd asked me when she came over to watch the girls was if she could have some friends over. I gave her a look. A look that shut her down fast. I ignored her. It had either been that or fire her before she even started.

"Annie's not picking up. None of them are. I think Sarah's phone is dead." Charles's tone tightened, the wind muffling his voice through the receiver. I could picture him pacing through the sand, the clear blue waters of the ocean his backdrop.

When they'd left, I had guaranteed them everything would be fine and stay under control. My brother deserved some time off, and for fuck's sake, he was a newlywed.

"I'm pulling through the gates right now. Calm down," I told him. "I'll call you when I'm home."

He would have fun on his damn honeymoon if I could

help it. Mason and I'd made a pact to not bother Charles for a single thing regarding the girls, and we'd made Charles promise he would call only once a day if that.

"Don't worry; everything is fine." Then, I hung up, waved to Jerry—our security guard—and drove through our gated community.

The large, grassy area and manicured hedges highlighted the beauty and massiveness of our neighborhood. I drove down the long driveway, which widened into a circle that encompassed Brisken Estate.

The first thing I noticed was that Annie the babysitter's car wasn't in the front. Instead of parking in the garage, I parked right by the steps of the house and hurried to unlock the door.

"Honey, I'm home." I punched in the code to the alarm and stepped into the foyer, my eyes flying to the chandelier above us and to the double winding staircase that led to my nieces' rooms.

Nothing.

No screaming. No laughing. No music. No TV.

Just silence.

Usually, my nieces were bickering or laughing or fighting. But never, ever silent. The babysitter had a schedule, and tonight the schedule meant homework and dinner.

Tiny goose bumps prickled my neck, and unsettling nausea built in my gut.

I plucked my phone from my back pocket, dialing Annie's number, but the call went straight to voice mail.

"Mary? Sarah?" I rushed to the winding staircase, searching for my little people.

My younger brother's car was not in the driveway. I called him, and when he picked up, I was breathless, already running upstairs to their rooms.

"Mason?" I pushed open Sarah's door. Nothing.

"Yeah?"

"You got the girls with you?"

My mind didn't usually go to the worst possible scenarios, but given that the babysitter that Charles and Becky had hired was absolutely inconsiderate and irresponsible, I had no choice. She didn't exactly calm my nerves.

"No! They're not home? Did you try Annie? Sarah's cell? Are they all not answering?"

I stopped in the middle of Mary's room and picked up her Ariel princess doll.

"Brad! What's going on?"

His panicked state was not helping my mood. *Shit. Wrong move.* I shouldn't have called the biggest worrier of the family. He worried about everything—what the girls ate, what they were watching on TV, if they were getting too much computer time, even what they wore. Mason was the type to put our nieces in all organic clothing as though anything else would burn their skin.

Honestly, he was worse than their own father.

"I'll call the school. I'm sure everything is fine." I tried to calm him down but knew nothing would when it came to my anxiety-ridden brother.

"I'm coming home."

And, before I had a chance to tell him that there was no need, the phone went dead.

I descended the stairs two at a time and went straight to the fridge, running my finger down the paper with all the emergency numbers and finding the school's.

I dialed, and it went straight to voice mail, understandable with it being after hours.

The tenseness in my neck reached my temples. There

weren't many things I worried about, but not having any children of my own, my nieces were at the top of that list.

My phone buzzed in my hand. It was Charles, and automatically, I pressed End. I wasn't going to pick up his call until I had his daughters right beside me so he could talk to them himself. I'd promised him that I had this under control. I had never broken a promise, and I wasn't going to start now.

I called Mason again. "I'm heading to the school. No one is picking up."

I was starting to get pissed off. If anything had happened to my nieces, there would be hell to pay. I'd be the devil incarnate himself.

His voice was riddled with worry. "No, I'll head over. Just stay there. I'm already in the car, and I will be at the school in ten minutes."

I had just called him. How fast was he going, ninety miles per hour? From Brisken, he was at least forty minutes from the school.

"You're not going to be any help if you're dead. Slow down."

He huffed like I was ridiculous. "Just call me if you hear anything."

I banged the phone against the counter.

One thing was for sure: I was going to take this babysitter by the tips of her ears and walk her out of my house and out of our lives once I found her.

Thirty minutes later, laughter bubbled through the foyer. Mary's laughter. It was the one and only noise I wanted to hear. Immediately, my whole body went lax as I rushed toward the joyous sound.

"Uncle Brad."

My adorable five-year-old niece, Mary, bum-rushed me,

and I scooped her up in my arms and inhaled deeply, taking in her baby shampoo scent. She was blonde-haired with ringlets that framed her face. Her cheeks were painted in an array of colors—pinks, yellows, and blues. She cuddled against me, and I, VP of Acquisitions, should have cared that she was getting paint on my five-hundred-dollar button-down shirt, but I didn't. This girl owned my heart, one of two in the whole world who did.

Annie sauntered in a moment later, followed by a not-so-happy, moody Sarah stomping behind her. Something was going on with Sarah. Becky, her stepmom, had said it was the beginnings of puberty, and I wanted to stay miles away from that.

"Where did you go?" My stare and my irritable tone were directed toward the babysitter.

"Six Flags Great America!" She smiled as though this were a good thing.

The theme park? Yeah, this girl is fired.

"Great. America," I rolled the words off my tongue like it was a curse word, steady and in movie-like slow motion. I blinked and then stared at her as though she were shit I'd stepped on.

Breathe, Brad.

I didn't even pretend this time. Pretending was long over. I had pretended the first couple of days when I arrived home from work, and they weren't bathed. I had pretended that it was okay for them to be up at eleven when I had a late work function, and it was a school night.

But now? I was done.

Sarah was always the voice of reason, but she didn't help the situation. "I'm the one who said you wouldn't be okay with this. I'm the one who said it's a school night, but

Mary insisted, and every single person does what Mary says!" she yelled, making me reel back.

"I just wanted to go." Mary pouted in my arms.

She blinked her long eyelashes at me, and I touched her button nose.

"See?" Sarah pointed. "This is exactly what I'm saying. No one wants to listen to what I have to say."

Then, she bolted up the stairs, leaving me speechless, wide-eyed, and stunned.

Hormones. Becky said she's going through changes. At twelve though? Isn't that too soon?

"Uncle Brad ... guess what I am. Can you tell from the paint on my face?"

Mary had two dimples, and when she smiled, she looked like an angel. An angel that never got yelled at. I could already feel my whole mood shifting into Mary Land.

I shook my head, needing to rein things in, so I placed Mary on her feet to deal with the help. "You're a princess?"

She pouted again. "No."

"A butterfly," Annie smirked, sipping some of her Starbucks coffee through a straw, one that she probably charged on the credit card that we gave her to use, specifically for the kids.

The door flew open, and Mason stormed in, hands on his hips and breathless. "They're not at the ..." He stopped mid-step, taking the scene in, his eyes landing first on Annie, me, and then Mary. "Brad, I tried calling you, but you weren't picking up."

Mary rushed toward Mason's side, this time charming him. "Look at me!" As though she were flying through our kitchen, she flapped her hands, using them as pretend wings. "Can you guess what I am?"

He knelt beside her and then kissed the top of her head.

"Butterfly." Then, he clutched her against him, closed his eyes, and released a long, heavy sigh for everyone to hear.

Dramatic much? With Mason, always.

His eyes flipped to mine. "Sarah?"

"Upstairs," I said. *And moody*, I thought but didn't add.

He breathed out again. "Okay. Okay." He patted down Mary's hair and kissed her forehead.

"They went to Great America. An hour away." My slightly enraged smile tightened.

His still and stoic features changed. His eyebrows pulled together, and he did one very slow blink. A Mason blink. The blink that said he wasn't a happy uncle.

He stood and then addressed the to-be-fired babysitter. "Hi, Annie."

At least he had manners; I had to give him that.

His gaze moved to my niece, most likely excusing her to yell at the babysitter. "Mary, why don't you get ready for bed? Did you eat dinner?"

"Yes! Cotton candy." Her eyes widened, and she jumped up and down in sugar-induced fashion.

Mason stared at me now and then again with a slow blink and the tilt of his head.

Internally, I laughed. This girl was a goner. Fired. Off on her ass. I'd gladly let him do it because he was the calmer and more professional one. I would have just told her to get out and stalked upstairs to change out of my work clothes.

After Mary galloped upstairs, I walked toward the kitchen island and leaned against it, waiting for a show.

"Annie," Mason began, using his disappointed tone that said *I'm better than you, but I won't make you feel like it*, "didn't you have your phone with you? We tried calling you."

"Oh, you did?" The straw hung at the side of her mouth

as she dug to the bottom of her purse. The annoying slurping sounds of her straw grated on my nerves. "Oh, you did." She reached for her cell, gripping the phone and showing us fifteen missed calls. She smiled and then shrugged. "Sorry." She didn't sound sorry.

Then, the slow blink happened.

I averted my gaze, suppressing the urge to laugh out loud.

"It's important that you have that cell phone accessible at all times. We were worried sick. And the girls can't be going to Great America on a weeknight. They're cranky in the mornings, and they need all the sleep they can get."

I sat on the barstool, texted Charles that everything was okay with the girls, and rested my chin on my hand, elbow on our center island.

Get this over with, Mason. Fire her ass already.

He continued, "What happened today is not acceptable." Mason proceeded to spit out statistics, being the numbers guy that he was, about how many people go missing daily and kidnappings, and then he went into the land of homicides.

I leaned in, wishing I had a bag of popcorn. Shit, maybe I could tape this showdown, post it on YouTube, and title it "Repercussions of an Irresponsible Babysitter."

This was going to be good.

"Trips like Great America and activities out of their normal day-to-day school functions have to be approved by us first, okay?"

Wait.

Did he just say okay? *Okay? Not okay.* I shot up in my seat. *What the hell is he waiting for?*

Annie nodded and smiled and continued to slurp her

coffee through her straw. For shit's sake, there was nothing left at the bottom of the cup.

"It's better if we are informed. The girls have a schedule that we have to adhere to." Mason pointed to the schedule on the fridge that he set up for the girls. "Especially during the weekdays."

Where is he going with this?

"Just please be considerate," Mason said.

Be considerate? How about using common sense? How about don't be an idiot?

This was not going as planned. What was Mason's deal? If anything, he was stricter than I was when it came to the girls.

I threw him one irritated look, the annoyance pinching my features. And, when Mason's shake of his head was directed toward me, I was really royally pissed, and it sent me over the edge.

"We were worried sick." My tone was sharp, cutting, like a blade through the skin. I emphasized the word *sick* with such force that Annie flinched. "Their father called, and we couldn't tell him where they were. How would you feel if you were in that situation? Not knowing where your own kids were, not knowing if they were safe, and being out of the country and feeling helpless to do anything about it," I slowly spat out. Maybe, by speaking slower, she'd understand me better.

Her calm demeanor faded quickly when I stepped closer, needing her to hear those two words that would end her employment.

"It won't happen again." Her voice was soft and repentant, but ask me if I cared.

I didn't. For some reason, I didn't believe her because

she was irresponsible, and you couldn't trust the irresponsible, not when it came to little lives.

"Damn straight it won't because you're—"

"You need to go home now," Mason cut me off. "Be here bright and early tomorrow morning." He framed her shoulders and pushed her toward the door.

What. The. Fuck?

He'd cut me off before I gave her an *Apprentice* exit, Trump-style.

I stared at his retreating, backstabbing back long and hard as he ushered the idiot out of our house, my nostrils flaring. I wanted to kill him. *Damn him.* I undid my tie and stormed to the fridge, reached in for a beer, and popped it open with my teeth, talented like that.

"Brad ..."

"Don't fucking *Brad* me when you let that girl off so damn easy. If you didn't have the guts to fire her, I would have. I was going to until you cut me off." I chugged the beer, feeling the cold liquid hit the back of my throat.

"What did you want me to do?" He exhaled a heavy sigh as though this were my fault.

I looked to the ceiling and around the kitchen, and then I opened my arms wide with my beer in one hand. "Hire someone else. Not. That. Hard."

"We can't." His expression was pinched. "I just need until the middle of next week. Don't you remember I'm flying to Ohio this weekend, and I won't be back till Wednesday?"

I lifted an eyebrow as if to say, *So?* I swore. I could speak with facial expressions.

"Becky and Charles will be back at the end of the month. It makes no sense to hire someone new and retrain another babysitter," Mason said. "It took me two weeks to feel comfortable with Annie after we trained her on the girls' schedule. If we had to do the same with a new hire, Charles and Becky would be back in town by then."

Felt comfortable? Yeah, right.

During Annie's training period, Mason had followed her to school on the very first day that she drove the girls to make sure that she indeed took the girls to school and wasn't going to sell them to sex traffickers.

"I'll watch them." Better me than that poor excuse of a babysitter.

Mason smirked and followed up with a peal of laughter. "You?"

My eyes searched the area. I looked left, then right, and then to the ceiling for an exaggerated effect as if there were someone else in the room. "Yes, me. Is there anyone else here?"

"No offense ..." Somehow, I knew whatever was going to come out of his mouth would definitely offend me. "You're the fun uncle."

"And? State the obvious, would you? And what the hell is that supposed to mean?" I scratched at my jaw and took my empty beer bottle to the recycling bin. The beer bottle that I had drained. I needed to eat something and cook something for Sarah and Mary because, apparently, they'd only had cotton candy for dinner.

"You can't even take care of yourself. Remember the puppies?" Mason reminded me.

Dickhead. Will he always bring up the puppies? We were ten damn years old. And someone had left the gate open, and because I'd had the puppies last, I had been the one blamed when it clearly wasn't my fault.

Mason strolled to the freezer, plucked out some prepackaged chicken breasts, and threw them in the sink. I guessed he had the same line of thinking, knowing the girls hadn't eaten yet.

"I know I'm a selfish bastard, but when it comes to those girls ..." I didn't have to finish my sentence. Mason knew I would do anything for my nieces.

I guessed he was making chicken strips because he plucked out the breadcrumbs from the pantry. Me, being the cool uncle, got out the ingredients for mac and cheese, one of the few things I knew how to prepare for myself. And let's get real; kids loved mac and cheese.

"She's staying on," Mason argued, using his work tone on me. "And, once I get back from Ohio, I'll be able to watch the girls more closely."

I tried hard not to shove him against the stove. This bastard would be the death of me. When he was in this type of mood, it was like trying to reason with a child.

With the set of his firm jaw, I knew there was no way I would win. He'd beat me down with words, and I would just want to throat-punch him because I couldn't speak as fast as he could.

"Fine," I grumbled. "But she messes up one more time, and she's out."

The smug, small nod of his head had me clenching my fists.

The safety of my nieces was nonnegotiable. "And, if anything happens to them, I'm going to blame you because I wanted her gone. You just remember that." I pointed to him. "It'll be your fault."

When the smile faded from Mason's face, I felt slightly vindicated. I'd won.

CHAPTER 3

SONIA

"I'm not going." I slammed the door to my one-bedroom apartment, holding the phone in my ear and talking to Ava. "It's not happening." I adjusted my glasses on my face and cringed. I didn't want to deal with any of this—my ex, the Replacement, or this stupid wedding.

Jeff had been the love of my life, the one I was supposed to spend the rest of eternity with. Also, the one who had broken my heart. And I was supposed to show up to this wedding and put a smile on my face, pretending to be okay when he was happily in love, and I wasn't? Yeah. Not doing it.

"You kind of have to go. You're in the wedding," Ava reminded me.

"As a reader," I reminded her right back.

Carrie could get another one. I plopped down on my brown leather couch, feeling the softness of the suede-like material under my knees as I curled into myself.

"We're only readers because she has five sisters; otherwise, we'd be in the wedding," Ava added. "We're kind of like her sisters outside of her family."

Sisters, my ass, I thought vehemently.

Carrie was a backstabbing, evil wench. I'd never forgive her for this.

"I don't care." I knew I was acting like a little child. But no one knew heartbreak like I did.

Jeff had ended it over eight months ago, but the wound was still fresh, the hurt very much present in my everyday life. Everything reminded me of him. His scent still lingered in my apartment, and every hand-holding couple reminded me of his absence in my life. Maybe I could fake illness on the day of the wedding or go on a mission trip to Africa or on a mandatory work trip. That would be perfect.

My forearm covered my eyes, and my glasses pressed against my face. Maybe if I could force myself to feel nothing, but everyone knew that it didn't work that way. Because, when I closed my eyes, he was there. His blondish-brown hair, his green-as-emerald eyes. His smile and that dimple in his cheek. And, now, he had *her*. There was no way I could show up, dateless. Might as well paint a red *Loser* sign on my head.

"I-I can't," I rushed out. Because I couldn't. I couldn't possibly pretend that him being with another girl didn't affect me. Why else would I be stalking her on social media?

Apparently, *she* was an ad exec at Mogul Media. Beautiful, blonde, booby. The three Bs that I was not. Maybe she was a bitch, too. That would make me feel better.

I hadn't even known she was Jeff's type. He and I had shared a love of food and Netflix and Harry Potter movies. I was skinny as though I still had to go through puberty and had glasses because I was legally blind without them.

His new girlfriend and I had no similarities. *What did he see in her? Is that why he'd dumped me?*

I flattened my limp brown hair and chucked my nerdy glasses to the side, my insecurities eating at my insides.

"You have to move on, Sonia." Ava's voice was calm and relaxing, but it didn't do anything to the tightness in my chest, the shortness in my breath.

"Easy for you to say." My voice shook with heavy, sullen emotion, an emotion I felt every time I thought of him. "He was it. My heart skipped for him. I didn't walk when I was with him; I skipped. Can you imagine that? Skipping into his arms because you're in love? That's the kind of relationship we had." I choked back tears threatening to escape. I hadn't cried about Jeff in a long time, yet thinking about seeing him in person with another girl gutted me. I could handle hearing that he'd moved on, but seeing him with another girl, holding her hand, kissing her, dancing with her —things that he had done with me—I wouldn't be able to handle that.

"I know it's hard." Ava's voice lowered to a soft and soothing tone, one my mother had used to console me after a failed track meet, a bad grade, a bad breakup. "I've been through heartbreak before. But, eventually, you have to move on. It's been six months."

"Eight," I corrected her, feeling even more pathetic.

I had counted down the days since I last saw him, the days since our breakup conversation. Every day, I thought the ache would lessen. *Time heals all*, they said. But, for me, unfortunately, it hadn't.

"Okay, eight. Which proves my point even more. It's time for you to move on."

I pushed myself off the couch and headed to my fridge. I'd eat my misery away in a pint of Baskin Robbins. The good thing about looking like I still had to go through puberty was that I didn't gain weight, and I could eat whatever I damn well pleased.

"How could Carrie do this? How could she do this to me?" I whined. I tore the ice cream carton open with my teeth. I jammed a spoonful of Jamoca Almond fudge in my mouth. "She's one of my best friends. She couldn't even ask me if it was okay to invite him? I mean, she doesn't even have to ask me because she knows I would have said no."

I stuffed more ice cream in my mouth. Maybe a brain freeze would hit, and I could stop thinking for a minute.

"This is your own fault, you know," Ava said.

"I hate you." I knew Ava was right, but I didn't want to own up to that fact.

"Well, it is. You wanted Jeff to be friends with everyone. You wanted him to get along with everyone. Now, look. After jamming him in our throats for years, he and Tim got close."

I pushed at my temple, finally feeling a brain freeze coming on, but it did nothing to all the thoughts running through my brain.

Why did Ava always have to be my voice of reason?

Then, it hit me. I lifted my head from the carton. "Did they double date? Have Tim and Carrie met the new girl?"

Ice filled my veins. That would be the ultimate betrayal and mean the termination of our friendship.

Ava's silence only confirmed it, and I left the ice cream carton on the kitchen counter to mope again.

"This is grounds for quitting her wedding." I was being absolutely serious now. Dead serious. I didn't care that we were weeks away from her wedding and that we had eight years of friendship behind us.

"Sonia ..." I could hear the pity in her tone. "Don't jump to conclusions. I'm not sure if they double dated."

"Who cares?" I stabbed the spoon into the ice cream. "She's still invited. After all I've done for that little wench. I introduced Carrie to Tim. How could she?" I paced my apartment back and forth and forth and back. It didn't take me that long to get from one side of the room to the other, given it was only seven hundred square feet from end to end. My bedroom wasn't even a room, more like a closet, but it was in downtown Chicago, so I was proud of my closet.

"Sonia, you have to pretend you're okay. For fuck's sake, save face."

I could tell she was losing patience with me.

Once again, I found myself on the couch, facedown this time, like I was dead or dying. Maybe it would be better if I were.

"Listen to me." Her stern, authoritative tone pushed through. "Do you want him to think you are not over him? Do you? Even if you are not, he's moved on. Pretend that you have, too."

I shook my head against the cushions, feeling the microfiber against my cheeks. "Oh, yeah, so easy," I huffed. "So, what do you want me to do? Get the finest guy alive to go with me? Show up to her wedding and pretend he's my boyfriend and that we're madly in love and I've moved on?" The laugh that roared out of me was like one from a rated-R Halloween movie, one that could raise people from the dead.

"Yes."

Her response had me shooting up from the couch.

"Yes? Okay, yeah, right."

She must think I was nuts. No, she was the nuts one. I was merely being sarcastic.

"It's either that or let him know that you're still pining

over him. He broke your heart, and you're going to make him regret it. It's the sweetest type of revenge. Been there. Done that."

I blinked and peered over at my ice cream melting on the counter. Damn it. That was my only pint.

I vacantly stared hard at the now-mushy puddle that was supposed to be my solace. I felt like my life was mush.

Why is life so unfair?

"Are you listening to me?" Ava's voice heightened.

You don't know what you have until it's gone.

"Fine." I sighed, resigned. "Say I even consider this plan. Where do I find the finest guy alive? Tinder?" An evil laugh escaped me.

"Hell if I know. Chris has a beer gut the size of Illinois. I'm a personality type of girl. Good-looking guys? I wouldn't even know where to look."

A slow migraine crept up from my neck to my temples. "I don't know."

I wasn't sure about this. Any of this. There were so many obstacles to overcome.

1. Find a good-looking man.
2. Be secure enough to approach said good-looking man.
3. Propose this absurd arrangement to this stranger because, hell knows, I know no one who was model fine.

Why will a perfectly good-looking stranger even want to do this?

I can buy you dinner.

Like that would work.

Most grown men could buy their own dinner. If not, then I wouldn't want to be taking them as my so-called date. It was weird, picking up a grown-ass man from his mother's home.

"You're doing this," she insisted, pulling out all her positivity. "We can make this happen, so commit to the plan. Now, we have to start looking."

A weariness filled my bones, and the mental fatigue rendered me unresponsive. I was too exhausted to try but even more exhausted to argue.

~

Brad

After dinner, Sarah helped Mason with the dishes while I ushered Mary up the stairs.

"I'm going to get you, you little monster."

She squealed and ran up the stairs on all fours as I pretended to chase her, my fingers curled and outstretched like monster claws.

Five years ago, when Mary and Sarah's mother had passed away, and then our parents, Mason and I had decided we would move in with Charles. Mason and I had made a pact long ago that we'd help Charles raise the girls. Natalie's parents were long gone, and our parents had raised us to know that family meant everything.

From a very young age, the three of us had been groomed by our parents about the business—how to run the company and the ins and outs of the firm—but no one had taught us anything about raising children, most especially girls. But we learned. There was no satisfaction from the day-to-day at work, but soon enough, I'd found out that my joy came from watching my nieces grow up.

Mary was brushing her teeth, and I was enjoying how the toothpaste and foam were getting everywhere—on the sink, on her Barbie pajamas, on the floor.

Mary was meticulous in brushing every tooth, just like

the dentist had told her. I didn't stop her five minutes in because good hygiene was important, after all.

"Did you have a good day at school?" Because I knew she'd had a blast at Great America.

"I ... I ... yeah ... pray ... play." Her words were muffled in the foam, and she had me chuckling.

Her eyes grew saucer-wide, and she giggled, spitting out the toothpaste from her mouth. After she gargled with water, she pointed a tiny finger my way and squinted like I was in big trouble. "Uncle Brad, you did that on purpose!"

I grabbed a towel from the rack, scooped her up in my arms, and dried her off.

"Hey ..."

Her laughter was like endorphins to my soul, and I needed to hear it again and again. It was my personal addiction. So much so that I had a video on my phone of Mary laughing uncontrollably when she had been just over a year, playing peekaboo. Every now and then, I'd watch it on replay just to lift my mood.

"I just want to make sure you're dry." I wiped off her face, rubbed the towel over her dry hair, and back to her face.

"I'm dry. I'm dry." She laughed, the sound muffled behind the towel. She pulled the towel off her head and wrapped her arms around my neck. "You and me and a bedtime story. You can tell me about Elsa and Anna or ..." She bounced in my hold. "How about a story about Grandma and Grandpa or ..." Her tiny fingers tightened around my neck as I walked out of the bathroom and toward her room. "Tell me again about that prince and all these princesses that chased after him because they wanted his crown jewels. I want to hear that story, Uncle Brad. I want to hear that story." She ducked her head and kissed my cheek. "Please, Uncle Brad. Please."

Shit. I really couldn't blame Annie. I would've taken Mary to Great America, too. This girl would've gotten me to buy her the biggest stuffed animal and eat all the cotton candy in the world for dinner just by her look alone. Not one woman had that kind of hold on me. Mary did though.

"Only if you tell me which part of dinner was the best."

"Your mac and cheese." She grinned and rubbed her belly in an exaggerated effect.

She is good. This girl knows how to read and work people. Watch out, men of America.

"Right answer, kiddo." When I reached her pink explosion room, I gently placed her on the ground.

She leaped up and down and jumped into her bed, kicking off its ruffled comforter. "Uncle Brad?"

"Yeah?" Fuck, she was so cute; my heart was melting all over the carpet.

"What's protein? Uncle Mason kept saying that mac and cheese had too much carbs and not enough protein."

I chuckled. "It's nothing you need to worry about right now."

I sat at the edge of the bed and pulled the covers up to her neck. She had the lightest blonde hair, just like her mother, Natalie. I wondered how Charles felt every time he looked at her—a walking reminder of his first love. Sarah, on the other hand, was the spitting image of Charles, but she held her mother's personality, genuine without any pretense with her dark brown hair and eyes.

"But Uncle Mason kept saying I need to eat more protein." She scrunched her nose, the way she did when she was worried about something.

I touched her nose with the tip of my finger, and she

relaxed. "Uncle Mason worries too much." If we were breathing clean air, if the water was pH-balanced, if our organic lotion caused cancer ... everything. "Now, did you want to hear the story about the prince and his crown jewels?"

Her eyes brightened, and I began to tell her my life story. The PG version.

~

Sonia

My fingers tip-tapped against the keyboard, nonstop and relentless, getting this memo done for Brad, but my mind ... my mind was on other things.

Carrie had called me—not once, but four times last night. Ava had probably told her that I knew, and she was trying to make amends. I was too angry to talk to Carrie, remembering how I'd cried for hours on the phone and at her place and in her arms as she tried to comfort me when Jeff and I broke up. How could she possibly do this after everything I'd gone through?

Ava had been right about one thing. When Jeff and I had first met, I had been madly in love. From the third date, I knew—or at least, I thought—we would last forever. And so I did what any girl in love would do. I'd integrated him into every aspect of my social and family life, introducing him to my immediate and big extended Italian family, double-dating with my girlfriends and their boyfriends, kissing up to his family. Wasn't that what couples did when they were madly in love?

"Sonia ..."

The annoying tone of the BILK echoed from his office.

Usually, I had a tolerance for Brad. I'd worked and

slaved for this man for over two years. I knew when to stay away and when to smile and just shut up. I knew what he liked for breakfast and lunch, the type of girls he dated. How he wined and dined and screwed them.

I'd previously found a bra in his office. He had called me from his car phone, seemingly sheepish and embarrassed for once. He'd asked me to throw it out so that the cleaning staff wouldn't see the evidence of his rendezvous.

Yes, he had the nerve. Brad had no shame. It was as though that one incident had broken the barrier, and I was just one of his buds like he was sharing stories with his new best friend. He told me everything now. Really, he liked to hear himself talk.

When that had happened, I had been offended to the max, but the next day, he'd bought me coffee and a box of doughnuts, and ... well, it didn't take a lot to make me happy.

"Sonia!"

I pushed off my desk, exhausted, and grabbed my iPad. I entered his office and slammed the door behind me. "Yes?" My tone was clipped, short, without its usual fake cheeriness.

He lifted his dark brown eyes to mine and tilted his head before speaking, "The meeting at Clarks has been canceled."

"All right." I swiped at my iPad and pressed delete on his ten o'clock. He could have called me on the phone like he usually did. I lifted an expectant eyebrow. "Is that it?" Then, came my smile. The forced smile that seemed like I needed to take a bad crap.

He twisted his pen between two fingers and then tapped it against the desk. The continual tip-tap of the pen against the mahogany wood grated on my nerves. "We're meeting with Thomas at Titan Printing next week."

"Oh."

This was news. There'd been an article on Brad's desk weeks ago that Titan Printing was going bankrupt. They were the biggest printing company that serviced the whole West Coast and also Brisken's biggest competitor.

"Are you really going to buy out the company?" Since we'd crossed that boundary, I felt I could ask him these questions now and then.

"That's the goal. If he wants to save his company and the thousands of jobs that could be lost, Thomas will need to make a decision. And we ..." He pointed to himself. "... are his best bet."

I made note of it on my iPad. "Anything else?"

He stared at me, as though he were studying me, and then he frowned like a little boy and let out a long sigh. It was almost comical.

"My date was horrible, in case you were wondering."

Oh hell, not again. Could this guy get married already, so I didn't have to hear about his god-awful dates?

Not only was I his secretary, his personal assistant, but more recently, I had also become his Dr. Phil. I tried hard not to groan, pleading silently with him to let me be on my way.

"You never said anything about it the other day." My tone was even as I pretended to be concerned.

He paused to examine me, his eyes expectant.

"What do you want me to say?"

My patience for Brad, for today, for my life was shot. Really, I hadn't wanted to know then, and I did not want to know now about his dating life. Listening to him gripe about his sex life was definitely not part of my job description. Though it would be interesting to hear he couldn't get it up.

He shrugged, and then, with a shake of his head, he replied, "You're always saying I'll find the one. *Don't worry. Maybe the next one will be it.* You're good like that. I don't know if you're bullshitting me, but it does make me feel better." His face clouded with an uneasiness that I wasn't used to, and he leaned in as though he were waiting for me to say something.

I blinked once. *Wow.* I guess I never really thought he listened to what I was saying.

That was what normal, sympathetic people were supposed to say when someone was down on their dating luck. Did I believe it? I didn't know. He never had a hard time getting a date, like the rest of us average folk.

"Sit down, will you?" He motioned to the chair in front of him when I kept silent.

I blew out an audible breath that I couldn't hide, and he carefully eyed me. If I didn't have more self-control, I would have stomped my foot, tantrum-style, for good measure.

Could I say no to the boss? Because I really wanted to at that moment.

"It sucks when it doesn't work out. I really liked this one." A long sigh escaped him, and his body went limp against his chair.

"You liked the one before that and the one before that." I tried to keep my face neutral, not sure what he wanted me to say.

"I'm being serious here." He rubbed at his brow and pulled at his necktie, frustration heavy on his features. "I'm not sure what's wrong with me, but every time I have sex with a woman, I lose interest. It's like sex is the kiss of death. It's to the point where I'm afraid to have sex." Then, he let out a small laugh and shook his head. "Well, that's not exactly true."

I rolled my eyes. "Okay, that's way more information than I wanted to hear." I stood, deciding to take the risk and be honest. "It's the chase for you, Brad. You win. You get bored. You move on."

"That's not true. I took my time with Olivia. I was searching for that connection, but something was missing between us." His mouth slackened, and he almost looked offended. "I'm looking for a relationship. I'm relationship material. My parents were married for over thirty-five years. Charles is married, and Mason has been in a long-term relationship. It's in my genes," he insisted, eyebrows raised as though my words had shocked him.

"Are you really now? Or is this what 'normal' people do?" I put normal in quotes. "Maybe you're just the black sheep?" I lifted a shoulder to my ear.

Out of the brothers, I could see that. Charles and Mason were even-keeled and in serious relationships and somewhat normal.

"You're the worst." He tossed the pen on his desk and crossed his arms over his chest, staring at me as though I held all the answers.

"Then, fire me." I knew he wouldn't and couldn't. No one would be able to last in this position long enough. "A minute ago, you said I was the best."

He pointed to the chair in front of his desk. "Sit. We're still talking."

I lifted my head to the ceiling, closed my eyes, and blew out a breath. With all that had been happening recently in my life, I didn't have any room in my brain or emotional bucket to take anything else in. When I rested my eyes on him again, all pretense disappeared. "I'm not your shrink,

Brad. Just take your Xanax, and all will be right in the world." The shitshow that was called my life was hindering my brain-to-mouth filter. I was being way too honest than I usually was.

"Are you okay?" He ran one hand through his dark hair, and his eyes teetered between the computer screen in front of him and the view of something behind me, as though he were uncomfortable to ask the question. "I feel like things have been going on with you lately."

Forget it.

He obviously wasn't letting me leave without getting whatever was off his chest out in the open.

I plopped down on the chair.

If *he* was uncomfortable, I wanted to crawl out of my skin.

I shifted in my seat, looking at him flat-on. "Yeah, why?"

"Well, yesterday ..." He averted his stare. " ... you looked upset. You've been looking that way for some time now."

He'd noticed? Odd.

"And you're usually less mean to me," he noted.

"You like it when I'm mean to you."

"Well ..." He shrank into his seat, looking like a reprimanded child. "Normally, you're funny, but now, you're just rude."

Crap.

That wasn't good. I liked to stay the utmost professional at work. I was careful not to let my personal life bleed into my work life. I guessed I should have tried harder.

I carefully composed my features. "Yes, everything is okay. Fine," I lied. Everything was far from fine. Tick, tick, tick, tock, tock, tock goes the countdown to the wedding.

"Okay. Well, if you need anything ..." His voice trailed

off, and he waved a hand. "Anyway, Kristin just went into labor early this morning ..."

I let out a silent sigh of relief, glad our conversation was off his dating life and my mood swings. "Really?" My spine went stick straight, and a genuine smile surfaced.

Kristin was Mason's secretary. She was sweet like candy and ready to pop.

"That's great." Then, I remembered her due date. "Wait, I thought she had a few more weeks."

"I guess not. But Mason will need some help booking his trip to Ohio this weekend to next week. Could you do that?"

"Of course." I swiped at my iPad and made myself a note. "I have access to his calendar and all of Kristin's files. Consider it done. Is Janice going?"

Brad's face scrunched up.

Whoops, I'd said Brad's bad word, the naughty word, the person he disliked the most—Janice.

"The gold digger," he scoffed. "I hope to God not. It's a work event. I wouldn't doubt it though, given that she likes to tag along on all his trips and spend his money."

I ignored his comment and kept on typing. Let's just say, Brad was not a fan of Mason's girlfriend. Honestly, I wasn't a fan. She did give off that gold digger, *I'm only into designer, but I can't afford it on my own* vibe. But still, it was Mason's choice who he decided to be with. Not mine. Not Brad's.

"Just ask him. I don't even want to broach that subject." Brad ducked his head back into his computer, already done with the Janice conversation.

"All right. Is that it?"

He rubbed at his brow again, one of Brad's many *I'm*

annoyed habits. "Last thing, could you book a double queen at Great Wolf Lodge for this weekend?"

I blinked. "The water park?"

That was a strange place to overnight with a woman pal. And he had a new one already? Maybe he meant Sybaris—that couples hotel with mini swimming pools in each room?

"Yes, the water park. I'm taking my nieces this weekend."

I nodded slowly. *Don't judge a book by its fine-ass cover*.

The smile that crept up my face was automatic. "That's sweet."

"Yeah, I want it to be a surprise."

"It's going to be a good one." I stood, but before I left, he called out my name.

"I'm not a total Scrooge, you know."

I peered back at him and threw him a sideways glance. "I didn't say you were." *Just an unsatisfied, woman-hunting dog.* But I kept my thoughts to myself.

CHAPTER 4

BRAD

The weekend flew by, and I had bonded with Sarah and Mary in a way that I'd never done before. We'd had a fun weekend at the water park. The girls had been fed and clothed and safe, and I had acted like a responsible adult all weekend.

Screw Mason and his *fun uncle* comment.

While he was on his business trip, I'd made sure to text him pictures of us—by the waterslide, eating nachos, pillow fighting.

I hadn't gotten a response, which only meant he was jealous.

Sucker.

"Girls," I yelled from the bottom of the stairs, "are you ready?"

Annie had called to tell me that she couldn't drop off the girls, so I'd told her I'd drop them off this morning. I'd wanted to fire her right then and there, but Mason would have been pissed. It had taken all my energy not to.

"Sarah, Mary, let's get going. You don't want to be late for school."

Mary and her cheery way hopped down each step until she reached the bottom. She dropped her bag, rushed toward me, and gave me her good-morning hug. These good-morning and good-night hugs from Mary never got old.

"Uncle Brad, that was the best weekend ever. Better than Great America, better than that cupcake tour I took with Uncle Mason." She tilted her head, looking thoughtful, and then scrunched up her nose in the cutest way. "But definitely not better than Disney World with Daddy. Sorry, Uncle Brad."

"It's really hard to beat Mickey." I rustled her hair and then nodded toward the kitchen. "Breakfast is ready. Go, peanut. You've gotta get going before you're late to school."

I peered up at the stairs, waiting for Sarah to appear. She'd been in a mood over the weekend. A much better mood than I was used to, but a mood, nonetheless. I hated that she was turning into a teenager—well, pre-teenager. Couldn't we go back to the days when she was sweet and happy all the time?

Hormones were to blame for her transformation. I couldn't deal with women's mood swings on a day-to-day basis, but I'd have to deal with Sarah's. There was no way to avoid it. Any other female and I would have left already.

"Sarah!"

We had fifteen minutes to go before I had to jet out of this house and off to drop them at school first before I went to work. Annie was supposed to take them today but had an errand to run. If Sarah didn't get down here in the next two minutes, we'd be late. I shook my head. Then, I rushed up the stairs two at a time and knocked on her door. I waited a second and then knocked again.

"Sarah? Warning, I'm coming in." I waited a little bit before I turned the doorknob and walked right in.

She was on her bed, clutching a pillow to her chest, her face wet with tears. My stomach sank and kept on going. Instantly, I rushed to her side but then stopped, unsure of what was the matter.

Crap. I didn't do well with crying women, and Sarah was turning into one. Mary was easy. Practically anything I did to cheer her up would work. And it didn't take much—ice cream, a good joke, candy, toys. But Sarah was more complicated.

"Sarah, what's wrong?"

She had always been closer to Mason. We had a good relationship, but it was different. Sarah was an introverted kid. Where Mary was outgoing and rambunctious, just like me, Sarah was just like Mason. She internalized a lot.

"What's wrong? Is it a boy? Do I have to get your dad's guns out?" I joked, attempting to make her laugh. Though, in all seriousness, if it were a boy, I'd kick his ass. That would be an easy fix.

She continued to cry, and that unease turned to a squeezing in my chest. My go-to tactics that would normally work on Mary would not work on Sarah, but I'd have to at least try.

I approached with caution, treading slowly across her plush pink carpet. The pink was the only remnant leftover from childhood. Now, pictures of actors and bands that I didn't really recognize were plastered all over her walls.

I sat at the edge of her bed as she cried into her pillow. She'd been crying about the stupidest things lately, but it didn't break my heart any less. Times like these, I could remember her mother so clearly. She had been kind and beautiful, and Charles had been so in love. Becky had stepped nicely into the motherly role, but I was sure there was nothing like your own mother. Sarah had been old enough to still remember Natalie; she had formed an unbreakable bond with her biological mother. Mary had never met Natalie, but Sarah remembered her mother so vividly at times.

"Sarah ..." My fingers touched the ends of her hair. "If you don't tell me what's wrong, I can't beat up whoever made you cry."

Her head popped up, and she swiped at her eyes with her forearm. "When does Uncle Mason get back?" Her voice was so sullen, so broken.

I understood their bond, but it gutted me that she needed him when I was right here. She had ushered Mason out the door when he left to go to his Ohio business trip and given him the longest, lingering hug as though he were leaving for a three-month trip to Africa. I was never jealous when it came to women, but with my nieces, Mason and I were always vying to be the favorite uncle.

"He'll be back Wednesday, but whatever you have to tell him, you can tell me. I'm your uncle, too."

Her eyebrows scrunched together. Then, with a slow shake of her head, the tears began to fall, and she dropped her head into her pillow again.

We were gonna be late. There was no doubt about it. But there was no way I'd rush her.

I brushed her hair from her face and bent down to kiss her forehead. Whatever she was crying about, I wanted to fix it, slay every one of her dragons.

"Sarah, please just tell me. You can tell me anything." I scooted closer. I wrapped my arm around her and brought her into my chest.

I wasn't sure if I'd be able to handle having kids of my

own. My heart broke enough just from my niece's tears. How would it be if my very own children cried like the world was ending?

"I'm bleeding." Her voice was so soft that I leaned in, straining to hear her.

"What?" I reeled back and searched her face. Then, my eyes scoured her whole body. "Where?" My voice heightened with concern, and I scooted away to get a wider view of her, my hands following my gaze—first, her arms, then her face, and then her shoulders. "Sarah, where?" I almost ran to the door to get the first aid kit. But I had no idea where she was bleeding.

"No ..." Her face turned tomato red. "I got ... I got my period."

I stood there, dumbstruck, mouth agape, and openly stared at her as though she were a wild animal that had grown horns. I blinked—not once, not twice, but three times. Then, I blew out a slow breath. "Okay ..."

She dropped her head into her pillow and began to cry again.

It was a wonder how these kids made me feel so clueless sometimes. I could lead conversations in the boardroom. Close out deals as I was eating a bacon cheeseburger. Handle a hostile takeover. But this ... *this*? I had nothing.

I lifted a finger and then slowly backed up toward the door as though I were trying to escape. My smile was strained, and perspiration formed at my brow.

Sarah tilted her head, waiting for some response from me but I had none.

"One second. I'll be right back." Then, I shut the door behind me.

Sweat coated the back of my neck. I paced up and down

the hall and then decided that I needed Mason's help after all.

I could call Charles and Becky, but Mason and I had made a pact not to bother them during their honeymoon unless it was an absolute *we can't handle it* emergency. This would constitute for a call, but still, I'd try Mason first.

I reached for my phone in my back pocket and leaned against the wall in the hallway. "Pick up. Pick up. Pick up."

When it went straight to voice mail, I left a message. "Mason, call me back. It's an emergency."

Then, I texted him.

Emergency. The girls. Call back. ASAP.

I took deep breaths as though I were hyperventilating. Then, I bent down, hands on my knees, and tried to control my breathing.

I called him again and no answer. Texted again and waited.

Yes, I'd freak him out, but I didn't care. I needed advice and stat.

Every second felt like hours, as I knew that I had my crying niece behind this wall, feeling all alone and helpless.

A few minutes later, my phone rang.

"Hey ..."

I pinched the bridge of my nose and waited to catch my breath.

"What? What happened?" Mason's voice heightened with worry. I pictured him pacing, wearing a hole into our Ohio office floor. "Brad, what the heck is wrong? You said it was the girls. What's going on?"

"Chill. Just relax." Even though I uttered those words, I was far from relaxed. "So ... Sarah ... she ..." My voice trailed off.

"What? What happened with Sarah? I swear to God,

Brad. I was in the middle of a meeting and just stood and left when I got your text. What's going on?"

I sighed and rubbed a heavy hand down my face. Maybe it was wrong to call him because this man was freaking out way more than I was, and I was in pretty bad form.

"She got her period, man. And, honestly, I don't know what to do."

The line went silent. The man who was never silent and always had words when it came to speaking to me suddenly had none.

"Mason? What am I going to do?" I needed help with this one, much as it hurt my pride.

"Give me a second," he mumbled into the line.

I tapped my head against the wall, waiting and waiting and waiting. My niece was still bawling her eyes out, probably weirded out at the way I had left the room, and here I was, waiting.

"What are you doing?" I shot out, patience gone.

"I'm Googling what to do."

I chuckled without humor. Clearly, neither of us had a clue.

Finally, he piped in, "Just tell her it's normal. Says to stay calm. Get her some supplies."

I pushed myself off the wall. "What do you mean?" I grumbled. "What supplies?" I was picturing pencils and paper and erasers and folders, which I knew wasn't right. "I don't want to do this."

He sighed sympathetically. "This is gonna get complicated, brother. I mean, has anybody ever talked to her about tampons, the changes in her body?"

I wanted to stick my fingers in my ears and make loud noises like a little kid. I'd rather do that than deal with this shit. "Don't they teach them this in school? What the hell are they teaching them then? Their tuition is high enough where this shit should have been covered."

"This is usually a big moment for kids her age."

"What does that mean, big moment? How do you even know this? Is that what it says on Google? Have you lived through your period?" I ran a hand through my hair, wanting to pull at the ends. "How the hell do you know?" My frustration was showing through my tone.

"Fine," he said, resigned. "I think we need to call Charles."

"Absolutely not." I paced the hallway next to her door, one hand on my hip, thinking of my next step. This was taking longer than I expected. "We will not call Charles. I told him we would handle this when they were planning their honeymoon. They wanted to take the damn kids on the honeymoon with them, but you and I agreed that was inappropriate, and we wouldn't allow it. And, we said we'd handle it, so we'll handle it. We've got this." I was rambling now and didn't even know what I was saying.

"Fine, I'm calling Janice then, and I'll ask her to come over."

His girlfriend? Yep, that will be a negative.

"Hell no. That's the last person you're calling. Why would you want your girlfriend around our nieces? To teach our girls to be cold-blooded, money-hungry—"

"You're an ass," he snapped. "Fine, you don't want to ask Janice? Deal with it yourself." And then he hung up.

I stared at the phone, blinking. *Well, great. Now what?*

It took me a couple of minutes to collect myself.

I was a grown-ass man. Vice president to the largest intercontinental printing corporation. Nothing scared me. I could handle this. Right?

Somehow, the internal pep talk I was giving myself wasn't working, but I had left Sarah alone for long enough. I pushed through her bedroom door. She was in the same spot. No longer crying, though her eyes were red, and she was still gripping the pillow against her chest like it was a lifeline.

"What did Uncle Mason say?"

She had to know I had called Mason. *Great*.

I cleared my throat. "He said we needed to have a little talk."

Sarah shifted on the bed, looking anywhere but toward my direction. She was uncomfortable with the situation, and that should've made me feel better, but it didn't. I wanted her to feel like she could talk to me about anything, even the stuff I didn't want to talk about. I wanted her to feel like she could trust me.

I tried to recall my early years as a teenage boy, but then I clamped those horny teen memories down. That thought backfired because, now, I wanted to lock Sarah up in a tower, just like that Disney movie I had watched with Mary.

"Do you want me to call your dad?" Because, if she really did want to talk to her dad, she could. This was a major change in a young girl's life, as Mason had said ... or Google, whichever.

"No." She dropped her head, staring at the hands wrapped around her pillow in a tight vise.

"So ..." I cleared my throat, dreading the words about to come out of my mouth. "When a woman hits puberty ... there are changes—"

"We're not talking about this, Uncle Brad." She let out a low laugh. A laugh that eased the tightness in my shoulders. At least she wasn't crying anymore.

"All right." I let out a giant breath. I was about to ask her if she knew what a pad was because we were not taking the tampon route. I was not about to give a tutorial. I wasn't explaining where to stick it in. Nothing was going up there until she was thirty, as far as I was concerned.

"I looked in Becky's room, and she had only one pad left." She peered up at me with confusion and nervousness and all things teenage girls going through hormonal changes had. "Uncle Brad, could you take me to get some pads?"

I cringed inwardly, trying not to let it show. Why was teenage life so hard?

With confidence I didn't have, I placed my hand on her shoulder. "Sure. Get ready. We'll get you some right now."

CHAPTER 5

SONIA

I stared at the time on the bottom left of my computer screen. Brad was late to work, and he was hardly ever late. Something was most definitely wrong. He had a meeting, one that would start via teleconference in fifteen minutes, and I wasn't going to cancel unless I heard from him first.

I was about to pick up the phone and call him when he stormed straight into the room with two girls trailing behind him. If I had to guess, I'd say they were his nieces.

"Sonia. In my office." He stomped to his desk without a glance and left the door open.

Great. He was in a good mood this morning. I never knew what type of Brad I'd get every day—sad-'cause-my-date-sucked Brad, angry-at-the-world Brad, cocky-and-I'm-the-king Brad.

"Have fun at the waterpark, boss?" I strolled into the office and shut the door behind me.

I smiled at the girls. One looked about middle school age, the other preschool or kindergarten. I'd only seen them in pictures on Brad's desk. There were only three photos on his desk. One of his parents, one of him and his brothers, and the other, in the largest frame, of him and his nieces.

"Sonia, this is Sarah and Mary, Charles's kids." His whole demeanor softened, the crease between his eyes disappearing as he introduced them. He was holding the younger girl's hand, Mary, and she smiled, revealing dimples on her cheeks.

"Best. Weekend. Ever," Mary exclaimed, hopping in her spot.

Her eyes were the bluest I'd ever seen. None of the Brisken boys had blue eyes.

The older one's eyes were puffy. As I examined her closer, I realized that she'd been crying. Automatically, my eyes shot to Brad's.

I'd seen him make women cry before and even grown men, but looking at the way he softened when he looked at them, I doubted he was the source of her problems.

I waved toward them, took a Jolly Rancher from my skirt pocket, and handed them each one.

Brad tipped his chin toward me. "Do you carry candy everywhere you go?"

"Yes," I replied, opening the wrapper for Mary when she let go of Brad's hand. "Here you go." I smiled, wondering why they were here with him. *Didn't they have school today?* It was a weekday.

Then, slowly, realization slapped me in the face, first one cheek and then the other, and reality punched me in the nose. There was only one reason he'd bring the girls to the office. My shoulders tightened, the tenseness rising to my neck. I could predict what was going to happen next. He wanted me to babysit.

As cute as the kids were, no. The definition of secretary did not include babysitting.

We had crossed so many boundaries already, and once he had me babysit them, there would be endless errands that would include his nieces. Picking them up from school, taking them to practice, feeding them lunches. I wasn't ready for that.

Brad paced the room, one hand on his hip, the other pinching the bridge of his nose. I recognized this stance, the anxiousness and frustration emanating from him. I'd worked with Brad long enough to know his tics and how he tocked.

"Sonia, I need you to cancel all my morning meetings." He rubbed at his temples and continued to pace the room.

I clenched my teeth together in a forced smile. "Sure."

"No school. No school. No school!" Mary bopped up and down and danced, her blonde curls bouncing side to side. She was like a hopping bunny.

"Are you doing something with the girls this morning?" Because I sure as hell would not be. I had work to do, and it did not include babysitting his nieces.

He shook his head and looked at Sarah, and then his eyes landed on me again. "No, no, I'm the only one here to take care of things. But I'll need to make my afternoon meetings." Then, he began to stare at me in that expectant way, as though he were going to ask me a very important question but wasn't sure how to frame it.

I could read all the thoughts running rampant in his head and also the reluctance in his eyes, knowing that I would reject his request because he knew me so well.

"Plus, Mason is in Ohio, and Charles is on his honeymoon, so that leaves me ..."

Then, he simply stared, opened his mouth, and shut it again.

His eyes flickered to Sarah and me and then to Sarah

again. Mary continued to suck on her candy, taking it out to examine it and then shoving it back in her mouth.

"Hey, I'm gonna be right back. I just need to discuss business with Sonia, but I'll just be outside that door." Then, he smiled the most awkward smile. His teeth were clenched so hard that his cheeks stretched like a woman who'd had too much Botox.

I followed him out his office door and over to my desk.

"We had a situation this morning." Brad lowered his voice as if he were afraid anyone else would hear.

I walked around him to sit in front of my computer and booted up.

He looked at the ceiling, placed his hands on his hips, and took deep breaths. "God help me."

He stood there, praying or whatever he was doing for far too long. To be honest, he was beginning to scare me, but I showed no mercy. Whatever he had to take care of regarding his nieces was his issue. I would handle everything work-related that was within my capacity.

"Sarah got her ..." He circled the air with his pointer fingers. "... this morning." Then, he blinked, taking deep breaths in. "And so, now ..." He tapped my desk twice. "... she needs ..." He widened his eyes as though I'd understand him better if he did. "She needs stuff." He moved his hands in some sort of box-like figure, looking at me as though I understood his weird language.

"Stuff?" I quirked an eyebrow.

"Yes." Weird box-like hand movements happened again. Then, he pointed to his private area. "Stuff."

"Um, a penis?" I smirked.

He obviously did not think my joke was funny.

"No. Women stuff." He nodded slowly as though I was supposed to understand him better.

I nodded, too, mimicking him and biting the inside of my cheek to prevent myself from bursting into laughter. "You mean, pads?"

"Yes!" He lifted his head to the ceiling, his whole body going lax once I'd uttered those words.

I let out a low laugh. "Feminine products," I simply stated.

"Yes. Exactly. So, will you get her the products?"

"No," I snapped, straight up, real, and without argument. I turned to my computer and opened up his schedule for the day.

He reeled back as though the answer shocked him. No one ever said no to Brad, but I had grown thick skin since I was hired here years ago. Except for where it came to Jeff, I guessed. But still, I already picked up his dry cleaning and took his shoes to get polished. I had to draw the line somewhere and feminine products was that line.

"No? No," he repeated as though testing out the word and hearing it for the first time. "That's interesting. I've never, ever heard that word come from a woman before. My nieces, sure, but definitely not a grown woman."

At least he'd looped me in with the big girls.

"I'd like you to reconsider."

His cocky self was back, and I realized I preferred the awkward, nervous Brad. He was less demanding.

I kept my face firm, but neutral. "No. I am not paid to get your niece's feminine products. It's not part of my job description."

He frowned. "I'm pretty sure it is," he countered.

This guy. The nerve. I reached in my desk, opened the drawer, and plucked out my original contract from two years ago. I placed the crumpled piece of paper on the desk, and I pointed to said job description. "Anywhere on here does it say that I am supposed to get your niece's sanitary napkins?"

He peered down at the piece of paper and skimmed. His pointer finger ran down the faded cream paper and then it stopped at the end. He jammed his finger against the sheet for emphasis. "Here. Right here. Run errands. I would classify this as an errand."

"I don't think it would." I faced forward, in front of my computer screen, and began to open Outlook to send an e-mail out. "Okay, so I'll cancel your meetings this morning."

I was just going to pretend that the last twenty minutes hadn't happened. When did it ever stop? Next, he'd ask me to pick up his condoms. Nope, not gonna do it.

"Okay, all meetings canceled." I rechecked my inbox, but he continued to stare at me. Maybe ignoring him would give him a hint.

"Sonia, I'm not kidding. I need you to do this. I *need* you. Please." He was pleading now. Brad never pleaded.

Stay strong.

I peered up from my computer screen. "No. Those are your nieces. So, you do it." I threw him my clenched smile and then dropped my head back to the screen.

I was walking a fine line here.

I blew out a breath and lifted my head. "If I don't do it, are you gonna fire me?"

I tried to show no mercy, but I needed this job. Needed it like he needed me to buy pads. If he said yes, I'd never forgive him, but I'd get the damn pads anyway.

He pinched the bridge of his nose again and closed his eyes, sighing. "Of course not. I can't fire you."

Of course not, jerkwad. Liabilities and legalities and all. I could imagine it now—getting wrongfully fired for *not* buying sanitary napkins.

He leveled me with a stare. "But I would really like you to do this for me since we're ... since we're friends."

I reeled back and barked out a laugh. "Friends?" Snickers escaped my mouth, and I snorted loudly. "You're my boss, not my friend."

"Hey, I'm offended here. We've known each other for a long time. You know practically everything about me."

"Which is exactly why we can't be friends." I bit the inside of my cheek to keep my face steady and pushed the annoyance aside.

"You're being mean again," he said matter-of-factly as though I were mean all the time, which I was certainly not.

It took all my effort not to be sassy, to smile and say, *Yes, boss*.

I softened my tone. "Is there anyone else you can ask? Elizabeth or Riley or ... what's her face who came by the office the other day?" I ticked off the names of some of our interns.

He looked dumbstruck, tilted his head, and assessed me. "No. I can't ask anyone else. I need you. I have no idea about periods and pads and teenage female hormones. I grew up with two brothers. Come on, Sonia." He placed both hands on my desk, his fingers interlaced as though he were praying.

I'd never seen him so desperate. Ever. Even when he'd lost the Cliffton printing deal.

He'd been in the boardroom, so close to winning in acquiring Cliffton from a competitor who was also vying to acquire the company. Brad conceded a little and upped the price the brothers were willing to pay. And, though I had known Brad wanted to buy Cliffton badly, he had done everything short of begging.

Here he was, begging.

"Please. I'll owe you. Anything you want, it's yours." He held my stare with those depthless brown eyes that women fell for.

Then, after remembering how damn beautiful he was, the brightest idea filtered through my head. It was where desperation met desperation in the direst of situations.

Ava's words pushed through. *"We can make this happen, so commit to the plan. Now, we have to start looking."*

There was no way he would go through with it, and to be honest, it wasn't a fair deal. I simply had to buy his niece some pads. He'd have to pretend to be my boyfriend for a whole evening.

"Anything, Sonia. Ask, and it's yours."

And, just like that, I sold my soul to the devil.

I returned his smile anyway because I was beyond saving now. "Fine. But you owe me. Whatever favor I ask you to do, you have to do it. No questions asked. No turning back. You just have to do it." I crossed my fingers—and legs and toes for good measure—hoping and waiting for him to be my savior for this horrendous upcoming wedding. Really good-looking people were not accessible in my life.

The devilish glint in his eye told me what he was thinking. That I was going to ask for some sexual favor. Um, gross. No. I mean, he was gorgeous, but no.

"Sure." The smile was still heavy on his face.

"And I don't mean sex," I clarified quickly. "Pigs could fly and there could be an apocalypse and you would be the last man on earth and I'd still not sleep with you."

He jerked back, and his posture turned rigid as though what I'd said was absurd.

"You're being mean again, Sonia."

I got up from my chair, slipped the bag over my shoulder, and ignored his last sentence. "There's a drugstore down the street. I'll take her." I glanced behind me. "But you're going with me."

He groaned.

"I'm buying them. All you have to do is stand there. What's the big freaking deal?" When he didn't answer right away, I quickly added, "You're going."

My comment did not amuse him.

"Anyway, about your favor, are you gonna ask me now?" he asked, genuinely curious.

"No. But I need your guarantee." Inside, I was fist-pumping, doing pirouettes, flips, and cartwheels. Outside, I gave him a stern look and lifted an expectant eyebrow.

He didn't hesitate. "I promise—or as Mary says, pinkie swear."

For all he knew, I could ask him for money or diamonds, to drive his Aston Martin or to give me half the shares of Brisken Printing Corporation, and he would have to give me that, which only meant this man was serious and also very, very desperate.

"Anything," he promised. "Just get my niece her products, and I will owe you big time."

"Fine."

He was satisfied with that answer.

So, I stuck out my right hand and smiled. "Then, we have a deal, boss man."

He just had no idea I was getting the better end of it.

∼

Sarah inched closer as we entered the drugstore at the corner of Clark and Nelly.

As requested by Brad, I had called their personal driver

to send Mary back to school. Brad had panicked this morning because he'd forgotten that Mary had an event at school that she couldn't miss out on.

Something about the way Sarah sidled up against me made me realize that maybe she wasn't entirely comfortable around Brad. Not like I was surprised. Brad didn't seem like the sentimental type, but I was a complete stranger, and we'd met only moments before.

We both perused the selection of pads.

"There're so many different brands. But they'll function the same way." I lightly tapped her left hand, and she cowered into me, linking her arm through mine.

Sarah wasn't a typical pre-teenager. I should know. I was the oldest of six and had seventeen cousins, ranging from seven to twenty-five, and the majority of those teenagers were hormonal and rambunctious. Sarah was quiet. She'd said five words since we left the office, and it was mostly one-worded answers to Brad's questions. I'd guess she didn't open up to people much. Where most of my teenage cousins were into makeup, skinny jeans, and heels, Sarah was a Converse, boy-jeans kind of girl.

Brad trailed behind me. His hands were shoved in his pockets, and his eyes perused the feminine product aisle, his face devoid of any emotion.

He plucked a few boxes from the shelves and began to read the labels because, of course, he had to know it all. "This one has wings. This one doesn't have wings. What do you prefer, Sonia, wings or without wings? What do you recommend?"

"Neither," I deadpanned. "I prefer tampons."

The color drained from his face, and he cleared his throat. "Um ... I don't think she's ready for that yet." Then, he plucked another box off the shelf. "How about these?

They come with a little packet that you can put your product in. Isn't that nice?" He ended that with a smile.

Sarah's lips pressed together, and her gaze flicked upward. She was not a bit amused.

"Look, these are scented." He gritted his teeth in the most uncomfortable smile.

I laughed under my breath when he lifted the box to his nose and inhaled deeply. I should snap a picture and send it to our company paper, which all the employees received. That'd be comic relief for the day—Brad sniffing a box of pads.

"Uncle Brad, please stop it." Sarah plucked the box from his hands and placed it back on the shelf.

"I'm just trying to help." He picked up another box and began to inspect the label.

Sarah completely ignored him and peered up at me as she bit her bottom lip. "I'll just take whatever you use."

Brad turned toward us, box abandoned, eyes wide. "No. No. No." He shifted with unease. "I don't think Sarah's ready for that. Like I said, we have to wait for Becky to discuss the ..." He pointed to the tampon box as though he was unable to say the word.

So mature.

"You know what? I use these sometimes." I snatched the regular maxi pads off the shelf. "They'll do the job."

Sarah's eyebrows pulled together, her gaze dropping to her black-and-white Converse shoes. "Thank you."

My insides softened a little, and I tucked an escaping strand of hair behind her ear.

I lifted my gaze to Brad, who was still intently studying his niece as though she were a wild animal that no one could tame. And, out of nowhere, Sarah covered her eyes and rushed down the aisle, crying.

"Shit. I just don't understand teenagers. Isn't that what she wanted?" He linked his fingers behind his head and stared at the ceiling. "I have no idea what to do here."

For the first time, Brad looked so helpless that I couldn't help but feel bad for him.

I placed a hand on his forearm and squeezed. "Let me talk to her for a second. Stay here."

I found Sarah in the nail section, studying a bottle of dark pink. She stared blankly at the label, reading it as though it had the secret to all her problems.

I sighed. The teenage years were tough. From feeling like you wanted to crawl out of your skin sometimes and not knowing who you were to the hormonal stages

"I know it sucks, and it's a little uncomfortable to be here with someone you barely know and, worse, your uncle. But at least, he's trying, and hopefully, your mom will come back soon."

"My mom's dead." Her voice was barely above a whisper, and I strained to hear her. "She died, giving birth to Mary."

My heart clenched. *Crap*. I had known that. I'd meant Becky, not her biological mom. Damn it, I should've been more careful. A heaviness settled in the pit of my stomach. I had known Charles's wife had passed, but I hadn't known the cause, but now that I knew, it felt more real—deeper—than hearing it through the grapevine at work.

"I'm sorry about your mom, kiddo. I'm sure you want her to be here instead of talking to me."

"It's not like I don't love Becky ..." Sarah's voice strained, and she dropped her lashes to hide the hurt. "I just miss her." Her lip quivered. "A lot of girls in my class were starting to get theirs already. And they'd say things like, 'My mom took me here, and we had ice cream after I got my period,' or, 'My mom gave me a book, and we went over it together.'"

My heart hurt for her and the sadness in her eyes and the longing in her voice at her loss because there was nothing like a mother. I knew because I had the best one out there.

My mother was my best friend, my confidant. I couldn't imagine my life without her. Thinking about Sarah and how she'd lost her mother at a very young age tore at my insides. I could feel her sorrow, this huge, painful knot inside.

I reached for her clenched hand and squeezed, needing to comfort her. The sadness was heavy in her big brown, innocent eyes, but eventually, her fingers relaxed in mine.

I swallowed the lump in my throat before speaking. "I'm nowhere near a good stand-in, but I know this awesome place that has the best rolled ice cream. What do you say?" I leaned in, tipping my head toward hers.

She nodded, and then, after a beat, she gave my hand a tight squeeze. "You're so much better than Uncle Brad. He just gets really weird about this stuff, and it makes me feel weird because he's weird. Then, everything is weird."

I nodded. Boy, did I know it.

I playfully tugged the end of her hair and then bumped my shoulder against hers. "I know. I've worked with him long enough to know he is just plain weird."

Sarah laughed, which lifted the mood.

I leaned into her, ducking my head to get closer. "And I want to let you know that, from this moment on, we are friends, and you can call me about any question or any thought or about random things. Because I'm a girl, and I have sisters and nieces and cousins, so I understand." I threw her a conspiratorial look. "Don't worry; I won't tell your uncle."

Sarah smiled. Then, she took a step forward, erasing the space between us, and gave me a soul-crushing hug that shocked me. As she relaxed in my arms, I rubbed her back, holding her tighter against me. To be so young yet to have experienced such tragedy made my heart hurt.

When I lifted my head, I noticed we weren't alone. Right behind us, down the aisle, Brad was staring with narrowed eyes. Except he was no longer looking at Sarah. He was looking at me.

~

Brad

"Ice cream?" I peered down at my Rolex. "Not sure we have time for ice cream right now."

We walked out of the drugstore and down the street, back to the office. Both girls had their arms linked and were practically skipping down the sidewalk in front of me. I couldn't help but smile, especially when my day had started so horribly, and now, my Sarah seemed happy, so content.

People dressed in their suits and business attire rushed past us to get to work. Where mostly everyone was carrying their cups of coffee, I was carrying bags of sanitary pads.

The crying fits and hormonal outbreaks seemed to have stopped—for now, at least—and now, I needed to get back to the office and do some real work. Today, I needed to contact my sources about Titan Printing. It would seem as though the deal was off the table, that they were no longer looking for a buyer, even though their bottom line and talks in the industry said they'd be bankrupt within six months. I needed to seal this deal. Titan was on my wish list, and I was eager to acquire them.

"You can pick up a tub of ice cream on the way if that's what you want."

"Does this mean I'm out of school the whole day?" Sarah's eyes brightened. "Because, if I am, I want to walk around downtown or something."

"By yourself?"

She obviously didn't mean by herself. She was twelve.

"Yes, by myself," Sarah sassed.

To be young and think you could fly and do anything you damn well pleased. Nope. Not happening.

"No." I shut her down quick. Just when I thought my day was looking brighter, I sensed Sarah's pouting face beside me, but I ignored it.

I had to get back to work. My morning meetings were canceled, but that didn't mean I could cancel my afternoon meetings as well. Charles and Mason were out of town, which meant that I had to keep the machine running.

"But, Uncle Brad," Sarah whined.

"No," I snapped, stepping through the revolving doors.

Twelve-year-olds thought they could rule the world and that bad guys didn't exist when, in actuality, in every corner, there was a predator. I read the paper every morning, and I watched *Dateline*.

"Most definitely not. You brought your backpack with you. Your homework—you can do that." I tipped my chin in Sonia's direction. "Maybe Sonia and you can go out to lunch while I work."

That seemed to brighten Sarah's mood, and Sonia nodded beside her.

"Of course. Sarah, I'd love to take you out to lunch." She bumped her shoulder against Sarah's like they were suddenly best friends.

I wanted to be jealous of their immediate connection, but I couldn't. It was too nice, seeing a smile on Sarah's face.

"Then, we can get some ice cream." Sonia eyed me with a smirk. "I'll grab the corporate card."

I shook my head as we entered Brisken Printing Corp. and passed by security.

"Hey, Tommy." Sonia waved to the security guard, an older male with salt-and-pepper hair in a navy-blue suit and tie. Then, she proceeded to wave to two more people who passed. "Jenny. Christine." She tipped her chin and greeted other people as we entered the turnstiles, heading to the elevator.

When we entered the elevator, I turned toward her. "Do you know everyone here?"

She rolled her eyes. "No. Just people who've worked here forever. Tommy has been here for twenty-five years."

I frowned. I'd thought his name was Ted. "I know Tommy."

She raised her eyebrows in a challenge. *Why is it that my secretary knows when I'm bullshitting her?*

Her tone was condescending and all-knowing—her typical Sonia tone. "Then, why don't you smile or say hi? Because I guarantee you'll want to know his name when you're in trouble. Sometimes, you have to move out of that bubble world of yours." She turned toward Sarah and smiled. "What kind of food are you into?"

"Tacos," Sarah said.

Whatever. I was close. Tom, Ted. I'd like to think I paid attention to the things that mattered most, not the little details. We had security, and they were well trusted and had worked for us for quite a long time. That was all that mattered, right? Sonia was responsible enough to get them all Christmas presents.

"Did those two girls work for us, too?"

Sonia made a face, visibly irritated. "Yes." Then, she turned to Sarah, and her smile was back on. "I love tacos, too. I know this awesome Mexican place I can take you to."

I scratched at my temple, and my expression pinched because I had never seen those women before. "Which taco place?" I turned my attention back to the conversation.

Her smile disappeared as though I were her off switch. "You wouldn't know it."

I clenched my jaw, annoyed. Just because I hadn't recognized some of my employees didn't mean I was clueless about downtown Chicago. "Try me." I'd worked downtown for years and tried every restaurant there was by myself, on dates, and on client calls. "You're talking about Mario's, right?" This time, I threw a challenging look back at her.

Her smile was smug. "No. You haven't been there."

"Try me," I repeated, hating that this woman was so sure when she was wrong.

"Gomez's Burritos." She watched for my reaction.

Shit. Well, that's a first.

I cleared my throat, pretending like it didn't bother me that she knew something I didn't. "That's down here? Is that a new place?"

"No, not new. It's been down here for years, just like Tommy and Christine and Jenny have been working for you *forrrr-ever,*" she dragged out.

If I didn't need Sonia so much, I'd be tempted to strangle her.

When the elevator opened, she reached for Sarah's hand and ushered her onto our floor. I blew out a breath, letting go of all this annoyance.

When we entered my office, Sonia picked up a pad of

paper and her iPad from my desk and gave Sarah a genuine smile. "I'll pick you up at lunch." Then, her smile slipped—again—as she probed me with a look. "Brad, about that deal. Don't forget about it."

"I won't." I scratched my head, wondering where the hell Gomez's Burritos was. I always wanted to be in the know.

And, about the arrangement I'd made, maybe I should have heard the deal out before I agreed. I was a businessman after all, and agreeing to something without ironing out the details was a bad deal. She could ask me for money or a vacation.

I dropped to my chair and booted up my computer.

I wasn't too worried. I'd known Sonia for two years. She was completely and utterly harmless.

CHAPTER 6

SONIA

My fingers tapped against the keyboard, updating Brad's schedule and ordering supplies for the office. After finishing my morning routine, I dialed Ava's number. I never called during work hours, so she had to know this was an emergency. And this was big, awesome news my best friend needed to hear.

Before she even had a chance to say hello, my excitement exuded over the phone. "Ava, I know who I'm taking to the wedding." Though I hadn't asked him yet, Brad had promised, so I assumed this was a done deal.

This plan was falling perfectly into my lap. Brad was the finest man that I had ever known. He looked like he'd walked out of a *GQ* spread with his dark, tousled hair, broad shoulders, chin chiseled from the Greek gods. My two single guy friends were not up to his caliber in looks, in height, in stature, and I had to bring my gun locked and loaded, pointed directly at my replacement. I didn't want to look like a loser who hadn't had a date since her breakup when, in actuality, I was a loser who hadn't had a date since my breakup—eight long months ago and counting. If the replacement was stunning in her pictures online, I dreaded meeting her in person. But, now, I had ammunition—the BILK.

"Who are you taking?" Her voice heightened with enthusiasm.

I peered up at my computer, looked into his office, and ducked under my desk.

I couldn't hold my excitement any longer. "Your BILF," I sassed.

Wait for it. Wait for it.

I pulled the phone away when she squealed loud enough to bust my eardrum.

She breathed heavily for a couple of seconds before she spoke again. "How did you get him to do that?"

"Are you having hot flashes now?" I laughed. "Anyway, we struck an arrangement."

I went into the details of our arrangement. Ava coughed up her morning joe when I mentioned the sanitary pads.

"This couldn't be more perfect if you tried. I can't believe you told him what you're going to do, and he's okay with it. I mean, buying pads for his niece and being your pretend date for the wedding is not necessarily an even deal."

My gaze dropped to the ground, noting the coffee stain on the carpet from over a year ago. "Well ... I haven't exactly told him yet."

So what though? Brad was a pompous ass, a womanizer, but a man of his word in business.

"You haven't told him yet?" She paused. "Well then, you have to have a backup plan."

There was no backup plan. Brad had to come with me. I

couldn't come with a dud. *Maybe I could hire someone?* But I didn't have that kind of cash.

"He'll agree to it." But, as those words slipped out of my mouth, there was no certainty in my voice.

Would he? This wasn't your typical boardroom deal, but he'd promised me.

Sarah rushed out of Brad's office. "Uncle Brad wants to go with us to lunch. Can you please tell him no? He's being so annoying today." Her eyes skittered behind her, her voice frantic.

I smiled at her and then told Ava I'd call her back.

"I can't. He's my boss." I dropped the phone back into the receiver.

"He's having the worst possible conversation with me right now. Like, how I'm turning into a woman now." She grimaced. "And I know he's reading a script because he's staring at his computer screen the whole time as he does it and pauses to ask me if I have questions."

I cringed, knowing how uncomfortable she must feel, but I had to give him some credit. At least he was trying.

Then, sympathy kicked in. My mother had gone through the motions with me, read me all the books, and we'd have long talks about puberty. Sarah's mother was gone. Her only info was from what she had been getting from sex ed in school or from Becky.

She plopped down in the seat by my desk. "And then, somehow, the conversation turned into a 'boy' talk." She placed the word in air quotes. "And about how I shouldn't date until I'm thirty. And to finish school. It's not like I'm *not* gonna finish school. I want to go and finish college." She slapped her forehead. "Doesn't he know that?"

It was amazing how kids were so animated with their

hands when they talked. My sixteen-year-old sister was the same way.

Yeah, Brad was taking this personal counseling session a little too far.

I placed a tender hand on her shoulder and squeezed. "I'll tell him you want girl time, alone."

My desk phone rang with two beeps that indicated that Brad was beckoning. I pressed the receiver and picked up. "Hello? I'll order your lunch. We are just about to leave." Direct and to the point, and I hadn't asked him to come with me. It was my way of helping Sarah out. I threw her a sideways glance and winked.

"I'm going to lunch with you guys." His tone was clipped, short, and brooked no argument. "You have to give me at least fifteen minutes until I call a couple of clients back." Then, he hung up.

Rude much? I stared at the phone. "He hung up on me. Again. Is your uncle always so rude?"

She nodded and then picked up my Harry Potter bobblehead at the edge of my desk. "Always. Mostly to Uncle Mason. They're close in age, and that's why they fight so much. At least, that's what Dad says."

"Nice to know he's consistent. I was starting to get offended."

I shot him an e-mail, stood from my chair, and then grabbed my purse from my drawer. "I'll get him lunch on our way back. I just e-mailed him." He'd be pissed, and I'd probably pay for this later, but ask me if I cared. Sarah and I were on a mission—to spend quality time together and get tacos, alone.

Sarah's face relaxed, and she placed down my favorite figurine. She linked her arm through mine as I led us to the elevators.

"And to Gomez's Burritos we shall go," I singsonged.

We were seated in a booth in the far corner of the restaurant, right by the window where we could people-watch outside. The scent of meats and spices and grease in the air bombarded our senses.

Gomez's Burritos did not disappoint.

"Mary loves quesadillas. We have to take her here." Sarah took an overly big bite of her burrito, the sauce dripping onto the tin foil wrapper it had come in.

I almost forgot how hungry teenagers were, but then again, it was her time of the month.

After putting her burrito down, she reached for a chip and dipped it in the salsa. "But she's weird. She puts sugar on everything. Pizza and spaghetti, and I bet she'd put it on this quesadilla, too. Funny enough, Brad is her dealer." The corner of her mouth quirked up, mid-chew.

After I spooned some of the best Mexican rice in the universe into my mouth, I leaned in closer. "Dealer?"

"Mary's sugar dealer." Sarah laughed, seeming to recall a memory.

She had the brownest eyes and an endless amount of curls that lay mid-shoulder. She was beautiful. I could see Charles in her features. In her square, delicate face and in her eyebrow that would quirk up whenever she was thinking a little too hard. But that was where the similarities ended, and I wondered about their mother and what she had looked like.

My heart clenched at her loss. I couldn't imagine life without my mother and father. Our family was crazy, and when one was missing from our get-togethers, it was like losing a limb.

"Dad tries to monitor Mary's sugar, but then you'll have Uncle Brad supplying her behind his back. He carries pouches of sugar or candy with him, just for her." She put down her burrito and swiped at her eyes as laughter escaped her. "Ask him about it. Ask him if he has some sugar. He stores it in his pockets, and one time, it was in his sock 'cause he had nowhere else to hide it."

Okay. A little over the top there, Brad.

Plus, this was the guy who had asked me about the Jolly Ranchers in my pocket. I couldn't have pictured it before today. In my head, Brad was a tough working/dating machine. Today was the first time I had seen him a little softer, with less edge. I guessed his nieces did that to him.

My phone buzzed next to me, and I groaned. "It's your uncle. Hurry, eat faster."

I started shoveling rice into my mouth like there was a shortage, and Sarah followed suit. When we lifted our heads from our plate, our eyes would meet, and we'd laugh.

"It's like he knew we were talking about him." Her cheeks puffed out, overfilled from rice.

I let the phone ring three times before I picked up. "Hello?" I crumpled the tin wrapper that had once held my taco and tossed it in my empty bowl of rice.

"You left without me." His voice was accusatory, as though I'd committed a crime.

"Sarah's a growing girl, and she needs sustenance. You wouldn't want to be the sole reason that her growth is stunted." I winked at Sarah. "Plus, I get hangry and need to eat on time." I reached for Sarah's napkins and tin wrapper where her burrito had once been in and tossed it in my tray.

"Where are you?" he asked.

The buzz of cars echoed around him. The honking of horns blared in the background, indicating he was already out of the office.

"I told you we were going to Gomez's Burritos." I stuffed a nacho chip into my mouth. "It's fine. We are just about done here. I e-mailed you."

"Where is that place?"

"It's on a side street. You'll never find it."

Sarah eyed my nachos, and I pushed it toward her.

"Never mind. I'll find you. I'll track Sarah's phone." Then, he hung up.

I pulled the phone from my ear and stared at it. I hated that he had done that. It annoyed the crap out of me.

"He's coming." I dropped my phone and dipped my chip into the most wonderful glop of salsa. "Someone should really teach your uncle some manners."

"Uncle Brad?" She snorted. "Yeah, maybe you should be the one to do that. It's funny how you give it to him right back. I've never seen anyone do that—well, besides Uncle Mason."

"That's kind of our relationship." I reached for another chip.

If I wasn't snippy, he'd flirt. I'd seen how he acted with the other women in the office. It was his natural demeanor. I'd bet he had been born a flirt. So, I was rude, showed I wasn't interested, and he left me alone and kept it strictly professional. For the past two years, that was how it had always been. I just prayed that our deal—my invitation to this wedding—wouldn't change the dynamic between us.

Ten minutes later, Brad strolled into the restaurant. Two women sitting in the booth next to us dropped their tacos midair, and their eyes followed Brad, in his crisp navy-blue Armani suit. A suit I'd specifically picked up at the cleaners three days ago.

He swaggered toward us, tie neatly in place, suit jacket and pants pressed to perfection. One would never guess his morning had gone sideways, except for maybe the scowl on his face.

"Thomas McCloskey is an a—ape." He undid his tie, glanced at Sarah, and then plopped down in the booth next to me. "He's not a very nice person."

He meant asshole. I'd worked with this man long enough that I could finish his sentences, which was pretty sad.

"Where's my food?" He frowned at the crumbled-up foil on my tray and the half-eaten chips.

"I was going to pick up your regular—an Italian sandwich—on the way back. I don't know what type of Mexican food you like."

He had picky tastes. I could guess his everyday sandwich and his black morning coffee. Anything out of his routine, I was at a loss.

I pointed to the mile-long line in front of us. "The line starts there."

He could boss me around during work hours, but my lunch was my time, my small reprieve from his tyranny.

"I thought you were gonna get me lunch." His scowl grew deeper.

"Yes, on my way back to the office, like I always do." I couldn't remember the last time Brad and I'd had lunch together outside the office. Never. Never in all the time I'd been working for him.

He took in the booths, the swarm of people standing and eating, the concrete floor, exposed walls, and workers crowded behind the tiny kitchen counter. I knew exactly what he was going to say next, so I beat him to it before he could insult my favorite place to eat in the whole downtown Chicago area.

"You'll love this food; trust me."

But my comment could not stop his snotty one. "Are you sure this place is up to code with the Board of Health?"

"It's no three Michelin star place, but it's more than fine." I pulled off my glasses, blew hot breaths on the lenses, and cleaned it off with my sleeve. "If you want to go, we can go."

"Uncle Brad ..." Sarah started. "It's one of the best tacos I've ever had. Just try it."

I stood, ready to leave, but Brad motioned me back to my seat and stood himself.

"I'm going to get some tacos. Do you guys want anything else?"

"I'm about to go. Did you want to stay with your uncle, Sarah?"

My hour lunch was nearly over, and I had to get back to work, but Sarah's face scrunched up, and she held my hand with sweet desperation.

"Please stay."

"Yeah, Sonia. Stay." Brad tipped his chin toward the counter. "I'll be right back—in an hour or so," he scoffed, noting the line almost out the door.

"Please," Sarah repeated, pushing out her lip.

I remembered the type of conversations that Brad was giving his niece this morning and squeezed her hand right back. "Okay, I'll stay."

Fifteen minutes later—not an hour later—Brad had the taco in his mouth, and I'd never heard him praise anything more.

"I can't believe I've never been here. You've been holding out on me, Sonia."

I simply smiled.

He said, "You're right. This is the best taco I've ever had."

I responded with, "I'm always right." Because there were rare occasions when I was ever wrong unless you counted my taste in men.

"If you are always right ..." He stuffed escaping lettuce into his mouth. "... then tell me what to do about Thomas from Titan Printing. He isn't budging on our deal, our potential buyout of his company. He wants more money, but his company won't bring back returns for at least a couple of years. And I'm not budging on the price."

I blinked at him. *He's asking for my advice? On business?* I tapped my fingers against the table. *Is there a wrong way or right way to answer this question?* I knew nothing about acquisitions, but I could offer honesty.

"I don't know anything about business, hostile takeovers, or anything like that. I can imagine that it's all a money game, but if this guy is like you and your brothers, you care about the people who work for you."

He stopped, his taco hanging midair, and intently looked at me.

I laughed. "Let's forget the fact that you don't know anyone's names, but you care that they are compensated properly, that the Christmas parties and promotional parties continue, and that everyone is happy and morale is high." I picked off a chip from his plate and stuffed it in my mouth. "That's why you send those questionnaires all the time."

He waved his taco toward his niece. "See, I'm not the mean one after all."

"I never said you were. But I think those questionnaires were Uncle Mason's idea," Sarah added.

He pulled at the end of her hair. "Playing favorites again." Then, he turned to me with that intense look as though my opinion really did matter. "Go ahead. You were saying?"

I blinked, surprised at his value of my opinion. Then, I cleared my throat and began again. "Well, besides the whole money part, I'm sure, even though he might be a dick like you said, he can't possibly be so heartless to not care for the future of his employees who have families to support." A gush of energy rushed through me as a thought pushed through. "So, next time you talk to him, go with that angle. That, although you can't promise the employment of every employee, you can guarantee that you would try to place all you could with permanent positions and that we have good benefits at Brisken."

He examined me and stopped eating altogether. After a beat, he let out a satisfied smile. "You're a smart one, you know that?" He pointed to me and then took another bite of his taco. "I knew there was a reason I hired you."

"Smartest cookie in the cookie jar." A flush warmed my cheeks. I wasn't used to getting compliments, especially from Brad. "And correction, Charles and Mason hired me."

Brad's phone buzzed on the countertop, and the screen read, *Worst Sitter*. The smile slipped from his face, and he let out an exasperated sigh. "Do I even have to answer this?" He placed his taco on the napkin, the grease of the steak seeping through. He took another napkin, wiped the corner of his mouth, and then picked up. "Annie."

No *hello*. No *how are you*. With Brad, you got what you got.

"Oh. So, you couldn't bring the girls to school this morning, and now, you can't pick up Mary?" His voice was low, menacing, yet he was smiling. "Mmhmm. Yep. Is that it? Mmhmm."

His smile widened, and he reached for his taco. Tiny goose bumps formed on the back of my neck at the evil glint in his eyes.

I glanced at Sarah, and she sliced her neck with her pointer finger in an *off with her head* motion.

"Don't worry about it." His tone hitched up in pitch, so un-Brad-like. "I'll pick up Mary myself. I'll just cancel my two, three, and four o'clock meetings today. I already canceled my morning meetings because you couldn't drop them off." This wasn't entirely true, but he kept on going anyway. "I'm assuming, since you didn't do your duties today, tomorrow will be more of the same and the day after that and after that, but it's okay because you're fired." Then, he hung up and retook a bite of his taco, as though nothing had happened.

My mouth slipped ajar, and Sarah bit her cheek and held her stomach, one second from bursting from laughter.

"I think I'm going to have to take another one of these tacos to go," Brad added, unaffected.

Sarah let out a peal of laughter and collapsed against the booth. "Oh boy." She cackled. "Uncle Mason is going to be pissed."

"I'll deal with Mason." Brad turned my way and placed down his food. "Sonia, cancel my afternoon meetings. I hate to do that, but the worst babysitter left me no other option ... unless ..." He lowered his gaze, almost to a puppy-dog look. Nope, this must be his seductive *do whatever I want* look. "My favorite secretary and friend wants to do me a huge favor and pick up Mary? Our driver is off Monday afternoons, and I don't trust anyone else to pick her up."

And to think, I had been in such a good mood only minutes earlier.

He added for good measure, "Then, we can discuss the deal you were talking about earlier."

I sighed overly loud. When he put it like that, how could I refuse him? I was the desperate one in this situation. "Fine," I grumbled.

He smiled. "Best. Secretary. Ever." He picked up his taco and took another bite.

CHAPTER 7

SONIA

After picking up Mary from school, I plugged in the address to their house on my navigation.

I needed a raise. Seriously, the things that I did for this man ...

I stopped by the guard at the gate, and after he greeted Sarah, he waved for me to pass. I drove past a wall of manicured hedges, all leading down a long path that widened into a circular driveway.

And holy freaking crap ...

My mouth dropped to the floor and kept on going.

"Nice house." I wished I'd sounded normal, but my tone was anything but.

I had only seen houses like this on television—the ones on my entertainment feed that celebrities bought or sold. *Wow de wow.* I knew that Brad was a millionaire, but now, this house ... was not much of a house. This estate only confirmed how wealthy his family was.

"Have you lived here all your life?"

The Brisken brothers kept to themselves. They were private people, and I knew that Brad had a place in the city, but I didn't know where, nor had I known where Charles lived. Until now.

"Grandpa and Grandma lived here before everyone moved in," Sarah said. There was an air of sadness in her tone, which reminded me of all the loss that this family had experienced. Not only had Sarah and Mary lost their mother, but they'd also lost their grandparents, too, in that horrific accident. It'd been all over the late-night news and newspapers.

I pulled in front of the house and placed the car in park. "Everyone lives here?"

"Yeah, Uncle Brad and Uncle Mason, too."

Mary continued to work on the sucker I had given her when I picked her up from school. *The sugar fiend*, I remembered Sarah saying. No wonder Brad called her sweet Mary.

"Wait, both your uncles live here?" *Why didn't I know this?*

"Yeah." Mary took out her sucker and bit down hard, cracking the solid in half. "He doesn't really stay at his other place in the city because he can't tuck me in." Mary had a glimmer of joy in her eyes as she crunched down on her candy. "Uncle Brad tucks me into bed every night, and he tells me stories."

"Yep. Their nightly tradition." Sarah unbuckled herself and stepped out of the car.

"Stories about Prince Charming and his royal jewels. That's my favorite one," Mary added, bouncing to the door.

I couldn't picture Brad telling princess stories. I wondered how much of the story was about himself.

Gag. Double gag.

They punched in a code to the garage, and I pushed my glasses farther up my nose. Seven vehicles filled the multicar garage. I only recognized one of them, but I could tick off the high-end types—Tesla, Range Rover, Mercedes. I assumed the joint prices of all the vehicles could have bought a small mansion.

When we entered through the door in the garage, a room that would most likely be described as the mud room welcomed us, except it was two times the size of my bedroom with a coat rack that spanned almost one whole side of the pale-yellow wall and little drawers that were lined beneath it.

I followed the girls as they put away their book bags and headed into the kitchen that was built for a *Top Chef* king. A marble island as big as my bed centered the room. Copper pots and pans hung from a rack from the ceiling. State-of-the-art stainless-steel appliances glistened against the sunlight peeking in through the floor-to-ceiling windows where I could see a massive-sized pool outside.

Holy freaking double crap.

Sarah pulled their industrial sized fridge open and grabbed three juice boxes. After handing her sister one, she handed me one and smiled. "I had fun today. Besides all that weird stuff this morning."

I plopped on the barstool by the kitchen island, and the girls plopped down next to me. "Yeah, it was, wasn't it?"

Sarah being in the office had definitely broken the monotony of my day. It brought me back to my twelve-year-old self—pimples and uncontrollable hormones that caused me to cry for no reason and getting angry at the stupid things. Those days had not been fun.

As Sarah sipped her juice box, I leaned in. "Anytime you need anything, I know we just met and stuff, but you just let me know."

Mary hopped off the stool and tugged at the edge of my

purple silk shirt. "Wanna play Chutes and Ladders?" She slurped on her straw wedged into the juice box.

She was breathtakingly cute. Mary's cheeks were round, and naturally blonde curls framed her heart-shaped face. No wonder Brad carried sugar everywhere. I'd give in to this girl, too, if I were him.

"I'd love to."

She reached for my hand and dragged me down the hall. "It's in our game room."

"Game room?" I could only imagine how massive this game room would be.

I took in a deep breath. Was I overwhelmed? Yeah, just a little.

~

Time flew by as we played Chutes and Ladders, Sorry!, Life, and a long game of Monopoly where Sarah and Mary were on one team.

A sound of a chime echoed in the room.

"Uncle Brad is home!" Mary jolted up from the floor and ran down the hall like a puppy waiting for her master to come home.

I strolled leisurely with Sarah next to me, and when I entered the kitchen, I nearly fell over at the cutest sight.

Brad had grocery bags in each hand, and Mary had her little hands wrapped around his neck and was kissing his cheek senseless.

"Can I have ice cream? Please. Please. Please." Each please was accented with a kiss.

Brad's laughter was free and natural, unlike his forced smile at the boardroom meetings. He dropped his bags on the floor and wrapped his arms around Mary. "Of course you can." He rubbed his nose against hers and then bent down until her feet touched the ground. "But, first, you have to eat dinner."

I felt like I was in *The Twilight Zone. Where is the stuck-up, stick-in-his-ass Brad?* I was used to Brad the Brute, unmoving, unsmiling, all serious and cocky. This guy was a totally different person.

"Thanks for picking Mary up." His voice was genuine, without its usual annoyance. His eyes made their way to mine.

"You're welcome." I teetered back and forth in my gym shoes that I had changed into in the car. The rest of my professional outfit stayed intact from earlier—purple silk top, plaid mid-ankle pencil skirt.

Brad reached into the bag and emptied the contents on the enormous island—chicken, broccoli, pasta, milk, eggs, ice cream, and cones.

Mary's eyes widened as she grabbed the tub of ice cream and clutched it to her chest.

"Mary, put it in the freezer, so it doesn't melt."

A pout formed on Mary's face, but she didn't complain. She simply did as she had been told.

"After dinner?" she asked with a hopeful light in her eyes.

He touched the tip of her nose. "After dinner, sweet Mary."

I was having an out-of-body experience, as though I were watching a television show. The actor in front of me was almost believable—almost. If it wasn't for my past experiences with him—yelling obscenities about a client and observing grown women and men leaving his office, crying, I might believe the guy in front of me.

When Brad placed a pan on the stove, I straightened,

ready to talk about what I'd come here for and then leaving. He was cooking dinner, and I'd obviously overstayed my welcome.

I'd already seen his house when I was pretty sure no one else in the office had, and soon, I'd be asking him the unthinkable—to be my date for my sorry-ass self.

I blew out a breath. "So ..."

"Want to help me cook dinner?" Brad placed a pot of water on the stove, next to the other pan, not looking up. When I didn't answer right away, he said, "Or you can play with the girls."

"Uh ..." I shifted in my spot and played with the front of my shirt. Dinner would be crossing some weird line for sure. "I really have to get going."

"You're at least staying for dinner." He lifted an expectant eyebrow.

It was a command made in the form of a request—one of Brad's tactics. *You're going to print that out, right? You made that appointment, didn't you?* Where you said yes to all of his questions because saying no would sound bad. It was like when your parents asked you, *Did you do your homework?* As if I'd say no to that trick question.

I bit my bottom lip, and though my mind screamed to get down to business, my stomach grumbled, contradicting everything my rational brain was telling me.

"You're staying, so come here and help me." His confident tone was not meant to be argued with.

Brad rolled up the sleeves of his crisp white button-down, and I couldn't stop staring at his elbows. No idea why. Maybe 'cause I hadn't seen his bare elbows before, and seeing him in this casual state was messing with my head.

Sarah and Mary left the room, and I took the liberty to

wash the broccoli and cut it into pieces. Brad was making chicken and broccoli pasta.

I noticed his feet were bare and had a strange urge to snap a picture for Ava. She'd appreciate the sight of his bare feet and elbows, too.

"So, about the deal ..." My voice trailed off, nerves getting the words stuck in my throat.

"Do you mind if we talk about this after dinner?" He flipped the chicken on the pan. "I have some stipulations."

"What kind of stipulations?" I asked, eyebrows shooting to my hairline.

"After dinner." Then, he smiled and poured the pasta into the boiling pot.

Great. Same old BILK. He'd made a deal with me, yet he was the one with stipulations. That was what I got for making a deal with the devil.

~

Laughter filled the kitchen. I knew there was an eighteen-person dining room because I had seen it when the girls took me on a tour, but we were all seated in the intimate table for eight in the kitchen.

"Do you cook every day?" I asked, making small talk. Over conversation with the girls and watching Brad interact with his nieces, the tension in my shoulders eased up.

Mary chimed in, bouncing in her seat. "No, yesterday, we had McDonald's, and the day before that, we had Taco Bell, and then we had mac and cheese yesterday, too."

Brad continued to cut up some more of Mary's chicken. "Mason is the stickler when it comes to everything organic and healthy. He called, and I promised I'd cook dinner tonight."

Sarah laughed and then stuck some pasta in her mouth. "He's the food Nazi. He wanted me to e-mail a breakdown of everything we had eaten over the weekend. He wanted pictures, too, for proof, but I told him we hadn't taken any."

Oddly enough, I could see that in Mason, him being the finance and numbers guy. He was meticulous in the office and picky about his lunch—from what his secretary had told me.

"I'm the cooler uncle, aren't I?" He teasingly pushed at Mary's side, his eyes playful.

"Yes, you are." Mary's cheeks puffed out, her mouth full of food.

"He's the one who hired the babysitter?" I asked.

"No. Charles and Becky did." Brad stabbed his fork into the broccoli and fed Mary. "Here, you didn't have enough broccoli." He slipped more onto her plate. "They didn't think Mason and I could handle the month they'd be gone on their honeymoon." A devious grin crept up his mouth. "Mason will be pretty pissed that I fired her. But, hell, she was irresponsible and late, and I didn't feel the kids were safe with her. She was always nose deep in her phone, and," he added, just above a whisper, "everything Mary says goes, which can't be good."

"I heard you," Mary said, mid-chew.

"You're just as guilty." Sarah outed him. "Mary gets whatever she wants from you."

"I don't know what you're talking about." Brad chuckled.

Mary reached into Brad's pocket and plucked out a sugar packet. She opened it and poured it on top of her pasta. When Mary shrugged, the whole table laughed.

"It's because you're so cute. I can't help it, now can I?"

Brad picked up a broccoli floret and stuffed another one in Mary's mouth.

"So, who's going to watch them now?" I asked.

"Charles comes back in three weeks, and Mason comes back Wednesday." He sighed heavily. "I'll have to deal tomorrow and then work with Mason until Charles get back." He reached for his wineglass and tipped it back. "We have Leilah, a teen who lives down the street. She can watch the girls until we get home. I'll have to do pickup and drop-off for a bit." He placed his glass down on the table, his tone turning serious. "I couldn't stand Annie watching the kids when I didn't have peace of mind. It had to be done."

Knowing how much he loved his nieces and putting myself in his shoes, I would've done the same thing. With family, I'd rather not take chances. And, with Annie not doing her job, it was affecting Brad's work schedule.

I sipped my water and crunched on the ice. "I can pick up Mary from school again if you'd like."

I was doing this guy way too many favors, but I felt bad for him. He'd been strung out lately with the Titan deal. Picking up the girls wasn't hard. It was a matter of principle, but I guess principle flew out the door when I'd made him make me a deal he still didn't know about.

His eyes locked with mine, and his look made me shift in my seat. "I'd appreciate that, Sonia. Really."

"Consider it done." I tore my eyes away from his, lifting my glass to my lips, giving myself something to do.

The niceness between us was just plain bizarre. When you were used to bantering with someone a certain way and then, all of a sudden, the mood changed, it was plain odd. More than odd. Crazy twilight-zone odd.

Sarah and Mary were excused from the table to do their

homework, and as I stood, Brad grabbed my plate and placed it on top of his.

"I can help do dishes," I offered, aware that it was just the two of us left in the room. Again.

"It's fine. We have a dishwasher."

He moved with grace and confidence, even to the sink. Some people were born leaders. Brad was one of these men. I could tell from how he led his meetings and talked to his staff. When Brad walked into a room, there was no way he could be ignored. When he was present, people noticed. Even how he did the dishes was powerful.

I walked past him and grabbed the pans on the stove. "I actually love doing dishes." I moved to the sink as he began to load the dishwasher.

"Of course you do. With five siblings, you must have done a lot of dishes." He chuckled.

I held the pan up midair. "How do you know how many siblings I have? I never mentioned it."

"You mentioned it to Charles one day." He shrugged as though it was no big deal, but it was. A huge deal to me. He rarely paid attention. I never thought he cared to know about anyone else, except himself.

Goodness, he couldn't even get the security guard's name correct, and he had worked for him forever. Today had been an eye-opening, period-pad-buying, almost-deal-making experience.

"What?" He lifted an eyebrow.

"Nothing." I turned on the faucet and began to suds up the pans while he rinsed off the dishes and then placed them in the dishwasher.

"This is being domestic," he said.

I felt a strange wave of déjà vu as we stood there, side by

side. We looked exactly like my mother and father, cleaning up after our large family dinners.

I choked on my own saliva. And coughed.

"You okay?"

"Yeah"—*cough*—"I'm"—*cough*—"okay."

"Do you need some water or something?"

I shook my head.

What? Where the hell did that come from?

Getting my mind off of it, I scrubbed the pots and pans hard enough to turn my hands pink from the pressure. I needed to leave—and, like, ASAP before I went crazy. All this domestication and seeing Brad in this element were throwing me for a loop.

"So, did you want to discuss the deal?" I had to steer this course back to the straight path and stay in my lane.

He wiped his hands on the towel next to him. "Sure, but with a glass of wine. After this exhaustive day with Sarah and work, I need a drink. Let's head to the living room."

Wine? Wine was not good. I still had to drive home. My heartbeat picked up in tempo, and I rubbed my sweaty palms against my skirt.

"You just had a glass." I glanced at the wine bottle still set on the table.

"I need another one. I'll open a bottle of Eagle Cabernet Sauvignon. Trust me. You'll like it."

We sat in their living room, which had a bar area comparable to what I'd seen in small restaurants. We talked about his upcoming meeting with Thomas and how he'd bring up my points on keeping his employees employed as one of the main reasons he should consider selling. We talked about his nieces, and for a little bit, Brad asked me about my family, all my siblings, and my parents.

Oddly, it felt nice, as though I were talking to an old

friend, as though I were talking to Ava, which was weird because Brad was not Ava. And because this was the guy I'd pictured torturing in different, excruciating ways.

Time had flown by, and by the time I looked at my watch, it was past nine in the evening.

Mary and Sarah said their good nights, and after Brad tucked them in, we continued our conversation.

After downing my first and only glass of red wine liquid courage, I straightened. This was it. No way to chicken out now. "So ..." I swallowed. "... one of my best friends is getting married at the end of the month, and I ..." I twisted my fingers around the slim neck of the wineglass, staring at the way the glass flared into an elongated tulip-like bowl. "And ..." I swallowed again. "... I kind of need a date." I dared to peer up at the amused look on his face.

Great.

His smirk was devilish, and there was that mischievous twinkle in his eye. "So, that's all the mystery?" He took a long sip of his wine, never breaking eye contact. "Why me?"

I blew out a breath and looked at anywhere but him. "Well, I can't just bring anybody to this wedding. I need a ..." It was getting hot in here. I adjusted the neck of my purple silk shirt, feeling the heat rise up my cheeks and to the tips of my ears. "I need a good-looking date."

His smirk widened. "Is that so?"

I narrowed my eyes. "Are you going to make this more difficult than it is?" With Brad, it was better to get to the point. "My ex-boyfriend is going to be there."

"Okay, so you're using me to get him back."

"No."

"No?"

"I mean, I don't know." My voice wavered, and I pushed a hand through my hair, frustrated. "He has a girlfriend already, a very pretty one, and ... and I don't want to look like a loser, okay?" I leaned back on my chair, already feeling defeated. "You already know I'm desperate if I have to ask *you*." I hated that I was in this situation, yet here I was, begging the boss I disliked to be my date.

For a beat, the room was silent, and my cheeks burned. I couldn't believe I had to degrade myself to this. If I had the money, I would just hire a date. I'd hit an ultimate low this time.

I poured myself another glass of wine because it was needed. Then, I chugged a big gulp back. I was past the sipping-wine stage at this point.

When I glanced up at him, I watched him sip his glass, and then he tipped his chin.

"Does this date entail after-wedding activities?" There was that smirk again—the mischievous, *I'm up to no good*, little-boy smirk.

I coughed, wine spilling on my shirt, and half-laughed. This was the Brad I could handle—the cocky bastard who thought every woman wanted him.

I wiped my lips with the back of my hand. "I don't want to sleep with you." I made a face. "Like, ever. I just need a date. You're not even my type."

He poured himself another glass, watching me with unconvinced eyes. "I'm everyone's type," he said.

I cringed and wiggled my whole body as though there were a spider on me. "Sorry, I don't want what everyone else has already had."

"For someone who's asking me for a favor, you're being awfully mean." There was no bite behind his voice like he was unaffected.

"Fine, fine. I'm sorry, all right?" I drained the last drop of wine, and I was tempted to ask for my third glass. "The man who broke my heart is taking Barbie to this wedding I'm in, and I don't want to look like an absolute loser, going stag. I want to show him that I've moved on, too." My fingers pressed against the neck of the glass. With any more pressure, I could break it. Fragile, just like a woman-in-love's heart.

"And have you?" He placed the glass on the side table and leaned in, resting his forearms on his thighs.

I frowned. "Have I what?"

"Moved on."

"No." I cleared my throat. "Well, yes. If you mean moved on as in starting to date other people, I haven't ... yet. But I'm over him." Why did the words feel so hollow, not real? A tightness formed in the center of my chest every time I thought of Jeff. Did that mean I wasn't over him?

"So, you can already see where this is going." I waved a hand, swatting at an invisible fly. "I need a date but not just any date. I need to one-up him, show him that I'm over him. I need you—specifically you because you're good-looking." I blew out a breath, happy that it was finally out on the table. "So, what do you say? Two dates."

"First, one and then two? Aren't we getting a little greedy now?"

It hadn't been in the plan from the beginning, but now that I was continuing to do him favors, I wanted a practice run before the real day. "Rehearsal dinner and then the wedding."

"You think I'm good-looking?" He grinned outright, straight white teeth and all.

Goodness, that was what he'd gotten from my rambling? I fell back against the couch. This deal with Brad was equivalent to making a deal with the devil.

Maybe I could hire a stripper from one of those sites. I

did have savings in a CD, but then again, there would be penalties if I took out the money.

I took off my glasses and rubbed at my eyes, resting one elbow on my knee. I didn't know what was more embarrassing: when I'd sat on ketchup and walked around half the day—to the office, to the restaurant, to run Brad's errands and mine after work—and no one told me I had something red on my skirt, people probably thinking it was period stains or now.

"You already know how embarrassing this is, but I'll be more humiliated if I show up, dateless, while he has *America's Next Top Model* on his arm."

The couch indented from the weight of him, and I lifted my head and slipped on my glasses. He smiled that devilish smile that would look good on his face at the wedding.

Then, he straightened my glasses. "He broke your heart?"

I groaned. "Yes, okay?" I decided this was more embarrassing than the ketchup-stain incident.

"All right then." He shrugged as though it wasn't a big deal. "I'll go."

Wait. What?

I did a double take, shot upright, and held my breath. "Really?"

His smirk only grew. "A deal is a deal. Plus, I enjoy saving the day."

I blinked up at him, and when he playfully bumped his shoulder against mine, I was convinced that crossing this secretary-boss line would be okay. And who knew? Maybe, after all of this was over, I'd dislike him less.

CHAPTER 8

SONIA

"Hey, you coming with me today?" I peeked into Brad's office.

Over the past week, he'd been coming with me to eat lunch. Oddly enough, I had been introducing him to places that he'd never gone to before, which had surprised me because, working downtown all his adult life, he'd never been to some of the greatest places I'd ever eaten at.

At lunch, he let loose. We were civil, and he gave me hope that we could pull off the wedding-date thing.

"Not today. Busy." His tone was short, curt. He didn't peek up from his computer.

I sighed. *Just when I was starting to like him.*

Mason was back and splitting niece duty, and Brad was back to his typical, annoying self at work. Maybe he was just a hangry man, and he needed to be fed.

"I'll grab your regular and bring it back."

I turned to leave when he said, "They're coming to pick us up at seven."

"What? Who?"

"My personal shopper." He lifted his eyes to mine while his hands tapped against his keyboard.

I blinked once. *Is he joking?*

He cocked his head. "Shopping. Personal shopper. Wedding suit shopping. Didn't you see my note on your desk?"

I glanced back behind me at my desk and then threw up both hands. "What note?"

Standing, he strode past me and went straight to my desk. He lifted the keyboard where a small piece of paper was placed, no bigger than two inches by one inch. He shoved it my way, the tiny piece of paper between his index and middle finger.

I huffed and then grabbed it from him, reading it aloud. "*Shopping tonight. Seven p.m.*" I looked up at him. "I can't tonight." For the sole reason that he was being super annoying. You'd think he would've mentioned it earlier than today, yesterday perhaps, or maybe he could've written it on a bigger piece of paper that was in plain sight.

"She's paid by the hour." Then, he stalked back toward his office, conversation over, as usual.

My hands fisted at my sides, posture stiff, corded neck. I wondered how I'd be able to get through two whole dates with him without wanting to stuff him in a body bag.

I forced myself to loosen.

This is for me, I reminded myself. *For me.*

"How do you know I don't have plans?" I argued.

He spun around and smiled. "Do you?"

A-hole. "No." For once, I wished I had the superpower to lie without my face giving it away—or, really, I wished I had plans. Real plans. Why couldn't I have plans?

I followed him back into his office, preparing for another argument.

"Well then." He sat behind his desk, leaving me an annoyed and a confused mess.

"Don't you have a suit? Any suit will do."

And why did I have to go with him? I wasn't his mom. I didn't need to approve his choice of clothing. We weren't a real couple, and I was not choosing his tie.

His fingers steepled by his lips. "This is a special occasion. I won't be wearing one of my work suits to a wedding."

"Okay ..." I didn't see what the big deal was. Buying another suit seemed like a waste of money. "I don't care. You can wear that suit." I gestured to his attire. "The one you're wearing. It's perfectly tailored, and I'm sure it's a very expensive suit." I'd seen the tag before I took it in to be dry-cleaned. And it wasn't cheap.

"What are you going to wear?" he continued as though I hadn't said a thing.

"A dress I've probably worn before." I knew I'd have to dress up to look decent next to Brad, but I wasn't worried about my clothing as much as I had been stressing about finding a date. And, now, I had one. Who needed a fancy dress when I would have the hottest guy on my arm?

He snorted loudly and then dropped his head back into his computer screen. "Seven o'clock. Downstairs. Can you order us some dinner beforehand?"

I simply stared at him. "I haven't even picked up your lunch yet." *Is this guy serious?*

Not caring, I slammed the door behind me.

Then, I grumbled around the office the rest of the day.

At six fifty-five p.m., I picked up Brad, and we rode the elevator down together. He'd been so busy that he'd eaten dinner at his desk.

"Great," I muttered, noting the thunderstorm pouring down tsunami-style outside the doors.

The rain pelted against the windows, and thunderous clouds roared above us. Of all the days not to have an umbrella. The forecast hadn't called for rain. Damn weatherman.

The scent of rain reminded me of the summers when I was younger, how the rain would wet my hair, making it frizzy when it dried. How the other kids would make fun of me and call me Medusa when my hair stuck out at all ends. Yeah, I hated rain.

When we walked outside, Brad opened his oversize umbrella. At least he had his. The rain trailed down the bottom of my long skirt, and beads of water soaked the gym shoes that I had changed into.

Brad tilted inward and lifted the umbrella over my head, shielding me from the downpour. "You should keep an umbrella with you."

"Thanks for the enlightening advice." *This man.* I wanted to stick his sarcasm and his umbrella where the sun didn't shine.

I could have, at a minimum, brought a pair of jeans and a comfortable sweatshirt if I'd known we were going to go shopping, and I was going spend the rest of the night sitting and watching him walk the catwalk in an array of suits that'd probably all look the same.

The rain, wet feet, and cold air caused my teeth to chatter. "Why can't we drive somewhere? Where's your car?"

"That's not how this works. Not how my personal shopper does things. It's a full-service experience."

"Getting wet and cold is part of this full service? Will they towel-dry us off?" I hugged my middle to get some warmth back into my body.

He angled closer and wrapped his arm around my

waist, bringing me against him and the umbrella directly above me to shield the rain. "There. Better?"

Heat spread down my arm, where we touched, and I reeled away. "Boundaries, hello? Are you purposely trying to make me uncomfortable?"

Brad being Brad did the opposite and leaned in even closer until we were flushed hip to hip. "Boundaries? Next weekend, I'm supposed to pretend like I've been balls deep in you, and you want to talk about boundaries?"

I jerked my head and stuck my finger in my mouth, pretending to vomit.

Brad shook his head, amused.

He did have a point though. I had to get over this closeness, but how could I when he was my boss?

"You need to get used to my hands on you."

His hands circled my waist, and I shoved a finger into his shoulder.

"Do you even realize you're flirting, or is it just natural for you?"

A long stretch limo stopped in front of us, and before he had a chance to respond, I opened the door and brushed inside to get in and out of the rain.

"Mr. Brisken. Miss Vanducci." The driver stepped out in the rain to hold the door open.

"Hello, hello," Brad responded as the driver took his oversize umbrella from him.

I scooted farther into the vehicle, down the wraparound leather seat. The leather stuck to my wet skirt, and I rubbed my hands over my arms. The chill cut through my bones.

LED track lighting created a light-yellow glow at the ceiling, and an ice bucket with drinks chilled on the side.

"Champagne?" Brad reached for two glasses in the drink holder.

Maybe some champagne would warm me, so I grabbed my glass, and he poured. The fizz bubbled to the top and almost spilled over, so I brought the glass to my lips.

"Mimosa in the morning with clients, drinks for lunch, and now, champagne in the evening. Is this something I should warn your brothers about? That you're a borderline alcoholic?"

He lifted his glass and then leaned back against the cushion, resting his ankle on the opposite knee. "I enjoy a little drink once in a while. Maybe you should try it. It'll loosen you up."

I kicked off my wet gym shoes and then my socks. My toes were pruned. Definitely less suave than him. "I am loose."

He barked out a laugh, his eyes telling me what he was thinking—me some ho.

I rolled my eyes. "All I meant was that I don't need alcohol to have a good time."

"I doubt that. When was the last time you ..." He coughed. "... got loose?"

"Hello? Inappropriate." I pointed the tip of my glass in his direction. "How about I ask you that question? Oh, never mind. I know since I'm the one making all your plans." I barked out a louder, obnoxious laugh. "Lucille ... Jasmine ... Stella ..."

The smile erased from his face, and his tone was stone-cold serious. "I don't sleep with every girl I go out on a date with. You can't have that kind of impression of me."

His mouth slackened when I didn't respond.

"You do, don't you?" His foot dropped to the floor, and he leaned in, his wineglass between us.

I shrugged like his closeness didn't affect me, which it

didn't. Mostly. But our thighs kissed this time, and warmth spread where we touched.

"It doesn't even matter. It's not like I'm your mom."

His stare seared a hole on the side of my face, and my cheeks flushed pink.

"What?" I snapped.

"I know I give that kind of vibe, and everyone else thinks of me that way." He inched in, and his brows furrowed. "But you?" With a slow, disbelieving shake of his head, he said, "I thought you knew me." There was hurt behind his soft tone.

Knew him? Is he offended?

He hunched over, dropped his gaze, and stared at the wineglass in his hands.

I was about to apologize but bit my tongue instead because I knew his stories. He of all people had shared them with me.

Maybe by making his countless dinner reservations, I had assumed he took them all home, too, but I wanted to assume and not know the truth because I didn't care. This was a job. He was my boss. Really, should an employee know this much about her boss?

I shifted in my seat, uneasy, realizing boundaries were being crossed, making me uncomfortable.

He got a little quiet, swirling the wine in his glass. "I'm going to change how you think of me."

"Please don't." I sighed. Boundaries. I needed to set up the border, the wall that separated personal from professional. "What I think doesn't even matter."

Again, he got quiet, swirling that wine, and then he finished off the glass. "It probably shouldn't matter." Then, almost under his breath, he added, "But it does."

We arrived at Saks Fifth Avenue on Michigan Avenue,

which was only a short ride from the office. We could've walked, but there was no way high-maintenance Brad would walk in the rain. I doubted he did that.

When we entered the posh shopping area, my eyes took in five female attendants dressed in all black skirt suits and a woman in a pantsuit that hugged her figure. They were impeccable with their non-smudge red lipsticks and tall model-like figures. Compared to them, I looked like Smurfette. They didn't look like they worked here. They looked like mannequins on display. Figured that he had an all-women team to help him pick out a suit.

The tall woman in the pantsuit with an even olive skin complexion had her black hair pulled back into a long ponytail that lay in the middle of her back. Not a strand of hair was out of place.

"Brad, it's wonderful to see you. I haven't seen you in a while. You're always calling in your orders nowadays." She pressed her cheek against his, and then she reached for me and placed her hands around one of mine. "You must be Sonia. It's so lovely to meet you. I'm Nadine." The inflection in her tone reminded me of a serious teacher—firm, articulate, and to the point.

"It's a pleasure to meet you," I replied.

She smiled, no teeth, like how the Britain royals did with an air of sophistication. "Let's get started."

An hour later, I found myself sitting in a fitting room large enough to rival my apartment with a wineglass in hand. Brad stood on a circular pedestal in the middle of the room as though he were the bride on the show *Say Yes to the Dress*. I rested against the chair—feet dead, body bone-tired, and mind drained from the long day. He'd been trying on suits for the whole hour, and they all looked the same. I almost jumped out of my seat and fist-pumped the air when he finally decided on one.

An older woman bent down to pin the hem of Brad's Kiton suit, a designer I'd never heard of before. To me, the suit looked great, but Brad needed one hundred percent perfection, no matter the cost—and boy, did it cost.

"The hem should hit just above the heel," he said as though the woman who worked here didn't know that even though that was her job and she most likely had years of experience under her belt.

I noted how the navy-blue suit stretched along his broad shoulders, casing in his well-defined arms. The way his pants accented his height made my mouth water a little. I'd still never date him—my feelings and morals hadn't changed —but I couldn't help but admire the package. I was a woman after all.

But then I caught his stare and noticed the smug smile on his face as though he knew I was checking him out, which only reminded me that he was, in fact, the BILK. And for all intents and purposes of this exercise, I had made the right decision and snagged the looker as arm candy at the wedding.

"Take that, Jeff," I whispered under my breath.

When Brad changed and stepped out of the fitting room in his regular suit, I released a breath, ready to be done with this night. I stood, prepared to leave and excited for a hot shower and my warm bed.

Nadine came in, and when I raised a hand to say goodbye, the slew of women suddenly shoved in racks of gowns in every array of colors and fabric and style imaginable— from silk to satin to lace.

Nadine snapped her fingers, and like a Santa's workshop, her model-like elves got to work. One took my jacket, another took my purse, and two more caged me in, on either side of me as though they were my bodyguards. My head flipped around, and I stared at the tall, flawless woman beside me.

"I'm not looking for an outfit. Just Brad. I'm about ready to go." I turned to face him, but liar was written on his face.

His hands were behind his back like a good Boy Scout, which made me want to wring his neck.

"You lied. We didn't just come here for your suit."

He simply shrugged.

"No way." My eyes went wide. "I am not doing this. I can't even pronounce half the designers you wear, let alone afford them." If I could afford one of these designer dresses, I could've afforded a good-looking stripper date. What was he smoking, crack?

"And I didn't lie," he said smoothly. "I've ordered my suit. I just left one little detail out—that we'd be shopping for a dress for you. It's not like I can risk us not matching, and anyway, who said you were paying?" Amusement was heavy in his features.

"Excuse me for a second." I sidestepped my female attendants and pulled Brad to the side by his elbow, like a naughty little boy in trouble. I would have grabbed his ear, if only I were tall enough.

This guy and his absurd ideas, I swear!

"If you are planning to reenact a *Pretty Woman* moment, let me tell you, I'm not falling for it. This was not part of the deal." I crossed my arms over my small chest and pushed out my bottom lip.

"Taking you to the wedding was part of the deal." He flicked my nose with his pointer finger like I'd seen him do to Mary. "This is just a little extra."

My teeth clenched. "I don't need extra."

"They closed this store down for me." Pride was heavy in his tone. "You can't possibly tell me they've all come here and I'm paying for Nadine to work extra hours for nothing."

"No. No. No." I shook my head back and forth, now sounding like a five-year-old Mary, as his face stayed utterly even. Of freaking course. Brad didn't know the meaning of the word *no*.

He leaned in and leveled me with a stare I was sure he frequently used to negotiate with clients. "Sonia, I know this is too much to ask of you, given the amount of pride you have, but I want to do this, okay?" He placed a soft hand on my shoulder. "I want to. Because you've helped me on more than one occasion and with my nieces and even more so every day. I've asked you to do things way above your job description, and when you asked me to do this one favor for you, I thought I could spoil you a bit." He took a step back and reached for my hand and squeezed. "So, please, just accept this. This one-time gift from me."

I peered up at his deep brown eyes, eyes that poured out sincerity. Still, my pride refused to accept this gift. He'd already agreed to too much, but I also knew he wouldn't take no for an answer. It was in his locked jaw and the steadiness in his stare.

"Fine," I conceded, practically pouting.

"Is everything okay here?" Nadine asked with a flash of a smile, approaching us.

"Yes. Everything is fine." There was my tone again, the tone that indicated that everything was not fine, but I didn't want to make a big deal out of it.

"Come on. This is Operation Get Your Boyfriend Back, so you'll need ammunition." He moved to the first rack of gowns, ignoring my lethal glare.

I felt way too much like Julia Roberts. Two women

greeted me with their smiles, and one handed me another glass of wine as we passed rows and rows of ballgowns fitted and flared.

My feet did the walking, but my brain could not wrap around how much money this guy had to shut down a whole department store for his bidding.

Nadine stepped in front of me and led us down the long hall of designer dresses. "How about we start at McQueen and then head over to Oscar? Does that sound good? With your beautiful skin tone and figure, I'm sure we'll find something wonderful."

I smiled through clenched teeth. If I were in a better mood or more comfortable, the compliments would've flattered me. But I was too irritated. "Oh, how fun." My tone turned sarcastic, ready for the "fun" to be over with.

~

Brad

I had found my new obsession, annoying the crap out of Sonia. Even better, making her cheeks turn crimson. It was the cutest thing, like watching a little pup growl. Her death glares were comical, as though she wanted to tear my eyes out with her fingernails. Every time Nadine turned away, Sonia would glare, nostrils flared, mouth pouty.

Fuck, she was adorable.

She'd tried on four dresses already, and as she stomped into the changing room, making it known she was not a happy camper, I laughed under my breath.

"Come out. I want to see."

"I hate you," she replied. "And no."

I winked at one of the attendants holding up the next dress for Sonia to try on. *She loves me*, I mouthed.

"Come out, or I'm coming inside that dressing room," I threatened.

It did not do the trick. She fired back, "Two words: *sexual harassment.*"

This woman. Always a snarky comment.

I shook my head as I sipped my wine. Domaine Leroy Chambertin Grand Cru. This was the good stuff from France. I swished the red wine and watched the liquid coat the bottom of my glass. "It's only sexual harassment if you don't want me in that dressing room."

The blonde attendant hid a smile, and her cheeks turned pink.

"Come out. One. Two ..."

Before three, Sonia emerged. My eyes widened. *Well, well, well.* That was an interesting dress—fluffy and full, and it reminded me of a comforter. I nearly scoffed out a rude comment but thought better of it.

Sonia was picking the dresses that my dead grandma would wear. If she wanted to outdo this new girlfriend, she needed to step it up a notch. Though the dress did accentuate her small waist, it flared out into a ballgown that looked like she was about to jump off a plane and engage the skirt as a parachute.

She trudged toward me, arms crossed over her chest, lips pouty, and eyes screaming revenge. She reminded me of a pissed off Mary, and I had the sudden urge to laugh, but I covered my mouth instead. I wasn't about to push my luck. Knowing Sonia, she'd deck me.

She pulled at the dress and twirled, the black-and-white floral skirt flaring out and contouring her body when she stilled.

It wasn't as though she wasn't attractive because Sonia was beautiful, and there was no doubt I'd give her a second glance, but everyone needed to give her a first glance. It was as if Sonia was trying to dim her beauty and hide her slim runner's body under that giant skirt.

I stood and pointed to the pedestal. "Up." I tipped my head toward the circular stand.

She groaned but followed directions, to my surprise.

"What's wrong with it?" She placed her hands on her hips, ready for battle.

Boy, was that the question of the year. I could make a full-page list, but I knew her response would be merciless.

"It hides your figure."

She frowned. "I don't have a figure—unless beanpole is a classification."

I couldn't hide my frown. *What in the world is this woman talking about?*

How was it she had a bucket full of sass and was confident in her abilities at work, but she lacked confidence in her looks? She was petite and the kind of cute that would be the envy of the majority of the female population, a pouty bottom lip that could model, and the loveliest set of eyes I'd ever seen on anyone.

"It's not the dress for you. I don't like it."

Sonia could do better if she wanted to stick out and shine, but I doubted that was her goal. She was bringing me as a date to do that job for her. Well, I was going to use this as an opportunity to show her how she could shine all on her own.

"This flares at the waist." She swiveled, forcing the skirt to fan out. "I thought it'd give me some curves."

"It doesn't."

She pursed her lips and then threw up her hands. "I'm not trying on a thousand dresses just to have you reject them all." She pointed a shaky finger my way, one hand heavy on her hip—a Mary move. "And who says you get a say? My friend's wedding. My body. I get to pick the dress." Then, she stormed back into the fitting room.

"You always know how to get the girls riled up, don't you, Brad?" Nadine laughed.

"It's what I'm good at." I pointed to a dress on the rack. "How about that?"

Nadine picked up the silvery-blue floor-length dress that I'd pointed out. I tipped my chin toward Sonia's fitting room. Anything was better than the number she had on now.

"I have one that I think you'll love, Sonia. One that I picked out personally for you." Nadine threw me a sideways glance.

That was why I'd hired her; she knew how to read people, what they wanted, how to appease without offending. If Sonia knew I had picked the dress, she wouldn't have tried it on.

A long five minutes later, I lifted my head from my phone as Sonia stepped out of the dressing room. *Well, shit.* On the hanger, it had been mediocre at best, but on Sonia ...

I stood and went to slip my phone in my suit pocket, but it fell on the ground. She was stunning. The dress accented her petite figure, clinging to every part of her. The neckline swooped down to an achingly low level that had my eyes dipping to the slender curve of her neck, the span of pale bare skin right above her breast line.

I swallowed. Hard.

"And?" She twirled around, and I nearly fell over because the back of the dress dipped into a V, stopping right above her perfect ass.

"It's beautiful, right, Brad?" Nadine sported a victorious smile.

"I'm not sure it's me." Sonia flattened her hands against the dress and stared back in the mirror.

I had no words. The cat had taken my tongue and swallowed it or fed it to the mice. Shit if I knew.

"Well?" She lifted an eyebrow, waiting for a response.

I snapped back to attention, reminding myself that I couldn't look at my secretary in that way. I wasn't allowed to want her. My brothers would kill me.

"That ... that's the dress." My voice was hoarse, unlike my confident demeanor.

I averted my stare and bent down to pick up my phone to hide these weird emotions.

She's your secretary. Damn it. Get it together.

CHAPTER 9

SONIA

As the week flew by, I could hardly believe the wedding was a day away. When I had asked Brad to the rehearsal dinner, he'd been more than up for it, not like he had a choice because it was part of the deal. I had to introduce my pretend boyfriend to a good core of my friends that would be in attendance on the big day so the wedding day would be less awkward if that was even possible.

I placed my Toyota Camry in park in front of Brad's palatial home and stepped out of the car. I didn't think I would ever get used to the amount of luxury that surrounded the Brisken family. Lights highlighted the pillars of the mansion that framed the door, and the window-height shrubbery that was etched against the building were like lines against a painting.

I walked into the house, and Sarah greeted me. Her Beats by Dre hung around her neck, and her eyes lit up before she leaned in and gave me a hug.

"Sonia!" Mary shouted from down the hall, rushing toward me.

I scooped her up—an automatic reaction—and held her close. "Goodness." I laughed. "What a greeting. I think I should come over more often."

"You should! You should!" Mary twirled her fingers around my simple silver necklace.

The last time I'd seen the girls was when I picked them up from school weeks ago. Was it weird to say I'd missed them?

"Why don't you come to visit?" Mary asked, pushing out her bottom lip. "I want to play Life again. I'm better now. I've mastered the roll where I twist my fingers and can control what numbers I want to get."

"Yeah, I vote for game night soon," Sarah added.

Brad walked into the room in jeans and a dark gray Henley. His hair was shorter. He must have gotten a haircut after work.

I stared for a second, feeling out of sorts. I didn't think I'd ever seen Brad in jeans. They were dark-washed and not overly tight but tight enough where I could tell he had definition in his thighs.

"What about game night?" Brad asked, giving me a once-over.

Why did it feel like Brad had been judging my choice in clothing lately? I wiped a sweaty, self-conscious hand down my knee-length jean skirt.

Every time I turned toward him when I walked into his office or any room, I always felt like he was watching me. Too closely.

"Sonia promised me another game night." Mary wrapped both arms around my neck, bringing herself closer and flashing me a *you can't say no to me* smile.

No wonder Brad fell for her antics. I doubted anyone could avoid the cuteness overload of this little blonde. Guys everywhere would be goners in the future. Talk about Heartbreak Hotel.

I cleared my throat, not waiting for Brad to respond. "We'll talk about it, okay?"

As I held Mary in my arms and with Sarah glued to my side, I could easily see that lines were getting more blurred by the day. Somewhere between me getting Sarah pads, Brad agreeing to go to this wedding, us shopping and having lunch daily, we'd gone from coworkers to oddly being almost friends.

Mary kissed my cheek. "Please? Pretty, pretty please with cherries on top? Game night. Game night!" She clapped her little hands to match her game-night chorus.

Brad chuckled. "Say yes now, or she'll up the cuteness."

I threw him a *help me* look, but he simply shrugged as if to say arguing was pointless.

"Okay." I gently dropped Mary on her feet and touched her nose. "I'll come over. Maybe I can babysit sometime, and we'll play."

"Wait a minute here," Brad gasped loudly, feigning offense. "Don't count me out. I'm the king of board games."

I gulped. The song "Blurred Lines" played in my head. Yes, we were definitely friends now if we were playing board games.

Letting it go, I suggested we leave, so we said our goodbyes to the girls and headed to my car. The rehearsal dinner was going to start at the church and end at a pizza joint. It was to be casual, so I wore a light-blue satin shirt, knee-length jean skirt, and boots, which, if I wasn't mistaken, Brad kept staring at.

I glanced down at my watch, noting that we were running a few minutes behind schedule. "We'll have to hurry."

"I'm going to drive. My car." Brad turned toward the garage when I gripped his forearm to stop him.

"Uh, no. That wasn't the deal. You agreed that I'd drive." My back straightened, and the beginning of annoyance seeped into my skin.

"That's before I reevaluated your vehicle situation," he rudely added. "Your car's not safe."

This guy!

Didn't he realize I drove the girls to school in this car?

Forced friends—that was what we were because I could guarantee that I wouldn't be friends by choice with this stuck-up, designer-wearing automobile snob. I wanted to put a mute button on him that I could control with a remote.

"Why is it that you like to constantly annoy me?" I glanced down at my 2010 Camry. "It's a perfectly well-working vehicle, and we've discussed this. I'm driving. Now, get in the car!"

If he didn't get in the car in the next minute, we would definitely be late. I glanced back at the house to make sure that no windows were open, and the girls weren't accidentally learning new words.

"Calm your panties. Fine." He held out his hand, palm up. "Compromise. Give me the keys."

I gritted my teeth and slapped them in his hand because there was no time to argue. I hoped this was the right choice, taking him to meet my friends and then tomorrow when Jeff and my replacement would show up. I hoped it was worth all this because he was killing me softly and slowly with irritation.

"You'd better be worth all this trouble," I muttered as I slipped in the car.

"Don't worry, baby. I'm a sure thing." He winked, and I wanted to slap him.

"I'm surprised none of your girlfriends has killed you in your sleep yet." I shot him a look. "Because you're so annoying!"

Forty minutes later, we were in front of the church. The light was shining overhead as the sun set in front of us in an array of pinks and purples that highlighted the sky. It was as if the universe was showering down its blessings on Carrie and Tim, but it still couldn't ease the tightness in my chest.

When he stepped out of the car, Brad reached for my hand. It was the first time our hands had ever met intimately, a fusion of fingers. "I promise not to annoy you for the rest of the night if you promise to relax."

"Relax? What's that?" I laughed without humor. My muscles were tense, the veins on my neck strained. Soon enough, a full-on migraine would attack.

I'd never lied this big before. Tiny little lies, sure. White little lies that didn't hurt anyone, I was okay with that. But this—pretending Brad and I were romantically involved—was different.

"Yes, just relax. Close your eyes and breathe." Brad stopped walking and pulled me in front of him, our hands intertwined.

I closed my eyes but still could not calm my nerves.

His thumb slowly made circles on the top of my wrist. "You're going to be fine."

I hoped and wished and prayed that was true. I took three full, calming breaths through my nose and out my mouth, and soon enough, the warmth of the sunlight on my face and the comfort of his hold eased me. "I don't even know why I'm going through all this trouble." That was another lie. I knew why … because looks mattered, and I didn't want to look like the loser I really was. "Everyone is engaged or married or in a serious relationship. I think I'm the only one in my friend group that isn't. And, now, Jeff is going to be there with *her*."

"So?"

"So?" My eyes flew open, and I openly gaped at him.

"I mean, why does it matter, Sonia? Who cares?"

"I care." Every muscle in my neck tensed, and I gripped my dress within my fingertips. "Are all your friends married or in a serious relationship? They have to be if you're thirty-three."

"Yes, most." His tone was even, unbothered, unfazed.

And I was jealous. I wanted to not care because then this would be easier, and I wouldn't need to pretend and lie and bring Brad to this wedding.

He peered at the church, noting the people already walking inside. "One of them is even divorced, but I don't care. Because that's them, and this is me. Why should what's happening in their lives have an effect on mine?" And this was Brad in all his blunt honesty.

My shoulders slouched, and my stomach churned. Why couldn't I force myself to not care? Why couldn't I be stronger when it came to this? "I wish I had your confidence."

He tipped up my chin with the lightness of his fingertip, his other hand wrapped around mine. "I wasn't always this confident."

I tilted my head and looked at him. Really looked at him. I couldn't picture it. Brad not confident would be like throwing the world off its axis. He radiated confidence, merely standing there and doing nothing.

"Really?"

"I know it's hard to believe, but, yes, really."

His fingers played lightly with mine, and I ignored the butterflies caused by the warmth of his touch. Must be nerves.

"My parents were always telling me how good I was, smart, handsome, but somehow, I would always compare myself to Charles or Mason, and in my head, I never seemed to measure up." His face turned wistful. "Mason was the younger one, the cuter one, the spoiled one. Charles was the boss, the leader of the family, the brother in charge. I never knew where I fit in."

He'd never talked about his parents before, and a little part of me ached to know more. More about his parents and what made up my boss's DNA. Weirdly enough, before, I didn't care, but now that I had a glimpse of his life, I realized I had placed him in this asshole box, one that maybe he didn't deserve.

"So, what happened? What was the switch?" Because I needed an internal switch, one where I didn't care where others were in their lives. I wanted to be content with my own.

He stared at me for a second, and his smile slipped. "A succession of things. I think I just grew up, but ultimately, when my parents died, I didn't care about anything else—what others thought of me, their accomplishments, or how I measured up. I think I wanted to remember how my parents had looked at me, and all else didn't matter."

I reached over and squeezed his hand. "I'm sorry. Sorry you lost them so young." Full emotion hit me as I remembered the loss of his parents. It only reminded me of how lucky I was to have a great relationship with my own parents.

He nodded and released a heavy sigh. He seemed lost for a moment, in his thoughts of his past, of his parents, his face wistful. "Yeah. Me, too. I miss them. Sometimes, I try to block it out, but there are big moments that I know they'll never see, and it makes me feel their loss even more." His stare turned distant. "If they could've only seen how Sarah and Mary have grown." His eyes dropped to where we were connected. "Or see Charles get married or me one day." His voice trailed off, and the quiet spanned the space between us, in the open air, when people passed us by to get to the church.

The whole world disappeared, and there was just us.

A moment later, he shook his head. That vulnerability that I had just witnessed disappeared and that cocky smile was back. "But my parents never did like Mason's girlfriend, even in college. They never said it to his face, but they would let things slip to let me know that they never liked her."

"Protective brotherly type, I see." I leaned in, playful.

"He just deserves more, and I know he can do better." His gaze dropped back to our intertwined fingers, and he gave it a cheerful little shake. "Feel better?"

I nodded. He'd diverted my crazy, worrying thoughts for a moment. My tiny reprieve from all this chaos happening in my head.

"Let's go meet your friends," he suggested, tipping his chin toward the steps to the church.

Before I could think further, he was pulling me toward our destination.

As soon as we entered the doors, Carrie lifted her head, and her smile was blinding. She rushed over to me and encased me within her arms in a bear hug that could rival my grandma's. "Sonia! I'm so happy you're here."

I patted her back, and all annoyance of the Jeff-and-Replacement thing eased.

"I'm so sorry. You're so right," she whispered against my shoulder, hugging me tighter. "If I could disinvite his ass, I would."

"It's fine." It wasn't totally fine, just a little fine now. "I'm not going to let a boy destroy years of friendship."

Because our friendship transcended boys and drama and gossip. It had been here before Jeff and I were even together and would outlast any other major catastrophe in my life. Good friends were hard to come by, and Ava and Carrie were the best kinds of friends. I hadn't been feeling it the other day, feeling betrayed by the sting of her inviting Jeff and disregarding my broken heart, but this here, this wedding, went beyond Jeff and my breakup. Because years from now, I hoped that Jeff would just be a memory, and I knew that Carrie and I would still be friends.

"I love you," she whispered in my ear, relaxing against me. "Thank you for being here. You don't know how many days I've spent worrying about this." When she pulled back, her mouth went lax, and her eyes scoured the over six feet of fineness beside me.

"I'm Brad." His voice was low, masculine, silky, and smooth.

Carrie's mouth fluttered open and then shut. "Carrie." She stuck out her hand to meet his. It happened in slow motion, as though they were in a film, meeting for the first time.

Internally, I laughed because this was precisely the reaction I had been hoping for.

Her stare ping-ponged between us, and then she pointed at him. "Aren't you ... aren't you the BILF? You work with Sonia." Her finger shook in front of his chest. "You are the BILF!"

I blanched, pale, pasty white, like the pasta I ate almost every other day.

She had not just said that out loud. My jaw locked, and I tipped my chin, indicating that she should stop talking. I would kill Ava for this.

"BILF?" Brad asked, confusion evident in his tone.

"Yeah BILF, like MILF." She motioned between us. "When did this happen?" She turned to me with accusation in her eyes. "I thought you hated him. She calls you names behind your back just so you know. She has these weird drawings of you and even has a voodoo doll and this dartboard thing." Carrie let out a little chuckle.

"I do not!" My neck, my face, and my ears felt impossibly hot.

To my utter shock, Brad played along, his face the epitome of amused. "Very interesting. Is that why I had numbness in my leg the other day?"

Carrie laughed, but I was far from entertained.

"Oh, look! I think Tim is calling you." I turned her toward the front of the church and shoved her. "Go. We'll be up there in a second."

She contested, but I gave her a look that said I would make a voodoo doll of her if she didn't keep on moving.

When she left, Brad's smirk widened. "BILF. Instead of Brad, are you going to call me BILF from now on?"

I rolled my eyes. "That's what my friends call you. I call you ..."I coughed. *BILK.*"... other things you'd rather not know." It was way too late for anything less than honesty at this point. Everything was out in the open. "So, if you ever bring this up again, I will literally poison your lunch. Now, let's go." I pivoted and headed to the front of the church, ignoring his smug attitude behind me.

Brad

There were many things I'd been noticing about Sonia lately. One of which was that she fidgeted way too much. Her knee bounced beside me as the priest in the front went over what would be happening today, a mirror of tomorrow. He explained the logistics, how people should walk in, where they should stand, and the order of events of the wedding. All during which anxiety poured out of Sonia in roller coaster waves.

"Hey," I whispered. "Relax."

I placed my hand on her bare knee to still her, and she gripped my hand with so much force that her strength surprised me.

"I know." But the quiver in her voice told me she wouldn't be relaxing anytime soon. "I hate public speaking." She gnawed at her bottom lip, and her eyes flitted to the priest, to the bride and groom, and to the podium where she was going to speak.

When it was time for the second reading, Sonia stood and then straightened her skirt. She walked to the podium with her head down and her hands fidgeting with the sides of her skirt. It was as if she wanted to disappear. Why hadn't I noticed this before? At work, she seemed so sure of herself, confident.

Sonia adjusted the mic, which screeched, and her cheeks reddened. Then, she paused, lifted her head, and recited the Bible verse, her voice steady, strong, and slow enough for others to understand.

And, just like that, Sonia had stepped up to the plate, confidence back in her tone and the set of her shoulders. This was the girl I knew.

When she sat down, I reached for her hand and gave it a squeeze. "You were amazing."

She peered up at me with that adorable little pout. "Thanks."

Her body sagged against me as though she was glad that it was all over, and she scrunched her nose in the cutest way. As I wrapped an arm around her, I got the oddest sensation in the middle of my chest—an unrecognizable feeling, a lightness. The first thing that popped into my head was the story I had told Mary, about a prince saving Princess Sonia—because Mary had insisted that I name the princess Sonia in my nightly fairy tale.

I leaned in closer, and though every ounce of sanity was telling me I shouldn't and that I should keep my distance and that she was my secretary, I couldn't stop the urge to be near her.

An hour and a half later, we were at Gino's East pizzeria in a private room reserved for the wedding party.

"So ..." Ava said, eyes wide. "It's great that you're doing this for Sonia. Being her date and all. Jeff is an ass. I never liked him, but Sonia seemed to be so damn in love. He's a jerk for leaving her, and that Barbie chick—whoever she is—is not cute. At all. Fake boobs, Botox lips, fake eyelashes. It's the opposite of Sonia, who screams all-natural beauty."

I never knew a woman who could talk as much as Mary, but Ava had my niece beat. Her mouth was like a machine gun, shooting words at full speed. I doubted I could get a word in, so I nodded and tipped back my beer.

My gaze drifted back to Sonia across the room, by the bar. She was surrounded by four girls, all stealing glances my way. Sonia's cheeks turned a crimson red, and I could only imagine what they were grilling her about. Maybe they'd made up stories about our after-work bedroom activities. Maybe Sonia had bragged about me and my skills after hours, but as she ducked her head, focused her stare on the floor, and dug the toe of her boot into the ground, my smile slipped. Once the bartender set down her drink, she grabbed it and stalked my way.

"Excuse me," I said to Ava.

I met Sonia halfway and wrapped an arm around her waist against my better judgment—again. "So, what were you talking about over there?" I tipped my head toward the girls still gawking at us.

She blinked up at me, and her forehead wrinkled. "Nothing."

I lifted her chin to meet my eyes. "With women, I know *nothing* means something. Spill."

"They want to know if you're single." She peered behind her and then shook her head. "The nerve, right?" She teetered back and forth in her boots, gripping the glass of whatever she was drinking too tightly within her fingertips.

What fucking nerve was right. "Nice friends you have there." My body tensed, the muscles in my forearms going rigid.

"They're not my friends, not my real friends. They're acquaintances, and right now, they're annoying the hell out of me." She tipped back her drink and swallowed three full gulps. "How are they going to ask me that? I came here with you." Her expression pinched.

The women continued to whisper among themselves across the room. One of them raised a flirty hand in greeting, beyond disrespectful. They didn't care, but I sure as hell did. I slipped my arms around Sonia's waist and brought her close, nuzzling her neck, and the sweet scent of her hit me. My heartbeat picked up in speed, like an adrenaline rush, and I wasn't prepared for the shock of my body reacting to being so close to her.

What was that scent? Apples? Something sweet, not perfume. I angled closer, getting a deeper sniff, and a sudden urge to bite her in the most tender part of her skin—between her ear and her shoulder—pushed through.

I restrained myself before whispering, "Who am I? Your boyfriend? To them, I mean." My nose grazed the shell of her ear, and she shivered. "If you want them to stop looking, you have to play the part." My gaze lingered on her throat, and my hands went to the soft curves of her hips.

She pulled back, her eyes searching, and with the smallest voice possible, so tiny that I strained to hear her, she said, "Okay."

And then I kissed the corner of her mouth, close enough to taste those lips but with just enough restraint not to go there.

The shock of the contact went straight to my dick.

I heard her sharp intake of breath before she blinked up at me.

It was the tiniest of pecks, but I felt it everywhere. I was right. She smelled of apples. It must be her lotion or her shampoo.

She stiffened when I didn't release her right away, and I meant to, but I couldn't. The oddest realization came over me, one I'd never entertained. I wanted more of that kiss ... but a real kiss. With her.

Damn.

What is happening to me?

Her hands moved up my chest, and slowly, she pushed and backed away. Her eyes were wide and questioning, and when I peered up behind her, I realized I'd accomplished the very thing I had wanted to. The women were shocked, and the woman who had waved at me earlier sported a noticeable frown.

My focus went to Sonia when she touched the corner of her mouth, staring at me as though she didn't know what to say.

She blinked a few times and adjusted her glasses. "Well, that was weird."

"I thought that was rather nice." I captured her chin with my forefinger, swiping her bottom lip with my thumb, again having the undeniable urge to taste her fully.

My breathing slowed, and my eyes flickered to her lightly glossed pink lips.

Can't go there. She's my secretary. My brothers will feed my balls to some stray dogs.

I coughed, and after a few seconds too long, I slowly inched away from my tempting, sarcastic, and sweet secretary. "Sorry about that. I thought that was necessary, given what you're trying to accomplish." *What is she trying to accomplish? Make her boyfriend jealous, win him back, or am I truly eye candy to save her pride?*

"It's fine." She shook her head. "I mean, we'll have to up the game tomorrow for the wedding, right?" Her voice was shaky, sexy, soft.

She took a step back, a step too far, and her fingers flew to her lips again. She blinked, doe-eyed and dazed, and was so damn beautiful that, with all the warning signs that told me not to, I did it anyway. I kissed her again, in the same spot. I meant for her lips, a direct connection, but I missed.

"Brad!" Her eyes searched the room. When I smirked, she leaned into me. "I think you're enjoying this way too much. I might have to tattletale and tell Charles."

I pinched her side. "You wouldn't."

"Don't test me. I totally will." The apple of her cheeks flushed pink.

I was tempted to do it again, but I held steady. Because I thought of all that was at stake—my relationship with my brothers, my work relationship with her, our friendship.

I swallowed.

I needed self-control.

~

An hour later, we were parked in front of my house. The car ride was silent, and thoughts of kissing her again played over and over in my head. Kissing her today, just a peck at the corner of her mouth, had been like sticking a fork in the most tempting chocolate cake, taking a lick of the frosting, and stopping, knowing there was a whole cake to gorge on, a sweetness, a rich, decadent, delicious devil's food cake to devour.

Shit, this was going too far.

As I watched her fast asleep beside me—her mouth slightly ajar, the moonlight highlighting the delicate planes of her face, her glasses slipping off her nose—the need to take a deeper taste of her was overwhelming.

After a few minutes of watching her like a stalker, I softly nudged her. "Sonia." I brushed the strands of hair from her face. "Sonia, we're here."

She stirred and slowly blinked awake. Lifting up her arms over her head in a satisfying stretch, she moaned loudly. "I really, really have to pee."

God, was she cute. "Your car needs a tune-up."

I stepped out of the car, and when I opened her door, she flew out of the car.

She jumped up and down in what I would describe as

Mary's pee dance. "I know. I know. Hey, can you move a little faster and get the door open?"

When I opened the door, Sonia sprinted to the bathroom and was gone.

I was greeted by boisterous laughter.

Mary was in her favorite outfit—Princess Elsa from *Frozen*, wig, dress, shoes, and all. "Uncle Brad!"

She propelled forward, and I caught her in my arms. There was no way I'd ever get tired of this type of greeting.

"Where's Sonia? Where did she go?" Mary adjusted her long white wig on top of her head.

"Wait, let me get this straight." I narrowed my eyes. "I come into this house, you jump in my arms, and the first thing you say is, 'Where's Sonia?' Well, where's Sarah?"

Mary bounced in my arms and pointed to the family room. "She and Leilah are trying to find a movie to watch. I think *Beauty and the Beast* is the winner."

I peered down at the overhead clock in the kitchen. "Leilah has to go home. Her parents will be waiting for her."

Leilah was the seventeen-year-old neighbor that we hired on and off to babysit the girls. A much better alternative to the fired Annie.

"Well then, you have to stay up and watch the movie with us. We already popped some popcorn."

In typical Mary fashion, she pouted, pleading her case, and in typical favorite-uncle fashion, I rubbed my nose against hers.

"Okay, just this once."

"Hey, Mary," Sonia said, her face relieved, her hair a bit frazzled from the car.

Mary immediately jumped out of my hold, and Sonia was the new object of Mary's affection.

She propelled into Sonia's arms. "Watch a movie with us." And then, with her pout, she pushed out her lip further for emphasis. "Please. Please. Please, Sonia." Mary had perfected the cute baby voice, one that didn't come out as whiny but sweet.

"Oh, honey, I can't. I have to get up early for a wedding tomorrow."

"Pleeeeeease," Mary strung out the word, not giving up yet.

Sonia begged me with her eyes for assistance, but there was no way you could deter Mary when she was on a mission.

"Pretty please. We have the popcorn ready and pillows and blankets all laid out, and we're watching *Beauty and the Beast*, which is my favorite movie in the whole wide world. Please, Sonia. I'll never ever ask you for anything again. Ever."

That was a lie that I'd heard a million times before.

Then, Mary went in for the kill. She squeezed Sonia tighter, arms wrapped around her neck, and kissed her cheek like Woody Woodpecker, kissing and alternating with pleases.

When Sonia sighed, I knew she was a goner "Okay. Just for a little bit."

Mary claimed victory. With a loud squee, Mary was on her feet, running toward the family room, screaming, "Sarah! Sonia is staying!"

"She definitely should go into sales." Sonia rubbed the back of her neck and pushed out her lip in a pout of her own. "I have to get up at eight to make a nine o'clock hair appointment."

"Come on." I threw an arm around her shoulders, bringing her close, taking in her scent again. "The movie is only a couple of hours. Plus, Mary will fall asleep before it ends."

She huffed audibly loud and rested against me. "I didn't have a chance, did I?"

"Nope."

Mary could lay on the charm hard, and I'd seen no one who could resist. Except for Charles, her father, but that was only on very few occasions.

"I'm tired."

"Me, too." I dragged us into the living room where pillows from the couch and from their bedrooms were laid across the carpet up to our knees.

"This will make me fall asleep for sure." Sonia yawned and plopped down on the floor on top of a bed of pillows.

"Don't worry; I'll wake you up when Mary is fast asleep."

CHAPTER 10

SONIA

I snuggled closer. The soft feel of cotton pressed against my cheek. The clean fabric-softener scent filtered through my nose, and I nuzzled against it. When my hands moved against the firm surface beneath me, I lifted an eyebrow, forcing one eye open.

Then, my head snapped back. "Shit! Shit! Shit!" I jolted to a sitting position from the floor, watching Brad stretch in front of me.

The pillows and blankets were scattered all around us.

That cotton was his shirt; the firm surface was the span of his forever-pack, which was now slightly exposed, as his shirt was pushed up to below his nipple—by me.

My cheeks heated. I wouldn't doubt it if the heat spread to my forehead.

I guessed I was trying to get underneath the covers.

"What time is it?"

The room had cleared. Sarah and Mary must've gone upstairs to sleep in their respective bedrooms, leaving Brad and me all alone.

I hovered over him, reaching to the other side of him to

get to my eyeglasses and my purse on the hardwood. He watched me with amusement as I straddled his middle, unable to get to my glasses because I couldn't see a damn thing.

"Time. I need the time." After putting my glasses on, I plucked my phone from my purse and screamed. "Omigod, it's eight thirty! I'll never make it."

When I stood, Brad followed.

"Calm yourself. The wedding is not until one."

I smacked him with my purse. "I have a hair appointment at nine! You were supposed to wake me up. *Last night.*"

"You look fine." He tousled my matted hair. "You can just go like this." The heavy smirk that was signature to Brad was on display.

"Screw you."

He laughed, and a slice of six-pack showed when he lifted his arms to stretch. "Only if you want to, but I think Charles might not approve."

"Brad!" I whined. "Not funny."

I'd never make it. Get my hair done at the salon and be late, or do my hair myself, look like the help, and be on time. I wanted to cry.

I flipped around, grabbed my shoes, and stormed off to the entryway.

"I'm kidding, Sonia." He shuffled behind me and took hold of my shoulders, moving me to face him. "Breathe."

When I shook him off, his hands framed my shoulders again.

"Brad, I have to go!"

"Breathe, Sonia."

I blew out a breath and puckered my mouth into a pouty fish face.

"There. Feel better? And, now, go brush your teeth. I think we have some extra toothbrushes upstairs." He scrunched his nose as though my breath stank.

Did it? Oh, who the hell cared?

"Brad! I'm serious."

He gently shook me. "And I'm kidding. Hey, let's just divide and conquer, just like in business." He tipped up my chin. "What do you need to do?"

"Hair, makeup, get dressed." My voice came out in huffed, broken puffs to match my rapidly beating heart. "I need to leave and race to my hair appointment."

He checked the clock on the wall. "You'll never make it."

I shrugged him off. "Duh. I need to beg the salon to take me, like, right now." I searched my purse and came up empty-handed and then rushed back to the family room. "Where're my keys?" I paced the room, throwing the pillows and blankets on the couch. "Keys? Where are you?"

He shuffled behind me, picking up his phone from underneath another bed of pillows.

"Keys, Brad!"

Is he purposely ignoring me?

Great, he is making a call. What the heck is this guy doing?

"Hello, Selene." He smirked and then eyed me with amusement. "Yes, I need a big favor." And another laugh.

"Brad!" I gave him my evil stare and then dropped to my knees, looking underneath the couch, hunting for my keys. I needed to go, and stat.

"I'm going to a wedding today, and my date needs hair and makeup done. Is your team available this morning?"

On all fours, I peered up at him, confused.

"Thanks. I'll text you her address. Yes. Nine-thirty will

work. I owe you. Put it on my tab." He ended his call and extended a hand to help me up. "There, done."

"Who's Selene?" I asked.

"She owns a salon on the Gold Coast."

My hand flew to the base of my throat. "Selene Clives on Michigan Ave?" I whispered.

This man knew *the* Selene. Selene was a household name. Where Martha Stewart was known for all things home, Selene was known for all things beauty. Her clientele included all the A-list stars who walked the red carpet.

I blinked. "I can't afford Selene."

"It's fine. I'll take care of it." He handed me my keys. "Nine thirty, Sonia. Chop-chop. They'll meet you at your apartment." Then, he pulled me up and slapped my ass.

I didn't have time to chastise him. I was already out the door and in my car without a good-bye. For once, I was grateful for his connections.

An hour and a half later, I straightened in a chair in my kitchen, held a mirror up, and gawked at the woman staring back at me. Her brown hair was swept up with curls on the top of her head, and her makeup was immaculate. Transformation was an understatement. With my contacts on, a fresh coat of mascara, my eyebrows freshly waxed and trimmed, and makeup by the magical Selene team, I didn't even recognize myself.

"Well, darling. Do you like it?"

I peered up at Juan, Carole, and Nette.

When Brad had told me a team of beauticians would be coming to my house, he wasn't joking. The three of them, all dressed in black, had strolled into my mini apartment, each armed with a suitcase and ready to beautify. Juan was hair, Carole was makeup, and Nette was wax and plucking and had interned with the great Anastasia, the eyebrow-plucking queen.

"I love it." I touched my newly waxed eyebrows and tilted my chin, taking in cheekbones I'd never known I had. Contouring did wonders.

I felt like a princess, pretty in a light-pink lipstick to match the blush on my cheeks. "You guys did amazing. Thank you so, so, so, so much."

When I offered to tip them, they waved me off.

"Please, honey," Juan began. "Brad has tipped us well over what is normal. You're good." He placed his brushes in his oversize pouch and zipped it up.

"Over is an understatement," Carole added with a wink. "I hope you have another made-up evening real soon. Have fun."

After our farewell greeting, they left, and I nearly skipped to the bathroom. I shut the door and took in the beauty in my full-length mirror that hung on the back of my door.

"Wow. Take that, Replacement Girl." I popped out a hip and pushed out my nonexistent chest. "This is going to be fun."

An hour later, I slipped into the body-hugging, boob-enhancing, floor-length, backless dress. The shimmery blue V-neck spaghetti strap dress fit tightly up to my thighs and then tapered off in waves of simple ruffled fabric and into a mermaid tail. But the showstopper was the back of the dress —or lack thereof—where the beginning of the fabric cinched at my tailbone.

The knock on the door had my body tensing.

"One second." I did one more mirror check. Then, I

grabbed my purse, slipped on my heels, and rushed to the door. "Brad?"

"Did you invite someone else to this wedding?"

Crap. There was no way he could come into my apartment. First and foremost, it was a mess. Second ... my eyes followed the poster of him full of dart holes on my wall.

Yep. Nope, can't let him see that.

"Coming." I hurried and slipped into the hallway, and my eyes took him in.

All of him. In a tailored navy-blue suit, a skinny gray tie, and a smile that could drop panties anywhere.

Goodness, Brad was a fine sight.

My thought from earlier popped back into my head. *Yes, this was going to be fun.*

~

Brad

I blinked. Whatever I was going to say got jammed in my throat.

From the curls to the light sheen of pink on her cheeks and lips and the dress that fit as though it had been made for her, Sonia was magnificent—a princess in real fucking life.

"You're beautiful," I whispered without a second thought.

She stared, quietly, and her piercing eyes locked with mine. Then, as though she snapped back to attention, she playfully slapped my shoulder. "You aren't too bad yourself."

Without her eyeglasses, her brown eyes shone brighter. She looked like a different woman—still Sonia, but enhanced—one who showed her beauty and didn't hide it.

She turned around and headed to the elevators, and I

stopped breathing. Her bare back was the sexiest thing I'd ever seen. I wanted to run my finger from the base to the top of her slim, pale neck and then back down again but this time with my tongue.

I swallowed.

Shit, I was in trouble. Deep shit trouble because I doubted all the self-control in the world and all the big-brother threats would keep me away from this woman.

This was going to be an interesting night. That was for sure.

When we stepped off the elevator and into the lobby, a low, hoarse whistle had me turning to the side.

"Hot damn, Sonia."

A taller male with light hair and dark gray eyes and a coffee mug in hand walked toward us. When he reached for Sonia, my whole body tensed.

"Kyle." She lit up, moved toward him, and wrapped her arms around his neck, hugging him in greeting. "You're back from South America."

My jaw locked, and I stifled a growl in my throat. *Where the hell did that come from?*

When he wrapped his arms tightly around her waist, my hands fisted at my sides.

"I am. Just got back yesterday." He held her at arm's length, and his eyes took her in from the curls on the top of her head to her sexy neckline.

When his hand skimmed the bare of her back, I gritted my teeth and forced my body to stay put even though every molecule in me wanted to pounce and pull her back against me.

He wanted her. There was no doubt. I could read it in the way he leaned into her, the look of longing in his eyes. I could also read that Sonia was utterly clueless about it.

They made small talk before I cleared my throat and introduced myself. I stepped between them and offered my hand. "Brad."

"I'm sorry," Sonia said. "Brad, Kyle. Kyle, Brad." She motioned between us, and his smile slipped as though he'd just noticed I was in the room.

For shit's sake, we'd walked down together.

"Hey, man." Then, he eyed Sonia with curiosity. "Date?"

"Wedding," she clarified as if tonight were nothing.

He blinked back up at me. "Brad Brisken?"

I smirked, wondering where he'd seen me. *Crains Business Magazine* perhaps. "The one and only."

He let out an all-knowing laugh that grated on my nerves and then turned to Sonia. "When did this happen? I thought you hated this guy."

All my muscles tensed. "Excuse me?" I stepped into him, but Sonia grabbed my arm, yanking me toward her.

"It's fine." An anxious, high-pitched laugh escaped her. "We're fine. Everything is fine." She was already making her way toward the door with me in tow when she yelled back, "Brad is doing me a favor. I'll explain everything later, Kyle."

I turned toward her and narrowed my eyes. "You really hate me that much?" *Am I that much of an asshole to her at work?*

"I'll explain."

I opened the door to my Porsche 918 Spyder, closed the door behind her, then hopped into the car.

"This feels like a toy car." Her hand brushed against my dashboard, and she adjusted her seat to give her more leg room. "I like that it has that new-car smell."

Talk about queen of diversion.

I turned to her. "Explain."

She averted her gaze, looking down at her hands that wrung in her lap. "I ... I complain about you sometimes."

"Why?"

That forced her head up. "Why? Because you're a jerk."

She pulled back as though that wasn't what was supposed to come out of her mouth, but I'd take it. I didn't want our normal glossed-over relationship. I wanted honesty from her.

"I'm not," I argued. "I treat you with the utmost respect."

"Yes, when you're in a good mood." The sass was back in her tone, and I welcomed it. "But the problem is, you're not in a good mood all the time, and you take it out on everyone around you. Plus, you make me do things that are not a secretary's job."

"That's our relationship. I push at you. You give it right back."

She thought I was an asshole. I'd never been a purposeful asshole. That was just our relationship. Fun and games, but work still got done.

My muscles turned rigid. "I want examples."

She reeled back. "What?"

"Yes." I tapped my fist against the steering wheel. "Real-life examples."

"Oh, let me count the ways." She lifted one hand and began to tick off instances. "How about when you were already home, and I had to come to the office to throw away the bra of your recent rendezvous because you didn't want to get in trouble with Charles?"

Shit. I'd made it up to her, right? Okay, that was a douche move. But I'd bought her favorite doughnuts and coffee the next day.

"Or how about when you made me get your dry cleaning, and it wasn't clean enough, so you made me go to another dry cleaner to get it done the same day?"

"They'd done a shitty job."

"Well, you know that's not a secretary's job, right?" She glared at me with burning eyes. "I was doing you a favor." She continued. "Or how about when you made Chris, the new grad accountant, cry, and I was the one who had to console him? You didn't know about that one, did you?"

I shrank back into my seat.

She ticked off a fourth finger. "Or how about when the coffee spilled at that important meeting with that big honcho guy and I was helping to clean it up, and you embarrassed me and told me to get out of the office?"

Fifth finger. "How about the many times I've gotten your coffee, your lunch, fixed your schedule, including your three-week haircuts, and I hardly hear a thank you? Do I need to go on? Because this could be an all-day event, and we have a wedding to get to."

Shit.

I hung my head because she was right. About everything. I stared at the couple walking past my car, checking out the vehicle, checking out Sonia and me. A woman in a skirt suit passed, carrying a Starbucks cup in each of her hands, and I was brought to months ago, to the boardroom where I had been leading a meeting.

I cleared my throat, coming clean about that day and spilling the coffee. "I didn't like how he was looking at you."

"Who?" She frowned.

I kept my gaze out the windshield, sighing loudly. "Bill Townsend. He'd spilled the coffee on purpose, and I know you wanted to help, but I didn't like how he was looking at you. He wanted to see you bend and clean up the mess, and the shirt you were wearing ... it was a little see-through."

"No, it wasn't." Her face lost its color.

I reached for her hand, meaning my next words more than I'd ever meant anything before. "I'm sorry. I know I was harsh that day, but I wanted you out of that room, out of his view." My thumb brushed over the top of her fist. "And I am thankful for you and what you do every day. The reason I ask those things from you is because I'm comfortable around you, Sonia, and I trust you." I did. There was no one in the office, other than my brothers, whom I trusted more. I was an asshole to them on the daily, but it didn't make it right. "So, I'm sorry. And, for future requests, you have every right to deny them, and I won't hold it against you."

She was quiet for far too long, and I waited for what seemed like an eternity for her to say something, anything.

"I forgive you."

Those three words had my body relaxing.

She squeezed my hand back. Then, she retracted her hand from mine and turned toward the road, shifting in her seat. "That was oddly refreshing, getting that all out in the open." She laughed. "Now, let's drive. We have a wedding to get to."

I quirked an eyebrow. "Who's the bossy one now?" I turned the key in the ignition, revved up the engine, and drove.

CHAPTER 11

SONIA

The ride to the church was the slowest, most agonizing ride of my life. Sweat formed between my boobs, in my palms, at my temples. Not because of the awkward conversation between Brad and me. No, that was long forgotten, replaced by memories of Jeff and me.

I did not want to do this. To see him with her, kissing and holding hands and dancing, all throw-up happy, the way we had been once.

When we stopped at the front of the church, my stomach churned.

"I can't breathe." I inhaled deeply through my nose and exhaled a ragged breath.

I gripped the dashboard of Brad's Porsche, closed my eyes, and dropped my chin to my chest. All I could see was darkness behind my eyelids as I clenched them shut. All I could smell was the leather new-car scent of Brad's automobile, and all I could feel was my manicured fingernails digging into the tender part of my palms. Sweat formed behind my neck even though the air was blasting on high and my hair was up in an array of curls pinned to the top of my head. The bodice of my dress squeezed my rib cage, limiting my airflow.

"I can't breathe," I repeated, concentrating on getting air to fill up my lungs.

"You're fine. You're exaggerating. You did fine during the rehearsal." His voice was calm and steady, opposite to my erratically beating heart.

I shook my head. This had nothing to do with the rehearsal and everything to do with Jeff. It had been months, and I knew, one look into my face, he'd know I wasn't over him. The humiliation would kill me, like a bullet.

Breathe. Why is it so hard to breathe?

"You're fine. You'll do fine," he reiterated. His hand went to the back of my neck, rubbing and massaging.

"I want to go home." The fear of seeing Jeff suddenly choked me, tears nearly warming the backs of my eyes. All the pent-up emotions and anticipation had built up to this one day, our first after-breakup meeting.

Brad's warm hand massaged between my shoulder blades, but it did nothing to calm my nerves. "I've never seen stage fright like this before. It's one reading. You'll do amazing, just like yesterday."

My eyes flipped open, and I stared at him, dumbfounded. He was clueless.

"This is not about a stupid reading." I clutched my stomach, trying to hold myself together, almost to the point of hyperventilating. "This is about seeing Jeff when I haven't seen him in forever. Seeing him happy and in love with my replacement, Barbie two-point-oh, when this ..." I motioned between us. "... is all pretend."

Brad's hold dropped from my shoulder to my hand. "It's not going to be that bad. That's why I'm here, right?"

His fingers intertwined with mine, and he gave it a squeeze.

I peered up at him, wishing and hoping that his words were true, and for a tiny moment, his touch relaxed me.

"How do you know?" My words came out as a breathless whisper.

"Because I do. Trust me?" There was sincerity in his tone, one that startled me for a second. The tone he used on his nieces to tell them that everything was going to be okay.

"Do I have a choice?" Because, do or die, I had to trust him at this point. I was banking that being seen with him would lessen the humiliation, maybe even lessen the hurt.

"That's true." Then, his sparkling smile made an appearance. "Let's go, my new fake girlfriend. Let's see if we can rile up the ex."

He stepped out of the car and opened my door. After he extended his hand, I placed my hand in his, and he hooked it through his arm, pulling me closer. With the most tender of kisses, he pecked my forehead.

I peered up at him, and a vulnerability I rarely ever showed pushed through. "Tell me it's going to be okay." I gathered the sides of my dress, flattened it, and then gathered it again, squeezing the fabric between my fingertips.

He tipped my chin with the flick of his thumb and hummed the beginning of "Everything's Gonna Be Alright" by Bob Marley, and I had a hard time not smiling.

He can be cute. Sometimes.

"Will you stop fidgeting? You're drop-dead gorgeous with that dress on. Though I prefer you with glasses on, too." He led us to the front of the church.

I made a face. "You like the glasses? Why?" The nerdy glasses. *Why would anyone like my nerdy Harry Potter glasses?*

"Because ... it's you." He said it as though it were fact, no inflection in his tone.

I didn't have time to contemplate what he meant by that before we were at the steps of the church.

I took one more breath.

It's showtime.

I forced a smile and kept my eyes steady on the door. If Jeff was here, I didn't want to see him yet. I wasn't ready, though I doubted I'd be ready anytime soon. I sent a silent prayer to the Almighty above to wait until the reception because it was inevitable. Maybe my nerves would be calm by then. Probably not.

The insides of my palms began to sweat when everyone's eyes turned our way—more so, Brad's way. Every woman gawked—women with dates, married, old, and young—and even straight men, taking him in, sizing him up, and then quickly turning away to realize that they weren't up to par.

And, in that instant, I knew that I had made the right decision, bringing him here. He was a showstopper.

The pews were decorated with an array of pink and white roses, and cascading white tulle swooped down each row. I gazed at the crucifix in front of me and the stained-glass windows that brought in the natural light through every part of the room.

Though I was practically naked, my body heated as though I were experiencing hot flashes. I shifted and adjusted my dress, centering my neckline.

"You're fidgeting again," he said quietly, dropping his arm to link our hands.

"I can't help it. I'm not used to wearing dresses this tight and revealing, and I cannot freaking breathe." I pulled at the front of the dress again. Honestly, it wasn't the dress that was restricting the air to my lungs; it was thoughts of Jeff and my replacement.

Since the runner was already laid down the middle aisle, we walked down the outer aisle and through the side, and as we passed a few people, they openly gawked.

A few ladies stood at the front pew. They seemed about my age, a taller blonde and a redhead. The woman smiled, a little bashful. After, their eyes perused me. I blew out a tiny breath. I could read what ran through their expressions. *What the hell is he doing with her?*

It was so obvious that they might as well have said it out loud, but I didn't care. I wasn't really with him.

So there. Eat that, everyone, with your judgmental eyes.

Brad ushered me down the aisle, and my eyes zoned into the seat where I needed to be, the third row from the front.

Focus. Focus. Focus. Keep your eyes on your destination.

I had one job: to read the second reading about love and marriage and how love was patient and kind and all that jazz, even when I didn't believe in things like that anymore. A broken heart would do that. It crushed you and changed your beliefs.

I stepped into my pew, followed by Brad; all the while, his hand was on the small of my bare back. Heat rose from where he touched.

He leaned into me, so close that the scent of his cologne filtered through my nose, hitting all my senses.

"You smell good." With anyone else, I'd be less honest, trying to front it. With Brad, that was all we were—honest and blunt.

"You look divine," he dished right back. There was a huskiness in his voice that surprised me.

I brushed it off. I knew him too well, with his lines and his lusty looks. If I didn't know him better, I would've fallen for it.

"Breathe," he said. The warmth of his minty breath brushed against my skin and pushed goose bumps to the surface.

"I'm okay." I twisted the shimmery fabric of my dress within my fingertips, wringing it as though I were crumbling a sheet of paper.

His look told me he wasn't convinced.

I straightened when we were seated in the pew, feeling the cold wood behind me, a contrast from the warmth Brad radiated beside me and the heat wave I'd experienced moments before. My eyes perused the beautiful church. The old wooden bench, the cross in the center of the room, the two floral arrangements in the front filled with hydrangeas and gladiolas and roses, all in an array of whites and creams and pinks.

Kelly, a college friend, waved to me, and when I turned to wave back, my eyes caught sight of Jeff sitting several pews behind me, next to my replacement, her beauty radiating against every light in the room.

My whole body went rigid, and my jaw locked. Jeff smiled, but I couldn't. When Blonde Barbie by his side met my eyes, I jerked back around before I could get a better look, and a gut-wrenching pang shot straight to my chest.

Brad followed my line of sight, sensing my change of mood.

I elbowed his side. "Face forward!" I whisper-yelled.

His eyes locked with mine. Then, he leaned in and kissed the tender part below my ear.

I reeled back. "What are you doing?"

His stupid smirk surfaced. "What I agreed to do—playing a part." He pressed another kiss to my cheek and tucked an escaping curl around my ear. "Is that him?" He subtly jerked his head behind us.

"Yes," I whispered under my breath, my cheeks burning bright from the lingering kiss. "Turn back around."

"I expected better. He's not all that." There was underlying disdain in his tone.

But Jeff had been. He had been all that, my other half, the butter to my bread, the yin to my yang. Until, one day, he hadn't been anymore, and he was all that to someone else.

Brad grabbed my face, squeezing my cheeks between his fingertips where they puffed out, chipmunk-style. "He's not." Then, he leaned in to kiss right by the corner of my mouth, the same place as last night.

Why does he keep doing that? Missing on purpose? Not that I wanted him to kiss me. It was just odd that he kept on missing the mark.

Of course—boundaries.

He wanted to maintain boundaries. Right.

I was about to say something when the processional of Pachelbel's Canon in D echoed through the church, and everyone turned to the groom walking down the aisle.

For a brief moment, all other thoughts disappeared, and I took in the groom walking down the aisle. Tim looked dapper in his three-piece suit, the royal blue in his tie bringing out the gray in his jacket. When I'd met him, he was a lanky freshman in college, skin and bones. Now, he was taller, broader, older. Though college wasn't that long ago, it seemed as though a decade had passed.

The doors closed, and the processional song changed.

The whole congregation stood. When the doors opened at the entrance, you could hear the whole crowd's intake of breath, mine included.

Carrie was stunning with her elaborate ball gown, which cinched at her waist and flared out into a princess skirt. Her hair was pulled up into curls at the crown of her head, and from underneath, her curls hung a mile long, lace veil with intricate designs outlining the edge. Her father, a linebacker-sized patriarch of the family, stood tall right beside her, tears rimming his eyes, which was so unlike his big and buff demeanor. But it was understandable since Carrie was the first of his many daughters to get married.

I snapped about five pictures when she passed by our pew, and I was so engrossed in her beauty and Tim's face at the end of the aisle. It wasn't until after that that I noticed Brad's warm body pressed against mine, his arms wrapped around my waist, pulling me in front of him, his fingers linked together around my middle.

When Tim shook Carrie's father's hand and took Carrie's hand in his, tears nearly burned the backs of my eyes, for her happiness and for their forever future together.

And, at that moment, I couldn't help but wonder about my own future.

One by one, my friends had been trickling off into the holy bonds of matrimony. We were all about the same age—twenty-five, twenty-six. And, for those who weren't taking the leap into marriage, they were making some sort of serious relationship commitment by either living together, getting a dog, or even having babies.

That should've been me. Or at least, I should've been on my way.

That familiar pang hit the center of my chest, harder this time. I didn't need to turn around and see Jeff to know he wasn't thinking the same thing—the what-could've-been between us—because he had moved on. Fast and hard with Miss Blonde Victoria's Secret model.

When it was my turn to read, I stood on cue, but before I left, Brad leaned in and whispered, "Kick some ass."

He winked, and I wiped the sleek sweat from my palms on the sides of my dress. With all the false energy I could muster, I straightened my back and put one foot in front of the other, slowly making my way up to the stairs and to the podium.

My eyes scanned the room, first landing on Tim and Carrie but then straying to Jeff and my new replacement.

I cleared my throat, but nothing came out, not a single word. My palms began to sweat like a dripping faucet. I closed my eyes for a quick second and took a deep breath through my nose. When I opened my eyes, they zoned in on Brad, who gave me a little smile, giving me the courage to continue and dimming my nervousness just a tad.

And I started, *"Love is patient, love is kind ..."*

I uttered the words of one of the most famous scripture readings of the Bible, my eyes still on Brad, and for a brief moment, all the noise in the room dimmed, and the people and congregation faded to a blur.

My pulse slowed to an even beat, and my voice was loud and clear. All my attention was focused on the man in front of me.

When I recited the line, *"It does not boast, it is not proud,"* his smile widened, which made my insides lighten because proud was the epitome of who Brad was and boasting was his pastime.

Before I knew it, I steadily uttered the last line. *"Love always protects, always trusts, always hopes, always perseveres. Love never fails."*

And, as I stepped down from the podium, I realized that this was also what Brad represented. When I thought of his devotion to his family and how he loved his nieces, this verse reminded me of him.

I waved to Carrie and Tim when I made my way to my seat, overjoyed that I'd had an opportunity to be a part of their wedding, contribute in this way as a reader.

When I entered the pew, Brad's hand intertwined with mine, and he kissed the top.

"You did beautifully." He smiled and fingered an escaping strand of hair, tucking it behind my ear. "I love that passage. We'll have to have it at our wedding."

"Har-har-har." I rolled my eyes.

We both watched as Carrie and Tim began their vows, pledging their love for one another, and a familiar longing pulsed in my chest.

When Brad squeezed my hand, the tender gesture had the first tear falling down my cheek. I swiped at my cheek, and when I did, his hold tightened.

Like an unpredictable gentleman, he plucked tissues from his pocket and handed me one. He said in a low voice, "I Googled what to bring to a wedding."

"You're such a dork," I whispered.

Soon, the officiant pronounced them as man and wife, and the congregation was on their feet. My smile could not be dimmed as the groom kissed the bride, and they practically skipped down the aisle and made their way back to the front to take pictures.

Two sweet little girls with a crown of flowers in their hair passed out little clear containers with bubbles. *Blow kisses for the new couple* was written on the label along with the newlyweds' initials.

Brad followed behind me with his hand on the small of

my back as we made our way outside to wait for the couple to make their rounds again.

"Sonia."

I froze from the sound of my name falling from his lips. I'd remember that voice in my sleep, in my dreams, after I was dead.

I inhaled deeply, turned around, and plastered a smile on my face. So wide that my cheeks hurt from the strain.

Jeff stood there, almost six feet in height, dapper in a black suit, red tie, and glasses very similar to my black frames. His girlfriend was in a skintight fiery-red dress, which hugged her figure like Saran Wrap.

My stomach rolled, and my heartbeat slowed. At that moment, I remembered what heartbreak was and was reverted back to months ago when I had cried for hours on my couch. I wanted to do it again, right here and now.

"Hey." I pushed confidence in my tone that I didn't have. There were so many things to say, so many questions to ask, but so much time had passed so that one word was all I had. My whole body froze when Brad slipped his arm around my waist and pulled me flush against him.

"Hey." Jeff's eyes immediately flew to assess Brad.

Funny enough, his girlfriend's eyes appraised Brad as well.

"Crazy how they got married, right?" Jeff said, attempting small talk.

"Yeah." Not really, given they'd been together forever. I simply nodded. My gaze focused on my pointy designer shoes, a name I couldn't even pronounce.

A short silence filled the awkward space between us, and of course, Brad was the first to speak. "Aren't you going to introduce me to your friend?" Brad moved his hand lower on my back, just above my ass cheek. He extended his other hand, introducing himself to Jeff and his date. "Brad." His smile was cocky and confident. "Sonia's boyfriend." The words rolled out of his mouth in a possessive, masculine manner that made me think he'd pound his chest, caveman-style, next.

I inhaled deeply and held my breath because, even though I had this fine man beside me, I wanted to cower and hide and run back home to the comfort of my couch.

Jeff smirked, but I knew this smirk; it was a tiny, forced smile that told me he wasn't too happy, which didn't make a lick of sense because he had dumped me.

"Nice to meet you, man." Jeff gripped Brad's hand in one of those manly handshakes. "I'm Jeff."

"Jeff?" Brad spat out the word like it was brussels sprouts in his mouth. Then, his eyes met mine. "Oh, is this *the* ex?" he asked, pretending to be quiet but fully knowing they could hear him.

I had to give Brad credit. In his former life, he'd probably been an award-winning actor.

My eyes widened, but Brad continued. "Oh." He let out a low laugh. "I guess I expected something ... different." His eyes scanned Jeff's suit as though he had a piece of dirt on it, and since it wasn't a designer, it wasn't good enough.

My face turned beet red, and blood pounded in my ears, reaching to my temples. Where was my genie in the bottle? My three wishes granted. I'd take one. *Get me out of here*, being my only wish.

Jeff's eyebrows furrowed, and the Barbie behind him cleared her throat. "Jean." She extended her nicely manicured hand to Brad, not me. "Pleased to meet you."

Of course, I'd already known her name. I'd stalker-stalked and Google-gawked this woman.

Brad met her hand and then dropped it, his face devoid

of any emotion. He made it seem like shaking Jean's hand was a chore. "Have you met my lovely Sonia?" he asked, basically pushing me in front of her double Ds. "Doesn't she look beautiful?" Then, he scanned her dress with distaste.

I raised an eyebrow, throwing him a look. *What is this, the Oscars?*

God, this is awkward. I glanced toward the door, but then Carrie and Tim were still inside. *Where were the groom and bride when I needed them?* I wanted to stay silent and blow my stupid bubbles.

Jean did a hair flip and then brought some of her long locks to one side. "Hi, Sonia. I've heard so much about you."

I sensed that it was such a loaded statement, given her condescending tone.

I shook her hand and couldn't stop staring at her pink bubbalicious lipstick staining her lips. "I hope all good things." Because that was what I was supposed to say.

"Yes, omigod," she gushed, adjusting her dress because she was spilling over the two-sizes-too-small gown. "Even when Jeff and I used to work together, he'd talk about you nonstop."

She lovingly gazed at him, and I wanted to stick my finger down my throat and gag.

A ringing in my ears initiated.

The fake smile I was sporting disappeared.

Wait.

They used to work together.

Work together.

The color drained from my face. My eyes were trained on Jeff, but he didn't make eye contact. *Were we still together when he started to have feelings for her? Did he dump me because of her?*

Jeff cleared his throat, looking only slightly uncomfortable. "Yeah, she left when I made partner at the firm."

I nodded and gripped my stomach, feeling nausea hit me straight in the gut. We'd still been together when Jeff made partner. I wondered if indiscretion had caused Jean to leave the office.

I rocked back on my heels, my equilibrium off. "Why did you leave?" I asked before I could even stop it.

"Complications." She giggled.

Jeff still could not meet my gaze, and my hands trembled at my sides as I ran down the timeline of our relationship in my head.

He wouldn't. The Jeff I knew didn't cheat, but the Jeff I thought I knew also wouldn't have left me.

Brad piped up. "Funny, when we got together, she never mentioned Jeff once, but then again ..." He kissed the side of my neck. "... I'm sure she can think of nothing else but me when we're together."

His hand slipped further down my back, to my ass, and he squeezed, but I didn't even react, didn't feel a thing, except for this burning sensation rising in my gut and a fear that my gut was never wrong.

Had Jeff and I ever been real? I searched Jeff's face, willing him to look at me when he was lovingly looking at her.

Just then, the bridesmaids made their way out the door, and so did the bride and groom. Bubbles were blown, kisses were exchanged, and I couldn't get out of Jeff's and Jean's sight fast enough. I walked steadily in the direction of the car, and when I knew I was out of view, I sprinted.

I rushed into the car and slumped against the seat of Brad's fancy Porsche. I gripped the warm leather beneath my fingertips, wishing, hoping, wanting to melt into the seat. Maybe I could forget that all of this was happening.

"So, that's Jeff," Brad said, his tone indicating he wasn't impressed.

"The one and only." My only, I had thought at one point. *Where did I go wrong? Where did I fail him in our relationship? When did I stop being good enough?*

My pulse slowed, and the hollowness in my chest widened.

"Interesting," he merely commented.

"Interesting?" I gave him a pointed look. "What's so interesting about our interaction? Was it the fact that I probably looked like I wasn't over him? Was it the fact that I'd never heard about Jean until today, yet she'd heard everything about me? Was it the fact that he was probably cheating on me the whole time we were together?" I slammed a fist against the dashboard and clenched my jaw to prevent the tears from falling.

"Who cares?"

I blinked, my mouth slipping slightly ajar. "Who cares?"

His face was devoid of emotion, even compassion, which a heartbroken girl could've used a little of by now. "I mean, why should you care? It's over."

"Because it still hurts!" I burst into a ball of emotional fury. "Have you ever been in love? So deeply in love that you want to be with them all the time and the sun rises and sets on their face and they're the last person you want to see at the end of your day?" I tore my gaze from his and stared vacantly out the window, watching happy couples hold hands and head to their vehicles.

"I gave my everything to that relationship. He was my *it* guy. The one for me, the one I was going to have children with. We shared our hopes and dreams for the future, our future. We talked about it. He talked about it, and then, one day ... it was like those conversations never existed." Tears warmed behind my lids.

"You wouldn't know anything about this because you've never, ever been in love before or had an *it* person." My trembling hands flew to my chest, and I visibly shook. "It does matter because everything I thought was real was fake if he was with her, and I refuse to believe our relationship was a lie." I dropped my head into my hands, not wanting to relive this nightmare of a day that had barely started.

I took deep breaths through my nose and exhaled through my mouth to calm the ache in the center of my chest.

I will not cry.
I will not cry.
I will not cry in front of my boss.

He drove, and I wallowed in the silence, in my thoughts of the life I had once lived with Jeff.

Brad didn't say a word. Good, because I needed the quiet, the tiny bit of rest that I knew would disappear once we were at the reception.

When we parked, I lifted my head from my hands and pulled down the overhead mirror to check my eyeliner. I swiped at my bottom lid with my index finger. You'd think I'd be embarrassed that I'd poured out all my insides on Brad's dashboard, but we'd crossed that line days ago.

Internally, I told myself that everything would be fine, and if not, I'd pretend for everyone else.

"You're right." His voice was quiet, resigned, without its usual bite.

I tilted my head to look at him.

"Sonia, I've never had an *it* person. I've also never had my heart broken before, so I can't relate."

My jaw tightened. Must be nice to be the breaker of hearts and never have had your heart broken. I swiped at my nose.

"But, when I said who cares ..." His eyes filled with uncensored compassion. "I meant that *you* shouldn't care. If he broke your heart, then your heart wasn't all that important to him. And, if he promised things, things of the future, and broke those promises, that only means he was a liar who wasn't worth your time. Just forget about him."

Our eyes locked for a second too long until I ripped my gaze from his. His words were meant to comfort me, but they did the opposite. They gave me unrest.

"Easier said than done," I whispered.

If I could forget him, I would've by now.

And, if Brad had ever in his entire life fallen in love, then he would've known that.

He sighed. "All I know is, in business and in all things, promises mean something. Integrity and honesty hold the utmost importance." He unlocked his door and opened it. "And, when I find my *it* person and someone by chance gives me their heart, I know I won't take that lightly, and I won't break it. Because some things cannot be undone."

CHAPTER 12

SONIA

When we walked in, I took in the reception hall, round tables covered by black tablecloths and chairs decked out in black-and-white satin in an old Hollywood vibe. Each table was adorned with tall arrangements of white hydrangeas, and streams of black-and-pink satin ribbons adorned each pilsner vase.

My nerves were shot, and I never, ever drank, but I swore tonight that I would. I couldn't remember the last time I'd gotten drunk—maybe tipsy, but never drunk. Tonight, as soon as I had food in my belly, I would make it to the bar and join the brokenhearted to drink my sorrows away.

A piano played softly in the background, and waiters in tuxes and white gloves greeted us at every corner of the room.

"Food." I grabbed a napkin from the blond waiter and also a bacon-wrapped date. I was on my way to getting my belly full. Soon, I'd be at the bar.

I grabbed two more appetizers and then turned to Brad. "One for you. Two for me." I smirked.

"Are you one of those people who eats when you're nervous or gets moody when you're not fed?"

Another waiter passed with shrimp cocktail, and I turned from Brad and grabbed four. "No, I just like to eat." Then, I leaned into him, cheeks puffed out and mouth full. "You have to promise me something."

The devilish smile was on display, the one that seemed to be permanently fixed on his face. "Shoot."

"Promise me that, when I get a little tipsy, you'll take me home."

His smile deepened.

"To my house, idiot." I smacked his shoulder and popped another shrimp in my mouth. "I trust you not to do anything inappropriate." Because, although Brad was a little manwhore, I knew he would never force himself on any woman. He didn't have to. "And please promise you'll keep me in check and prevent me from embarrassing myself or my friends."

"And why would I do that?" He laughed.

I rolled my eyes, and just like I'd seen him pinkie promise with his niece, I stuck out my left pinkie. "Promise."

He curiously eyed me. "Fine. Promise." Then, he wrapped his pinkie finger around mine and pulled me into a kiss.

A real one. Mouths closed, lips to lips, and his one hand on my hip. My shrimp was still in my mouth, for heaven's sake! My eyes widened, and my whole body stiffened into a wooden pole.

He held me there for a second before he moved his free hand up the length of my body to cup my face. "Breathe."

Breathe? Shit! What I need to do is swallow the shrimp in my mouth.

"Don't turn around," he said discreetly, his breath hot on my cheek. "We have an audience."

So, what did I do? Yes, I turned around to see Jeff and Jean staring directly at us.

I gulped down my shrimp, and my pulse increased in tempo.

Brad linked our fingers together. "Do you live to do the opposite of what I tell you?" he asked.

I wanted to slap his amusement away. "Whatever. I do practically everything you tell me to do."

He frowned. "What do you mean?"

"I do everything you say."

"You do not," he argued lightly but looking just a little slighted.

"I do, too," I said, raising my voice a little.

"If you do it, it's not without complaint." He shook his head. "You don't think I hear you whisper stuff under your breath, but I do." He ducked his face close to mine. "You think I don't know what you say to your friends about me, but I know that, too."

I popped the last shrimp in my mouth, chewed slowly, and pretended not to react.

Well, shit, that couldn't be good.

"And don't pretend you don't make stuff up at work," he continued, making his point. "Like they didn't have my sandwich at Bello's or that restaurant was fully booked when I requested reservations when it was clearly not."

Busted. I looked away. "Sometimes, you're a pain in my ass." Honesty leaked out of me. And I wasn't even drunk yet. Was there any hope for me tonight?

"I know," he sighed. "I'm trying to be better."

I blinked up at him. "Since when?" I asked, noticing the seriousness in his features.

He scratched the back of his neck and shook his head. "Since Sarah said I should try being nicer to you."

"Oh." Recently then.

"I'm just wired the way I am, and sometimes, I don't realize I'm being an asshole, okay?" A waiter with a display of ham croquettes passed us. Brad grabbed one off the tray and handed me the little wrapped appetizer in a napkin. "But I'm trying at least."

"Okay." I took a bite of the croquette, noticing the grease staining the napkin. "I'll be nicer, too."

"You? Nice?" A louder laugh escaped him. "To me? That'll be a first."

I barely contained a growl. Maybe this was too much honesty for one day. "I think I've filled my belly enough." I reached for his hand, dragging him toward the bar area. "Let me buy you a drink." I winked.

"It's an open bar."

"Exactly! I'm being nice already."

We stopped by Krystal and Helen and Brandy on our way to the bar. They were a few girls that I knew, acquaintances from college. I didn't miss the way their eyes scanned Brad from his head down to his shiny designer shoes.

"So, you're in business?" Krystal said with a little lilt in her tone. She flashed Brad her pearly whites even though her date stood right beside her. "I was a business major in college, minored in international finance."

She began to tick off her résumé while Brad smiled but looked not a bit impressed.

Brad being polite? This was new. He stayed silent, but I could read his thoughts.

I was surprised, given Brad's ego, that he didn't just shut her down and tell her he owned one of the biggest printing companies in North America.

When she placed her hand on his forearm, I stiffened. She was blatantly flirting, but I didn't know what to do because it was clearly in front of me, and we were playing a part. Any other normal girlfriend would be livid.

When I stepped back, Brad's arm circled my waist. "It was nice meeting you, Krystal. I should get my bae a drink now."

I choked on my own saliva and coughed. "Bae?" I whispered when we approached the bar.

"Before Anyone Else. Like babe." He reached for my hand and intertwined our fingers. "I learned the lingo from my niece."

I laughed. "Who are you right now?"

"Your bae." He chuckled darkly before lifting his arm up to get the bartender's attention. "Long Island?" he asked, his eyes never leaving mine.

I scrunched my face, wondering how he knew my drink of choice.

"I pay attention," he said, answering my silent question.

"When have I ever drank in front of you?"

"Christmas party. Last year." He placed a five-dollar bill on the counter and handed me my drink.

Wait. What? He remembered that?

I didn't have time to ponder that further because, as I turned around, I once again heard my name being called out.

It was Jeff.

∽

Brad

Sonia's whole body stiffened. I'd never in the two years that I had known her caught her speechless and so off-kilter, and it uneased me.

"Hey, Jeff." After she placed the tall glass of liquor between her lips and took a big gulp, she grabbed a handful of her dress, crumpling it within her fingertips.

I hated how this man had this kind of effect on her.

For a brief moment, I took him in. The light-blondish-brown in his hair, the emerald green in his eyes, hidden behind square-framed glasses. The way his suit hugged his tall, lanky frame. He looked like a hipster, and although I didn't want to admit it, I could see them together. Sonia and him.

If there were a lineup of eligible bachelors and I had to take a guess on who she'd pick as her match, this guy would be it.

Jean smiled my way. Her short red tube dress hugged her figure and stopped right below her ass. If she wanted to make a statement, she was making it loud and clear. She was here with Jeff.

With her red dress, his plain suit and white shirt, they both looked regular. Nothing spectacular. But they certainly were an oddly paired couple, opposites in every sense of the word.

"What table are you guys sitting at?" Jean asked, but when she did, she was looking at me the way women looked at me, as though if given a chance, I'd be their choice of date. What bothered me was that it was like Sonia wasn't here.

I pulled Sonia close, the movement so quick that her

Long Island swished, and some of the liquid slipped over the lip of the glass.

"Where are we sitting, babe?" I asked, leaning in so close to smell some of Sonia's shampoo.

She blinked up at me and pulled a small white paper from her purse. The paper that we had picked up at the center table before we walked into the reception area.

"Table ten." Her voice quivered, and it took all my energy not to sweep her away from this mess, go back to my house, and spend the rest of the night playing board games with Mary and Sarah.

"Oh poo, we're at a different table," Jean uttered.

The slight tightness in Sonia's shoulders relaxed.

She was always so put together, so organized, so focused. Being around Jeff undid her, and I didn't like it.

"So, how did you guys meet?" Jeff asked, studying me. He'd been doing that since I met him.

I recognized the scrutiny in his eyes. It was the same scrutiny that I had met with many business associates, right before I was going to take over their company.

"At work, just like you guys."

He shuffled back a step. "So, you work at Brisken. You're admin?" he assumed.

My smirk tightened. "No. I own Brisken."

Jeff's eyes went wide for just a second. "You own Brisken Printing Corporation?" he asked as though he didn't understand English. He scratched at his temple. "Sonia's your secretary? Aren't there rules about dating your subordinate?" Jeff asked, his face unreadable.

"I wouldn't call her my subordinate because it's Sonia who runs my office."

Then, his face transformed, first with contempt and slowly with recognition. He let out a peal of laughter.

"You're *the* boss? Oh my God. Sonia ..." He pointed to Sonia, "... you hated this guy. You drew doodles of him and had stakes going through his heart."

His laughter heightened, and it took every ounce of my energy not to clock him out cold.

Of all the people she complained to about me, this had to be the worst. I hated that she'd, at one time, complained to *him* about *me*.

"It's different now." Sonia's voice was low, without the usual strength and sass. Her face was beet red.

Jeff coughed to stop his laughter when he realized no one else was laughing with him. "Sorry. I didn't know your real name, just a bunch of names Sonia used to call you." Then, his eyes passed over both of us, and the fit of cackles started up again. "So, she's your subordinate? She still works for you."

My jaw tightened. I didn't know where this guy was going. Did he by chance think that I had forced Sonia into our pretend relationship all because she worked for me?

I kept my voice even. "No. She's most definitely not my subordinate—unless you count when we're in the bedroom, and she likes me to boss her around."

Sonia coughed up her Long Island, and the humor on Jeff's face dissipated instantly.

I handed her a napkin, my devious smirk heavy on my face. If we were playing the game of whose balls were bigger, there was no competition.

Jeff blurted, "Well, there are clear rules at the office I work at that, once a couple gets involved, one has to quit."

"Is that why Jean quit?" Sonia snapped, her tall glass now empty. "Because you were screwing her when you worked together? Possibly when we were together? Late-night meetings, my ass."

Well, that had come from nowhere.

Jeff sputtered, "No. That's not ..."

But, by the look on Jean's guilty, reddened face, I could only assume that was indeed what had happened.

"Asshole," Sonia whispered before turning and storming off. And the Sonia I knew and adored was back and in full force.

I didn't excuse myself from their presence. I simply went after her, down the hall and outside.

A row of green shrubs led us to a massive fountain outlined with concrete benches. Sonia dropped on a bench and faced away from the reception area, away from me.

"He's such a fucker." A deep sob escaped her, and it gutted me.

It was the first time I'd ever heard her drop the F-bomb. But I preferred a pissed off Sonia over a sad Sonia or a fidgety Sonia or a no-backbone Sonia.

"I won't disagree with you."

Then, she stood and faced me, and I clenched my jaw as though I'd been knocked in the face with a barbell. Her eyes were red-rimmed with tears. And, at that moment, I wanted to kick Jeff's ass, shove my foot so far up it that he'd taste the rubber in my sole.

"Everything makes sense now. Those late-night meetings that surprisingly increased right before he dumped me." She swiped at her eyes with the back of her hand. "How could he? After all I put into our relationship. After I introduced him to my parents and after I swore to my dad, who has guy radar, that Jeff was a good one." Her hands were clenched at her sides. "How could I have been so stupid?" She pointed back at the reception hall. "That new girl, my replacement, isn't even his type. Fine, if you're going to upgrade, but to someone totally not his type? Who does that?" She swiped at her tears streaming down her face. "I wonder what they have in common. Bunny sex? We had great bunny sex."

Sex with Jeff was the last thing I wanted to hear about.

I took a step toward her, pulling her in by the elbows. "Stop."

This was worse than seeing Sarah or Mary cry. I didn't know why, but it was. Maybe because I hadn't seen Sonia cry before, and my Sonia was strong and sassy and unbreakable.

"He didn't deserve you." My hand moved up to cup her face, my thumb brushing away her tears. "I wish you could see what I see." I leaned in closer, taking in the scent that was signature to only Sonia, the scent of sweetness, wholeness, and honesty. "She's not smarter than you or even remotely more beautiful. She can't hold a candle to you, Sonia. And you know I never bullshit about anything."

We stood there for a beat until she placed her hand on top of my mine on her cheek and let out a small, shaky breath.

When I heard a noise, I lifted my head to see that Jeff had rushed through the doors, and I didn't think. I simply reacted. I wouldn't let him win. I couldn't let him see how he'd affected her, and I knew she wouldn't want that either. Sonia had too much pride.

So, I leaned down to press my lips against hers. I heard her intake of breath before our lips met, but me? I thought I'd stopped breathing altogether because I wasn't expecting the shock of her kiss.

Undeniable heat, uncontrollable lust, and one hundred percent desire—unlike the pretend kisses I'd planted on this woman before. I hadn't expected her lips to be so soft, so delectable, a contrast to the friction of heat fused between our lips. I hadn't expected her to taste like strawberries, even when she had just had a Long Island iced tea. But, most of all, I hadn't expected to be so aroused.

When she didn't stop me, my other hand moved to her waist, bringing her closer, flush against me. My lips moved over hers, and when she kissed me back, I flicked my tongue, outlining the seam of her lips. She didn't fight me, and a moan escaped from the back of my throat, a sound I didn't recognize. I bit her bottom lip and angled closer, almost bending her backward. She tasted exquisite, like a sweet wine, and I couldn't stop.

I didn't want to stop.

Sonia

Holy mother-freaking crap. Who knew if it was the liquor or my moodiness or even revenge that had me kissing Brad? All I knew was that this kiss, his kiss, was beyond magnificent. His lips were like magic, as though he had been born a kisser. As though he'd gone to school for it, studied it, perfected it, and now, women everywhere stood in line to get a taste.

The movement of his lips over my top and bottom lip was soft but urgent, lulling me into a stupid kissing stupor. Maybe it was all the practice he'd had before me, or maybe it was just raw, natural talent.

His mouth moved against mine in uninhibited want and need and pure, unadulterated lust, and I gripped him harder, more desperately, clutching his arms, pulling him closer. I deeply inhaled his masculine scent, filling my senses, making me dizzy and light-headed.

I can't believe I'm kissing Brad—my boss. And, as soon as that thought filtered through my head, it was as though I'd been doused with a bucket of ice water, and slowly, I pulled back.

Our eyes locked, and he leaned in again for another kiss until I put a hand on his chest.

What the hell did I just let happen?

I pressed one shaky palm to the hollow of my neck. My heart was beating a mile a minute, my breaths coming in short, broken puffs, as though I'd just run a marathon.

This is crazy. Crazy, crazy, crazy!

And Charles, his brother, was going to kill me, kill me, kill me.

And Brad was going to fire me, fire me, fire me.

"What was that?" I asked, not expecting him to answer.

He blinked as though he were just as dazed and confused. Then, he stepped back and ran one shaky hand through his dark locks. "I don't know." He eyed me for a nanosecond and stepped into me even though we were already toe-to-toe.

I didn't know how to get us back to our normal when I couldn't even get a solid thought through my head because all I could think about was that kiss and his lips—his magical, talented lips.

Then, Brad pulled at the edge of his suit and straightened, and the boss man was back. "Jeff was there."

"Where?" My eyes perused the area, looking everywhere behind me.

A few people had congregated around the garden, and by the looks on their faces, we had caught their attention.

"He was here, and I knew you wouldn't want him to see you crying."

"Oh," was all I could say. "Thank you."

Brad laughed deeply. "No. Thank you," he said with a devilish smirk gracing his lips.

My cheeks warmed. I could feel the heat rising to the tips of my ears. "That is so against the Charles rulebook."

He nodded. "And my rules, too, but I think, since I agreed to this and am playing a part, kissing you is an exception."

"So, you're going to kiss me again?" The question flew out before I had a chance to stop it. Crap, I didn't think I could handle another one of his kisses.

He paused, as though debating on what to say. "Only if I have to," he said, his emotions now hidden.

I guessed kissing me was a chore then. My heart sank, and I didn't know how to take that, yet I didn't want to think about it too much, too deeply.

And, with those five words, we were back into the normal world of secretary and BILK.

Once inside the cocktail area with multiple highboy tables, the first people I spotted were Jeff and Joan across the room.

I grabbed Brad's hand and headed toward the bar. "I need another drink."

"Shouldn't you eat a little bit still? Maybe after dinner."

"Okay, Dad." I grabbed a shrimp cocktail from a server's tray that passed by. "I have been eating. See, food. In my belly. Now, drink."

Brad shook his head, amused, and followed my lead.

"Sonia," I heard someone call.

When I lifted my head, I saw Ava and her boyfriend, Chris.

I nearly bum-rushed her and pulled her in. "Where were you? I tried looking for you after the church."

She flattened her pink dress with a tulle skirt. "We took

a little detour after the ceremony." Then, she leaned in, her cheeks flushing a pretty pink. "We got a little delayed when Chris saw me in this dress."

I laughed but couldn't ignore the pang of jealousy in my chest. "It's quite a beautiful dress." I stepped back to take in the way the tulle flared out by her hips.

She shimmied with an exaggerated effect. "Brad, you're looking good."

I had to bite my lip to prevent my laughter at her over-the-top flirtation in front of a boyfriend she'd dated for years. Chris knew she was harmless, but if it were the other way around, I didn't think Ava would be too understanding.

"Thank you. Thank you," he said with a little bow and not at all modest. "I have to say, I have a great tailor."

"Yes, you do." Ava pointed her nose in the direction of Jeff. "Better than that loser wannabe. Did he come over to get your attention yet?"

Brad snaked an arm around my back, pulling me close. And a shock of warmth filled me. I wanted to deny it but couldn't because it felt different since we'd kissed.

"Yes, he did, and I have to say, I don't know what my little bae ever saw in him."

Ava's eyebrows shot up to her hairline. *Bae?* she mouthed toward me and in front of Brad.

"Nicknames already. I like," Ava said, flicking my shoulder. "Your bae is a nickname kinda girl. I know she also has a nickname for you."

If my look could shoot bullets, Ava would be on the floor.

"I've heard." He smirked and dug his fingers into my waist. "I want to know what it is."

He didn't know the extent of it.

I wasn't about to tell him I had a picture of him on my

wall that I threw darts at daily and that he was nicknamed BILK—Boss I'd Like to Kill—on my phone.

That was a secret I'd take to my grave, except for Ava knowing.

"I'm your bae, and you're my babe." I nearly choked on the word.

Jeff and I had never given each other nicknames. We'd dated for years, and he thought the gooey couples that made up nicknames were losers.

"Chris calls me babe, too, don't you?" Ava said, slipping her arm through his.

He nodded, mute as always, and then kissed her cheek.

"No, really." Brad rubbed my arm, and tiny goose bumps sprang to life. "What's your particular nickname for me?"

Ava's eyes widened, and a chuckle escaped her. "Maybe we won't go there today. Tomorrow maybe, but not today."

Brad turned on the charm. "Come on, Ava. Do tell. I want to know what Sonia calls me when I'm not around." Brad's seductive voice was soft and coercive, and in any minute, I had no doubt that Ava would spill.

I tugged Brad toward the bar. "Drinkie, drinkie time, *babe*." I threw a single wave Ava's way and led us to our drinking destination.

"Smooth, but you know I'll find out anyway." He popped my nose with his pointer finger before we stopped by the bar. "I like your friends," he said after he handed me another Long Island.

"Thanks. We go way back. I've known Ava since the first day of college."

Brad thought on that for a second. "I've only really had Charles and Mason. I was in a fraternity in college, but when it comes to knowing me and knowing who I can trust, there have only been my brothers. And, after my parents died, we've only grown closer."

He tipped back his beer that the female bartender, who was eyeing him, had placed on the counter. It was unnerving that he hadn't paid attention to her when she was blatantly staring. Maybe the beautiful were immune to the attention. But this was Brad, so he knew. He was probably ignoring the attention.

"You have a big family, right?"

"Yeah, a big extended family. My mom came from a family of five, and my dad came from a family of seven."

Brad raised his brows in appreciation. "Nice."

I scoffed. "Crazy is more like it. Everyone wants to get a word in when we're all together. If you were an outsider, you'd need a Tylenol right after."

"Sounds like my type of party." He smiled, looking thoughtful. "It's only my brothers and nieces. Sometimes, after a day with them, I drink a whole bottle of bourbon."

"So, you know what I mean."

A commotion erupted from the far end of the room, and when I peeked up, the bride and groom and whole bridal party had strolled in.

"I want to congratulate them. There was so much commotion at the church." I grabbed Brad's hand without thinking. Crazy how, in a day and a half, it had become so natural for me to reach for him. I led us to the crowd and waited like everyone else to squeeze the bride.

Carrie was stunning. I had taken her all in at the church, but being this close, I noticed every tiny detail of her wedding gown. From the pearl and crystal beading flowing down the bodice of her princess ball gown-style dress to the matching crown that held her veil with a similar pattern of pearls and crystals dotting the headpiece. Her makeup was immaculate and not overdone with shades of pinks that highlighted her cheeks as though she'd been kissed by the sun to neutral-toned eye shadow that complemented her complexion and brought out the hazel in her eyes.

Tim looked dapper beside her in his fitted tux, but it wasn't what he was wearing that took my breath away. It was the sweet way his eyes studied her, as though he'd never in a million years find someone as beautiful.

Pang. Right in the center of my chest. You'd think the jealousy would dim, but watching them together only made it hurt more.

It wasn't as though I hated them for their happiness because I wanted the same thing for myself. They had dated throughout college, and there were no two people born on earth who were more made for each other.

I sighed, but in the next second, we were up in front, and I went in to hug Carrie. "I'm so happy for you, friend."

I pulled her tight against me, squeezing her boobs. She laughed but returned my suffocating hug.

I stepped back and held her forearms as I took her all in. "You're stunning. Gosh, I don't even have words for how great this reception is or how beautiful you look or how heartwarming the ceremony was."

Her eyes brimmed with tears, and she looked up and blew out tiny breaths. "Sonia, don't make me cry again. I've been crying all day."

I turned toward Tim. "And you. I don't think I've ever seen you in a suit actually." I patted his lapel, trying to recall but coming up short. "Looking good, Timmy boy."

He grinned. "I'm only looking this good because I'm standing next to her."

Carrie rolled her eyes. "He's turned up the corniness

today." But then she tiptoed and met his lips. "But it's kinda cute."

I couldn't help but smile, cheesy-style. "Super cute." Another pang.

Someday. I'll have that someday.

At least, I hoped so. I had hope that, with time, I'd realize that Jeff wasn't my last relationship.

Tim placed a strong hand on Brad's shoulder. "Are you ready to drink tonight? Carrie's dad's requirement for our reception was top-shelf liquor."

Brad tipped his head toward me. "I think I'm the designated driver tonight."

"You guys didn't book a hotel?" Carrie asked. "We have a bus service that will take you back to the hotel."

I could feel the blush rushing to my cheeks. "No. Not tonight." Goodness, thinking of Brad and me in the same hotel room had my heart racing.

Flashbacks of his lips on me and his slow, shivery kisses had warmth pooling in the deepest part of my gut.

I swallowed, knowing I needed something cold and strong to drink. "We'll see you guys in a bit. It looks like you have a long line forming."

I turned to see the slew of people waiting to hug the couple, including Jeff and my replacement.

"I can't catch a break," I said under my breath.

Brad's line of sight followed mine, and then he said, "Let's get you another drink."

I fluttered my eyes and then smiled wide. "And, to think, I was worried you wouldn't be the perfect date."

CHAPTER 13

BRAD

A drunk Sonia was a hilarious Sonia. She was a nonstop chatterbox, talking with feeling and elaborate hand movements. We were at a table with her college friends. Ava and her boyfriend and four other couples that had been together for a long time.

Sonia engaged and laughed with her former classmates, I could empathize with her, knowing what she wanted and knowing that she wasn't there, relationship-wise. Two of the four couples at our table were engaged, and if she were with Jeff, there would be no doubt that they would be engaged by now, too.

Still, as I stared at Jeff and Jean, who was all over him, I couldn't help but cringe at the thought of him and Sonia being together. No doubt, she was way too good for him. Too good for his cocky, sorry ass who had left her and had probably been two-timing her all the while.

I smiled as I listened to her rant.

"And, one time, I said that the dry-cleaning place had ruined his favorite shirt, but in all honesty, I had thrown it out." Sonia laughed, retelling the stories.

I merely smiled, thinking back to how I had known about that little debacle. I'd been so pissed off that my favorite shirt could not be found that I went to the dry cleaners myself and was told it never made it there. Not like Sonia had known that. The whole table was laughing at her little joke, but little did she know that the joke was on her because I'd known all along.

Dinner was over, and dessert was being served. I'd been shoving water down Sonia's throat and had to cut her off since her last glass of wine an hour ago. Sonia was feeling good, and I didn't want to have to carry her out.

I stood, realizing her water was drained. "Let me get some water for you, bae." The nickname rolled out of my tongue, automatic. It was odd and weirdly normal at the same time. Words like that never slipped out of my mouth. Plus, I was a grown-ass man using kid language. Still, my little nickname for her made it seem as though we were together, on the same team, just the two of us.

She groaned. "I hate that word. It's the name teenyboppers who don't know how to speak English give their significant others. They make up their own words, this new generation, and it's such bullshit. You can't just make up words."

She'd read my mind.

Damn it. If she weren't so cute, I'd strangle her.

Cute. Adoringly sassy. Petite.

I grinned. "Fine. Shorty—that's your new nickname. You're my Shorts." Then, I kissed her forehead and proceeded to the bar.

But not before I heard Clarisse, who was sitting next to her, say, "You guys are the cutest couple ever."

I laughed, and as I stared back at Sonia, I staggered to a stop. She was stunning. Not like I hadn't noticed earlier because I had definitely noticed. But, with color in her cheeks and her smile that had been absent earlier when Jeff was around, she was drop-dead beautiful.

It took me a few seconds to collect myself, and then I headed to the bar and raised a hand to the bartender. She'd been openly flirting with me all night, but I was blatantly ignoring her. With her hair swept up in a curly ponytail and her tight white button-down shirt accentuating her perky breasts, I would have given her a second glance if Sonia wasn't here. But, for once, I preferred Sonia's sweet innocence to the bartender's in-your-face beauty.

"What are you having, handsome?"

"Guinness and two bottled waters."

Sonia was going to be living in the bathroom tonight, given the amount of water I was shoving down her throat.

"Is that it?" she asked with a lilt, a voice that sounded sweet as sin and promised more.

"Yes. Thank you." I placed a couple of bills on the counter, and when I tipped back my Guinness, Jeff sidled up beside me.

And, to think, I had been having such a good time thus far.

"Hey, Brad," he said, raising his hand to the bartender. "Midori sour and gin and tonic, please." Then, he winked at the bartender, who was in no way interested in his sorry ass.

"Where's Sonia?"

Why did this guy care where his ex-girlfriend was? The question irked me.

"At our table," I snapped.

He smiled, teetering and using the bar for support.

Someone couldn't handle his liquor.

"Yeah, Jean went to the restroom. I think she's checked

her makeup at least twenty times. I mean, I told her she's gorgeous, but still."

Why is he talking to me like we were fucking pals? We weren't.

He took the drinks from the bartender, placing the Midori sour on the bar, closer to himself. "When she started flirting with me at the office, I couldn't believe it. Have you seen her?" He hiccupped. "She's way out of my league."

What a prick. It felt like a jab to Sonia, and tension rose to my shoulders. "I prefer the simple beauty."

He knew what I meant.

"Yeah. I mean, that's nice and all. But I've had that." He gestured toward the table where Sonia was sitting. "And, between you and me, Jean is crazy in the bedroom." He laughed and tipped back his drink, spilling some on his shirt.

I smirked, though my eyes were hard. I had an undeniable urge to knock him on his ass. "I know what you mean. Sonia ... fuck ..." I let my voice trail off. "I don't know why you let her go, man. I've been with many women, but no one like her."

Take that, asshole.

He straightened, all of a sudden sober. "What do you mean?"

"Well, you know ..." I followed his line of sight to Sonia's direction.

"No, I don't." He leaned into me and pushed up his glasses, as though to see Sonia better.

"Maybe she just needed a different guy to unleash her." I condescendingly patted his shoulder.

Before he had a chance to respond, Jean walked up to us. "Thanks, baby," she cooed, grabbing her gin and tonic.

I chuckled to myself. So, Jeff preferred the girlie drinks,

not like I was surprised. And I knew I'd gotten to him because he couldn't stop staring at Sonia, and all I wanted to do was rip his eyes off his face.

As though Sonia knew we were talking about her, she lifted her eyes to me and smiled. I'd thought she'd be pissed, but she began to walk our way, almost skipping and definitely shimmying her hips to the sound of the live band.

"Hey, guys. You talking about me?" she asked, her eyes lazy in that *I'm feeling good* kind of glow.

I was so glad I'd cut her off when I did.

"Yes, we just were." I grabbed her chin with one hand and leaned into her, meeting her lips for a brief kiss. "I was telling Jeff here how you have the sweetest mouth." And it was sweet with a touch of liquor that I could taste. I bent in again, my whole body tingling with need, and kissed her. "I can't get enough of these lips."

Instead of backing away, she smiled. Guessed the liquor had loosened her up.

Then, she grabbed my hand and proceeded to drag me to the dance floor. "Let's go, go, go and dance, dance, dance."

To my surprise, Jeff and Jean trailed behind us and met us on the dance floor.

"I Wanna Dance with Somebody" by Whitney Houston was being played by the live band. Sonia lifted her hands in the air and moved to the rhythm of the beats. Not like I'd had any doubt she had coordination, but still, I was surprised at how Sonia could really dance.

Me? I had been blessed with many things. Rhythm was not one of them. I stood there, bounced a little, and tipped my head, all the while holding my drink—just how I had in my early twenties at the bar.

"Come on, Brad. Dance with me." She tugged me forward and then began to twirl herself around.

I laughed, watching her shimmy and dance like no one was watching. Maybe my favorite Sonia was the free Sonia. Then, she dropped her hand and circled me. And the way her hips moved heated me up, making my thoughts turn seductive, thoughts I shouldn't be having about my own secretary—a secretary that I adored and couldn't fire.

When she backed up into me, my cock stiffened, and I froze. I didn't know what she was doing, but shit ... it was bad. My free arm wrapped around her waist as we both moved in sync to the music.

When the beat changed, she grabbed my Guinness and tipped it back, draining the bottle. Then, she ran to the closest table and left it there.

Rules, rules, rules. I drilled the words into my head because I wasn't drunk enough to blame wanting to be close to her on the liquor.

Against my better judgment, I wrapped my arms around her center, and we were grinding—her ass to my straining cock—on the dance floor like we were in the club and had just turned twenty-one.

My head dropped to the crook of her neck, and I could smell that strawberry perfume or soap or lotion she used. I leaned in and kissed the tender part of her skin, and then I took a swipe with my tongue. She tasted of salt and sweetness, the right combination, and it wasn't enough. I needed more. She was like a new drug I hadn't known about, a drink of choice I had just discovered. My fingers gripped the silk dress, right by her thighs.

Soft. Smooth. Sexy.

I wanted her. There was no doubt. There was wanting and knowing you couldn't do anything about it. It was a foreign concept for me because, everything I wanted, I took. It was always within reach, and it was mine. But this ... I couldn't do it. I couldn't have her, though I very much wanted all of her—in my arms, in my bed, beneath me.

I swallowed hard.

When a slow song broke through the noise, she turned around and wrapped her arms around my neck. Our eyes locked, and my heart stopped.

Her eyes sparkled with a gleam that knocked me breathless. For once in my life, I was mesmerized by a woman. This woman.

When she pulled at the ends of my hair, and I peered down into her endless pools of brown, I couldn't resist. I needed another taste of heaven, and I kissed her. She kissed me back, harder, without restraint. Her breasts were pressed up against my chest, and I knew this was a terrible idea, yet I couldn't help it. I couldn't stop kissing her. The reception hall could be burning down, everyone around us could be screaming, all the women in the room could be stripping, yet nothing would stop me from kissing her.

Her lips were soft, the bottom lip plumper than the top, and she tasted of liquor and mint and a sweetness I couldn't put my finger on. She was exquisite, and her body molded against mine, as though it were meant to fit there.

She was drunk, and I was taking full advantage. I very well knew that. Sonia wouldn't be kissing me in her right mind, and the thought shoved a pang of annoyance in my gut. But that annoyance disappeared when she swiped my bottom lip with her tongue.

Fuck. Fuck.

"Sonia," I whispered, my eyes falling shut.

Now would be the time to stop. Now would be the time

to put some space between us. End this. Clear my muddled head.

You know that little voice in your head that told you something was wrong, so wrong that you needed to step back and reevaluate things? Well, this was that moment.

But, instead, I opened my mouth and swiped my tongue against hers. Purely fucking delectable.

Both of my hands skimmed down her bare back to right below her tailbone, where I pushed her against me.

We shouldn't be doing this with her friends and their parents around. We weren't in a club. This was wrong. But why the hell did it feel so right? And so damn good.

She pulled back, sporting a lazy smile when the music changed, and her fingers continued to play with the ends of my hair while her arms were wrapped around me.

We stayed locked in our own moment for a few seconds before the song changed, and so did her mood.

Suddenly, she jumped up and down, searched the room, and grabbed Ava's hand right beside me. "Let's dance."

Her change of mood gave me whiplash. I sort of liked horny Sonia.

Jeff approached with Jean, and my eyes widened when Sonia, who'd previously bawled her eyes out over her two-timing ex, released Ava to grab one of his hands and then Jean's.

Jean enjoyed the attention and began to dance to some upbeat version of some Adam Levine song, moving like an awkward duck that had rolled out of its mother's womb.

"I thought I was mad, but I'm not mad anymore. Everything tends to work itself out, ya know," Sonia slurred.

Shit, this was bad, really bad. I had pinkie-promised that I wouldn't let her make a fool out of herself.

"I mean, he hated the way I ate, and I hated the way he couldn't last more than three minutes," Sonia said loud enough for Jeff to hear.

"She's drunk," I heard Jeff say.

"Sonia." I reached for her, but she pushed me off and continued to dance and move with Jean following her lead.

Jeff and I stood awkwardly by the side, watching our dates interact. Jean was laughing hysterically. Then, without warning, she handed Sonia her phone, and Sonia proceeded to plug in what I could only think was her number.

Fuck. This isn't good.

I walked over and wrapped one arm around her waist. "Okay, Shorts. Maybe it's time to go home."

A full-on pout escaped, and a big part of me wanted to bite her bottom lip again.

"No, we have to dance," she demanded.

"YMCA" played next, and before I even had a chance to deny her, I was on the dance floor, laughing and twirling her with my hands up in the air, YMCA-ing. If my brothers could witness me dancing, they would never let me live this down.

"Aunt Chelsey!" Sonia shouted, hugging a short, stout woman beside her. Small brown curls encompassed this woman's head, and I imagined that she wore curlers overnight.

"Sonia ..." Aunt Chelsey said, mid-YMCA. "Who is this? I didn't know you had a new boyfriend."

"I do." She tugged me forward, almost making me trip. "This is Brad. My man."

All right then. Isn't Sonia cute?

I extended my hand. "Nice to meet you."

"Well, well, well. Does your mom know?" Aunt

Chelsey pulled me into a bear hug, and I had to bend forward to hug her shorter frame. "You will have to go to the monthly family dinner. We have one on Monday."

"He is; don't worry," Sonia said, eyes crinkled, smiling with all teeth and definitely drunk.

I cringed. She'd hate me in the morning if I didn't fix this.

"If I don't have work, honey." I raised my eyebrows and stared at her, doing the silent-speaking thing that Mary and Sarah did when they had done something bad and didn't want to get in trouble. "You know how work is."

She tiptoed and surprised me by kissing me on the lips. "Don't be silly. You love your Shorts."

Shit. This is so bad.

After twenty more minutes of dancing, I grabbed more water for her. Maybe she would be able to dance and pee herself to sobriety. But, after the electric slide, the chicken dance, the cha-cha slide—which she taught me—I knew there was no slowing down.

I was practically dripping sweat, but I couldn't help but smile. My mood was in between enjoying the night with Sonia and stopping her from talking to Jean and Jeff as though they were all best buds. I hadn't ever danced so much, nor had I ever been more entertained by another human being.

I thought Mary was amusing. Drunk Sonia was a totally different level.

At one point, the bride had me in the center of the circle, doing some Michael Jackson move that I hadn't known I had in me.

When a Frank Sinatra song came on, I twirled Sonia around and brought her close to my chest. Like before, her body melted against mine, her softness to my hardness.

"Thank you," she whispered against my cheek, and nothing felt righter.

"Don't mention it."

Her eyes were closed, her breathing even.

"No, really. Thank you. I've been dreading this day for weeks, but I don't think I've ever had more fun."

Tiny breaths escaped her, and when my hand moved to the small of her back, I pulled her closer.

"I don't think I've ever had this much fun either." Because it was the truth.

I'd never experienced a whole spectrum of emotions in one night like I had tonight. I'd never laughed so hard. I'd never been so pissed before than I was at Jeff, at Jean. I'd never danced like no one was watching. Most of all, I'd never felt this undying need to be this close to someone else.

She nuzzled her nose against mine, and then she kissed me, sweetly, passionately. This time, her kiss was the end of me, the end of everything platonic, an end of everything I had ever promised my brothers. But it was the beginning, the beginning of a hope that I wanted to explore. A hope with Sonia.

~

Brad

It was almost midnight, and the band's music was all slow jams, indicating the end of the wedding. Sonia was hunched over with her head on the table, asleep. Her mouth was ajar, and I could hear soft breaths escaping her mouth. I wouldn't doubt it if she was drooling. She had knocked out mere minutes ago, but as soon as she was down, she was down for the count.

Ava and her boyfriend had left, and only a few college friends remained.

Jeff and Jean had left an hour ago. From everyone looking in, Jean and Sonia had become good friends, dancing and laughing and drinking. She was going to hate herself in the morning when I told her.

When the music finally ceased, I knew it was the end. Carrie and Tim made their way over.

"Looks like she had fun." Carrie rustled Sonia's hair.

"I've actually never seen her like this before, and she drank in college," Tim added.

"Yeah, but never that much." Carrie bent down and kissed her forehead. "Take care of my girl, okay?"

I stood and proceeded to lift Sonia into my arms, her head resting on my shoulder. "I will. It's bedtime."

Tim patted my back, and I ushered my sleeping beauty to the car. She was passed out, dead weight, and I wondered if she'd remember what had happened tonight—the drinking, the dancing, the kissing.

You would think she'd smell like a piss-poor drunk, but she still smelled sweet through the liquor, her natural strawberry scent pushing through.

She stirred in my arms. "Brad?" She opened one eye.

"Yeah?"

"I drank too much, didn't I?"

"You did. But you're allowed. It's not like you do that every weekend. Unless you're undercover. Do you keep bottles of tequila in your desk?"

She smirked, and then her eyes fell shut. "No."

I opened the passenger door, placed her in the car, and buckled her in. Her swooping neckline had me enjoying the span of her pale neck, and I had a sudden urge to bite the tender part of her skin. After I shut her door and entered the car, I drove us back to her apartment. I'd actually never been inside her apartment, and I'd be lying if I said I wasn't curious to see where Sonia lived, how she decorated her home, what pictures of her family members she had hanging on her wall.

As I parked in front of her condo, I wondered how the hell I was going to get in her place. I reached for her purse that she'd brought to the wedding, unzipped the top, and dug to the bottom. After jiggling the contents around, I found a slew of keys attached to a Canada keychain.

"It's a go, Shorts."

I exited the car, made my way to the passenger side, and unbuckled her from the seat. When I lifted her in my arms, her head lolled to my shoulder.

"You smell amazing." She sighed into me, inhaling deeply against my skin.

I laughed. "And you are officially drunk."

"Are we home?" she asked in a barely audible voice.

I kissed her forehead without a second thought, not knowing where the hell that had come from. "Yes, we're here. You're home."

Sonia weighed nothing, and it was easy to carry her past the doorman and up the elevator, but getting us through her apartment door was going to be a challenge because I had to put her down.

"Shorts, you're going to have to stand while I get the door open."

She nodded with her eyes still shut, and when I placed her on her feet, she nearly wiped out. With one hand around her waist and anchoring her against me, I used my free hand to fidget through the keys. I prayed it was the first one I grabbed, but it was the fourth key I tried.

I kicked open the door. I swept her up, and she was

weightless in my arms again. Then, I entered her apartment.

Inviting gray walls welcomed me into an open area. I could see her living room and kitchen all at once. There was one room to the right, which was the bathroom, and on the far end of the room, I knew it had to be her bedroom because it was the only room left. I staggered to a stop right before entering her room.

An eleven-by-fourteen poster of my face hung on the living room wall, like a tortured piece of art. I recognized the picture from the company website. This thing had darts around my eyes and a few other darts lying on a table right next to it.

"Nice." A low laugh escaped me.

I should've been mad, offended at the very least, but I couldn't after today, after being with Sonia.

Oh, how times had changed. I'd bet she hadn't predicted this. After tonight, I hoped I'd proven myself, and she no longer hated me. I wondered how things would be tomorrow or even the next day at work. I didn't know how I would be because there was an internal shift in me after the multitude of kisses and spending the day with her. I knew I no longer wanted her to be just my secretary. I wanted to explore the idea of more.

I shook my head and proceeded to the bedroom. After I kicked open her door, I turned on the lights and laid her on her dark purple bedspread. No pretty in pink or frilly bedspread for Sonia, but I could've almost guessed that.

I made my way around her neat room, which screamed organization. I'd bet her panties were even color-coded, just like her Post-its and pens. And, for the life of me, I had to know, so I walked over to the dresser and opened the drawer. Socks, all coordinated and separated by dividers—white, black, and multicolored.

I opened the second drawer. "Jackpot."

Not only were her underwear sorted by color, but they were also sorted by type—thongs, lace, satin—and her organizers were labeled.

I lifted a black lacy thong. "Well, well, well, my sexy little undercover devil. I would have never guessed this about you." A chuckle escaped me. "Only you would label your underwear."

But that was why I needed her, didn't I? She was organized where I wasn't, and she had a photographic memory where she could most likely recite my address book.

"Brad?" She stirred on her bed, and I slammed her underwear drawer shut, not ashamed one bit.

Her eyes were closed, so I doubted I had gotten caught.

When she reached for the strap of her dress, still lying down, and slipped it off one shoulder, I froze.

"Can you get me out of this?" She squirmed awkwardly against the mattress, like a fish out of water.

"Sure."

I approached the bed, bending over to help her to a standing position, and she wobbled within my hold.

"Whoa." Her eyes were still closed. "Dizzy."

"Easy." I framed her shoulders to steady her.

She was feverishly hot, and in a minute, she'd be half-naked. The thought had me unbelievably aroused. Was she wearing a lace thong right now? The thought of seeing her pink nip—

Stop! I needed to stop.

I was wrangling my restraint here.

"Um." I sat her against the edge of the bed and lowered her to her back.

"Brad," she whined, "I said, help me."

I swallowed, noting that her dress had slipped lower. "I'm going to grab you a T-shirt." My mother would applaud my sense of respect at this point. If it were any other girl, I wouldn't have bothered.

I tugged open her drawers and chucked a Def Deception band T-shirt onto the bed.

I lifted her again, and she leaned into me, practically hugging me, front-to-front, and I slipped the other strap of her dress off her shoulders. Like magic, her dress dropped to the floor.

Holy shit.

I held her at arm's length because any closer, and I wouldn't be able to control the urge to touch her all over.

My gaze raked over her body with a hunger I'd never felt before, and her nearness sent my senses spinning.

Her almost-see-through bra, a bra that crossed to her lower back, and panties were all she had left, all lace and all fucking sexy.

I swallowed.

"Wait." I was scared she would topple over.

I lifted her almost-naked form up in my arms and gently placed her on her back. When she held on to my neck, I fell on top of her, bracing myself against the mattress.

I balanced on my fists, hovering over her, trying to think of workouts and planks and burpees.

Tight core. Straight back. I could plank over her for over five minutes. But trying to divert my mind wasn't working. Nothing was. Because thinking of working out only pushed through thoughts of how Sonia and I could burn more calories together. Naked.

My cock stiffened as I peered down at her lacy bra that

crisscrossed to her waist, the pink of her nipples peeking through. Nipples I wanted to bite.

"Uh ..." I was at a loss for words and in the most compromising position, hovering inches above her. It was so hard not to let my hands roam, to touch every inch of her, to let my lips fall to the crook of her neck and go fucking wild.

"I fantasized about you once." Her voice was seductively low.

My cock twitched.

Are you kidding me?

I stilled, looking down at her lustful deep brown eyes. We were so close, a millimeter away from our lips meeting.

"Was it after you threw darts at my face?" My voice didn't sound as steady as it usually was.

"No," she replied, unfazed. "It was in a dream and so unexpected. I never thought of you that way."

Her tongue darted out, licking my chin, and I held my breath. I couldn't take much more of this.

"They say that, in the subconscious, the truth comes out." My chest seized, and my cock strained against the inside of my slacks.

She wrapped her legs around my waist, and I fell into her, my heart pounding an erratic rhythm.

Jesus, Mary, and Joseph, Mom and Dad, help me resist.

"Kiss me, Brad." She lifted her head and met my lips.

I froze.

I needed an intervention. I was on the last string of self-control. My breathing was labored, and my body flooded with warmth. I could kiss her in a room full of people, knowing nothing else could happen. But here, with her so fucking sexy and practically naked beneath me, once I kissed her, I doubted my ability to stop.

"Brad ..." Her tongue traced my bottom lip.

And I gave in. Gave in to what I wanted. Gave in to her.

Game over.

I kissed her back, needing some of that sweetness, needing another taste of heaven, of her, knowing full well it wouldn't be enough.

"We should stop." Because we should.

She was drunk and we worked together, and I was about to ruin one of the best relationships that had ever graced my life.

She pushed at my chest, went on her knees, shoved off my jacket, and ripped opened my shirt. Buttons flew everywhere. My ruined five-hundred-dollar shirt was the last thing on my mind.

She fell back on the bed and leaned back on her elbows, staring up at me, taking me in.

Her eyes were hooded and glossed over. Her curls untamed on the top of her head, strands falling over the side of her face.

She looked like a damn angel. An angel I was about to corrupt.

She pushed up her hips, grinding my hardness against her softness, creating this sensual friction that drove me mad. Soft moans escaped her lips as I gripped her ass and moved against her, my head dropping to the crook of her neck, my hands roaming from the swell of her hips to cup her breasts.

"Sonia ..." I breathed, my voice shaky and barely controlled. "This is a bad idea."

Because she was drunk, and she wasn't in the right state of mind. If she were sober, this would be a totally different game plan.

"I didn't know you were so sexy underneath your suit,"

she whispered, licking the seam of my ear, sending a jolt of pleasure to travel straight to my groin.

I cupped her face. "You're the sexy one." I placed a chaste kiss on her lips and took in her body. All strength and beauty in her long, slim legs, her tight stomach, and subtle but firm ass.

We were all lips and mouths, sucking and tasting. I flicked my tongue all over every inch of her.

When she reached for the buckle of my pants, I grabbed her hand. It was like a douse of water had been thrown on me. I froze, breathing heavily.

"I haven't had sex in eight months, Brad, and I want to feel you inside me."

I squeezed my eyes shut. How could I say no when she was basically begging me? But, if I let this happen, everything would change. I would be forced to fire her because it wouldn't work in the workplace. Charles and Mason would kill me. Absolutely kill me.

I hated that I was thinking about them when my cock was hard against her thigh. But above those things ... she'd hate me, and because of that, I'd hate myself. She was drunk. And, when we had sex—which we definitely would—I wanted her to remember.

Shit. My thoughts were a jumbled mess.

I squeezed her hand between us. "We can't."

She whined and pushed her pelvis against mine, locking her legs behind my waist, tighter, harder. "Please ..." she begged.

I groaned. "You'll regret this in the morning."

"I won't." She rubbed her hand against the top of my pants. "You don't want me?"

If she only knew.

"That isn't it. If you were sober, I'd give in to this, give in to what I wanted. I just don't want *you* to regret this."

She peered up at me with sad, lustful eyes. "Why doesn't anybody want me? Why am I not good enough?"

Her words gutted me, a butcher knife to the heart. *Why is this beautiful, smart girl so insecure?*

"Don't say that. You're beautiful. Stunning. And, if some dumbass of a guy isn't smart enough to realize it, then it's his loss, okay?"

When my thumb brushed tenderly across her cheek, her lips trembled, and her eyes fell shut.

She wouldn't remember this conversation, but I had to make her understand.

I gripped her chin with one hand, making sure we were eye to eye. "Look at me, Sonia."

And she did.

"You keep calling her an upgrade, but she's not." My hand brushed the apple of her cheek. "She has nothing on you. Nothing."

I was awarded with a sweet, slow smile. Her hand ruffled the top of my hair and then landed on the back of my neck. "Brad, will you kiss me again?"

I arched an eyebrow.

"Just kiss me and nothing else."

Her lips were plump, swollen, and sexy.

My willpower was shot.

I kissed her as though it were my first kiss of the day and the last kiss of my life. We kissed for what seemed like hours, exploring each other's mouths and tongues. I loved the little moans that escaped her mouth when I nibbled on her bottom lip or the way she gripped my arms tighter or arched her breasts into my chest when I flicked my tongue on the roof of her mouth. Her delicate lips struck a vibrant chord in me. I lost focus, and kissing her was the only thing that mattered. I hadn't known I could enjoy the art of making out so much.

Or maybe it was just with Sonia.

Her kisses slowed, and she pushed me to my back. I thought she was going to ride me, but she laid her head on my chest instead.

"I'm tired," she whispered, snuggling against me.

My hands trailed up and down her bare back. "I'm horny." My cock was rock hard, straining against my pants.

She merely laughed. "Of course you are. You're always horny."

This time was different. But I knew she wouldn't believe me. I'd had drunk sex before, lots of times. I wasn't drunk now. But, this time, the stakes were higher, and I didn't want to risk it because I could lose it all.

"You're always so honest." I kissed her temple.

"Want honesty?" Her tone was soft, her breathing evening out, "You're the best kisser I've ever had."

"Really?"

She might as well have told me I'd won an Olympic medal.

"Really. But don't be too impressed. There weren't that many before Jeff."

What she didn't know and what I didn't tell her was that she was the best kisser I'd ever had, too.

I ran my fingers through the ends of her hair, repeating the motion over and over. She was still in her bra and panties, and I debated on getting her that Def Deception shirt from the edge of the bed, but I was again replaying what she'd just said, and I was too comfortable and content to move or care.

Soon, we were both asleep, and I knew I'd have to deal with everything else in the morning.

CHAPTER 14

SONIA

"Shit." I gripped my pounding head, which felt as though a sledgehammer were playing Beethoven's Fifth on the inside of my brain. I lifted my neck and then let it fall again, unable to open my eyes. My pillow wasn't soft. It wasn't fluffy, and it didn't smell like my laundry detergent.

I opened one eye and shot up to a sitting position, nearly toppling over again from the wild pounding in my head. But then I realized I was straddling Brad, who was clearly smiling.

Why must I always find myself in the most compromising situations with this man? Always on top of him.

"Morning, Shorts." He stretched his arms over his head and yawned. He was shirtless and sported the sexiest bedhead I'd ever seen on a man.

I stood straight up on the bed and then realized I was only in underwear and a bra.

I covered myself with my hands, walked off the bed, and face-planted on the floor.

"Shit! Shit! Shit!" The pain from landing on my elbow shot up my arm.

Immediately, Brad was beside me, scooping me up and placing me on the bed.

I pushed at his chest. "No." The dizziness took over, and I fell back against the mattress. I threw one arm over my eyes. "Please tell me we didn't sleep together." I rubbed a shaky finger against my temple. "Please. Please. Please."

The bed indented by the weight of him, and he grabbed my hand and pulled it from my eyes.

"We didn't," he said, all humor gone from his face.

I squinted against the sunlight peeking through my curtains. I exhaled in relief. "So, we didn't?"

"No, Sonia." There was that *I'm up to no good* smirk again.

I swallowed hard. "Do I still have a job? Because I really, really love my job."

He blinked, and for a moment, I thought he was going to say no. And then I would cry or throw up. Because I loved my place and being on my own, and I still felt sick from all the liquor I'd had yesterday.

His eyebrows pulled together as though he were contemplating, but then, with a tip of his chin, he answered. "Yes. You can't get rid of me that easily."

"Thank God." My eyes flew to the ceiling and then back to his face. "Why am I practically naked then?"

"You asked me to help you out of your clothes." He rubbed his thumb at my bottom lip, and I pushed his hand away.

I tilted my head. "I did? I don't remember that." *Shoot, when did this happen?*

I tried to replay my last memory from the night before and realized I didn't remember coming home. Well, this couldn't be good.

His expression was tender. "You don't remember a lot of things from last night, do you?"

A whole slew of scenarios filtered through my head, but the worst one—where we were both doing the naked dance together—had been avoided. Thank goodness. Nothing would've been worse than that.

"What else happened?"

He swallowed, and then the smile slipped from his features.

"Tell me, Brad!" I held my breath. My voice was whisper soft, and my body lay still, as I was afraid of what he was going to say. "Brad ..."

"Well, what's the last thing you remember?"

I paused, trying to recall. "I remember the ceremony and ..." I cringed. "... part of the reception but not too much. I had a lot to drink."

"You didn't throw up. I'm pretty impressed."

"I never throw up," I said matter-of-factly. "But I never black out either." I guessed there was a first for everything. I blinked up at him.

"Well, I'm sure you've never had that much to drink either."

He lay beside me, one arm behind his head. It should've been uncomfortable that I was practically naked beside him, but shit, I simply lay there as though I were fully clothed. Plus, he wasn't looking at my body like a creep; he was scouring my face.

"I have never, ever been that drunk." I rubbed at my temple, and the pain seemed to subside. "And I never will again."

Brad held this secret smile as though he were replaying all the embarrassing things I'd done last night in his head.

I narrowed my eyes at him. "What else did I ask you to do? You're holding back. I know you are."

He held a secret smile. "Kiss you."

My eyes widened. "When?"

"Last night, after you told me to undress you."

"All right then." But then I remembered he had kissed me. "We kissed after the ceremony."

"We did." He dipped his chin. "There was more." And his stupid smile appeared then.

"When, where, how? Just tell me." The back of my neck turned unbelievably hot, warmth spreading down my body. Could your stomach flush with color? 'Cause I was pretty sure mine was right now.

I didn't know what was worse—not knowing or having to relive the whole ordeal by him repeating it.

"Kisses on the dance floor and some more back here." He laughed.

"Like peck kiss? Muah or ... more?"

"So much more." His tone was cocky and indulgent. "So much. We made out for hours."

I groaned and threw one arm over my eyes again. "You are so enjoying this. I hate you."

He chuckled, a deep sound in the back of his throat. "You wouldn't be able to tell from how you were acting last night."

This was way too amusing for him. I slapped his chest, and when I tried to hit him again, he held my hand and intertwined our fingers.

Awk-freaking-ward.

There were boundaries, and we had broken every single one of them. I tore my hand from his and sat up, surprised that my hangover had quieted to a dull hum in my head.

I decided it was better to not know.

"Well, since that crapfest is over, you'd better get going. It's Sunday, and we have work tomorrow."

I moved to the edge of the bed, reaching for an old T-shirt. After putting on my Def Deception band T-shirt, which was thankfully long enough to cover my butt cheeks, I placed one hand on my hip, expectantly looking at Brad. I raised an eyebrow and tapped my foot against my worn carpet. He needed to get out of here ASAP.

Amusement shone in his eyes. "You're cheapening the moment and everything that happened last night."

I wanted so badly to wipe the damn smirk off his face.

"Get out." I pointed to the door and watched as Brad slowly sat up, his hair a disheveled mess but his face still *GQ* handsome.

He was probably the only male who didn't have morning breath.

It was a sin to be that good-looking.

"But, Shorts," he said in jest, "we had so much fun last night." He walked toward me and reached for my waist. He was playing and eating up every little second of it.

I pushed his hand off me. "Get out. And Shorts? Where did that come from?"

"Your new nickname."

He kissed the tender part of my neck, and I flinched.

"Stop it. Charade over. Out. Out. Out." I pushed him out of my room, and panic seized my chest when I spotted my dartboard of his face. "Close your eyes."

His laugh rumbled, echoing through my small apartment. "I've seen it already. Your shrine to me."

"Shut up," I groaned. *Could this guy get any more annoying?*

He walked over and picked up a dart, noting the tiny holes that marred his face. "Using me for dart practice?"

"No," I said, eyes wide and blinking. I schooled my features and lifted a finger. "Actually, how can you be sure that's even you? There are a lot of people who look like you."

"Is that so?"

"Yes." I plucked the dart from his hand. "The pizza boy, for example."

He nodded, still way too amused. "That must've been one really good-looking guy."

I crossed my arms over my chest. "Nope. But it was really, really, *really* good pizza."

I pointed to the door again, and he laughed.

He slipped on his shoes, and I opened the door to escort him out. When he turned to give me one final good-bye, a scary thought filtered through my head. *Last night changed everything between us.* Our exchanged kisses and a make-out session I didn't remember.

After everything that had happened, I needed to confirm one thing.

"Brad ..." For once, I turned sheepish, digging my toe into my carpet. "Thanks for being my pretend boyfriend." I couldn't look him in the eye for obvious reasons. Things had shifted between us, but I needed things back to normal. "But everything on Monday morning will be the same, right?" I twisted my hands in my shirt, needing him to agree. He'd said I still had a job, but I needed him to confirm this last request.

He was silent, and then his smile slipped. His eyes studied me for far too long. "Yeah, Sonia. It'll be the same as before." There was a heavy disappointment in his voice, which confused the heck out of me.

I rushed into him then, throwing my arms around his neck, hugging him as relief flooded me. "Thank you."

His arms wrapped around my waist, tighter than my grip around his neck, and then loosened. His head dropped to the hollow between my shoulder and neck, and for a brief second, I thought he'd sniffed me.

After a few long seconds, my hands moved to his chest, and I was the first to pull away. "Thanks again."

All the awkwardness was back.

"You're welcome."

Then, we were in some weird eye-lock action that made my stomach clench, and a dizzying current rushed through me, causing me to sway, so I slowly shut the door.

Hangover central. I blamed it on my consumption of way too much liquor last night, which would never happen again.

~

Brad

I stared at her condo door and the numbers 323. It must have been at least five minutes of me standing like a stalker outside her apartment. I'd been on this side of the door before, but I'd never hesitated walking away. Now, I waited. For a few more seconds, just to see if she would open the door again. Maybe she'd remember last night and how amazing it had been, how great we were together, and she'd let me taste her sweet lips again.

Fuck ... I am screwed.

I'd promised her normalcy on Monday, and right now, I didn't know if I could give her that. I rubbed at the back of my neck, feeling the tension rise to my shoulders. I headed toward the elevator with my tail between my legs.

There was an absence in the car that was undeniable. I could still smell the faint scent of her perfume that lingered in the air as though the universe were tricking me, and if I looked over to the passenger seat, I'd see Sonia smiling or asleep, cuddled into herself.

An unnatural tightening in my chest occurred, a feeling that I hadn't ever experienced before, and that was when I knew Monday could not be normal because the feeling could only be described in one word—longing. I missed my annoying, sexy little secretary.

I banged my head against the steering wheel, waiting for the light to turn green. "Fuck! Fuck! Fuck!"

I needed an intervention and stat, so I rushed home as though my life depended on it. I knew the exact person who would talk sense into me.

When I walked into the house, Mason was seated at the kitchen table, paper in front of him, with Sarah eating breakfast.

"Where's Mary?" I asked, searching the room.

"Still asleep."

I didn't know why I'd even asked. Mary was the female version of me when it came to our sleeping patterns. We'd sleep till one in the afternoon if we could.

"Mason, living room. I have an emergency." My tone was clipped and serious, meaning business.

He took note of my new suit, probably rumpled from it being tossed on the floor. Inside my suit, my shirt was buttonless.

"What happened to your shirt?" He shook his head. "Where did you go?"

"To a wedding," I said.

"Nice." Then, his head was back in the paper, and his cup of joe was on his lips again.

"With Sonia."

He coughed up his coffee, splattering some on the paper, black coffee stains dotting what he had been reading.

"Sonia, your secretary?" he asked as though we knew more than one Sonia.

He shot up from his chair, rubbed his forehead, scratched the back of his neck, and itched his arm.

Have you seen two-year-olds drop to the floor, kick their feet, and do circles, all the while trying to rip off their clothes? That was Mason but till he was eight. And, boy, did I like to watch him get all riled up. Most of the time, I was the cause of his tantrums because I had taken his toys.

I tipped my head in the other room, noting little teenage eyes on us. "We need to discuss."

"Where did you spend the night last night?" He pushed his hands through his hair. "Tell me it was at your apartment." His eyes widened when I didn't answer, his mouth slimming to a thin line.

"Other room," I urged.

"No. No. No. I want to hear what happened," Sarah said, hopping off her chair. "I love Sonia. She's cool and sweet and ..."

"This is an adult conversation, Sarah," Mason said, cutting her short and heading to the study.

I followed, but so did Sarah.

"I like her," she said behind us. "I really do. Seriously, you'll never find any other girl who puts up with your crap. No offense."

"Out." Mason pointed to the study door. "Finish your breakfast."

A stubborn-faced Sarah did an about-face and stormed out the door. After Mason slammed the door shut, I faced his wrath.

"You slept with your secretary." His hands flew to his hips. He was in scolding mode. "The only one we've been able to keep on forever to work with you. Why the hell would you do that? Are you dumb?" He shook his head and answered before I could. "Shit! I already know the answer to that. Charles will have your balls on a stick. Of all the girls you could sleep with, she's the one girl who was off-limits!"

He gripped a fistful of hair, wanting to pull it out. If I weren't so desperate, I'd have laughed at his over-the-top reaction.

"Why the hell can't you keep your pants on?" His face reddened.

I simply stood there and took it, watching him flare up.

"I didn't sleep with Sonia."

He paused, mouth open as though his words were stuck in his throat. He took a breath, and then his whole body slackened like a balloon releasing air. "Well, that's good."

"But I want to."

His whole posture turned rigid again.

"And you're not going to," Mason said gruffly. "So, stop having those thoughts right now."

"I think I like her, Mason." The words flew out, uninhibited, pure, uncensored honesty.

A cynical laugh from one of those horror movies escaped him. "*Like* her? Please, the only person you like is yourself."

My frustration bubbled underneath the surface. "I'm being serious. Every single time I kiss her, I want more."

Maybe I hadn't come here for an intervention. Maybe I needed permission, his blessing, someone to tell me that this was okay and that I was merely experiencing symptoms of being in love.

Love? Shit. I'd have to analyze that later.

The sane part of me wanted him to convince me that what I was feeling wasn't wrong. It was the war of my two worlds—one where we worked together and the other where I was falling for her.

Mason ran one frustrated hand through his hair. "Listen to me. You do not like her." He stepped into me and spoke slower, as though I were an old person hard of hearing, "What you like is the chase. In business and in women. And, because Sonia won't look at you, which is exactly why we hired her, you see her as a challenge you want to conquer."

His words were all wrong. I didn't want to conquer her. I wanted to be with her. *Her.* No one else.

I shut my eyes and let out a shaky breath. My world as I had known it was discombobulated, turned upside down and inside out, and it'd all started with that damn kiss. "I don't know."

His eyes narrowed into angry slits. "You do know, or you wouldn't be coming here, straight to me. You know I'm your voice of reason, and I'm telling you, once you sleep with her, you'll have to fire her because things between you will be a mess. You'll ruin your relationship and never talk again."

His words shot me in the chest. The last thing I wanted to do was ruin my relationship with Sonia. To never talk again? I couldn't imagine not hearing her smart mouth or seeing her stunning face every morning.

I hung my head, staring at the lines in our hardwood floor that seemed so suddenly interesting. "I don't know."

His hand rested on my shoulder. "You know I'm right, Brad. Deep down, you know I am."

Brad

The next morning, before I walked through my office doors, my chest tightened. I recognized the feeling—anxiety. The same feeling before I walked into a meeting to seal the deal and acquire another company.

This time, the anxious feeling was intensified, a rattling in my chest, my palms sweaty.

I inhaled deeply. The best thing to do was to face my fears head-on, so I walked through the doors, my eyes already searching for her because she was always there before me. Always. When my stare was met with the vacancy of her chair, the tightening in my chest rose to my throat.

What if she quit on me, all because of what happened at the wedding?

I flipped around, my eyes wide, and the tension instantly eased out of me. I took in all five feet two of Sonia Vanducci. Her brown hair was pulled back into a sleek ponytail, exposing the span of creamy white skin that I had kissed a few days ago. Her yellow silk shirt was tucked into a fitted skirt, one that hugged her slim figure, the same slim figure that I'd had beneath me.

Shit! Get it together, Brad.

I swallowed and croaked out, "Good morning." I sounded like a teenage boy who'd just hit puberty.

Real smooth.

She quirked an eyebrow and held out a cup of coffee. "You okay?"

"Sure. Why wouldn't I be?" I schooled my features, but my pulse ticked up.

"Okay." She sounded unsure. "Anyway, you have a

meeting at nine with the McCarthys and then a meeting with that China supplier at ten."

I nodded, keeping it casual. "Aren't you going to come into my office for my morning brief?"

Flashes of papers scattered on my office floor and Sonia on her back on my desk, naked from the waist down, pushed through.

Normal? We were far from normal.

My voice was hoarse and horny. "Come into my office."

She blinked up at me. She wanted normal, and that was our normal routine. *Is she avoiding me now?*

"Oh. Yeah. Of course." She fidgeted in her spot, pulling at the edge of her shirt. "I'll be in, in a bit."

She let out a shaky breath, and I was a bit relieved that it wasn't just me who was anxious.

"Okay."

I walked into my office, sat behind my desk, and powered up my computer. I swung my chair around to take in the Chicago skyline at my feet.

Challenge. Sonia is simply a challenge, as Mason put it.

And what male didn't love a good challenge, right? This man sure did. Wasn't that why I ran faster on the treadmill, sprinting, upping my incline and speed? Wasn't that why I always tried to increase the weight that I benched? Wasn't that why I volunteered on every deal Mason and Charles thought was too farfetched to win?

I was the epitome of a conqueror.

Maybe Mason was right.

A small knock came at the door, and I tucked away any emotion from my face, plastering on a nonchalant smile. "Hey."

"Hey." She stood by the door for a bit, not her usual

style, before I tipped my chin toward the chair in front of me.

"Don't be shy. I'm not going to bite." I smirked. "Unless you want me to." And then I was back to flirting, which never happened between us. I cleared my throat. "Sit down, Sonia. We're going to go over my schedule for the day because I have that nine o'clock."

"Yeah. Okay. Sure." She sat down and rattled off my boring meetings of the day. Then, she reminded me to send Sarah's and Mary's teachers a teacher-appreciation present that Mason had tasked me to do. Teacher appreciation was tomorrow, and Charles was back at the end of the week.

As her eyes focused on her iPad, my gaze zoned in on her delectable lips. I could still taste the sweetness, feel her smooth, silky tongue against mine. I pictured me on top of her, grinding against her, my hardness against her softness. I shifted in my seat as my cock slowly came to life.

When she was done, she stood. "Anything else you want to make note of?" She held the iPad against her chest, as though using it as a barrier between us.

I smiled casually. "Nope. I'll let you know if I do."

She nodded and then turned to walk to the door. My eyes dropped to her tight ass, and I swallowed.

She was just about out of eyesight when she flipped toward me. "Does this ..." She motioned between us. "... feel weird? Because it totally feels weird. Sometimes, I regret taking you, but then again, I don't because Ava said everyone was talking about us and how hot you were, and so ..." She raised one hand in the air. "... yay!" She gritted her teeth. "Go, team, go, right?"

"Do you think I'm hot?" I asked, carefully watching her and wondering why her opinion was so fucking important to me.

I usually didn't care what women thought of me. Well, that wasn't true. I usually *knew* what women thought of me. With Sonia ... I wasn't sure about anything really. What she thought, felt. She was a mystery, which was partly terrifying and mostly exciting as hell.

A flush crept up her neck. "Can you please stop that?"

"Stop what?" I very well knew what I was doing, and despite Mason's warnings, I couldn't stop.

"Wipe that shit-eating grin off your face and stop flirting with me." She walked toward the chair again and plopped down. "Here are the facts. You are my boss, and I am your employee. I took you to a wedding, and, yes, we kissed and ... okay, made out from what you told me." She bit her bottom lip, and her knees bounced.

"Anything I did under the influence cannot be held against me. Listen, I promise not to stalk you or act weird, like all those other girls who date you and flip to the psycho side because I'm just not that type of person. But you ..." She gave me a pointed look and extended her forefinger. "... you have to act normal, and pretend to flirt just to make me uncomfortable is not acting normal. You promised, Brad, remember?" She sagged against the chair as though that whole speech had wiped all the energy from her.

"I want everything to go back to how it was when I hated you and I annoyed the hell out of you." She blew the bangs from her eyebrows. "Can we do that?" Her hands flew to her chest, her eyes pleading. "I need this to all be normal between us."

I searched her face, and there were so many things that I wanted to say, like the fact that she never annoyed me or that I didn't want her to hate me. Ever. And the fact that I'd had such a great time on Saturday night.

My heart felt as though it were shrinking. "Yes, Sonia,

we can do that." I tried to hide the heavy disappointment in my tone because I didn't want normal. I wanted the opposite of normal between us.

The crinkle between her eyes eased. "Thanks, boss man. I really do love it here."

"I'm glad." And I was.

But I couldn't help feeling like things were never going to be the same. Mostly like I was never going to be the same.

∽

Brad

When she left, I plowed through my day, but I couldn't stop thinking about her. But, when she came in and dropped my lunch on my desk, I waved her off, keeping my eyes steady on my computer screen. I noticed that her smile widened at my gesture because she thought we were getting back to our normal, but it was anything but. Because, every chance I got—when I went to the restroom, when I went to drop something off at her desk, or when I went to make a copy at the machine by her desk even though I never made my own copies—I'd steal glances at her when she wasn't looking. I'd admire her profile and the natural poutiness in her lips when she was concentrating on her computer screen. Something that I had never noticed before.

And it wasn't nearly enough. I had a crazy thought of making an excuse to move her desk into my office so I could have more time to study her features.

I felt like a stalker.

As the time moved closer to five, quitting time, my stomach churned. I wanted to think of an excuse to see her again. Catch a movie. Have dinner. Shit, staring contest. Any-damn-thing.

Wasn't this Karma for all the broken hearts I'd left scattered around the city? This was what I got for dating girls that I never truly liked.

I pinched the bridge of my nose. I hated not feeling like myself.

Again, I tried to think of an excuse to keep her here, but I hadn't asked her to work after-hours for a while. She knew everything on my schedule and all the big deals I was working on. There was nothing on the pipeline.

"Shit. Shit. Shit." I knew I was acting like a little pussy who kept thinking about her pussy.

"OH MY GOD!" Sonia rushed through the doors, cheeks flushed, eyes blazing. "What the hell, Brad?" She stared me down like she was about to jump on me and wrap her arms around my neck.

That would be fine as long as her legs were wrapped around my waist. Pissed off Sonia, nervous Sonia, now fucking angry-as-hell Sonia. I decided the hottest one was the angry firecracker in front of me.

"Why would you agree to our monthly dinner?"

"What?" I quirked an eyebrow. *Monthly dinner?* My mind went blank.

"Aunt Chelsey." She lifted both eyebrows. "Ring any bells? Because I don't remember her inviting you to family dinner. That doesn't ring any bells on my end."

Laughter escaped me. Of course, she wouldn't remember. She had been drunk beyond oblivion that night.

"It was your idea."

She slapped her head and rested one hand on her hip. "Of course it was." She groaned. "But why the hell would you agree to it when you knew I wouldn't remember?"

"Have you met your aunt Chelsey?"

The woman hadn't looked like she understood what the word *no* meant.

She groaned again. "You're only my friend, okay?" She gave me a pointed stare. "They think otherwise, but these people are my family, so remember, you're only my friend. I don't want them getting any ideas."

"Sure thing." I smirked, silently fist-pumping inside. It was like God had answered my silent prayer because this was my way in.

She glared at me. "Wipe that smug smile off your face."

"You know your aunt did see us holding hands at the wedding, right?"

She groaned louder.

"And kissing," I added, trying to minimize my amusement.

She rubbed her temples with two fingers. "Okay, okay. I get it. I'm never drinking again. Ever."

I chuckled. "Why not? You're quite cute and affectionate when you're drunk."

God, she was adorable. I'd never noticed how she bit her lip when she was frustrated, but now, I could commit to memory all her mannerisms.

"You ..." She pointed. "... shut up. I'll meet you at seven."

She turned to leave, but my question stopped her.

"Do you want me to pick you up?" I stood, waiting behind her, feeling anxious and eager and excited, all at once.

Who is this guy? I didn't fucking recognize him. With women, I was never anxious. It had always been the other way around.

She flipped around and squeezed her eyes shut for a moment. "Sure, whatever, fine."

Not exactly the reaction a guy wanted. But I wasn't deterred.

As soon as she shut the door behind her, my butt dropped to the chair, and I grinned. Guessed I didn't have to make an excuse to spend more time with her after all.

CHAPTER 15

SONIA

Brad never made me nervous. Not his fancy, swanky car or his gorgeous looks. He'd always been the BILK to me—a self-centered, pompous ass who didn't care about anyone or anything other than himself. But, since I'd seen him with his nieces, my opinion of him had already started to shift. And, now, as he jumped out of his car to open my car door, nervous butterflies stirred in my belly.

"Where to?" he asked, giving me a once-over. He'd never done that before. "You look nice."

I barely refrained from groaning in despair. He needed to stop.

"Elmwood Park. It'll take us thirty minutes to get there." I proceeded to punch in my address in his car navigation.

"Did you do something different with your hair?"

I scrunched my eyebrows together. "Yeah, I pushed it up into an after-work, *don't give two shits* bun." I shook my head. "What's up with you, Brad?"

"What?" His eyes went to the road.

"You're being too ..." I tried to search for the perfect word. "... nice. It's weird. Cut it out."

He went quiet. No comebacks. No cutoffs. Just silence.

Then, he said, "Maybe I want to be the nice guy for once."

I scoffed. "Since when?"

"Since recently."

I sensed a tiny bit of hurt behind his tone.

"And why would that be?" I was completely thrown off by his demeanor.

"Because I don't want to die a grumpy, old man. How about that?"

This man wasn't making a lick of sense.

"Are you fatally ill, or is something up that you aren't telling me?" I asked.

We were stopped at a red light, and he turned to look at me, really look at me. "You said something the other day that made me rethink a lot of things."

I tried to jog my memory. "What things?"

"About being nice for once. About nice guys."

I threw up both hands. "I was just kidding." No, I hadn't been, but still, this different Brad was a strange beast. I wasn't used to this side of him.

He jerked back, almost looking offended. "Are you saying you want me to be an asshole? Because that makes absolutely no sense."

"No. I don't know." I wanted this conversation over and done and shoved in the glove compartment.

I stared at the traffic forming in front of us as he swerved onto the highway. I just wanted things to be normal between us, which meant him being his dickish self and me giving it back to him.

Silent minutes ticked by, and I watched the clock, knees bouncing, like a kid waiting to get to their destination, asking, *Are we there yet? Are we? Are we?*

Brad was the first to break the silence. "Is there anything to be aware of, things that should be off topic for tonight?" He stared at the road straight ahead, never turning to me, as though he were talking to the windshield. "Strong political or religious views, for example?"

"Well, just that my family is too Catholic, for lack of a better word. They believe abortion should be illegal and all the other things far rights believe. We go to church almost every Sunday together. They are *the* over-the-top Italian family. Lots of hugging and kissing and talking over each other. My parents come from a big family. I come from a family of eight and that's the average. And my extended family is insane. It's like all my aunts were trying to top each other by procreating."

"Interesting." He turned to me then, almost smiling. "I want to know a little more about your immediate family before I'm thrown into the fire. Tell me about them."

I eyed him. "Really? This is just dinner to placate my aunt."

"Just answer the question," he snapped.

And the bossy boss man was back. I'd take it.

"There's Marco, Anna, Laura, Rosa, and Stella. I'm the oldest, and then my parents just kept popping out more kids. Marco is a nurse. Anna and Laura go to the University of Michigan so they won't be there. Rosa and Stella are in high school and hormonal as hell."

I gave him the lowdown on each of my aunts, Aunt Chelsey being the loudest and sweetest chick of the litter, and before I knew it, we were in front of the house.

"Anything else?" He turned off the engine, reached for the door handle, and pushed open the door. One foot was already out of the car.

"Oh, and my father hates you." I shrank into myself. It

was mostly my fault, being the child who shared almost every detail of her life to her parents.

Brad scoffed and then shut his door. "Why?"

I tried to shrug, though my face flushed pink. I could feel the warmth, as though a heating pad were placed on the apple of my cheeks. "Because I complain about you nonstop, and you're kind of a dick to me."

"Which is exactly why I'm trying to change," he pointed out.

I sighed. Maybe it was a good thing he wanted to better himself. I just hoped it had nothing to do with me.

"Duly noted." I opened my door and couldn't jump out of the car fast enough.

We strolled to the front door, and his hand awkwardly fell to the small of my back as I rang the doorbell. The noise and commotion of people talking and laughing could be heard from outside.

I pushed his hand off my back and patted his shoulder. "Good luck. If you survive this, I'll marry you," I joked, embarrassed that had fallen out of my mouth. If I wanted normal, I couldn't be joking like this. *Am I flirting? Shit, maybe I was still drunk from two days ago.*

The door flew open, and my mother's smiling face greeted us. "Sonia!" She pulled me into an embrace so quickly that I tripped over my own two feet.

Seriously? I'd just seen this woman last week.

She held my cheeks between her two hands and squeezed, making my lips puff out like a fish, before leaning down to kiss my cheeks.

My mother was a big woman with hips that didn't lie and hair that was short and with curls that were teased like we were still in the eighties. She'd been stick skinny in her younger years, but she had grown into her skin, the more children she had and the more pasta she'd made.

When her head tilted up to take in Brad, her eyes lit up. "Hello, boss man turned boyfriend. Come on in."

"He's not my boyfriend," I groaned.

She ignored me and pulled him in, holding his cheeks so that his lips puffed out like a puffer fish, too. "Such a skinny man. Does your mama feed you?" She pressed her cheek to his cheek. Then, she started feeling his biceps for more meat and frowned. "You need to be eating more pasta, but don't you worry; I have cooked a feast for tonight."

When she linked her arms around his, I left him to the wolves. Maybe this would cure the weirdness between us.

"I'm Lydia, and let me introduce you to our clan."

"Sonia!" Rosa and Stella rushed toward me. They were Irish twins, born eleven months apart. There were days when I couldn't tell them apart with their silky, shoulder-length brown hair, their same brown eyes—my father's—and their similar choice in clothing—Hollister hoodies and Vans.

"We made the school play." Stella leaned against the couch and crossed her ankles.

"And I'm second chair," Rosa added, almost jumping up and down.

Stella grabbed my hand and pulled me to the couch, and they began to tell me about the play, who had gotten cast as whom, about their hot-to-trot theater teacher, and all that was high school drama–related.

Like me, they were late bloomers and weren't dating anyone seriously. Must be a Russo thing.

When I peered over at Brad, all the aunties and my mother were grilling him.

Aunt Kim went up on tiptoes to touch his hair. "Is that a natural curl?"

"Doesn't he look like a young John Travolta and James Dean mixed into one?" Aunt Clara asked beside him.

They were studying him like a new animal they'd never encountered.

A part of me debated on saving him, but when he caught my eye and smiled, I shrugged and decided he was a big boy. Plus, a little revenge wouldn't hurt.

"You guys make the cutest couple," Aunt Clara said.

I shouted back, "We're not together!"

They completely ignored me and prattled on about how adorable our future children would be.

"Like I said, we are not together." I rubbed at my forehead, feeling exasperated already.

"That's not what it looked like at the wedding," Aunt Chelsey added. Then, she proceeded to whisper to her sisters so I couldn't hear her.

"It's called too much to drink and just a date and nothing serious," I muttered, ambling to the kitchen.

The thing about my aunts was that they were relentless, so I gave up. Temporarily.

I went straight to the fridge where I knew our boxed wine was waiting for me.

My mother was a fan, a lush for boxed wine. Any kind of wine actually, but because she liked it cold, she'd get the boxed kind because she was convinced the taste lasted longer.

"Poor guy. He's never going to make it out of there alive." Marco sat at the kitchen island, eating a slice of tiramisu.

Out of all of my siblings, Marco had the biggest sweet tooth, yet he was stick skinny. He'd been a lanky teenager and never changed as he grew into adulthood. You wouldn't have guessed that the skinny gene ran in our family, judging by the size of my father's Santa Claus belly. Or maybe it was because my father had married an Italian woman who thought pasta was God's gift.

"He's fine." I tipped the box to pour some wine into my glass. All the way to the top.

Marco chuckled, and his fork stopped midair. "If he makes it through tonight, I might actually like him for you."

"Did you meet him already?" I shut the fridge and staggered over to my brother, sitting by him on a barstool by the long kitchen island that split the room.

"Not yet. I snuck past the herd to get a piece of dessert before dinner."

"And we're not dating," I huffed, irritated and already tired of repeating the words.

There was no doubt I'd have to repeat it a dozen more times before the night was through, though it wouldn't matter. When he no longer came around, my family would get the hint.

"In the beginning, Jeff used to be attached to your hip. And then he stopped going to our monthly dinners altogether. He smartened up." Marco pushed his fork through the tiramisu and slid it in his mouth.

"He always had to work." The muscles in my neck tightened. I felt the need to stick up for him, though I wasn't sure why. Jeff didn't deserve my loyalty. That was for sure.

Marco lifted two fingers in air quotes. "'Work.' Yeah, sure. During almost every monthly dinner. How coincidental."

I thought about the new information I'd learned Saturday night. Jeff had been working all right. Little had I known, he'd been working on my replacement.

"I never liked that guy." And Marco never had. He

wasn't overly talkative, but when he said something, it meant something.

"Why?" I settled my wineglass on the marble island and grabbed Marco's fork.

"There was something about him."

I sliced the tiramisu with my fork and stuffed it into my mouth. As soon as the cake touched my tongue, I sighed. *Heaven on a plate.* "You know I hate when you say that. What does that even mean?" I'd never asked Marco to elaborate, but seeing that I was obsessed with my ex-boyfriend, I needed to know. *Did others know he was cheating all along? Could I have predicted our end? What signs did I miss? How could I guarantee it never, ever happens again?*

Marco peered over at me, his face thoughtful. "You were way too in love with him."

I laughed. "Well, duh. We were in love."

He shook his head and then retrieved his fork from me. "No, I mean, you were way more in love with him than he was with you."

There was Marco in all his honesty, saying how he had seen it.

"No, I wasn't." It hurt to hear it, and I didn't want to believe it, but it had to be true because I'd loved him so much that I couldn't fathom leaving him. "Jeff was in love with me, too." I stared blankly at the dessert and then picked up the wineglass, tightly gripping it within my fingertips. If I squeezed tighter, I would break the neck. It wasn't exactly the neck I wanted to break, but it might help ease some of the pain, the pain of finding out that my ex-boyfriend had cheated on me. "He did things for me, too. Wrote love letters, bought me nice dinners, surprised me with gifts ..."

Jeff used to talk about forever, how our children would

look, how they would be legally blind because we both were.

I swallowed hard because Marco was only speaking his mind, and deep down, I knew it was the truth because, if Jeff had loved me as much as I had loved him, he wouldn't have left me.

Marco bumped his shoulder against mine. "Hey." He dipped his head closer to mine, getting eye to eye. "Stop overthinking things. It's over."

I wished it were that easy.

A low breath escaped me, and I smiled a little for his benefit. "How did you know? That he didn't love me the same way?" So, I'd know not to do it again. To fall in love with a guy who wasn't that into me.

"It's how you looked at him. Like he was your whole world, and you would do anything to keep him in it."

I sighed and bit my thumbnail, thinking deeply. "Isn't it always that way though? When people are in love, there is one person who always loves the other person a little more? I mean, look at Dad and how he looks at Mom. You can't tell me their love is even." I wanted an excuse, someone to tell me it was okay that I had fallen in love with Jeff and at one time was fully and deeply committed to him. That I wasn't stupid and that it was okay if I fell in love again sometime in the future. Because I wanted to believe in a forever love after heartbreak, in a love that led to marriage and kids and endless happiness. I wanted to believe in love for me in the future and that my love life hadn't ended with Jeff and that failed relationship.

"See, that's the thing." His brow crinkled, and he absently tapped his fork against the plate. "Love is not even at any one time. Yeah, Dad dotes on Mom, but then once in a while, roles are reversed, and you can just tell Mom can't get enough of Dad, as though he's her world. It's gross really." He cringed.

I was thrown back to when we'd caught Mom and Dad making out in the car, in our garage, windows fogged up, but thankfully, they were fully clothed.

"That makes no sense."

Then, he pulled back and took a sip of my wine in the Marco nonchalant way I was used to. "But it does. With you, you always looked at Jeff that way, but ..." He trailed off, and the silence was deafening. Though it wasn't said, I heard it in my head. *But he never looked at you that way*.

"What the hell is he doing here?"

The boom of my father's voice had me jumping to my feet.

"Oh, crap."

Marco chuckled. "I guess he's back from work. You'd better save your non-boyfriend over there before Dad gets his shotgun."

"Shit." I was out of the kitchen and back in the living room, rushing toward my father in less than a second. "Daddy," I cooed, wrapping my arms around him.

"You." He pointed a stern finger toward Brad, like the barrel of a gun, steady and firm, knowing its target. "Who the hell invited you?"

I wrapped my arms tighter around my father, teeth clenched in a tight smile and blood pounding in my ears. "I did, Dad. I thought it would be nice for the family to know who I worked for."

Brad teetered on his newly shined shoes, a timid smile forming. "Sir." He stepped forward, steadying a hand to shake. "It's great to finally meet the patriarch of the family. Sonia has told ..."

My father narrowed his eyes and took a step toward

him, glaring at his extended hand as though it had crap on it. "Yeah, I've heard a shit-ton about you. Slave driver, mean womanizer who makes my little girl cry."

My face turned all shades of red. Why, oh why, did I have the best relationship with my parents and tell them everything?

Brad's smile evaporated, and it looked like he'd been punched in the gut. And the aunties ... well, they stared at Brad like he'd suddenly fallen off his pedestal.

I waved a hand at Brad. "It was one time. Nothing really. Plus, it was when Jeff dumped me. Any and every little thing set me off."

How the hell did I get out of this one?

"Honey, I'm sure Brad has realized the error of his ways." My mom reached for my father's face, placing one large palm on his cheek. "And I'm sure he's sorry." She patted his cheek. "Because they're dating now." She beamed at him as if this was the best news she'd heard all year.

I groaned internally. *Kill me, someone. Quick.*

"Dating?" My dad flipped toward me so fast that I thought he would topple over. "*Him?*" The muscle by his neck twitched, and his vein pulsed in his neck.

And now was the moment of false truths. I could say I wasn't dating him and have my father kick him out and beat him to a pulp, or I could say all was forgiven and lie because he wouldn't kill his potential, possibly future son-in-law.

I gulped. "It's true." The pained smile surfaced again, the one that made my cheeks hurt from the strain. Then, I stretched a hand out and tilted my head for Brad to come toward me.

The aunts laughed with murmured confirmations of, "I knew it."

Brad hesitated, but then I stretched my pained grin farther, and he walked toward me and intertwined our fingers. And, at that moment, I regretted ever lying and taking him to that stupid wedding and getting butt-ass drunk. Because one thing I never, ever, *ever* did was lie to my family. Our bond was real and strong and built on honesty. And, now, I'd have to lie about the breakup.

~

Brad

"... who makes my little girl cry."

It took me a moment to realize what she was trying to do or even what she had said, that we were now pretending to be together because all that rang in my ears was, *"... who makes my little girl cry."*

I tried to search my memory, trying to recall a time when I'd seen Sonia unhappy. My mind came up blank. Yeah, I'd been a dick to her, like I was a dick to everyone, but with Sonia, I knew she could take it, and she gave it right back.

She knew me, not only my likes—like the way I liked my sandwiches with little mayo and no lettuce—but also my dislikes, my pet peeves, but she had to know I wouldn't treat her like shit and intentionally make her upset.

I searched her face, the way she was smiling to ease her parents, the smile she held for me when she was annoyed. And I knew deep in my gut that she was upset right now, right here.

I never cared what others thought. Maybe it was because I was the boss, and it didn't matter. But, as I stared into the almost-six-foot-tall, stout man who held the same warm eyes as Sonia, I realized that I cared what this man thought about me.

I mustered my most apologetic, contrite tone. "Sir, I never meant to make your daughter cry. Trust me when I say that I appreciate everything Sonia does for me day to day at Brisken. If it weren't for her, I wouldn't run as efficiently as I do."

I squeezed her hand and peered down at her to see her biting her bottom lip. It was an apology sincerely meant for her, as it was meant for her father. "I'm sorry. Sometimes, I think you're made of steel, and I forget you're not like those cutthroat CEOs I battle with."

I exhaled, and before I knew it, my hand cupped her cheek. "I'm sorry, Sonia. Know that I do appreciate you. I promise to be more conscious of my mood and to never take things out on you." Because it wasn't fair, and one of these days, I'd push too far, and I'd hate to think of what would happen if I did.

We were locked in a stare, and even though her whole family was in the room and I could feel the hostility oozing out of her father in waves, all of me wanted to kiss her, without hesitation and in apology. Just as I had at the wedding and in her apartment.

The urge was so strong that I leaned into her and brought her close but kissed her forehead instead. She smelled of strawberries. The sweet, light scent of her shampoo had me leaning closer.

Coos and awws echoed from the women in the room. It wasn't a reaction I had expected or wanted because all that mattered was Sonia's reaction.

She pulled my hand down from her face and tilted her head to look at me. "All's forgiven." Her eyes bled with sincerity, with forgiveness, and I eased up. "Just don't be an asshole to me anymore, and I'll no longer throw darts at your head at home."

I smiled a little and nodded. At that moment, I promised to never give her a reason to forgive me. "I kind of like that picture of me. I was thinking I could practice, too, and get better at my aim."

Sonia's face broke into an irresistibly devastating grin. "We can work on that. I've actually become very good at playing darts. Constant practice and all."

"See, all's forgiven. Now, go shake his hand, Vinny." Lydia gave her husband's shoulder a shove. "If they end up getting married, you're going to regret being a dick. Remember how my father hated you. You want to be him?"

Vinny flinched.

"Mom," Sonia yelled, her cheeks turning a shade darker. "We're not getting married."

"Yet," Aunt Chelsey finished, her eyebrows waggling.

Sonia groaned. "I hate all of you."

Vinny stepped forward, and I took in his stature. His chest was three times the size of mine. He reminded me of one of those WWE pro wrestlers, and judging by the size of his fist, I'd bet he could knock me out cold. Still, I straightened and met his gaze straight on. I wanted him to know that I was sincere, but more than that, I wanted him to believe I was worthy of his daughter.

And the realization pushed through.

I wanted to be worthy of her because I wanted a future with her.

And because it was Sonia, and I wanted more of her. More than our platonic relationship now. I wanted all of her dislikes and likes. I wanted every one of her future kisses and arguments and annoyances. I wanted it all. All in.

"Vinny," he spat out, sticking out his hand.

Great, a mob boss name. I wouldn't doubt it if Vinny was connected with the Italian mob.

"Nice to meet you, sir. I'm Brad."

I tried not to wince when Vinny squeezed the living shit out of my hand, smiling as though he didn't want anyone to know. When he released me, I wiggled my fingers to get the blood flowing again and reached for Sonia, who was right beside me.

"And so, everyone, sit. Dinner is ready and needs to be served because Mama is hungry. Girls?" Lydia disappeared to the kitchen, followed by a trail of females.

"Take a seat. We'll be right back." Sonia pointed to a seat at the far end of the table, and then she about-faced and followed the other ladies.

The women all filtered out of the room, toward the kitchen, leaving all the men at the table.

Their dining room was not big by any means, so each chair was right next to the other. The normally twelve-seater dining room table now sat sixteen, some chairs in the corners of the table.

I took a seat as far from Vinny as possible. Oddly enough, I craved confrontation, didn't show fear and was never intimidated by others in the boardroom. This time though, this was different.

An uneasy feeling crept up my spine, forcing me to sit straighter even though I wanted to cower.

Vinny was talking to one of Sonia's uncles, who was equally as tall and as muscular as Vinny. Other males were scattered around the table, but no one paid attention to me. In the boardroom, from the opposing team, I never felt welcome, but at least I was acknowledged. Here, it was as though I weren't even in the room.

"Hey." A hand clasped my back, and then a chair was

pulled out. Down sat a lanky male with hair that flopped over his eyes. "Marco." He stuck out his hand.

And, boy, was I relieved to meet someone who didn't radiate hostility.

"The younger brother," I noted.

He nodded. "I see Sonia has been bragging about me." He eyed me with curiosity, the once-over that other CEOs would give me when I stepped in the boardroom, wanting to decipher what my intentions were with a friendly smile.

I shrugged one shoulder. "I told her to give me the four-one-one on your family before we arrived."

"And let me guess; she didn't tell you about Dad." He tipped his chin at his father, who was at the head of the table, in deep conversation with the uncles.

"She did, but I guess I wasn't expecting a full-on war."

There it was again, the curiosity in Marco's stare, and it was as though the words had been spoken out loud; he wanted to know my intentions with his sister.

"I like Sonia," I said, bluntly, answering his silent question. "I was a dick before because I didn't realize it, and now, I'm trying to set things straight."

He crossed his arms over his chest. "Hmm." As though to say, *So what?* He added, "Just so you know, I know Sonia allows you to run your business smoothly. She also runs this family smoothly. She is our go-to person for problems, to divert confrontation, for anything." His tone was heavy with pride. "She's our girl, so you can see how we are *all* protective of her."

I didn't miss his emphasis on *all*, and I wasn't surprised by his admission. Sonia was selfless; she gave herself fully to her job. I had no doubt she did more than that for her family.

I picked up my napkin and placed it on my lap, not

wanting to seem too nosy. "Is Jeff the only one she's brought home before?"

Marco scowled. "Yeah."

But, by the look on his face, I didn't have to ask what he thought about her ex.

Well, that made me feel better—that not everyone was on the Jeff-Sonia team, hoping for a round two.

"She doesn't date a lot. Jeff was her first serious relationship, and, yeah, he was the first boy she brought home, maybe because she thought she'd end up with him. Otherwise, she wouldn't have put him through the family torture, and also, our family gets attached. She still gets the question, 'How's Jeff?' practically eight months later, and you can guess how that makes her feel." His gaze dropped to the table, his stare distant, empty.

Right on cue, Sonia stormed through the door, two mitts on her hands, carrying one major pan of lasagna. Her smile was blinding, and if I weren't sitting down already, the sight of her would have knocked me off my feet.

Normal? There was nothing normal about this, about how I felt, just seeing her smile. I loved that smile. And quite possibly the girl who held that smile, too.

CHAPTER 16

BRAD

Yesterday was the first night that I'd ever had where I didn't pay a fortune to take a woman out, all to see if we were compatible in bed.

With Sonia, that wasn't the end goal. The end goal wasn't an orgasm; it was simply her. And, though I knew it was a bad idea through and through, I wanted another date with her, outside of work.

I had dropped her off with a lightness in my step and a cheesy smile no alpha male should be sporting. I pulled into my driveway, thinking of ways to ask her out but not ask her out because, if I told her it was a *date* date, she would flat-out tell me no.

As soon as I walked inside, Mason looked up from the stack of papers on the kitchen table. The girls were fast asleep, but Mason was always up, going over the financials and reports. Mason had a fascination with numbers, always wanting to double- and triple-check and reconcile what our accountants had turned in.

I walked straight into the kitchen, noting his hair was in disarray and him tip-tapping his fingers against his laptop.

His head lifted when I approached. "Hey."

"Hey." I pulled open the fridge. "Want a glass of milk?"

He curiously eyed me. "Yeah, sure. Can you warm mine up?"

And, suddenly, we were ten all over again, having a stressful day and couldn't sleep and our mother was warming us a cup of milk to calm us.

After the microwave dinged, I strolled over and placed his NYC mug in front of him. When I sat across from him, he shut his computer.

"So ... did you settle things with Sonia?" He eyed me as though there was only one way to answer this question.

"Yes." I nodded, tipping back my glass of milk.

"Thank God." Mason reached for his mug and took a sip as though he were drinking wine.

"It's settled. I like her."

Now, this was comical. The way he flinched and his facial features dropped into a definite frown and the way his eyes turned cold, dead, flat.

The mug dropped on our kitchen table with a thud. "What?"

My confident stare didn't waver. "You asked if things were settled, and they are. I like her. I've settled that much."

Past that point, I didn't know what to do next, besides wanting to see her again. I'd never been in a relationship longer than a month. That had been in high school, and the girl had been psycho. Since then, I'd basically sworn off relationships. Too complicated.

Mason threw up both hands and pushed himself up to a standing position. "That's not what I meant, and you know it."

And here was the beginning of the Mason show.

I loved my brothers. Both of them equally, but Mason

tended to fly off the handle. Still, I needed him to be on my side for this one because, if he wasn't, my older brother, Charles, wouldn't be either.

Plus, I needed advice. Desperately. And, since Charles wasn't here, the default was Mason.

"This is not happening. Didn't we discuss this?" Mason paced the room, trying to keep his temper at bay and failing miserably.

We had discussed it. I'd tried to keep things purely platonic, but I couldn't.

"I like her. More than I've ever liked anyone." And I wanted more, whatever that more entailed.

"Oh," he sighed, exasperated. "And that means a shit-ton, right? Brad, when it comes to women, you have an attention span of a four-year-old boy. *Oh, look! Shiny new toy!*" His condescending smile surfaced.

Now, he was starting to piss me off. My jaw clenched. Yes, I had a reputation, but you'd think, of all people, my brother would give me the benefit of the doubt. He'd see things were different this time. That I was different.

"I sound like a broken record." He gripped the kitchen table and leaned in. "It's the chase. That's all it'll ever be for you. That's why you're so good at your job. You like to win and conquer. But, once it's over, it's done. It's the same for women."

Mason stalked to the fridge and grabbed a beer instead. Long forgotten was the milk that I had warmed up in the microwave for him.

"It's different this time. She's not just a game for me, Mason."

I had a hard time expressing my emotions. Truth be told, I wasn't an emotional guy at all, but I needed my brother in this situation because I wanted to know how I could win Sonia over. My flirty ways with other women wouldn't work with her. She thought this whole thing was a facade, but I didn't know how to tell her, make her believe me. She'd think it was all bullshit.

"I met her family today."

He spat out the beer, and it trickled down the side of his mouth. "Why the hell would you do that?" He stalked to the counter to grab a paper towel.

"Because I wanted to." My expression pinched, and I could feel my patience slipping. "Because I wanted to spend more time with her after work."

"That's the stupidest move in the history of fucking dumb moves." Mason rubbed at his temple as though a massive migraine was making its way to the forefront of his brain.

His negativity was taking a toll on my self-esteem, and my gaze flicked upward. I cracked my neck from side to side, already regretting that I'd sat down for a little brotherly chat.

"You're going to ruin everything. Do you know how long it takes to train a secretary?" His eyebrows flew to his hairline, and his face reddened.

"It's not going to come to that." I had promised I wouldn't fire Sonia, and I would keep my word. "The problem I have now is, how to ask her out without her thinking I'm talking out of my ass."

And that was the truth of the matter. She'd witnessed my bullshit tactics with other woman—the flattery, the flirting, the outright crassness that turned some of them on—but none of that would work with her.

Mason pinched the bridge of his nose, and he was no longer looking at me. His eyes were clenched shut, and he was breathing loudly. I could almost hear him counting to ten to calm down.

I thought of Sonia, her soft locks, her no-bullshit personality, and her laugh that was contagious, uninhibited, uncensored, and all real. Not like the fake laughs that women used to look cute. When Sonia laughed, there was no way I couldn't.

"I like spending time with her." My tone was quiet, soft, honest. "And being at work with her isn't enough, which is why I crashed her family dinner." I stared into open space, hating that I had a reputation and never caring before. Because, now, I cared, and all my shitty antics in the past could cost me my chance. If I had a theme song, it would start out like this, *To all the girls I've screwed before*. And it would end with, *I'm sorry*.

"After I dropped her off at her apartment tonight, I wanted her to invite me in. Not for what you're thinking, but just because I wanted to spend more time with her." I was officially going crazy over this woman.

Mason stared at me, wide-eyed, his mouth open. "You really believe this, don't you?"

My hand clenched against the mug, my patience running thin. Here I was, the brother who was never emotional and only asking for advice, and here was Mason, telling me not to feel what I was feeling—or, worst of all, telling me what to feel.

"It's not going to work." There was finality in his tone that had my blood heating.

I stood, my legs planted wide apart. "That's where you're wrong."

"Ah, fuck. I just threw a challenge in your face. Wrong move." He slapped his head again.

"Forget it," I grumbled. "Sorry I came to you for advice.

I've never been in this situation before, and I turned to you because you're my brother. I should have known better, knowing you've never had faith in me." I wanted to keep fighting. My voice itched to yell. But then I remembered my nieces were sleeping.

"I gave you advice, and you didn't want to take it," he snapped back. "I've been in a relationship for five years, and I know what it takes to be in one. Sorry, Brad, but you don't have it."

I'd had enough of this nonsense. "Relationship? You mean that shithole you're stuck in? You hardly ever smile when you're with her. Half the time, you're frustrated. To be honest, I doubt you're even happy."

"You don't know anything," he shot back, his eyes livid.

"Then, lie to me and tell me you are," I challenged him. "That you love her, and it's not the fact that you've invested time into a relationship and that's the only reason you're with her."

The silence stretched between us, and we warred without words, stiff and stuck in some sort of blinking contest.

He was the first to break contact.

His arms dropped to his sides, and he didn't say a damn thing. And, yeah, he knew me, but I knew him, too. He built things from scratch, invested time and energy to make things work, and he'd forever be in an unhappy relationship with the worst kind of person simply because he didn't want to give up. Mason was the type to see things through to the end even if it destroyed him.

I narrowed my eyes, going for the kill. "You know, if we went broke all of a sudden, she'd leave you. Or, if you were dying, the first person you'd call was Charles or me and not her. So, thanks for being the biggest asshole to the one who would save your ass in the end."

I stormed out of the room and straight up the stairs, hating the fact that he was partly right. I knew nothing about relationships and how they worked, but I was determined to find out.

"Uncle Brad."

Sarah startled me in her GAP T-shirt and sitting at the edge of the stairs.

"You have school tomorrow. Get to sleep." I waved my hand, and she moved off the stairs so I could pass.

"I couldn't sleep." Her hair was piled up on top of her head, and it reminded me of Sonia's *don't give two shits* bun.

"If this is about your womanly issues or boys or school, we can chat about that in the morning." I didn't want to be an asshole, but my patience had been spent on Mason. I gritted my teeth, not wanting to say the wrong thing. Not to Sarah, who was innocent in this situation.

I walked right past her to my room, but stubborn Sarah followed.

"You're going to be cranky as hell tomorrow, so why don't you go to sleep?"

"I was sleeping until you guys started yelling at each other."

I pushed open the door and stepped over my pile of laundry that I needed to send to dry cleaning. "Blame it on your other emotional uncle." Now, I was really being mature. I stopped, picked up the pile, and threw it with force into my laundry basket right by my bed as though the laundry basket were the cause of my foul mood.

"All you have to do is tell her the truth," she said like it was so simple.

"What?"

"Sonia. All you have to do is be honest with her." Sarah stood by the door, leaning on the frame.

"Sarah ..."

"Just listen to me, Uncle Brad. Please?" she begged.

My features softened, and I let out a long sigh and dropped my ass on the bed.

"Okay." I scrubbed one hand down my face, feeling the weight of not knowing how this would turn out on my shoulders. Then, I let it out, to the only person who would listen.

"I know Sonia. She won't think it's genuine." I was like the guy who'd cried wolf.

The bed dipped beside me, and Sarah dropped her head on my shoulder. "Then, you tell her that. That you're new to this, but you like her."

As I peered down at my twelve-year-old niece, still so innocent in the world, I wondered ... *Could it really be that easy?*

"Uncle Brad, take a chance. I really, really, really like Sonia."

I touched the tip of her nose. "I do, too, Sarah. I do, too."

∾

Sonia

I placed my elbows on my office desk, leaning into the phone and reading *the* text.

Sonia! I'm so glad we were able to finally meet. Let me know when you're free so we can do dinner.

Who is this? I texted the unknown number.

Jean. :)

I blinked and stared at my phone. *Jean. Jean. Jean.* But there was only one Jean that I knew.

Then, tiny, invisible spiders prickled my skin. It couldn't be. *How the hell did she get my number?*

The phone blinked red, right by my keyboard, indicating an incoming call for Brad, but I ignored it.

I bit my pinkie nail, and after staring at the phone for far too long, I texted back.

Dinner? I typed back, hoping it was another Jean, some long-lost classmate or acquaintance that I had forgotten about.

Yes! I can't wait. Jeff and I are free this Friday. Will you and Brad be available then?

Holy shit.

I typed, **I'll check.**

Then, I flew off my chair and straight into Brad's office for the second time this week.

His head peeked up from the sea of red roses in front of him. Oddly, they weren't in a vase.

"How does Jean know my number?"

His eyes flipped to mine and back to the dozen red roses simply lying on his desk.

"Who are those for?" I shook my head. "Never mind. I don't want to know. But what I do want to know is how Jean got my number." My hands rested on my hips, and my heels tapped against the marble floor. "Brad?"

He stood, stumbled, and approached without his usual confident swagger. *Was he drunk this early in the afternoon?*

"This ... these are for you." He stepped into me, toe-to-toe, and held out the roses wrapped in tissue paper and pulled together in a red bow. He teetered on his heels, his eyes meeting mine and then darting to something interesting behind me.

I followed his line of sight to the emptiness behind me and inhaled deeply, trying to see if I could smell liquor.

I blinked. "Me? Why?" My voice croaked and choked on my words. I stared at his hand as though it were on fire.

"Uh ..." he stammered, and Brad *never* stammered. "I'm not used to this type of thing. This sort of thing."

I blinked again. I'd never seen him like this. It was like he had grade school dance nerves. Why?

Then, a lightbulb went off in my head. *Oh!* "I forgive you." I smiled and reached for the beautiful bouquet.

He had apologized up and down and left and right for making me cry at work after my family dinner, and now, the flowers were an extension of the apology. I got that.

"No. That's not what I meant." He pulled at the flowers now in my hand.

"So, you're not sorry?"

Now, we were playing tug-of-war with the roses.

"Of course I am."

"Well then, let go!" I almost fell back from the force of tugging too hard. I blew out the hair from my face and steadied myself on my platform heels. *What the hell is wrong with him?* "Anyway, back to Jean."

"Jean?" Brad stared at the flowers, breathing unsteadily. "Who the hell is Jean?"

"Jeff's girlfriend." I popped out my hip. *Did this guy have short-term memory loss or something?* "I guess I plugged my number in her phone and pinkie swore with her that we would have dinner?" I narrowed my eyes. "Can you confirm that this happened?"

He laughed, looking more like himself. "Well ..."

"And, in my drunken stupor, did you ever once ..." I

shoved the flowers in his chest. "... think to stop me? Or think, *Goodness, this can't be a good idea.*"

His smile widened—damn guilty culprit—and he grabbed the roses between us and tugged at them, bringing me closer. "Actually, I did try to stop you, and you waved me off."

"Well, you should've tried harder." Annoyance settled deep in my gut.

I'd trusted him that night, and he'd promised. I'd almost guaranteed him that I'd act like an idiot that night. Either that or feel sorry for myself. He was supposed to be the one to keep me in check.

He peered down at me with that look again, the look that made me feel queasy and light-headed. I felt like I was underwater, and my lungs constricted.

"Well ..." I didn't know if I was expecting a response. I just needed to break the silence between us, the weird locked look we had going on.

"I'll try harder next time. I promise." He leaned in closer, his breath a hot whisper against my face. "Sonia ..."

The way he uttered my name was as though it were a new word he'd discovered. My heart began to beat louder in my chest, in my ears, at my temples.

"I need to tell you something ..." He leaned in closer, pulling me in by my elbows, the roses now crushed between our chests. "I'm not used to this sort of thing, but I need you to know that ..."

The world stood still.

I breathed in and forgot how to exhale. He erased the space between us. My eyes flickered to his mouth. One more millimeter and our lips would meet. Again. But, this time, I'd be sober. Then, suddenly, there was a knock at the door that had us both peering up, and Charles walked in.

Brad

Talk about the worst possible timing ever.

Sonia jumped back, almost falling in her heels. She then proceeded to step back farther, but it was too late. My brother wasn't an idiot. He could sense the sexual tension between us. He'd seen us a moment before. And, forget Sonia's flushed cheeks, my semi-boner also gave it away.

"Hey." I waved a hand in an awkward greeting and ran it through my hair. "Welcome back stateside."

His eyes flickered between Sonia and me, and in that instant, I knew he already knew. That Mason had gotten to him first.

"Thanks. So, what's changed since I've been gone?" There was a careful undertone in his voice, careful not to give away that he knew because he did. Charles knew everything. It was why his daughters couldn't get away with anything.

"Hey, Charles." Sonia tectered on her heels. "How was your, uh ... honeymoon?" She shrank into herself.

"Sun was shining; wife was happy. What more could I ask for?" Charles threw Sonia a smile, but then his eyes slid to me, and his smile slipped.

Charles was the scary brother, never emotional, even-keeled. When he got mad, it was a brewing silence, the kind of anger that was silent but deadly. All you wanted to do was talk yourself out of the mess until he said everything would be okay.

Sonia shifted forward and clutched the roses in one hand and tried to hide it behind her.

Isn't she cute?

"Can I order you lunch? I'm about to put in an order

for Brad at Sunrise Diner. Did you want anything?" Her eyes skittered around the room, landing anywhere but on my face, and all I could think about was how close I'd been to kissing her, to tasting those beautiful, succulent lips again.

"No, I think I'm good," he answered her, but Charles's focus remained fixed on me.

Then, he flipped like a light switch, eyes light, and addressed Sonia, "But can you make a posting on our website and submit a newspaper post for Kristin?"

"Kristin?" I asked, wondering what had happened to Mason's secretary. Maybe she wasn't coming back because of his annoying ass.

"Yeah." Then, like a coin toss, he was back to brewing Charles, his eyes steady on mine. "She's decided to stay at home with her new baby, and she won't be coming back to work. We'll need to find a replacement immediately."

"Will do."

Sonia was almost to the door when I called out, "Thanks, Sonia." Because I wanted the last word with her. And I'd officially lost my balls.

The door shut, and Charles and I were left alone. My big brother and me.

"So, is there something you have to tell me?" Charles adjusted the chair facing my desk and plopped down.

Tell him? There was so much I wanted to tell him, but I didn't want to risk sounding like a pussy, looking like a pussy, and worst of all, I didn't want him to disregard my need for Sonia, just as Mason had.

I scratched at my temple. Why did it feel like I was in the principal's office?

He lifted an eyebrow, and the silence choked the air out of the room. Charles did that. With one stare. Maybe it was the fatherly stare, that innate look that frightened not only the children, but adults, too.

I sat behind my desk, dropping my head against the custom-made mahogany wood. "I know you know, and I know what you're going to say, so why should I waste the effort or your time?"

"I want to hear it from you, or do you want me to just repeat Mason's version?"

I could hear Mason's voice in my head, picture his animated face, his over-the-top hand gestures ... and so I began. Again.

I told Charles everything. I started at the beginning and told him how Sonia had helped Sarah get her pads; how, in turn, I had promised her that I would accompany her to the wedding and how it had been the game changer for me. I told him I liked Sonia, more than I ever had any other woman. That there wasn't a waking moment that I didn't think of her and how I had spent most of my days wondering how I could ask her out and tell her how I feel but was afraid of rejection. I told him that I was obsessed with kissing her, and if kissing her was all I would ever do in life, I would die a happy man.

I laid it all out on the table, looking at my hands, at the pen marks on my desk, my mouse pad with our logo, anywhere but his face. I was being a coward, afraid to see contempt, disgust, or even disbelief because I had never been more honest than I was being right now. And I'd never been more vulnerable when it came to another woman.

"I can't sleep or eat." I dug my hands into my hair, repeating the motion. "I'm honestly obsessed, and I just need advice on how to win her." I lifted my head and dared to see his reaction.

Charles was covering his mouth with one hand, and then, when our stares met, he let out a peal of laughter.

"You're an asshole," I grumbled. "Thanks."

If I could disown my brothers, I would, but then we'd have to break up the company.

"I never thought I'd see the day." Charles's laughter heightened, and he rubbed at his eyes.

"Shut up." My parents were most likely turning over in their graves from all the support I was getting here. "I'm getting my lunch, and just so you and Mason are clear, I promised I wouldn't fire her, so I'm not going to. We'll work it out." I stood and made my way around my desk as I shook my head. "Thanks for kicking me when I'm down, bro."

Charles stood and pressed a heavy hand against my shoulder, humor dimming from his face. "Listen, I've been in love twice, so I know a thing or two about women."

I glared at him. "I'm not in love."

Charles chuckled, as though he didn't believe me. "Acceptance is the first step to recovery."

"Whatever." I leaned against the end of my desk. *Am I in love? Shit.* I rubbed my neck with my hand, suddenly feeling like I wanted to throw up. I didn't think love happened that fast. Didn't it take months of dating?

"Being in love isn't a bad thing, Brad. I wouldn't have gotten married twice if it was."

"I don't know what I'm doing here, Charles."

The walls were closing in. It was as though the longer I took to act, the more I was afraid someone would act before me, as though I'd missed my window of opportunity and someone else would snatch her up.

"Why didn't I notice her before?" I said out loud, not expecting an answer.

"I guess it was because you didn't give her a chance. I

hired her specifically because she wasn't your type, but then again, maybe you don't even know your type. You've been looking at all the wrong women, brother." Another disbelieving laugh escaped him. "She's a feisty one. And here I thought, I had my hands full."

When he started for the door, I straightened. "Wait. Where's my advice?"

"Your advice?" His eyes were amused. "Talk to her. Tell her how you feel."

Exactly what Sarah said.

"Easier said than done." I tipped my chin. "I'm not letting her go." I had promised her, and I'd keep my word that her job would remain intact.

Finally, there was certainty in his face. "We'll work it out. First, I suggest you get your girl."

Sonia

Bringing the bouquet of roses to my nose, I inhaled deeply, taking in the scent.

What was he going to say before we were interrupted? Whatever it was, it seemed important, and every part of me wanted to know what it was.

One thing I did know was, our relationship was shifting. Coming to work no longer felt as though I were walking into a war zone.

I touched the soft petals with my fingertips. I couldn't place my finger on what exactly was happening, only that the mean old Brad was long gone.

I pressed my cheek against the soft petals and skipped and staggered to a stop.

Skipped?

I looked behind me, searching for something that I'd tripped on. The floor was clear. Then, I looked at the bottom of my shoe to see if gum was stuck there or if I'd broken a heel. Nothing.

My eyes widened, and my hand flew to my neck where my rapid pulse thumped. After dropping to my chair, I placed the roses on my desk, pulled out the mirror in my desk, and touched my flushed cheeks.

Crap. Crap. Crap.

Then, I dropped my head against my desk.

Tap. Tap. Tap.

How could I be so stupid, and when the hell did this happen?

What I'd said to Ava weeks ago about Jeff played loudly in my head.

"He was it. My heart skipped for him. I didn't walk when I was with him; I skipped. Can you imagine that? Skipping into his arms because you're in love? That's the kind of relationship we had."

Maybe I was confused from the whole charade of being in love that, now, I was mistakenly starting to believe it but this time with Brad?

"Are you okay?" Lucy, Charles's secretary, placed a stack of folders on my desk, and her eyebrows pulled together.

"Yeah. Sure. Why wouldn't I be?"

Because I couldn't possibly be in love with Brad. There was no way.

A few minutes ago, I'd felt like I was underwater; now, I was drowning.

I stood, needing to get out of the building and to the open outdoors to think clearly.

"Sonia, you don't look too good." She placed a light

hand on my shoulder and then felt my forehead.

"I'm fine." I stood and reached for my purse.

I chucked my bag across my shoulder, already heading to the elevators.

"Please tell Brad I'm not feeling well." Because wasn't that the truth?

I shouldn't be leaving without telling him myself. There would be consequences, but right now, consequences be damned.

~

Brad Charles left me no better than when he'd come into my office. But I was on a mission, and after a beat, I stormed straight out of my office in search of Sonia. I didn't care that my lunch was on its way. I was taking Sonia to lunch, and we were going to hash it all out. But then I saw Lucy at Sonia's desk, sorting through a stack of papers, and stopped mid-stride.

"Sonia is out sick."

"Sick?"

She'd looked fine a minute ago.

"Yes, she went home."

Four words that told me where I also needed to be.

CHAPTER 17

SONIA

Maybe I really was sick. That would explain the heat in my cheeks and my light head earlier. But why were all my symptoms gone now? I refused to think it was anything else. I sat on the couch, flipping through the channels. I had just finished drinking a crap-ton of orange juice and played ten rounds of darts on Brad's poster, thinking it would make me feel better. It didn't. Even after marring his face, it didn't erase the flutter in my chest every time I thought of him. Whatever was happening internally or even externally had to stop and stop fast. I loved my job and my life and my sanity and had to do everything in my power to keep it that way.

The banging on the door had me jumping up. At least my food was here.

But, when I opened the door, it wasn't the Tex Mex delivery guy. It was the BILF.

I mean, the BILK. BILK! I want to kill him, remember? Not fuck him.

"What are you doing here?" I snapped, hating how handsome he looked today, how his crisp white button-down hugged his powerful shoulders, his strong arms, his broad chest.

"I brought reinforcements." He lifted two brown paper bags. "Soup, crackers, and chocolate."

That stupid pitter-patter in my chest intensified. This couldn't be a good thing.

"I heard you were sick. Soo ..." He peeked around me. "Can I come in?"

I shouldn't let him in, but I opened the door, and he strolled in.

"What's wrong? Did you call a doctor?" His tone was overly concerned, but I didn't need my primary physician to fix this. I needed a shrink.

The whiff of his cologne had me teetering on my bare feet. This was shithole bad.

"I can't breathe." *Shit. Did I say that out loud?*

"Do you have asthma?" He leaned in and touched my forehead, making the ability to get air into my lungs worse. "You don't look too well."

I shook my head when he took my hand and led me to the couch.

Then, he let out a low chuckle. "Well, that's interesting."

"Shit!" I flew to the poster of him on the wall, but he tugged my hand, bringing me cascading into his chest.

"Stop. I saw it the other day when I was here, remember?" Then, he approached closer, laughing harder. "But this unibrow is different, and this beard ..."

I groaned silently. With a Sharpie, I had tried to make him less beautiful, but it was impossible. No amount of Sharpies could de-beautify that face.

"Do you think I can rock that beard? I'm not sure about the unibrow." He tipped my chin up with the lightness of his fingertips, and a tingling sensation traveled down my neck.

His eyebrow furrowed, and all humor erased from his features. "Lie down," he commanded in his authoritative boardroom voice.

And I did because then the dizzying sensation might stop.

"Did you even eat?"

He frowned when I shook my head again.

He sighed and made his way to the kitchen, placing the can of soup on the counter.

"It's fine. I ordered Tex Mex."

Breathe. In through the nose. Out through the mouth. Why the hell did it feel like I was hyperventilating?

"Chicken soup fixes the sick. According to my mom." Brad was already sorting through my cabinets. He took out the soup pan, opened the can, and poured the contents into it as though he lived here.

What alternate universe am I in?

"I'm not sick. Plus, what the hell are you doing here? Shouldn't you be at work?"

Brad never missed work, and this could not be a good thing. Him being here with me in my apartment and not working? If Charles found out, my job would be as good as gone.

"I'm fine. My job will be there tomorrow and the day after that if it takes you longer to get well."

His back was turned to me, and I realized he wasn't wearing his suit jacket. Trying not to drool, I stared at the expanse of his broad shoulders and the muscles on his back. My mouth felt dry, and for the first time ever, I wondered how he looked without his shirt on.

I groaned and threw one arm over my eyes. "Why are you doing this, Brad?"

And why am I doing this? Wasn't I stronger than this?

It was silent for a beat before he said, "Because I like you." The words were spoken softly while he stirred the ladle in the pot.

Okay. Great. I didn't know what to do with that.

"Yeah, but still, I really don't think you need to be taking care of me when I can take care of myself, and you have meetings all day."

I knew his schedule. Once he missed a meeting, I'd have to reschedule it, which was a pain.

"I don't think you understand ..." His voice trailed off.

With my eyes closed, I could only hear him coming closer. When I lifted my arm, he was right in front of me, above me, and for the life of me, I couldn't stop picturing him shirtless.

I gulped. Hormones. I was sure I was going to get my period soon. That had to be the reason.

"I don't think you get it ..." He smiled then, a small smile, subtle, sweet even. Then, he sat on the couch, scooting me back against the cushions. "I like you, Sonia."

I lifted a brow. "Yeah. You have to. I work for you."

He moved closer, and the way he was looking at me made my heart hammer in my chest.

What is happening here?

~

Brad

And here was the moment of truth. Where I laid everything out on the table. I had to admit I was scared shitless because she had no clue what I was going to tell her and also, if she didn't feel the same, it would gut me. It wasn't like I could blame her. I'd built a reputation and put her in a no-touch box for so long. Now, it'd be hard to change her mindset because that was all we were to each other. Employees. Acquaintances. But I was about to change all that.

I reached for her hand and caressed the top of her fist with my thumb as I swallowed. "I like you, Sonia. More than my secretary and more than a friend …"

Her eyebrows flew to her hairline. I couldn't even finish my spiel that I had practiced in my head numerous times before I walked up to her door because she shot up to a sitting position, eyes wide, and moved as far away from me on the couch as humanly possible.

Fuck, did that burn!

"You can't," she spluttered. She rapidly blinked and pushed the hair out of her face. "I'm not even your type."

I swallowed hard. "So, smart, witty, funny, and beautiful is not my type?" My chest concaved. I had known it would be hard to convince her of us, and I'd expected her to go on the defensive, but still, it hurt.

She looked at me like I was an alien being. "I'm not blonde, I'm not five-seven or taller, and I'm not a D cup. I'm not your type." She was adamant, her voice rising with a certainty I didn't feel.

I couldn't deny what she was saying. I'd always dated the same type of girl, the Jean types.

I carefully chose my words, afraid I would scare her off. "I think about you constantly, Sonia, and ever since the wedding, it's gotten worse." I angled closer and pulled her right next to me. Her eyes went wild, and I used everything in my ability to calm her. "Listen. Don't freak out. Just listen." I cupped the side of her face, staring into her beautiful eyes that I'd known for years. "I couldn't have predicted this. Me ... you ... falling for you."

Her hand covered mine on the side of her face. "Brad ..." Her breathing came in and out in short, broken puffs, and she eyed the door behind me.

I didn't give her a chance to utter another word because I leaned in and met her lips with mine.

And it was explosive.

Better than the first time or the second or the third. She tasted like the finest wine, the sweetest chocolate, the most delectable cake.

I could kiss her for hours, and it would never, ever be enough. I'd always want more. Her hands moved down my chest, and she slowly shoved me away, eyes dazed and wondering and straight-up sexy.

"Tell me you didn't feel that," I whispered, our faces a breath apart.

Our connection was undeniable and electric, and there was no way she couldn't feel that spark between us.

"I'm sorry." She inched away and blinked up at me, bewildered. She scraped her hand through her hair. "I didn't feel that."

Wait? What!

This was not happening. I sat there, shocked and still and waiting for someone to come through the door and tell me that I'd been punked. But, of course, no one would walk through her door, and of course, I knew deep down that an incredible kiss would not win her over. This was a woman I had to wine and dine and cherish.

"I'm sorry ..." she started again.

"No, don't ..." It was too much of a blow to the ego to hear her apologizing for not feeling anything when I felt everything.

She stubbornly lifted her face. "No, I'm going to say what I have to say. See?" She motioned between us. "It's this whole charade. Our feelings aren't real."

"I feel everything," I insisted, eyes steady, voice sure.

"You don't." She pushed her finger into my chest. "You're still confused, and I get it. I'm confused, too. Like earlier, when I pictured you with your shirt off, and I was like, *What?*" She scrunched her face, confused. "Why would I want to see him with his shirt off? Then, you came closer, and I was thinking, *Goodness, he does have nice shoulders, and he really needs to take off his shirt.* Now, really?" She tilted her head and let out a low laugh. "If we were both in our rational minds, would you really want to kiss me, and would I really want you to take off your shirt?"

She was looking at me like it was all supposed to make sense, and I was trying my damnedest not to laugh.

Sonia has been thinking about me shirtless, possibly naked?

She kept babbling, like she always did when she was trying to prove a point, but when I undid the top two buttons of my shirt her breath hitched, and all humor slipped from her features.

And, now, I was back in the game.

"What are you doing?" She raised both hands as though she were under arrest, and dirty little thoughts of handcuffs and police outfits filtered through my head.

"I'm taking off my shirt." It was getting harder not to smirk.

The panic was back. "Why? What? Okay, this is getting ridiculous."

"You did say you were picturing me shirtless."

"I told you how absurd it was," she yelled.

My shirt was completely unbuttoned now, and her

mouth slipped slightly ajar. I'd been shirtless that wedding night, but she'd been too drunk to remember.

"Uh ..." Sonia was speechless.

Ding. Ding. Ding. I could hear the winning bell faintly in the background. Now, how could I make it ring louder?

I reached for her hand. "Here. Touch me."

"No!" She tried to retrieve her hand, but my hold was tight and kept her hand between us.

"You accommodated my kissing experiment, and now, I'm accommodating yours." My tone was soft, calm, but I felt anything but.

She shook her head and squeezed her eyes shut, as if she couldn't handle my naked chest. "I never said I wanted to kiss you or touch your body."

My cock jumped to life at her words because, shit, did I want her to touch my body.

"Just humor me here." I tugged her closer and placed her fist across my chest. Her touch awakened every horny cell in my body, and I swallowed. "Nothing?"

"Yep. Nothing." It seemed as though she was holding her breath.

I didn't believe her for a second. "Listen, Sonia. I tried. I really tried with that kiss a minute ago. You're not giving this experiment a real shot."

I opened her fist and pressed her palm flat against my chest, and she let out one low sigh. Her hand trembled as it trailed slowly down my abs, and my body was flooded with warmth. Shit, I felt her touch everywhere.

"You could iron on this thing. One. Two. Three. Four. Five. Six." She counted every single ab muscle and swallowed. Hard. Then, she tucked her hand in her armpit. "See, nothing." Her smile was strained and forced, and she had to be the worst liar I'd ever met.

Her eyes trailed the length of my body, and I felt victorious.

Drink it up, baby, because I'm going to romance the hell out of you.

I wasn't giving up that easily. I wanted to take her on a real date, where we could be ourselves and not pretend.

"Don't lie, Sonia. It's not like you."

She blew the bangs away from her face "Fine. I'm attracted to you. There. Happy? Really though, you'd have to be blind not to be."

"I never thought you noticed before." I wished I had.

She frowned. "Because you were a jerk. Now, you're being all sweet, and it's confusing me." She pushed out her lip in a signature Sonia pout.

God, all I wanted to do was hold her and kiss her and do naughty things to her. But the latter would have to wait.

"Come here." I pulled her by her forearms, and she landed on my chest. She relaxed into me, and I was thankful she hadn't pulled away. "Why can't we just see where this goes?"

"Because everyone—*everyone*—knows this is a bad idea."

"Who?"

"Your brothers and ..."

I grinned. "Your parents love me."

Even her dad had warmed to me by the end of the evening. Or, at least, he glared less.

"They do not," she argued.

"Your siblings love me." I tipped her chin with a light fingertip. "Don't lie."

"Fine," she said. "They do, but still ... that doesn't mean a thing."

I gave her my most serious face. "Just give me a chance, Sonia. One date, and I'll never ask you for anything again."

I waited ten torturous seconds for her answer.

"Okay."

"Okay?"

"Yes, because, before you got here, I agreed to go on a double with Jean and Jeff."

I scoffed. "You did? Why?" I didn't want to see that prick again, let alone go on a double with him.

She rolled her eyes. "Because, when Miss Barbie texts with, *I understand if you change your mind. I wouldn't want you to be uncomfortable with Jeff being your ex,* I couldn't let her have the last say."

I thought on it for a moment. It wasn't what I'd had in mind, but I'd take it.

I smirked. "Deal."

∽

Sonia

Brad's revelation had kicked my world off its axis. In between him trying to convince me that we'd be good together and me trying to convince him that these feelings would eventually pass, my life had turned upside down.

Truth was, this was my fault. A lie that had snowballed into an avalanche, and now, I was asking him to lie for me again on our double date.

We were out to lunch—Brad working on his computer, me staring out the window, people-watching. In typical weekday fashion, when I had been about to grab his lunch, he'd stood and clutched his laptop, saying he'd just go with me.

I didn't know what the point was. He had mounds of

work to do and an unprecedented amount of meetings this afternoon until tomorrow morning.

I peered over the table and took him in. Whenever Brad was concentrating really hard on something, his brow would twitch and then furrow and then twitch again. It took every ounce of energy not to reach out and smooth the lines.

"Are you going to eat that?" I tipped my chin toward his food. "It's getting cold."

His eyes slowly lifted from his computer. Then, he smiled, and my heart flipped and flopped and then went into cardiac arrest.

Stop, stupid heart. Stop. Stop. Stop.

"You're absolutely right." He shut his laptop and threw his attention on me, reaching for his turkey and ham and cheddar cheese sandwich. "You're done with yours already?"

I rubbed my belly and gave it one big pat. "Like, twenty minutes ago. Ate my cookie and yours, too, but you didn't notice."

He chuckled when he looked down at his empty cookie bag.

"I was still hungry. Sorry." I lifted my shoulder to my ear, unapologetic. "Anyway, do you think you're going to win over Titan Printing?" The current account he was still working on.

It was the talk of the office, the big merger we foresaw happening.

"I sure hope so. Our big meeting is this week. I think I've been distracted lately, and you know exactly why that is."

He playfully waggled his eyebrows, and there went my heart again, pitter-pattering without my consent.

"Do you live to make me uncomfortable?" I crumpled up his cookie bag and placed it on the tray.

"I live to make people, particularly you, accept the truths." He placed his sandwich down. "And the truth is ... I think you like me." Though he didn't sound too sure.

I let out a peal of laughter. "I do. I like you enough to let you lie for me and be my pretend boyfriend at the wedding and even Friday night on our double date."

I smiled, all teeth, and he frowned.

"Oh, yeah. I almost forgot about that."

There was no way I was showing up to the double date without him on my arm. "You'd better not."

He grimaced, studying me for a second as though he were debating on saying something. "Why are you doing this, Sonia?"

"Well, you did say that you wanted a date, so ..." If I could put a wink emoji at the end of that sentence, I would.

Brad was not amused. "I meant, a real date, and don't worry; I'm still collecting on that. But I mean, with Jean and Jeff. Why did you say yes?" He leaned in, elbows on the table, eyes intently fixed on me.

There were so many things that ran through my mind. *Why am I even wasting my time? It is over with Jeff, so why do I even care?* But, ultimately, I was going on the date because I didn't want to seem as though I wasn't over him. I didn't want him to think I was a loser. I wanted him to know that I was so much better off without him. I wanted him to regret ever leaving me.

There were a slew of reasons, and it seemed as though Brad could read me so well.

"Why does any of it matter? Unless ..." His forehead crinkled, and he rubbed the back of his neck, his face thoughtful. "Are you not over him?" When I didn't answer fast enough, he added, "Do you want him back?"

Do I? Do I want Jeff back? I hated him for what he had done, how he'd left me, possibly cheated, yet why was it so hard to just forget about him and move on?

"You do, don't you?" His voice was whisper soft, and his face flipped like a deck of cards—surprise at first, disdain, and then ultimately hurt.

"No. Of course not." It was the truth, wasn't it? How could I possibly want him back after he'd left me the way he did, so easily, so brokenhearted? But, if I didn't want him back, why couldn't I get over the fact that he'd left me?

He stared at me far too long. After a beat, he stuck his laptop back in his bag, stood, and rubbed the back of his neck. "I have to get back to the office. I have to prep for this meeting at two and the meeting with Titan later this week."

His abrupt change in mood gave me whiplash.

"Is something wrong?"

He sighed and averted his stare. Not able to read his eyes unnerved me.

"No. Just have a lot of things to do." His standoffish demeanor, the one that hadn't made an appearance in a while, was back in full force.

Normally, I'd call him out on it, but I didn't because I was afraid he'd continue to ask me questions that I wasn't ready to answer.

We walked back to the office in silence, side by side but as though we didn't know each other, an odd contradiction to how we'd been since the wedding. When we were finally in the office, I rushed behind my desk. He was about through his office doors when he about-faced and walked straight toward me.

He dropped his bag on the ground and placed both fists

on my desk, leaning in. "I have to say this because you can't see it, but he's just not good enough for you. He's just not, Sonia." The way he uttered my name had my heart staccato stopping again. "You're wasting energy on someone who isn't worth a second of your time. If you love someone deeply, care for them infinitely, then you would never, ever let them go. I know I wouldn't." His eyes were feverish and bright, and there was an underlying desperation in his tone.

I could read all his emotions with his one look, and shit, it intimidated me.

We locked eyes for longer than what was comfortable. I didn't know what to say. I had no words because Brad was right.

But Jeff had hurt me, and I didn't want him to know how much, which was why I just needed to drag this charade out for just a little bit.

The worst thought popped into my head. "Are you not going with me tomorrow night?"

He shook his head, and then his tone turned sharp. "Yes. I already agreed, and I'm not one to back out."

Then, he marched to his office and slammed the door shut.

My chest tightened. The last time I remembered that door being shut was weeks ago, before everything had changed between us. Even when he was taking conference calls, he'd leave it open. There was no one around me, and no one could hear him, so it didn't matter.

I hated this side of him. Funny how I'd prayed and hoped everything would go back to normal between us, and now that it was, I wished it weren't. Because I liked our new relationship—the cordial one, the fun-loving one.

I knew this was my fault, this change in him.

I should have been careful what I wished for.

CHAPTER 18

BRAD

I was tapping my pen against my desk, looking out my office window. People dotted the streets below me, like little ants in an ant farm.

Jeff has nothing on me. Nothing. I compared every physical feature between us and knew I one-upped up him substantially—in height, in broadness, in weight. But, even though I repeated that mantra in my head, I knew it wasn't true.

He had everything because, at one time, even possibly now, he had Sonia's heart, and because of that, he'd won.

The knock on my door had me peering up.

"Hey." Charles walked in, unbuttoned his suit jacket, and strolled to my desk with the confident swagger he'd been born with.

Better Charles than Mason. I hadn't talked to Mason since our fight. He was an asshole, and I was waiting for my epic apology. Knowing Mason, it would come. Later. Way later. But I'd decided I was going to wait this one out.

"You look like we already lost the deal."

I straightened, flattening out my hair. I'd run my hands

through my hair one too many times, and my hair was a disheveled mess. I'd undone my tie hours ago. If how I looked was any indication of how I felt, I looked like shit.

I shook my head. "We have this deal in the bag. We'll be giving them a little over fair market value. There's no way they can resist. Unless he's an idiot and he doesn't care about his three hundred employees."

This was an easy decision for the company. They hadn't been making their bottom line and weren't as profitable as they had been in prior years. Instead of closing shop completely, we could integrate their company into Brisken Printing Corp.

He plopped down in a chair in front of my desk with that Charles, older brother, knowing look in his eyes. "How did it go?"

"The meeting is tomorrow and I'm prepared."

"That's not what I was talking about."

I rubbed at my temple, knowing exactly what he had been asking about. I exhaled. "Not good."

With Charles, there wasn't any pretending, no beating around the bush, but it was as if my older brother already knew the answer to the question he'd asked.

"We have another date tomorrow."

He nodded, pleased. "That's a good sign."

I tried not to groan aloud. "Double-dating with her ex."

That pleased look disappeared. "Oh."

I flipped the pen over and over between my fingers and glanced out my windows again. The sun was shining, and the sky was blue. It was a perfect day, opposite to the storm happening in my life.

What could I say that Charles couldn't already read on my face?

Defeat.

"I don't think she's over him." Saying the words out loud was like a fucking brick to my head.

"So?"

I let out a laugh. That was Charles, and maybe that was why he made a good CEO. Nothing was impossible for him. But didn't he know I had already lost the fight before it even started? Maybe that was the reason she wasn't giving me a chance, blaming it on work when it was really because her heart belonged to someone else.

"Did she say that exactly?"

I swirled my chair around. "That she was in love with her ex? No. But she couldn't deny it either."

Charles lifted up a palm, his face incredulous. "Wait, is Brad giving up?"

Nostalgia hit me directly in the chest, and I suddenly remembered Charles kicking my ass when I was twelve. I'd stolen his ex-girlfriend, thinking he was over her. He'd chased me into our backyard with our parents in the house. His eyes were begging for blood.

Charles was taller, buffer, and stronger than me. Puberty had hit him early. He had me on the ground, his knee on my chest. I was all out of energy and full of guilt. I called defeat before I could even get the first punch in.

"Are you a quitter now? Is that all you've got? You're going to let me beat you, lying down?"

He called me every derogatory name in the book to get me to toughen up.

It had worked because I had flipped him over, my knee on his chest, and I hadn't let up until he'd heard my whole apology and forgiven me.

Talk about no choice in the matter. I'd had him pinned to the ground.

"So, are you?" Charles said, breaking me away from the past. "Are you giving up?"

Was I? This time was different though. I had known I could take Charles. Jeff, on the other hand, had history with her, and I couldn't compete with that; therefore, he had me beat.

"It's like fighting to take over a company when the owner isn't willing to give it up. The company isn't for sale."

Charles laughed. "You are giving up then. I didn't think it was in you."

I huffed and ran a frustrated hand through my hair. "You don't get it. I can't win if I'm not even in the race."

Charles's eyes narrowed, challenging me. "Who took you out of the race?"

"Her ex-boyfriend." I threw up both hands, beyond exasperated.

"What does he have on you?"

"Nothing. Absolutely nothing. Maybe a law degree, but shit, I could get that if I wanted to. And, if that would win her over, I would. He doesn't deserve her."

If Jeff had been stupid enough to let her go, then he hadn't known what he had in the beginning.

"Well then ..." He lifted an expectant eyebrow. "Why don't you jump back in the race?"

"Charles ..." My tone was tired, already defeated.

"As I see it, you're the one choosing to be out of the race. Sonia hasn't said she's still in love with him. And, even if she is, change her mind. An owner will sell his company for a price even if it's not for sale." He smirked, and years of being the older brother showed on his features. "Everyone has a price. The question is, how hard are you willing to fight to get what you want?"

Brad

I didn't emerge from my meetings until six o'clock. Sonia had been long gone since five. She'd usually tell me she was leaving, but I'd had my door shut, preparing for our meeting with Titan Printing.

After I shut down, I jumped into my car and headed to her place. My mind should've been on this very important meeting that would add a twenty percent increase to our bottom line in the next few years, but it wasn't. All that occupied my brain was the woman I'd been obsessing over. When the doorman told me she wasn't in her apartment, I texted her.

Where are you? We need to talk.

There were so many things I needed to say, but I needed to say them in person.

I tapped my head against the wheel.

Come on. Come on. Come on. Text me back.

A long minute later, my phone pinged.

Sonia: Can this wait until tomorrow? I'm at my parents' house.

I didn't respond to her text. I just reacted. I drove to her parents' house like the stalker I really was, using what was saved on my navigation from our previous dinner.

Rosa, Sonia's sister, opened the door when I arrived. "Hey, Brad." Her eyes widened right before she grinned.

At least someone was happy to see me. I hoped Sonia would have the same reaction.

"Hi, is Sonia here?" I shifted in my spot like a boxer ready to pounce. I wanted to barge in, given my normal lack of restraint, but remembered that her father had a gun. I needed to live through the next few minutes to say what I needed to say.

"Yeah, let me get her. Come on in." She opened the door wide for me.

"No, I'm kind of in a hurry." My fingers flexed at my sides, and I peered behind Rosa, getting a glimpse of the family party inside. "I can't stay long. There's just something I have to tell her."

"All right. One second."

My palms began to sweat, and I shifted with unease until she was right in front of me.

Sonia walked through the door, forehead wrinkled and as beautiful as ever. She was still in her skirt suit, a gray color with a fit that hugged her slim figure and had me staring nonstop earlier in the day.

"Brad?" She stopped mid-stride when she first saw me and then walked toward me until the door shut behind her.

I cleared my throat. I had words, tons of them. I had practiced a speech in the car, making note of every reason she should give us a chance, ticking off reasons we would be good together, but, as I watched her stand there with all the questions in her eyes, my words got lodged in my throat.

And so, I did what I wanted to. My hands threaded through her hair, and I tilted her head back as my mouth descended on hers. When I kissed Sonia, I never wanted to stop. I gave my all in that one kiss. Knowing what she had said earlier about not feeling a thing, this time, I wanted her to feel everything. I poured every single unsaid emotion into that one sweet kiss.

She stiffened at first and then melted into me, and I claimed victory. My free hand held her at the waist, bringing her closer. She tasted divine and smelled of sweet strawberries. I concentrated on her bottom lip at first and then the top, cherishing every bit of her. When her breathing hitched, I remembered we were in front of her house, and her dad had a gun.

Instantly, I pressed my foot on the brakes.

As I stared down at her, everything that I had been afraid of disappeared. I rested my head against hers, framing her face within both hands.

I didn't use the rehearsed speech that I'd made up in the car, but pure honesty gushed out of me in waves. "I like you, Sonia. I don't know when it happened or how it happened, but it just did. And I know you're unsure about me, about a possibility of us. Maybe it's because you have feelings for your ex, or maybe you're so afraid to be hurt again. I don't know, but what I do know is ... I'm not giving up on you or us, and I'm going to fight to make you see that we could be great together." My eyes locked with hers, as I needed her to listen and understand. "Because what I feel for you, I've never felt for anyone else."

I tipped her chin with a gentle flick of my wrist, and then I kissed her again.

When she pulled away from me, there was no sarcastic comeback. She simply stared at me with wonder and confusion and another emotion I could place because I recognized it—fear. Fear of the unknown, fear of our relationship changing. But, for her, I could imagine she was afraid of getting hurt again.

Good thing I didn't plan on hurting her.

A giggle had us both peering up at the window. Her aunts and sisters and mother were all blatantly hovering behind the curtains.

And the windows were open.

"Get inside!" Sonia yelled, making the crowd scatter like ants. "Good God, is nothing a secret in this family?"

Then, her mother opened the door and popped out her head. "Brad, are you staying for dinner?"

I loosened my grasp on Sonia. "I'm sorry. I really should get going." I'd already embarrassed myself, and I wanted to give Sonia time to think over everything I'd said.

But then Sonia dropped her hand to mine and threaded our fingers together, smiling sweetly, and she uttered one word that made my evening, "Stay."

The one word was a plea and my answer.

There was no way I could say no.

~

Sonia

"I can't believe she's been throwing darts at your face." Rosa held her stomach, laughing.

We were seated at the dining room table, and Brad was ripping into me, reminding me of how much I'd hated him at one time. Fast-forward to today, and my whole face blushed as I recalled the way he'd kissed me on my parents' front porch.

It was difficult not to be jealous of him as I watched him win everyone over. Brad could fit anywhere, compel an audience, successfully lead a meeting, and now, at my family dinner, he was the life of the party. Even my father's lips tipped up in a small smile. If Brad hadn't completely won him over yet, he was on his way.

"She could have at least gotten a better picture," Brad chided, as if I'd been concerned about how handsome he was when I was releasing all my fury.

I scoffed, "Please, I made the picture better." I picked at the last of the broccoli on my plate. Being so close to him and seeing him win over my family did weird things to me. It warmed my heart, but more than that, it turned me on.

Brad's plate was spotless. He'd eaten like a pro, vegetables and rice and chicken. Judging by my mom's beaming face, she was a Brad lover.

But she'd loved Jeff, too.

My heart seized, and I wrapped my arms around my stomach. I'd been here before. Right at this dining room table with all my family gathered. The only difference was the man next to me.

I dropped my gaze to the few broccoli florets on my plate, worried. Was I repeating history? I'd thought Jeff was a sure thing, and look how that had turned out. Brad was even less predictable and not long-term relationship material. If someone had asked me a year ago who would be marriage material, Jeff would've been my answer without hesitation. Guess I'd have been wrong there.

So, now, was I judging Brad without giving him a chance? Could we be good together? Could we possibly work?

I was confused as hell and still reeling over that kiss. I'd never met a man who had perfected the art of kissing as much as Brad had. I was sure he'd had lots of practice before me. Still, his kisses were unforgettable. I'd had to take a long, cold shower after he left my apartment the other night, and it had taken all my energy to pretend like that kiss hadn't affected me when it affected every part of me, the hot parts that wanted more.

I squeezed his hand before standing up to grab the dessert in the kitchen. Marco stood also, and on our way in with tiramisu and lemon meringue pie, he bumped his hip against mine.

"I like him."

I laughed. He never said that about Jeff. "And why is that?"

"He looks at you like you're his whole world, and he would do anything to keep you in it."

I stopped and blinked up at my brother. Marco had said the same thing before, but it was how I'd looked at Jeff, about how I'd loved him more than he'd loved me.

That made my heart skip two, three, four beats, and I knew then that I was in trouble.

CHAPTER 19

BRAD

Talk about killing it.

Charles slapped my butt the way football players did as we made our way out of the boardroom. "You nailed it!"

I shrugged before heading to the elevator. "Like there was any doubt." Because I sure as hell didn't doubt myself. I had sealed the deal with Titan Press, which would expand our capabilities in the west and would eventually increase our bottom line by twenty percent.

"We'll need to visit their plant within the next few weeks."

The buyout and integration of their facilities into our infrastructure would take nine months to a year, and that was being optimistic, but I was determined to get it done.

I raised my fist to fist-bump Charles and walked into the elevator while he proceeded back down the hall to his office.

Boy, did that feel damn good, nailing this deal.

The doors shut but not before Mason slipped in right beside me.

Great.

Mason pressed his floor and moved to the back of the elevator. "Good job in there. You've always been good at that."

"Thanks."

Our relationship since that day we had our blowup had been awkward. We only spoke to each other during work, and at home, we avoided each other like a married couple in the midst of a bad fight.

"About the other day ..." His eyebrows gathered in, and he let out a heavy sigh. "I'm sorry."

I'd been waiting for an apology, but I had already forgiven him long before. Even when we were younger, my fights with my brothers hadn't lasted long. Either we'd box it out, yell it out, or it hadn't been a big deal to begin with.

This time, I was going to do what I wanted to do anyway, so it wasn't worth the wasted effort.

"I understand your concern, but I'm not going to jeopardize work and what grandfather built for a quick lay." Maybe, at one time, I had been that guy, but I wasn't anymore. What Mason had to understand was what I had with Sonia was different. There was no way I was letting her go. "I'm different with her."

"I know." He leaned against the elevator and stuck his hands into his pockets.

I faced him directly, but he stared at the door, waiting for it to open.

"Maybe I was just ..." He paused. "Maybe I was just jealous."

What? I reeled back to study his reaction.

"I saw you and Sonia at lunch. I passed that place on Wells, the one you guys always go to. I saw you through the window." Mason's gaze dropped to the ground as though he were thinking deeply. "Janice and I aren't like that."

Fucking finally. But I held in the reaction. *Don't be an asshole. Don't say anything. Bite your tongue.*

"I don't think we ever were." There was a sadness in his tone, a vulnerability that Mason hardly showed.

Charles and I were on the same page when it came to Janice, but Mason would stick up for her until his face turned blue. Hell, my nieces weren't very fond of her, and those girls liked everyone.

There were a million things that I wanted to say, tons of reasons Mason and Janice shouldn't be together. I wanted to list them out and highlight each and every one—the most important being that she was a selfish gold digger who only cared about him because of the status he could give her. But I didn't.

"You should be happy, bro." I placed a heavy hand on his shoulder. "You already know how I feel about her, but in the end, it doesn't matter. It's your choice to make."

I understood it all in that second. How everyone could tell me that Sonia and I wouldn't work and her father could intimidate me and she could still possibly want her ex back. All the forces could be against me, us ... but in the end, it was my choice to pursue her.

"We've been together for years, and, yeah ... she's put on the pressure of marriage," he said when the elevator pinged open.

"She's not too shy about it," I muttered, stepping onto my floor.

He followed right behind me.

If the bridal magazines and Tiffany and Cartier catalogs were any indication. I bit my tongue before some asshole comment slipped.

"And I realized, she's right."

I winced. *Please, for the love of God, do not make her my*

future sister-in-law. My parents would be turning over in their graves.

"That's the only step now, but when I think of it ..." He stopped in the middle of my floor, where I would turn to head down the hall to my office, and stared behind me into the air. —"... I can't picture myself with her forever. Can you see Janice as a mother?"

I laughed. *Yeah, the evil stepmother.*

"So, I'm breaking up with her."

I stared at him, dumbfounded. *What is going on?* "You sure?" I was tempted to take my brother's temperature. "You're breaking up with her?" I asked again, almost like I couldn't believe it to be true.

Mason frowned. "I thought you of all people would be happy about this."

I blinked, still shocked into silence.

"But, yes, I am sure."

∼

Brad

After work, I headed to the only place I wanted to be—Sonia's.

Just when I'd thought my day couldn't get any better, Sonia opened the door of her apartment. I didn't think I'd ever met a woman who could make jeans and a T-shirt look so damn sexy. It was double-date night, which I wasn't too excited about, but spending time with Sonia would make up for it.

"Hey."

"Hey." She stepped into the hallway and let the door shut behind her. "I heard someone did good today."

"It's all in a day's work."

Then, she poked my side and locked the door before leading us to the elevator. "You were never one to be modest."

Is she flirting? I cocked my head. *Shit, I think she is.*

We entered the elevator, and I inched up beside her, our shoulders touching.

"If I'm being honest, it was a slam dunk." I threw her my cockiest smirk. "I'm just the best at my job, which is why Charles and Mason wish they were me. The company would be in ruins without me. Bankruptcy." Her laughter fired me up to keep on going. "People would lose their jobs. I could never have that on my conscience."

"Of course not." She rolled her eyes and angled toward me, and shit if I wasn't having the best day of my life, just being by her.

I kept on bragging about how I was God's gift to Brisken Printing Corp. and how everyone needed me. I proceeded to tell her how lucky she was to work with the finest and smartest man at the company. She scoffed playfully, and when the elevator pinged open to the lobby, I took the leap and risked rejection as I reached for her hand.

Her smile faltered a little, but she didn't push me away, and I continued to keep up my banter while my insides soared. Baby steps were good.

We held hands throughout the drive, and when we parked in front of the pizza joint, I faced her. Her eyes looked outside, scanning the area, her knees bouncing. It reminded me of the day at the church when she had been fidgeting in her seat, nervous to see the ex. I realized I didn't want to do this, have dinner with Jean and Jeff and pretend I was having a good time, when all I wanted it to be was Sonia and me, alone. I didn't want to share her.

Thinking of him and her and the past they'd shared had me itching to jump out of my skin.

"I don't even know why I'm here." Sonia bit her bottom lip. Her stare skittered outside, watching the people walk past our car.

My sentiments exactly, but today, silence seemed like the key. The key with Mason and now with Sonia.

"I didn't want to be the loser. I didn't want it to seem like I was too hurt to meet up. I didn't want him to know that he'd hurt me ... that he'd broken my heart so badly, so that's why I agreed to come."

I wanted to ask her again why it mattered. Why she cared about his feelings or what he thought months after they had broken up, but I was afraid to hear the answer.

"Do you want to go home?" I so badly wanted her to say yes. To ditch this fool and his blow-up Barbie. So that I could take her on a real date, to a movie and dinner, something better than second-rate pizza.

"It's too late. We can't." Her voice was so achingly low, hopeless even.

I tipped her chin my way, staring at her pink lips and needing so badly to kiss her. "You can. We'll do whatever you want to do. I know this Italian restaurant that makes a cloud of tiramisu."

All she needed to do was say the word, and it would be done; we'd be on our way.

Come on.

The knocking on the window had her jumping and me giving a death glare to the culprit—Jean.

Her wave turned frantic as she bounced on her toes. "Hi, guys!"

Jeff was right behind her, looking ... pissed?

Whatever he was, he wasn't happy, but it wasn't my concern.

Sonia rolled down the window. "We'll be right inside."

I leaned back in my seat, letting my head relax against the headrest, watching Jean and Jeff walk down the street. I rarely went where I didn't want to be, yet, for Sonia, I was going to go into that pizza joint.

"If we're going to get out of this, now would be the opportunity," I none too subtly reminded her.

She laughed, her eyes trailing the two bobbleheads walking into the pizza joint. "Now, we can't for sure. We've been spotted. There goes my excuse that I'm sick, and life is over." She bit her fingernail, watching their retreating backs. I wished I could read minds to know what she was thinking. "Do they match?"

"What do you mean?"

"Never mind." She shook her head. "Maybe it's true what they say; opposites do attract." Then, she turned my way. "Is she your type? Do you think she's attractive?"

I scoffed, "No."

And, from my one answer, I knew she didn't believe me.

"I'm being serious. You walk down the streets of downtown Chicago, and you'll see five Jeans."

"You're just saying that because I'm here, and you're trying to get in my panties." The corner of her mouth lifted into an almost smile.

Now, it was my turn to laugh, and then I angled closer. "Even though I am wanting in your panties, my answer would still be the same. Not interested."

She let out a low sigh and then stared back at the pizza joint. "Then, why do you think he picked her over me?"

I tilted her chin to face me, and I spoke with all the conviction and truth I had in me. "He messed up, Sonia, because what you don't understand is that Jean's not the upgrade; she's most definitely the downgrade."

Her eyes flashed for a second, and then she placed her hand on top of mine that was holding her face. She smiled and then pulled my hand down. "You ..." She squinted. "... are really, really good. So good that I almost believed you."

"I'm going to make a believer out of you, Sonia." And that would be my goal for the evening—or weeks or months if it took that long.

~

The date was horrible, and I'd been on plenty of bad ones. But this was by far the worst because I didn't want to be there.

Somewhere between walking into the pizza joint and after shaking Jeff's hand, I'd determined he was my enemy. Shit. He was the dumbass for leaving Sonia, so his misfortune was my fortune, but Sonia hadn't satisfied the burning question in the back of my mind. Was she still in love with him? My insecurity made me hate this guy that I hardly knew.

I pushed the half-eaten pizza farther away from me.

Chicago was known for its pizza, but not soggy pizza. Whatever this place was, it was horrible. With its bland red chairs and black-and-white-checkered floors that gave the vibe of an older soda shop, there was nothing spectacular about this place or its service or its food.

The pizza was cold and tasted like a box, bland and without flavor.

Jean kept talking with animated hands, and while I was not impressed and not even trying, what was surprising was, neither was Jeff. He looked above Jean, never at her when she was speaking, as though he were watching a television show he was not even remotely interested in.

"That was one of the best weddings I'd ever gone to," Jean said, eyes bright.

She reminded me of a sorority girl—the lilt of her voice, the way she talked with her hands. Maybe it had been cute in her early twenties, but it was annoying now. Like watching one of those talking baby dolls that you wanted to lock in the closet.

I pushed two fingers into my temple, feeling an oncoming migraine. If it wasn't for Sonia, I'd up and leave.

"Right?" Sonia nudged my shoulder and threw me a smile.

Shit. I'd missed the whole conversation, and I wasn't sure what I was saying right to. Immediately, I reached for her hand, needing to touch her.

"It's so romantic. Like *Pretty Woman*," Jean added.

"The dress at the wedding. How you surprised me and took me shopping. You tricked me, remember? Saying we were going for you."

Ah, that. See, I could be romantic, even when I wasn't trying.

"You wouldn't let me take you shopping otherwise." I kissed her hand.

And that was the truth of the matter. If I'd told her I was buying her a very expensive designer dress, she would have refused. Because that was just how she was, simple and happy with wearing one of her old dresses.

"Oh my God. It's like pulling teeth when I ask Jeff to go shopping. I'm always like, 'Let's go. Let's go. It'll be fun.'" Jean bounced on her seat as she talked, and I was surprised her seat didn't tip over.

"Jeff hates shopping. He's the type who will wait

outside the store, looking at his watch the whole time," Sonia stated. "I don't think I've met another male who hates it more."

They both laughed, and I added my ugly laughter, the one meant to come out for Halloween.

I clenched my teeth. *Who cares about Jeff?* I could hate shopping. I didn't because I had a personal shopper to do it for me, but I could.

"I do," Jeff stated, not even arguing. "You still know me so well." His laser focus was on Sonia, and my shoulders stiffened.

In my line of business, during a takeover or a buyout, the number one quality that I possessed that always worked in my favor and guaranteed that I won the deal 99.9% of the time was my uncanny ability to read people. And the way he'd uttered those words and the way he was looking at Sonia made me want to get up, reach for his collar, pull him in, and punch his pretty face until I messed it up.

For the next thirty minutes, he stared at Sonia, laughed at her jokes, and leaned in as though he could get closer.

How did I miss this earlier?

I only noticed how Jeff was annoyed by his date, not how much attention he was paying to mine.

My jaw clenched. I reached for Sonia's hand and brought it to my lips, meeting his eyes in the process.

Yeah, asshole. I'm watching you. You had your chance, and you blew it.

I leaned in to pull her in, paying extra-special attention to her, treating her like the queen she was in front of *him*.

The waitress dropped the check in the middle of the table, and immediately, I threw my black Amex with the unlimited line on top. The sooner I was out of this hellhole, the less likely I would ram my fist into Jeff's face.

"Thank you," Jean said.

Jeff grabbed the check underneath my card. "No, I have it."

I gritted my teeth. *Really? He is going to play this game right here?* "Maybe you should save your money since your girlfriend likes to go shopping." I plucked the check from his hand, and as the waitress passed us, I put it in her hands. "Here you go."

Jean's and Sonia's eyes ping-ponged between us. The tension between us was noticeably high. Jeff glared at me. Me? I threw him one condescending smile.

I could take this guy. Outside. One punch, and I'd have him out. I needed to leave or else I'd do something I'd regret, and I knew that wouldn't work in my favor with winning Sonia over.

"It's been a pleasure," I lied. Then, I reached for Sonia's jacket slung behind her seat. "Let's go, Shorts."

An awkward smile surfaced. "Okay, let me go to the restroom really quick."

Jeff stood. "Actually, I have to go, too."

Count backward. That was what I'd tell Mary to calm down during her tantrums.

I tipped my chin, afraid I would say some asshole comment, and sat back in my seat, stewing as they both walked toward the back of the restaurant. And then I was left with Barbie Jean.

CHAPTER 20

SONIA

"This was fun," I deadpanned.

Jeff let out a tired laugh, one I knew so well. "Was it? 'Cause I thought that was torture."

We walked into the narrow hall toward the restrooms.

"Maybe you should have told your girlfriend not to push it. She texted and left a voice mail. Do you think I wanted to be here?" I returned his honesty with equal sarcasm.

"She's an idiot," he said, letting out a breath.

I wanted to ask him why he was with her then, but he beat me to the question. He reached for my arm and pulled me to the side to let people pass us. The hallway that led to the restrooms was dark and secluded, and the light flickered overhead.

"What are you doing with him, Sonia?"

I reeled back, shocked at his directness. "What kind of question is that? I could ask you the same thing." I shook my head. "Never mind. It's none of my business anymore, and it sure as hell is no longer yours."

Jeff stepped into me, toe-to-toe. His tone was sharp,

pissed almost. "He's not your type. He seems like an asshole. You hated him when we were together, and now, you're a couple?" he spat. "How does that make any sense?"

Deep-seated courage seeped into my veins, and I lifted my chin. "I never saw this side of Brad before because I only knew him at work. Since then, I've met his nieces, and he's met my family. He's only an asshole to people on the outside." I gritted my teeth, not realizing I was justifying my relationship to someone who didn't deserve it. "And he's not an asshole," I snapped, my back straightening.

Even though Brad was an asshole, no one could call him one. Except me because he was my asshole.

My asshole. The moment the thought pushed through, I blinked.

When Jeff's hand fell to my waist, I pushed his hand off.

"You're the one who left me, remember? Jean? Funny how she worked with you and then quit close to the time you dumped me."

"We weren't together then." He ran one aggravated hand through his hair. "I made a mistake, okay? It's all wrong with her. It was only ever right with you."

He erased the space between us, resting one arm over my head, and I flushed myself against the wall, hating his closeness.

"I've missed you. Being with her has only made me realize how much. Every time she laughs, I think about your contagious, never-ending laugh. I messed up, and now, I want to make it right." There was a softness in his tone and sincerity in his eyes that I recognized from the old Jeff I used to know.

But this—him being so close—unnerved me.

I stared up at him, dumfounded.

Wasn't this what I'd been waiting for? I'd been

dreaming of this day, wishing for Karma, and now that it was here, it felt all wrong. Because why the hell did it have to take him to be with someone else to realize that it had been me all along? I had never doubted us. When I'd been with him, I'd never wanted to be with someone else.

"I've missed you so much."

He cupped the side of my face, and I flinched.

And, for the second time tonight, he shocked me as he bent down and met my lips with his.

~

Brad

I'd had to go to the restroom, but any urge besides the urge to get far away from here disappeared.

I stood there, in the hallway, so very still, and it took all my effort not to storm down the dark hall, punch Jeff in the face, and throw Sonia over my shoulder. I tore away my gaze and about-faced. I felt like I'd been sucker-punched in the gut. If I'd wanted to know my answer, I'd just seen it with my own two eyes.

I marched back to the table where I'd left Jean. My shoulders slumped, and my mind was reeling. *Why him? What the hell could he give her that I couldn't?*

"That was the fastest restroom break ever," Jean mused as I approached.

I didn't know what to do. I wanted to leave, go to the bar, get a drink, anything but stay here, but I couldn't exactly leave Sonia here. *Is she going to go home with him? Were they going to ask me to drive Jean home?*

The thought enraged me. If it came to that, I'd refuse. Shit, I'd go postal.

I dropped to the bland red booth and closed my eyes, rubbing at my temple.

"Is everything okay?" Jean's high-pitched tone grated on my nerves.

"Yeah, fine," I growled. Pretend time was over and done.

She was up, rubbing my back in the next second. "Are you sure?"

"I'm sure," I snapped. I raised my head and held a hand up. "Don't. Touch. Me. All right? I said I'm fine."

I was far from fine.

Whatever I had done, how hard I had tried, was all for nothing. *How could I claim a girl who belonged to someone else?*

Shit, because I wanted to claim her, make her mine, follow her like a lovesick puppy, knowing it would be me looking like a pussy. But who cared? I wouldn't even be able to do that now.

An overwhelming loss draped over me. The old Brad, before falling for Sonia, would have left her to fend for herself, to find her own ride.

This pathetic Brad sat there, waiting and wishing this was over. Hopeless. That was the only word that I could think of.

∼

Sonia

With force, I pushed Jeff off of me and immediately swiped at my lips with my sleeve. "What the hell, Jeff?" I spat out.

To think his kisses once were how I'd wanted to start and end my day. Now, it felt as though acid had burned my lips.

When he took a step forward, I ducked under his arm to move away.

"Sonia, tell me you don't feel the same." His face turned incredulous. "Tell me you didn't feel that kiss."

He was on drugs. He had to be.

I scoffed. *When did I give him any indication that it was okay to even do that?*

"I don't, and I didn't." My response was quick, automatic, honest.

And the truth would set me free. That kiss was like kissing a piece of furniture, no feelings attached. What I had felt was an overwhelming sorrow of what could've been.

"I don't believe you." His voice was emotionally choked, his eyes feverish. Then, he kissed me again, his body flush against me, his arms gripping me with more force.

"Get off of me!" I shoved him off and was about to knee him in the balls, but he backed away with his hands up.

I couldn't believe it was this easy, but that one kiss had told it all. I was over him. Truly and utterly over him.

Who is this guy? Where was the Jeff I had known? Or maybe I hadn't known him at all.

I flung a finger in the direction of the dining room. "Your girlfriend is out there. I'm not doing this."

When I turned to leave, he gripped my hand, and I jerked it back.

"And, even if she wasn't out there, I'm still not doing this." I motioned between both of us.

"I still love you, Sonia."

I inhaled deeply and squared my shoulders. "I'm no longer in love with you, sorry." But I wasn't sorry that I didn't feel the same way anymore. I was sorry that he'd lost a damn good girl because he'd wanted to see if there was someone better out there for him. It was a choice he'd made, a risk he'd taken, but now, it had backfired.

He opened his mouth to speak, but I didn't hear a word as I stormed back to our table. Brad was slouched over his chair, sitting with his elbows on his thighs, head down, staring at the floor.

When I approached, he looked up. He looked ... defeated. I'd analyze that later. Right now, I needed out of here, far from Jeff and Jean and a past I never wanted to revisit.

"Let's go. I want to get out of here. Where's Jean?"

Because she wasn't at the table anymore.

"No idea."

"I don't care. I just want to leave."

"Sure." His voice was soft and resigned when he stood to face me. "You don't have to do this, you know? Pretend and spare my feelings. I'm a big boy."

I reeled back. "What the hell are you talking about?"

His eyes focused behind me, and he tipped his chin toward the restroom. "I was back there. I saw—"

"Him kissing me against my will," I cut him off, pissed off and annoyed. Now wasn't the time for me to console the wounded soldier. Later maybe, but not now. "And then trying it again."

"What?" Brad growled, his demeanor changing like a light switch. "You didn't let him kiss you?"

I rapidly blinked, wanting to pull my hair out. *Am I on an episode of The Twilight Zone?*

"Um, no. He's in a relationship, and even if he weren't, I still wouldn't let that asshole touch me." I shook my head. "Let's just get out of here. I need to leave before I go crazy and tell Jean she can do better than his cheating, lying ass."

When Brad moved past me, his focus toward the

restrooms, I gripped his wrist. "He's not worth it. Let's go."

"I'm not letting this go." Brad's body was tight as a rope, his eyes promising revenge. "I just need to set him straight."

"Brad ..." *Seriously, what was a black-and-blue Jeff going to help my situation?* As far as I was concerned, this was part of my history that was officially closed.

"I swear, I'll only have words."

I gulped, though the evil part of me wanted Jeff to be put in his place. I had earlier, but I doubted he'd heard me with his focus on attacking my lips. Maybe repetition was the key. So, against my better judgment, I let Brad go. It was like releasing a bull into the ring.

∽

B**rad**

I stalked down the hall, straight into the restroom, and right by Jeff's urinal.

"What the hell, man?" He pushed his pathetic dick back in his pants and zippered himself up.

I took a step forward, my hands fisting. Maybe there would be more than words.

"Do you mind?" he snapped.

"Yes, I do fucking mind." My tone was cool but barely controlled. "I mind you kissing my girlfriend." Because, in every meaning of the word, she belonged to me even though we hadn't formally talked about it and we hadn't had sex. Sonia was mine the moment I'd agreed to her deal. "And I just want to make it perfectly clear that you're not going to touch her ever again."

"Whatever." He walked to the sink and rinsed off his hands. "She has her own mind to make her own decisions."

I chuckled. *Well, well, well. And, now, this tall guy has*

grown a spine.

Grinning somewhat psycho-ish, I pushed him against the wall, and his eyes went wide. "I think she's made her decision, and it's not you," I ground out.

I couldn't remember the last time I'd punched a guy. Those days of drunken brawls had ended in college, but I'd never wanted to bust a perfect face more than I did right now.

I stepped into him, nose-to-nose, so he'd understand my next words. His body turned rigid.

"You fucked up." I shoved him against the wall. "And, for that, I want to thank you because I know what not to do." I stepped away because he wasn't worth it, and I didn't trust myself. I had a girl waiting for me outside this door, ready to go home, and right now, that took precedence.

When I walked out, I reached for Sonia's hand and pulled her out of the pizza joint.

"What happened?"

I nearly dragged her down the street toward my car, silent the whole way.

"Brad! I'm talking to you."

When we reached the car, I pushed her against the door and kissed her. Hard.

Shit, I couldn't help it. Adrenaline pumped through my veins—from the high of her not wanting him anymore to the almost fight. I kissed her as I had the last time—with a passion of promises and the future I would give her. And the only difference was, this time, she kissed me back without restraint, an equal player. Her hands gripped the back of my shirt, and she tilted her head to give me better access. Shit, I took it, all she was willing to give me, because I'd waited for this. Waited for her to kiss me back. Not in pretend kisses or drunken kisses, but in a real kiss. This kiss.

Her small moans were a direct hit to my cock. She smelled of everything sweet and innocent in the world, and I wanted her in my bed. More than that, I wanted her in my life. The kiss accelerated from zero to one hundred, hot and heavy and hands everywhere, cupping her face, down her arms, gripping her waist. I pushed into her, and she met me head-on, holding the back of my head.

I kissed her as though I wanted to devour her, have her right here, right now, with no cares in the world.

People yelled around us to get a room, but I ignored them, flicking my tongue against the seam of her lips. Our tongues tangled, and when her hands went under my shirt, I rocked into her.

It took all my strength to slow down. If I didn't, I would have her on the hood of my car, and she deserved better.

I pulled back and rested my forehead on hers, panting, breathing hard. We both were. I wanted to ask her if I could come over. Judging by her body language, I was ninety-nine percent sure she'd say yes, but I needed to take this slow.

"Go on a date with me. Tomorrow. A real date, you and me and no one else." I had to do things differently with Sonia.

She peered up at me with the sweetest smile on her face and a lustful glow in her eyes. "Okay."

"Okay." The adrenaline from earlier rejuvenated me. Shit, this was better than winning the deal.

I bent down to kiss her once more.

∼

Brad

On the drive home, I took the longer way to drop her off. I wanted to savor every minute together, which was so unlike me. I slowed to catch every stoplight, let every pedestrian pass. I drove like a grandfather, days from giving up his license.

Sonia stared out the window, pinching her bottom lip. I wanted to continue to bite that sexy lip and vowed to do just that tomorrow after our date.

"Are you going to tell me what happened?" she asked when we were stopped at a light.

"Yeah, I saw his dick, and now, I know why you don't want him back." I smirked.

She slapped my shoulder, laughing. "I'm being serious."

"So am I."

"Come on, Brad."

I reached for her hand and rested it on the middle console when we parked in front of her apartment.

It was no wonder he was still pining for her. Jean was nothing compared to Sonia. Where Jean's looks were upfront and in-your-face sultry, Sonia's appeal was subtle, and the longer you stared, the more beautiful she became. To think, all this time had passed with all my wasted efforts and nights with other women when the right woman was in front of me all along.

"I just told him he'd messed up, and he now had to deal with the consequences of never getting you back."

Because you're mine now.

"He's an idiot." She squeezed my hand harder and scrunched her eyebrows together. Murder was heavy in her eyes. "To do that. Kiss me. What if Jean had walked in on us?"

Shit, my hand hurt from the pressure.

"He doesn't want her anymore, so he doesn't care."

Maybe he wanted to get caught.

"It makes me wonder ..." Her voice trailed off, and then

her tone lowered. "If he could do that to her, he surely could do that to me." Then, after a beat, her voice found its strength again. "What an asshole! A total living, breathing asshole."

"I can't deny that." I readjusted our intertwined fingers and brought her hand to my lips. "An asshole with a small dick."

That made her laugh. "Did you really say those things to him about me? Because ... that was sweet."

"It is, isn't it?" I angled my head closer, laying on the charm, pushing out my lip. "Does that mean I get another kiss for being so sweet?" Shit, it was officially over. I'd officially turned into Mason.

"Is that how you think relationships go? Tit for tat? You do this, and then I give you that? Because that's not how it works."

I didn't miss what she was saying. "So, we're in a relationship now, are we?" I didn't think I could smile any bigger.

A blush touched her cheeks, and she waved a hand, pretending to be unaffected.

Can I say, Freudian slip? I dare say I can.

"No, I was just explaining how relationships work. It's not about receiving. It's about giving ... of yourself."

The blush brightened to an almost red. She was so unbelievably cute. I couldn't resist, so I bent down and placed a chaste kiss on her lips.

"I don't mind being the one to give."

She rolled her eyes. "You're horrible."

"You're beautiful," I countered, thinking of all the other things I could give her, particularly in the bedroom. I only hoped it was sooner rather than later with the way things were going.

CHAPTER 21

BRAD

Working with Sonia was harder than I'd imagined. *Harder* being the key term. I had a hard-on every time she walked in the room. And her voice—what I had thought of before as a plain Jane voice was suddenly so fucking seductive. Everything about her had changed—or more so, how I saw her had changed. Being in love with Sonia had altered my whole outlook. I was becoming pathetic. I couldn't stand not being around her anymore. When she wasn't in my office, I'd stand at her desk, rambling about random things.

The need to see her and know every aspect of her day was overwhelming. I wanted to know what she'd had for breakfast, how she'd slept, what her plans were. I asked about her family and if she'd talked to them. I didn't know what was happening to me.

I would watch her lips when she talked, when she drank her coffee, and I'd fantasize about those lips on my cock. When she was in my office, typing away on her iPad, I'd stare at her breasts, watch them rise and fall, and I'd stop the urge to imagine how they'd feel in my palms and in my mouth.

When she stood and walked away, I'd watch the sway of her hips, admire the curve of her ass, and imagine slipping down that skirt, anchoring her against my desk, and pounding my flesh against hers. Half the time, I was struggling to walk normally through the office.

Minutes seemed like hours till our date. I wanted to take Sonia to a nice restaurant—a twelve-course, three-star Michelin place. One she normally wouldn't go to. Then, I wanted to have drinks on top of the Clement Hotel. The restaurant that turned slowly, so you could enjoy the view of the Chicago skyline.

I wanted to wine, dine, and impress her. But my way of wooing other girls wouldn't work on Sonia. She was simple in what made her happy, in the things that mattered—family and friends.

And, as I searched high and low and with the help of my niece Sarah, I finally found the solution that I had been hoping for—a solution to the perfect date.

"Where are we going?" Sonia asked, stepping into my car after work.

"Somewhere. Everywhere." My nerves were shot.

I couldn't concentrate at work, and I'd kept checking to make sure that I had my reservations confirmed. I felt like a teenage boy on his first date when I'd been on a shit-ton of dates since then.

"Do you think I'm underdressed?" Sonia flattened her cream satin shirt, and I swallowed.

I knew what was underneath that shirt. I'd seen her practically naked the night of the wedding and every night since I'd fantasized about that shirt, unbuttoned and on my bedroom floor.

"You're overdressed."

She was. Part of my date included getting her an outfit for this occasion—not a clubbing outfit, but something that would add to the ambience.

"Overdressed?" She looked over her clothes, frowning, her hand skimming down her skirt. "Crap, I thought I was playing it safe with a semi-casual look."

"You'll be fine." I reached for her hand and intertwined our fingers, needing the warmth of her touch.

During the workday, it had taken every ounce of energy not to reach her, touch her, kiss her. And, fuck, did I want to kiss her. Long and hard until she was breathless, panting, flushed.

"I'm nervous." She fumbled with her hair and pushed up her glasses, fidgeting again. Her eyes focused on the forming traffic in front of us.

That was one of Sonia's best qualities—honesty. If she didn't voice it, her face would tell all. I knew this because I'd been the target of many of her annoyed looks.

"Don't be. We'll have fun."

Thirty minutes later, we pulled into a park district where lights had been strewn from tree to tree. Cars were jam-packed into the parking lot, but when her eyes took in the countless people in robes and wands and hats, she flipped my way.

"Brad ..." Her smile widened, and it did things to me—not in the horny way that it had all day, but in a deeper, more momentous way, where I couldn't fucking breathe. "Where are we going?" Her eyes scoured the area in front of us again, and she squeed. She knew but only wanted me to verbally confirm it.

"I heard someone likes Harry Potter." I shrugged, seeming unaffected, but I knew I had scored big, and this was the perfect date for Sonia. I'd have to take Sarah shopping later for the idea.

"No shit! Omigod." And, just like a little kid, she pushed herself out the door, and I followed. Her eyes lit up like Mary's on Christmas morning—bright, wide, and adorably cute. "I have nothing to wear." She glanced down at her outfit again. Then, she jumped up and down and clapped her hands.

"There is a Harry Potter themed restaurant this week." I grabbed her Hermione robe from the back of my car, the one Sarah had picked out and I'd bought online, and walked around to meet her.

"Brad ... what's this?" The joy bubbled in her laugh as I handed over the robe.

"Courtesy of Amazon."

"And this event ... it's been sold out for months." She beamed, shoving her hands into the robe and zipping it up. "I can't believe this."

I wasn't telling her I'd paid ten times the price from some fans who were more than reluctant to let the tickets go.

"Unreal." She motioned toward me. "Where's your outfit?"

Reaching into my shirt pocket, I grabbed the thin, round Harry Potter eyeglasses and slipped them on. "Ta-da!"

She framed her hands on my face. "So cute. You're so cute!"

Now, I was beaming. Like a fucking idiot. I'd wear these damn glasses to work if I could get a reaction like this from her every day.

"This will have to be written down as my best first date ever!" She squealed and flung out her arms wide, taking in the scene.

A Hogwarts Express train passed us, taking people from the parking lot to the restaurant.

"The night hasn't even begun." I tried to play it off, cool and collected, but inside, I was on an ultimate high, high on her joy, high on being on our official first date together.

In my mind, I had planned to change out of my shirt in the car, but Sarah had said I had to make this date memorable.

"Let's get this night started." Just like Clark Kent saving the day as Superman, I ripped open my Brioni shirt, revealing my Gryffindor shirt with the lion crest underneath. Buttons flew everywhere, scattering onto the concrete.

I couldn't help but laugh. "I've always wanted to do that."

The fact that I had shredded a five-hundred-dollar shirt didn't matter because the elation on her face was priceless.

∼

Sonia

Brad's fingers were intertwined with mine as I skipped—yes, skipped—back to the car. I'd never laughed so much with anyone, let alone Brad. It was hilarious, explaining every single Harry Potter drink and character who had passed us by. The makeup artist who had gone around even drew a little scar on Brad's forehead. He twirled me and pressed me against the car, acting boyish and free, unlike his normal, serious demeanor I was used to.

"I can't believe you have never watched the movies. If you can't read the books, at least watch the movies," I insisted.

His eyes twinkled under the moonlight, and he brushed

strands of hair from my face. There was a zoo of butterflies in my belly, which came alive every time he touched me. And the way he looked at me, it made me feel ... beautiful. He hadn't noticed our waitress, who was blatantly flirting, or the other Hermiones who were busting out of their robes. His sole focus throughout the evening was me.

"Ask me about princesses. I know them all and their little sidekicks. A few times, I pretended to be Flynn Rider because Mary was stuck in a Rapunzel phase. Or Eric when she was in her Ariel phase. I even dressed up as Eric for her fourth birthday. But Harry Potter? I know nothing."

The fact that he played dress-up for his nieces increased his sexiness tenfold.

He dropped both hands to the edge of the car, caging me in. "I want to take you to Universal Studios in Florida."

I laughed. "Actually, I haven't made it out there yet." That would be my ultimate vacation of a lifetime. Forget Europe or Bali or Tahiti. Take me to Florida, and my life would be good as set.

"Let's go tomorrow. I'll charter a jet."

He angled closer, and I tiptoed and wrapped my arm around his neck, feeling things I hadn't in a very long time. I was hyperaware of him whenever he was near, and having him this close, flushed against me, made my heart hammer in my chest.

"We can't tomorrow." I laughed. *Him and his silly dreams. And his riches.*

"Why not?" His fingers trailed down my cheek and pinched my chin.

"Because I want to go for a whole week."

I'd planned my trip years ago but never had enough money to go. If and when I did go, I was going to drag it out and enjoy every second of it.

He grinned as if that was all he'd needed to hear. "Great. I'm taking off, and you can have a whole week off, too. I think I know your boss." His hands went to my waist, and he lifted me onto the hood of his fancy, schmancy car. "Did you have fun, Hermione?"

His eyes flickered to my lips, and he unzipped my robe, exposing my cream satin shirt and black skirt underneath. I sucked on my bottom lip, taking him all in—from his Harry Potter glasses and painted scar above his right eye to the way his Gryffindor shirt hugged his broad frame. He was so out of his element and all for me. What he'd done tonight was exceptional. I couldn't remember having a date like this, solely tailored to me, even with Jeff. He'd never gone this far to please me.

His fingers framed my face, lightly trailing down my arm and reaching for my waist inside of my robe. Every single trail of his fingertips—on my face, against my waist, at my hip—shot shivers through me.

And the way his eyes scoured my face made my heart beat faster.

"Just so you know, Hermione never dated Harry," I deadpanned. "But today was the perfect date. Thank you."

Because it had been, and I was enchanted and enamored with this man.

He cupped the side of my face, his eyes searching mine for permission, and then his fingers went to the back of my head, threading through my hair. Without a second thought, I closed my eyes and lowered my chin to his silent question.

When his lips descended on mine, it was soft, delicious, and erotic, all at the same time. Of all the boys I'd ever kissed before, this man was the best. His lips moved with purpose, sucking on my bottom lip and then moving to my top, paying lip service to each equally. I moaned against him, both of our breaths entangled into one. God, he tasted like mint and beer and all manly goodness. His hand dropped from my face and then moved to my ass, pushing my legs open so that I could cradle him. He was hard and erect, and every part of me pulsed with want and need and pure, uninhibited lust. Who knew how long we made out on the hood of his car. One minute bled into the next.

"Get a room!" someone yelled.

It was as if he hadn't heard a word as his lips dropped to my neck, making it to the shell of my ear. "Your lips are my new addiction."

I heard someone else muttering in the background. "There are children here, jeez. Come on, Darren. Let's go."

We both turned at the same time to see two kids about Sarah's age laughing and walking with their mother.

"Great," Brad muttered.

My heart thrashed against my rib cage. "Yeah." My voice was a breathless whisper. "I think we were just about to give them a lesson on sex ed."

He assisted me off the hood and then adjusted his pants, his well-endowed length pressing against the front of his slacks. "I can't seem to stop kissing you." He tipped my chin with his finger and placed one more peck on my lips.

I reached for his face, cupping his cheek. "I think I like the glasses on you." I adjusted them on his face.

His smile was BILF beautiful, and my heart staccato-stuttered.

"I think I'm going to permanently keep these glasses now."

And I think I want to permanently keep you.

The words rang loudly in my head.

There was no denying how I felt now. It was in the rapid patter of my pulse every time he was around. It was the way my eyes searched the room to look for his. It was the way my body craved his touch and the way my soul needed him to be fulfilled.

All hell had frozen over because my BILK had officially turned into my BILF.

~

Sonia

Silence overtook the car.

He stared into the parking lot as people started to file out. We'd been sitting in the car for two minutes. You could feel the tension in the air, taste it even. I counted every breath that left my body and every second that passed by. The passion-filled moment from earlier had disappeared without a trace and was replaced with a brewing tension, a sexual one that had us both quiet but thinking the same thing.

Brad turned to me, eyes conflicted. "Are you tired?" His voice was so soft, I wondered if he'd even said it.

I swallowed and wrung my hands in my lap, clenching my teeth and throwing him an awkward smile. "Not really."

Given tonight's date and how badly I wanted him, the deed would undoubtedly get done, but my nerves were shot. I crossed my arms over my chest and then uncrossed them, repeating the motion as though I didn't know what to do next.

The engine roared to life, making me jump, and I was glad that there was noise to break the silence.

"You've got some power on this thing." I straightened my skirt, pulling at the back, which lay mid-thigh.

"Power just like its owner." His stare flickered to my mouth, and his tongue darted to lick his bottom lip.

The tension from deep in my gut tightened like a rope being knotted over and over again. It had been forever since I'd had sex. Almost a year. I was practically a virgin again.

"Is your condo by work?" My nipples pebbled against my shirt and I swallowed, wondering how I could give a hint without being too forward.

"Downtown. Ten minutes from the office." His eyes flickered between me and the road ahead of him. His hands gripped the steering wheel, his knuckles white. He tilted his head from side to side as if to release some tension from his neck.

"In a high-rise?" I'd bet he owned the penthouse suite.

"No. House. I own a three-story flat. I live on the top floor."

"You have a house in downtown Chicago?" The money this man had access to was Christian Grey–worthy.

"We own the building I live in. It's right by Michigan Avenue." His voice was guttural and low. "Do you want to see it?" He visibly swallowed, but his face didn't give anything away.

I sucked in my bottom lip, blinking rapidly. "Okay."

He was my boss. Was I really going to do this?

Staring at his profile, I knew I was. Not only because I was horny, but also because I liked him—Brad, the guy who had planned the Harry Potter date, the man who had lied to all my friends to be my date for the wedding, the man who radiated strength and kindness and drew me in like a magnet.

"Okay?" He didn't sound convinced. "If you're tired, I can ... I can take you home."

"No, it's fine. It's early anyway."

A noticeable tension filled the silence and spread through the tight space. It was like we both knew what we wanted, but neither was willing to say it out loud. I tried to dim the dizzying current racing through me but couldn't.

He linked our fingers and kissed my inner wrist, right by the pulse, and the intimate gesture sent shock waves of desire straight down my thighs. His touch lit me up like a live wire.

I'd never been the aggressive type in my prior relationships because, like all men, they'd taken the lead, but I knew Brad was playing it safe, taking it slow with me, and I was done with slow.

I rested our hands on my upper bare thigh, and the air was sucked from the car. The electricity between us was undeniable and thick in the air.

The pulse on his neck ticked, ticked, ticked away. He eyed me when we were stopped at a red light. He rubbed circles on my thigh, slow at first and inching higher as though he were testing to see how far he could go.

When my right leg fell to the side, his fingers trailed up farther until I was pushing the seat back and angling toward him.

His eyes were on the road the whole time, and if it weren't for the deep breaths escaping him and his hard length pressing against his pants, I wouldn't even guess he was barely holding it together.

When his fingers grazed the edge of my panties, my eyes locked with his hooded ones when we were stopped at a light. I bit my bottom lip, watching as his fingers slipped past my underwear, touching the light patch of trimmed hair. When he slipped a finger between my folds, my right arm braced the car door when the light turned green.

My breathing increased in tempo to match the movement of his fingers making circles around my clit and then pumping into me, fast and steady.

I moved against him, against the sensual friction, yet it wasn't enough.

This man had endless talent—to drive and finger-fuck me and keep his eyes on the road the whole time. It was deliciously erotic.

I'd never done anything like this before—foreplay in the car. Hell, I'd never had sex in a car or any other place other than a bed.

When he extracted himself from inside me, he placed the two fingers that had previously been in me in his mouth and sucked.

Then, we were plunged into darkness as we entered a small tunnel and into a garage spot where the overhead light shone a dim glow on his hungry face.

Within seconds, I was unbuckled, and he reached over to pull me to straddle him on the driver's side. He kissed me with unrelenting passion, threading his fingers through my hair and tugging slightly. The pain shot straight between my legs. My blood was boiling with lust, and my body ached for release.

We were all tongues and breaths and passionate kisses, hot, horny, and hungry for each other.

"I want to taste all of you," he panted, chucking off my robe, unbuttoning my top, and kissing my neck. He sucked my neck, licking a path down to my collarbone and up to the shell of my ear again. "You taste amazing, Sonia. I need more." Soft, urgent caresses went underneath my shirt, his fingertips undoing my white cotton bra. I hadn't been expecting to get laid tonight or else I would've worn my matching lacy *do me* ensemble.

But I was beyond reason to stop him and too horny to care.

He pushed my bra to my neck and cupped my breasts

with both hands, his thumbs playing with my nipples. His lips were on my neck and then went lower and lower until he took one breast in his mouth. I bucked, feeling the warmth of his tongue against my sensitive nipple.

I reached for his hair and rode him, wet underwear against his hardness. The tightness in my gut was in double knots, triple Boy Scout knots, and I needed a release so badly.

I rubbed against him, feeling friction against my clit, needing the contact to send me over. When he lifted me by my waist and the contact was lost, I was a madwoman.

"Wait." I was a panting, aroused mess. "Brad ..." I begged, peering down at him.

He pushed a finger in me. One. Two. And three.

"So fucking wet."

My head flew back, and I pushed against the friction, impatient.

When he extracted his fingers and put them in his mouth again, I was about to yell at him for being a tease, but he slowed his kisses and adjusted my shirt.

"Not here. We can't do it here." His fingers trembled at my waist.

"What?" I'd take him anywhere. I didn't care. Car, train, plane, outside, inside.

"Sonia ..." My name was a tortured, ragged whisper from his lips. "Let's slow down."

My eyebrows flew to my hairline. "Slow down?"

"Yes. I'm not going to have our first time be here, where my neighbors could walk by."

He had started something in me, back on his hood at the parking lot, and now, we couldn't stop.

I froze above him, and his hold eased up. He peered up

at me and then guided me back down on his lap, wrapping his arms around my waist.

"I had no expectations tonight, Sonia. I wanted to take you on a date. Show you a good time. Maybe get a hand job on the way out," he teased, "but you know I'm patient."

I laughed and let my nerves ooze out of me. Maybe he was right. Maybe this was going way too fast. I wasn't against taking this to the next level, but the truth was, I needed to know I was not another repeat of the past, my past and his.

"Where are we going with this?" I brushed back my wild hair and buttoned up my shirt.

His gaze was as soft as a caress, and I felt it everywhere—my lips, my face, my cheeks.

God, I was falling for him.

"I need to know I'm not just another girl to you."

He cupped the side of my face. "You're not. I promise you that. This time, this—everything—feels different." I heard the sincerity in his voice and read the emotion behind his eyes.

I nodded. It did feel different. More raw, real, unpracticed.

"They're not just words, right, Brad?" I'd been here before, believing Jeff, believing his false promises. I needed to know that, this time, it wasn't all lies.

"No. I can't even adequately put into words what I feel for you."

"Promise me nothing is going to change. With us, with my job."

"I promise." His burning eyes held mine, and then he sealed his promise with a kiss.

And I knew I was going to let him have me, all of me.

"I want to see your apartment." More so his bed.

CHAPTER 22

BRAD

The heat had lowered, not died down, but lessened when we walked into the elevator. We didn't have a choice but to cool it because Mrs. Kennedy on the second floor walked in right behind us, followed by her three Pomeranians.

"Harry Potter? I didn't know that was you." Mrs. Kennedy was almost eighty, the sweetest woman, with too many dogs. Every stray was too cute to send to the animal shelter. "And Hermione. How cute." She stuck her hand out to a smiling Sonia. "I'm Maria. I've never met one of Brad's female friends."

Maria had failed to mention she'd never met one of my male friends either. I never took anyone to my place, friends included. We always met out somewhere.

And my dates? Yeah, I never took any of the girls I dated to my place, worried they would go postal if it didn't work out. It was bad enough that half of them knew where I worked.

This, with Sonia, was entirely something else, something different. The enormity of it all had me gazing back at the beautiful woman beside me.

"Sonia." Sonia took Mrs. Kennedy's hand and then bent down to pet the dogs, her whole face lighting up. "They're so cute."

Was it possible to be jealous of animals? Because I was. I wanted to be petted, too.

Mrs. Kennedy flashed me a grin. "She's a pretty one."

"The prettiest."

Mrs. Kennedy went on to introduce her dogs. "Oh, yes. There is Minnie and Mickey and Donald." She had an obsession with everything Disney, which amused Sonia.

I tried not to growl aloud with impatience. The elevator could not move fast enough.

When it pinged open, Mrs. Kennedy flashed us a smile. "Want to come over for tea? I could set a pot in no time."

I'd had tea with Maria numerous times. I had known her husband. They'd been married fifty years until he'd died a few years ago, and she'd replaced him with dogs. Any other day, I would, and I'd bring Sonia, too, but not today.

"Maybe another time," I said before Sonia could agree and answer for the two of us.

My fingers itched to touch Sonia, every part of her, and I was about to do it in front of Maria.

"Okay then." She smiled sweetly at us and then said to Sonia, "Nice meeting you."

When the elevator closed, I pulled Sonia in by the waist. I didn't want to move too fast, scare her off. I was overthinking things, but I didn't want to ruin what was happening between us.

All I read was want and lust in her eyes, in her body language.

But still ... I was functioning on my best behavior and using all my self-control to let her take the lead.

"We should have tea some other time." Sonia's arms wrapped around my neck.

"She bakes great cookies."

"Really?"

"Yeah, next time," I croaked out. Because I'd be feasting on something other than cookies tonight.

We walked through the door of my condo, and she took everything in—from the grand piano in the far corner to the plush leather couch in front of the hanging plasma TV to the bar to the fish tank that spanned one whole wall, which she was the most fascinated with.

"It's like an aquarium in here." She pressed her nose against the tank, looking like Mary when she became fascinated with a new toy. "How did they build this thing?" Her eyes flew to the ceiling. Tropical fish swam above us.

"I hired a guy." My hands wrapped around her center, and I pulled her against me, my lips dropping to her neck, my erection pushing against her ass.

She smelled amazing, like a field of strawberries, and I wanted to lick every inch of her flesh. My fingers trailed up her waist and cupped one breast, my thumb flicking over her sensitive nub.

"Tell me to stop, and I will." Because all self-restraint had flown out the door as soon as we stepped into my condo.

Her breathing was labored as I trailed my tongue from the hollow of her neck and up the vein that led to the pulse below her ear.

"Sonia, I want you."

"I would never be able to tell." Her tone was breathy

and sexy. She pushed her ass against my hard-on, grinding and moving with a delicious friction. "Why?" she asked. "Tell me why you want me, Brad."

Soon, I wouldn't be able to make out a coherent word. I flipped her around and held her arms above her head, pushing her against the fish tank. She gasped.

My lips descended on hers, and my thigh pushed her legs apart. "Because you're beautiful and smart."

"That's a generic answer." Her voice was horny and husky. Her hands tightened against my arms as she rode my thigh. "I want more."

"Because I love everything about you. Your work ethic." I lifted her skirt and grabbed her ass. "How you love your family." My lips found the hollow of her neck again. "How you are with my nieces." I pushed at her panties, and she shimmied them down her legs. "How you are when you're with me."

She found the button of my slacks, unzipped me, and grabbed my length. She stroked me from base to tip, and nothing had felt more amazing. I growled into her ear, nipping at her lobe.

"More." Her voice was breathless, hot against my skin.

"I love your sass, your smart mouth." I flicked my tongue over her lips.

We were all hands and lips and tongues and spoken words.

Soon, we were both naked, touching but not going too far. It was the same push and pull we had in the office, teasing yet not going too far.

When I lifted her by the ass, she wrapped her legs around my waist, and I carried her back to my room. I sucked on her breast, and she grabbed the tips of my hair, moaning loudly.

"More," she gasped out.

I bit down on her nipple, just enough for her to feel a tinge of pain but not hard enough to break skin.

"More."

I backed us into my room and kicked the door shut. I gently laid her on the bed and placed her glasses on my nightstand. Her hair was splayed on my gray down comforter, and she'd never looked more magnificent.

I covered her with my body, resting on my elbows. There was no hesitation on my part, no fear that this wouldn't work out because I knew as certain as I was going to wake the next morning that she was it.

The normal need to run and flee was nonexistent.

"You're everything I want and everything I never knew I needed." I pressed my heavy length against her wetness. "Worst part is ... I've wasted all this time searching when you were right here all along."

Our breathing was ragged, our eyes connected as though we'd known all along that this was exactly where we were supposed to be.

She touched my brow and trailed her fingers down my cheek. The gesture was sweet and tender, and I knew before I even entered her that, once we did this, my fate would be sealed. Unshed tears outlined her eyes, and the heat and lust in them transformed into something more—trust. She reached between us and positioned me at her entrance.

"Wait."

I needed a condom. I'd never had sex without a condom. Though I was cleaner than a virgin, got tested monthly, pregnancy and getting some disease scared the shit out of me.

"I'm on the pill," she whispered in my ear.

She released her hold, and our eyes locked. I realized I didn't care because I trusted her, too. I entered her in one swift movement and stilled because her tightness around my shaft felt so damn good.

She shifted below me and sucked in her bottom lip. "Next time, can you wear the Harry Potter glasses?"

I pulled back and studied her face, her features, the way her lips were parted, the way her breathing was labored when I thrust back inside her. "Are you going to pretend I'm Harry when we have sex?"

Her fingernails dug into my ass, and she moaned. "Technically ... I'm legally blind without my glasses, and I can't see a thing, so I can pretend you're whoever I want you to be."

I pushed into her deeper, harder, faster.

She groaned. "I'm kidding." She lifted her head, her eyes heavily lidded, her cheeks flushed. "It's only you. Only you, Brad."

I kissed her with unrelenting passion, and we fell into a delicious tempo of back and forth and push and pull. Every moan was mine. Every word of praise was mine. Every shiver and kiss was mine. I wanted all her pleasure, and in that moment, I knew that no one mattered before her, and there would be no one after her. With every push and pull of our bodies against each other, I knew I loved her, truly, madly, and completely.

A hot tide of passion raged through both of us, and I gave everything to her as she shivered in ecstasy, letting go and screaming my name. I sank deep inside her one last time, clutching her to me as I had my own release.

Moments passed.

There was no itch to leave, no urge to get up and run

like there had been in the past with other women, just an overwhelming need to hold on to her tighter and never let go.

When my heart rate slowed, I opened my eyes and brushed my nose against hers. I kissed her soft and sweet. "I love you." It needed to be said. "So much."

She took one savoring breath and brushed her thumb against my lips.

She didn't respond, so I kissed her again. If she wasn't ready, I'd wait. I'd wait forever for her to feel the same.

I flipped her over, so she was lying on my chest, and we were both breathless and content. I was on the craziest high.

I tightly wrapped both arms around her, and I knew I'd fight differently this time, for her, for us. I had lived my life fighting to win—in games, in arguments, in takeovers with other companies. I'd never fought with something to lose, and holding her in my arms, I knew life would be different. You fought differently when you had something to lose; you fought with every fiber of your being and until your very last breath. I'd fight for her happiness, her joy, her feelings for me.

When the shine of the moon highlighted the curve of her shoulders, it only confirmed that I was truly in love, just how she'd once described it.

"Have you ever been in love? So deeply in love that you want to be with them all the time and the sun rises and sets on their face and they're the last person you want to see at the end of your day?"

Now, I knew what she'd meant weeks ago because I wanted the sun to rise on her face, to see the morning glow on her every feature.

I gently kissed her at her temple because I wanted to

live in this moment, have her in my bed, in my life, and for her to be the last person I saw every single night.

"I love you," I whispered again, now knowing what it felt like and hoping to God I'd never lose it.

CHAPTER 23

BRAD

"Girls," Becky yelled, walking back into the kitchen. "Get down here, please. You're going to be late."

"They're dragging this morning." Charles kissed his wife and continued to make Sarah and Mary's lunches on the kitchen island.

Becky flipped the pancakes on the stove onto the plate already full of eggs and bacon. It was interesting, watching how they moved in domestic completeness, Charles with his sandwich-making skills and Becky with her perfection of the pancake.

Becky was a cook, just like my mother. It was nice, having them home, and I was enjoying being back at home. I'd been spending most of my nights at the condo with Sonia because the things I did to her could not be done in the vicinity of my nieces, my brothers, or sister-in-law.

Truth be told, Sonia was a screamer. There was no doubt, my neighbors heard us multiple times a night. I could tell by the knowing looks in their eyes, the blush in Maria's cheeks when she passed me on the street. They couldn't exactly say anything to me when I owned the whole building.

I flipped through *The Wall Street Journal*, sipping my black coffee. Mason was sitting at the kitchen table, opposite me, reading the same paper, only his coffee was a creamy light brown, full of sugar and milk and more like a dessert. I called it his girlie drink.

My parents had always wanted a girl. They'd prayed, gone to church, promised God things that they couldn't possibly deliver. After Charles and I were born, I had known they were hoping for less testosterone, and they'd gotten it in the form of Mason.

The way he combed his hair, pressed every article of clothing, even his undershirts, and his choice of a margarita over hard liquor or beer proved he was the answer to their prayers. I chuckled, just thinking about it.

My favorite laughter and footsteps echoed from the other room. Sweet Mary was coming. On cue, the table was set—eggs, bacon, and pancakes on every plate—and the lunches were made.

We all sat down together, as a family, which had become our weekly routine. Not every day, not every breakfast or dinner, but at least three to four times a week.

This was what I had missed over the last few weeks when I was spending my time with Sonia. I only realized I'd missed it now that I was here because I'd been consumed by everything that was Sonia, my girlfriend. I was almost tempted to ask her to move in, into this house, so I could have the best of both worlds. But I had guessed it would have come to this eventually, me moving out.

I'd always thought that Mason would be the first to go, marry the gold digger and move out. Who knew what their relationship status was now? I guessed it surprised me that I would move out before him.

"Uncle Brad ..." Mary pouted, swirling her pancake in a pool-sized puddle of syrup. "You haven't been home to tell me the story of the prince and his crown jewels."

Becky spit up her coffee. Mason glared at me.

Charles simply asked, "Crown jewels?"

I'd been telling the same story to Mary for years. Had they never paid attention?

"Yeah, crown jewels." Mary pushed out her lip. "I don't like it when you stay in the city. That's not your home. This is." She crossed her arms over her chest and glared at me, mad like the kitten she was.

"It's different now, Mary. He has a girlfriend now," Sarah added with a smile too happy for her own good.

"Girlfriend? Who? I thought I was the only one who's supposed to be your girlfriend." She slammed her fork against the plate, and I laughed.

Boy, oh boy.

I eyed Charles, and he simply shook his head, amused.

We'd thought that we had issues with Sarah's teenage rebellion. Wait till Mary turned into a teenager. I imagined she would be worse.

Sarah threw Mary an *are you dumb* look. "Sonia? Remember her?"

"Oh." Mary relaxed back against her chair, and her smile resurfaced. "When are we going to have dinner with her here?"

"Soon." I sipped my coffee. "Real soon."

Becky reached over and fixed Mary's white collar on her blue plaid uniform. "Maybe ... if Uncle Brad is up for it, you can go spend the night at his place on a weekend."

Mary sat straighter and bounced in her seat. "Oh. Can I, can I, can I?"

With a nod of my head, I once again had a happy Mary. "Now, go eat your food, sweet Mary. You'll be late."

After breakfast and in typical weekday fashion, we all stood. The girls got their backpacks ready for school. Becky assisted in giving them their lunches. I cleaned up the table. Charles washed the dishes, and Mason loaded the dishwasher. We were a well-oiled, domesticated machine.

The girls made their rounds with good-bye hugs and kisses. When Becky grabbed the keys from Charles, I turned toward him.

"You're not taking the girls to school?"

Because he always took the girls to school, right before driving straight to work. We all drove separately.

"No, Becky will take them." He pecked Becky on the lips before turning to me. "We have to talk."

My spine straightened, and I blinked up at him. I knew who and what this conversation was going to be about. Had they caught us having sex in the utility closet? Or my desk? I swore, my door had been locked. My hands clenched and then unclenched.

Was it my fault that I was in love and addicted to every part of her body?

I'd deny all the sex. We'd be fine. Sonia and I would simply keep it to after-work hours. It was hard, hard being around her and not wanting to be inside her, but I'd make sure things were strictly professional at work, going forward.

"If this is about Sonia, there's nothing to talk about. I'll meet you at work." I reached for my briefcase and turned to leave.

"Brad." One word. Loud. Authoritative. It was the tone he used on the girls, the tone that meant business.

"Yes, Brad, we need to talk. This isn't working out," Mason added. "Everyone at work is talking."

Mason's even tone was my cue to leave. He grated on my nerves. And, to think, we had been getting along.

"I don't care." I was already walking, but he blocked my direct path to the door leading to the garage. I was now sandwiched between both of them.

"Did you really have sex on the copier?" Mason's tone was condescending, and his face scrunched up, disgusted, as though he'd never, ever had sex in the office. "That's crossing the line."

Yes. "No, and if I did, it's my fucking copier. My company. My life." The muscles in my neck tensed, and my hand tightened around my briefcase.

"*Your* company?" Mason chuckled without humor. "That's funny. I think we all have one-third equity share."

I tilted my head from side to side, releasing the tension from my neck. "You'd better stop, Mason. You're pissing me off."

"I'll stop when you fire her," Mason spat out.

That turned a switch in me. I stepped into him, pressing a finger into his chest, eyes narrowed. "Sonia is my concern. Not yours. So, you don't get to decide what happens to her, what she has for lunch, where I take her on dates, and most definitely, *if* she's still working for me, which she still is, by the way."

He glared. "It's too late. You're outnumbered, and we've already decided. We've already hired her replacement."

The air knocked out of my lungs, and I stepped back.

I flipped around and narrowed my eyes at Charles. He never went above me—ever. He'd have discussed it with me first, but decision was written on his features.

My mouth went lax. "Don't I have a say in this,

Charles?" There was no bite in my tone, no strength in my voice. Once Charles made a decision, it was as good as done.

Charles sighed. "Brad, you're not thinking straight. People are talking. This is as much for her as it is for you. Women talk and can get nasty. They're already starting to say she only got where she was by sleeping with the boss."

I cringed. Maybe I'd fire all of them then.

I threw up a hand. "She's been working for me for two years, and she has had the same damn position." I walked to the kitchen and dropped to the chair, already tired. "Who? I want names." No one could talk about Sonia like that. "Names. Because they're fired."

"See? See how stupid you're being?" Mason shook his head, as if he was exasperated with me.

"Mason," Charles scolded in his fatherly tone, "stop."

Then, Charles's attention was thrown back my way. "You know this isn't going to work. How are you going to give the woman you love her annual review?"

"Based on how many times she gives him head," Mason muttered, and I wanted to fucking throw him through a window.

"Mason, just get out." Charles pointed sternly to the door. "If you can't be an adult about this, just get the hell out and go to work."

"I can be civil," Mason said quietly like a chastised child. He dropped to the seat opposite me at the kitchen table.

He was here for the show. *Damn bastard.*

"Brad, listen ... this is for the best. Deep down, you know it is." Charles placed a heavy hand on my shoulder, but it wasn't the strength of his arm that weighed me down; it was the enormity of the truth.

When Sonia was around, all I could think about was being near her, inside her. With her, my normal work ethics were thrown out the door.

"I promised I wouldn't fire her. I promised her nothing between us would change." I begged him with my eyes.

"But it has, little brother. It has changed. It changed the moment you fell in love with her." Charles was always the one to tell it how it was, straightforward and honest, just as he saw it.

I rubbed one hand down my face, knowing he was right.

"It's fine. I have the perfect solution," Mason added. "I've already set things in motion."

∼

Sonia

I strolled to my desk from the elevator. It took every ounce of energy not to skip all the way to work and look like a happily-in-love dope. Because, yes, I was happily in love with the BILK turned BILF—which I did multiple times a day.

I hadn't told him yet, knowing, once I said it, I couldn't take it back. A part of me was afraid, of giving myself so fully. But everything with Brad felt so right, so real, so forever.

If someone had told me months ago that I'd fall in love with Brad, I'd have denied it and bet my life savings and 401(k), too, that it would never, ever happen.

But yet, here I was.

Le sigh.

If there were a cloud nine, I was on cloud one million. Every morning was brighter, and my mood could not be dimmed, no matter how crappy my day was going. Traffic? No problem. Schedule gone wrong? Not a big deal.

This was the feeling of being in love—utter, true love. And I was here. In the present, working the best job I had with the perks of seeing my beloved day in and day out, in and out of work.

Tonight, we were having a Harry Potter marathon at my place. I was beyond excited, still in crazy awe that Brad hadn't watched a single movie.

The stack of boxes placed by my desk made me skip to a stop. I tilted my head, taking in Phala, an intern for Mason. Her stick-straight Asian hair lay by her shoulders. She spoke with a little lilt in her voice, her natural intonation, to match her petite frame and small features.

"Sonia?" Her eyes went wide. "I thought ... I thought ..." If her eyes widened any farther, her eyeballs would pop out of their sockets.

"Whose boxes are these?" I walked around to see two more boxes on the floor. "Are these Brad's?" Did he have extra files laying around that I didn't know about?

"No ... I ... uh ..." Phala's cheeks burned bright enough to almost rival the red on her lips.

I blinked and noted a plant placed on top of the boxes —*her* bamboo plant. The one I'd seen on the third floor, on her own desk, by Mason's office.

An intense ringing initiated in my ears, the kind that I knew would blow up, bomb-style, soon, real soon. Call it premonition.

I carefully framed my next words. "These are your boxes." My voice came out so softly, I doubted she heard. When her gaze drifted to the floor, my chest seized, and I gripped the desk for support. "It is, right?" I spoke louder this time. "Phala! Are these your boxes or not?"

When she tipped her chin, I exhaled, feeling as though someone had knocked me on my ass, yet I was still standing.

I stared at the desk, the clean lines of my tape dispenser, right by my stapler, right by my phone. My desk. A desk I had spent the last two years working at.

This couldn't be Brad. This had to be Charles. I'd broken my part of our agreement, and this was the consequence. *Or is this Brad's decision? Did he know? Was he already tired of me, just as he had been of the other women before me?*

But this was different. Between Brad and me, it was different. He'd promised. He'd said he loved me.

I swallowed hard, heat burning my eyes. *Breathe.*

But there was no point. I clutched my chest and rocked back, resting on my heels.

Phala's arms wrapped around me, hard and tight. Though I didn't know her that well, I rested against her, using her body to keep me upright.

"I thought you were smarter than this, Sonia." Her tone was apologetic, sad even.

I pulled back and swiped at my tears. Anger replaced the unbearable sadness as I reeled back, and with a firm voice, I asked, "What is that supposed to mean?"

She twisted her hands and fidgeted with the edge of her silk shirt, staring at her pointy red shoes that matched her ruby-red lipstick.

"Speak, Phala. What do you mean?"

She spoke to her shoes as though the pair had asked her the question, "You of all people know how Brad is. How he treats women. You know how many women have gone through that door." She motioned at his office door. "And out the company door. You warned everyone who walked through his office."

I stepped into her, eyes burning with a fury that churned in my gut. "You don't understand a single thing," I promised. Because she didn't. Brad and I had made love yesterday and the day before and the day before that. How he felt for me was different.

But it was her look. The same look I'd given other interns and account reps. And hadn't they told me the same thing? Hadn't they told me what they had with Brad was special?

I staggered back, and both hands flew to my chest.

Is this time different? Am I just another girl to him? Was he already bored? My mind was a tornado of thoughts, pulling me every way possible.

"Does he know?" I rubbed at my forehead and took deep breaths, feeling the walls of my world closing in. *Isn't this exactly where I was with Jeff? Right here, thinking he loved me all along, but really, he was screwing my replacement at his office.*

I shook my head. The need to get out of this horrid place was unbearable.

"Does he know?" I blinked up at her through clouded irises. "Does he know that you're his new secretary?"

She nodded again in confirmation, and that was when I ran. To the elevators, out of the building, to my car and straight to my apartment.

The tears were hot and heavy and endless. When Jeff had done what he did, I'd sworn I'd never end up here again, never be that girl again ... and yet, here I was.

∼

Brad

"What do you mean, she just left?" I stared at Phala, a former intern of ours because, after this, she was definitely fired. By me.

She stood there, teetering in her four-inch heels, looking anywhere but at my face.

"Brad, chill out. It's not her fault," Mason added, not making it better.

"And these?" I pointed to a stack of boxes by my Sonia's desk. "What the hell are these?"

"Boxes?" Her voice was timid and unsure, and she searched Mason's face for answers.

"Why are you moving in now?" Mason asked. "I said the sixteenth."

She blinked, doe-eyed and clueless. "I thought you said the sixth."

Fuck. My muscles tensed, and I gritted my teeth. I was so fucking livid. "Smart move there, Mason." I pinched the bridge of my nose and took deep breaths, willing the blood boiling in my veins to chill.

"It was a simple mistake," Mason said, though his voice was without its usual authoritative flare.

I pushed my finger against his chest, using all my restraint to keep steady. "If she fucking takes this out on me, I'm taking this out on you. If she fucking leaves me for this ... you are a dead man." I pushed a finger in his face. "Dead." Then, I turned to Phala. "And you're fired."

Mason opened his mouth to speak, but I shut him up real fast. "Don't even think of it. Since I'm not sticking my dick in anyone but Sonia, my previous secretary issues are no longer a concern."

I stormed out of there, running to the elevators, out the building, and driving to her place.

The doorman let me up, and I banged on her door, relentless, pounding like it was a punching bag. She hadn't been picking up my calls, and I expected her to be an angry, hell-raising mess, but when she opened the door, her face was eerily calm.

I stepped into her place, and immediately, I dropped to my knees. "I'm sorry. Mason and Charles didn't even consult me."

She lifted a shoulder, unaffected, and averted her gaze, walking farther into the apartment while I pushed myself to stand.

Her indifference gutted me. If she didn't care about her job and could leave work altogether, maybe it would be that easy for her to walk away from me. I wanted her angry or even upset because that would only prove that she was as affected by this as I was.

"I want you to know I had nothing to do with it. I'll find you another job." I reached for her, but she flinched, and I dropped my hand. A deep, dire desperation I'd never felt coursed through my veins. "I love you, Sonia. I won't let this get between us."

She walked toward the other side of the room, arms crossed over her chest. I couldn't read her face or see her eyes, my guide to know how she was really feeling.

"I can't afford this place anymore." She spoke quietly, mostly to herself.

"Move in with me then." I didn't hesitate when the words fell out of my mouth. I didn't even flinch or second-guess what that entailed. I had hopped on the love train, running full speed ahead, and there was no stopping now.

She flipped around, her hands fisted at her sides, eyes blazing. "Don't say stuff you don't mean."

Yes! A reaction. I'd take it.

"I mean every word."

Where her features hardened, mine softened. Where she tensed up, I eased up and stepped into her. I wouldn't touch her until she was ready, though my need to touch her was unbearable.

She shut her eyes and shook her head as though she were trying to shake things off in her head. "Stop, Brad. Just stop." She hugged her stomach, her gaze dropping to the ground. "Please. Just stop."

Stop what? Stop being with her? I couldn't do that.

"Why?" I swallowed, my voice emotionally choked. I took another step closer, needing to be nearer.

"Because ..." She trembled and gripped herself tighter as though she were trying to keep herself upright. "Because I want to stop believing you."

I pulled her in by her waist, unable to resist the urge any longer despite whether she rejected me or not. She fell into me, and I promised myself I wasn't going to let her go.

"Believe it. Because it's true. All of it."

She buried her head in my throat, and she shivered. "I'm scared," she whispered, true and honest and one of the very reasons I adored her.

"Do you think I'm not? I'm scared about every little move I make. I'm scared that one stupid, idiotic move could ruin what's happening between us."

She lifted her head, searching my face.

"I'm not talking other women or things like that because, believe me when I tell you, no one has captured my heart like you have." My hand went to cup her cheek, and I grazed my thumb against her cheekbone. "I'm talking about your job, what I've been saying to my brothers, what I'm saying right now. Asking you to move in with me. Knowing it sounds crazy and not caring that it does. Because it's what I want, what I want you to want. Worrying about saying how I feel because it might be too much. It might push you away."

Her eyebrows pulled together, her look pensive. "I've been here before. And it didn't pan out, and I'm scared to do it again because, this time, our relationship is moving faster. It feels different, deeper." She released a breath. "I knew there was so much at stake when I took the leap into us. My job at first, but now, it's more than that." She shuddered against my hold. "I don't give my heart easily. The last time I did, I was heartbroken."

I hated that she was comparing me to that asshole of an ex. I would've never let Sonia go if I'd had her then, and I sure as hell wasn't letting go of her now.

I'd remembered our conversation after the wedding ceremony where she had seen Jeff for the first time and cried in my car.

"I mean, why should you care? It's over."

She'd responded with my question with such honesty that I truly understood only now because I was in love. *"You wouldn't know anything about this because you've never, ever been in love before or had an it person."*

Sonia was my *it* person. Now and until forever. I knew this with everything that I was. And, as far as I was concerned, I was *it* for her, too. I'd prove it to her day in and out because nothing mattered more than being together.

And the thought ... the thought of losing her ... having her walk away from us ...

I swallowed.

"I've never done this before either. I'm scared shitless,

but more than that ... I'm more scared to live without you." My voice was fragile, shaky, honest.

She rested her forehead against mine and let out a deep breath. "Same. That's the scariest part of being in love, one day living without the other person."

"Love? Not being together is never going to happen." My insides soared. "Say it again. That you're in love."

She laughed, and it eased every part of me. "You're such a narcissist, you know that?"

"Say it." I pulled her in, staring down into eyes I'd grown to know so much.

"I love you, jerk." Her tone was teasing but tender, and I knew she meant it.

"Say you'll move in with me."

"It's too soon!"

"Who says? The rules in the dating handbook?" The look I gave her was skeptical.

"Me. My dad. My mom. Probably your brothers. Ava ..." She tilted her head, mulling something over. "Well, not Ava. She'd help me move in."

"And who the fuck cares what people think? The only thing that matters is, what you want and what I want. So ... what do you want, Sonia?"

I held my breath while the seconds ticked by. She held my happiness in her one-word answer.

She swallowed hard as she thought of it. "I don't have a job."

Boy, she was reaching far, thinking of every possible reason she shouldn't move in with me.

"I'll employ you." I grabbed her ass. "As my personal sex slave."

She laughed again, and it was the most glorious sound.

"You'll have to insure a certain body part then. Jennifer Lopez insured her butt. It's possible."

I grabbed a handful of ass, and she yelped. "I can make that happen."

I lifted her in my arms, and her legs wrapped around my waist. I guessed I was going to be late to work. I might not show up to work at all. "I think I might insure every part of you—your lips, your ass, your beautiful hair."

"My hair?" She touched the top of her head, smiling.

"I love your hair. Your arms, your hands, your toes."

She giggled as my lips went to the crook of her neck.

"Your neck."

I stopped a few steps from entering her room. "Is that ... is that my poster?"

The life-sized poster that had previously been her dartboard was on the floor. My formerly darted face was now sliced into shreds. A knife lay on the carpet, right by the poster.

"And here I thought, you weren't upset." I laughed. "A knife, Sonia?"

She bit her bottom lip, looking sheepish. "I couldn't find a pair of scissors."

"Remind me to never piss you off."

She wiggled in my arms and angled closer to lick the shell of my ear. "Are you going to kiss me, or are we going to continue talking about your poster?"

Fuck. Game over.

I leaned into her, met her lips with mine, carried her into her bedroom, and shut the door behind us.

EPILOGUE

Three Months Later
Sonia

"Brad, where are the tickets?" I was elbow deep in a plastic bag, which was supposed to contain all the Harry Potter items that we were supposed to put in the girls' gift bags for their secret surprise.

"Tickets?" He peered up at me from our leather couch.

I tasked him with making it every morning, and he still needed reminding.

As my former boss, he was disorganized. As my boyfriend, his discombobulation had doubled.

"The tickets. You bought them. You opened the mail. Now, where did you put them?" I stood and placed my hands on my hips.

"Look at you." He smirked. "All trying to pretend you're angry at me."

And, just like that, I laughed because that was how our relationship went. Endless laugher, lots of alone time, but enough big family time. And lots and lots of sex.

He pushed himself off the couch and pulled me in by

the waist, his one arm snaking around my lower back. He looped his pointer finger at my neckline, peeking in my shirt. "I think I left them here. Guess not." His lips fell to my neck, licking a path to the shell of my ear. "I wonder where they could be." Then, his fingers trailed down my arm to my ass. "Maybe they're right here." His hand skimmed my hip, moving to my stomach and trailing farther down. "Or here," he said, his voice husky.

He lifted me by the ass, and automatically, my legs wrapped around his waist.

"We're going to be late." My voice was a breathless whisper against his skin.

"So?"

His lips made their way back to the crook of my neck, and I arched into him, feeling an ache of want and need and desire coursing through me. I had turned into an insatiable beast.

"We have tickets to the play tonight. We can't be late." My fingers threaded through his hair, my breasts pushing hard against his chest. All of this was for nothing. My mouth said one thing, but my body screamed for another. "Brad ..."

"We have time." His mouth descended on mine, slow and seductive, and I was already a goner as he led us to our bedroom.

Yes, ours.

Two hours later, we emerged, completely satisfied and showered and in the car, on our way to our other home to see the girls.

The palatial mansion came into view, and after we parked in the front, I gripped the girls' bags in my hands. From Hogwarts T-shirts to bobbleheads to socks and scarves and necklaces, I'd filled the bag with all sorts of Harry

Potter goodies to match our super-secret surprise. Harry Potter, the Broadway play, was in town for a few days. Brad had scored rock-star center-row seats, which had cost a pretty penny. Not only did he spoil his nieces, but Brad's whole purpose in life—so he'd said—was to spoil me as well because he loved me. And also because I gave him sexual favors daily, sometimes twice daily, three times on weekends.

He held my free hand as we sauntered toward the garage, entered the code on the keypad, and walked right in. The scent of steak and potatoes and something sweet filtered through my senses.

"Honey, I'm home," Brad announced.

We were bombarded with squeals of a little five-year-old. Mary rammed into me, arms around my center, and I laughed.

"Wait a minute," Brad said, stepping away. "Wait a minute here." He pointed between the two of us as Mary still clung to my side. "What's going on here?"

Although Brad was joking, I could sense the jealousy in his eyes.

"Do you have a new favorite? Sweet Mary, have I been replaced?"

Her eyes went wide, guilt clouding her precious features, and she bum-rushed him next. Brad scooped her up in his arms, and he was awarded with tiny Woody Woodpecker kisses on his cheeks.

I placed the gift bags on the floor, next to the door, and walked farther into the kitchen. In typical weekend fashion, Becky was making dinner, Mason was on the computer at the table, and Charles was setting the table.

"How can I be of service?" I gave Becky a little side hug and then proceeded to hug the boys.

"Oh, I just put the steak in the oven. It should be done pretty soon."

I made my rounds, taking in the scene, my weekend normal scene. It was crazy how my life could change in an instant, in a matter of months.

This was now my extended family, one that had blended into my biological family. Everyone had already met in the short time Brad and I'd been together.

Becky insisted that she hosted one of our monthly family dinners. I guessed she wasn't prepared for my big and rambunctious Italian family, who brought over their homemade pasta for the event. There was an abundance of leftovers for the whole week after.

"Sonia, that meeting on Monday morning with Tyson Papers is canceled." Mason peered up from his computer, smiling, before dropping his head back to the screen.

"No talking about work after work." Brad slipped an arm around my waist and tucked me against him, my favorite spot in the whole world. "Or else I demand you give my girlfriend a raise for working after hours."

"I should give her a raise for dealing with your dumba— ankle," Mason said, throwing Mary a smile.

Right after I'd been fired, Mason had called me, apologized up and down for the Phala debacle, and offered me a secretary job since his secretary never came back from maternity leave. I wasn't sure if I should take it, given that I was banging my former boss, who happened to be his brother, who happened to own the company.

But, after some persuasion on Charles and Mason and Brad's part, I'd agreed, and I couldn't be happier. Being a secretary was my calling. I was an organized freak, a match to Mason's style, and I had enjoyed my job of playing Tetris with schedules and keeping everyone on task.

Mason was the opposite of Brad. He was organized, focused, and strictly business. Yes, he was neurotic and a complainer, especially about my boyfriend, whom I adored. I didn't take his jabs so easily when he talked about Brad, but that was tame, and the rest of his craziness I could handle. Mason and I were a perfect match in secretary-boss heaven.

Dinner was set on the table, and once everyone was seated, Mary held Brad and my hands, leading the prayer of grace. She insisted on sitting in between us, her usual spot. And, when Mary slept over, she'd sleep in between us, too.

"Sarah, phone down." Charles threw her that fatherly look, the one that brooked no arguments.

She huffed, teenager-style, sticking her fork in a potato wedge in front of her.

"Sarah has a boyfriend," Mary cooed.

"Shut up." Sarah glared.

"Sarah ..." Becky began.

"You have a boyfriend?" Mason's tone turned incredulous. "Is that even allowed?" His eyes made their way to Charles. "Didn't you set rules for Sarah?"

"Can we just eat?" Charles asked, avoiding the topic.

This was the normal banter between the brothers. Mason overanalyzing, Charles serious and wanting to stick to the task, and then my boyfriend, who did everything to annoy Mason.

"I don't have a boyfriend," Sarah argued.

Mason's shoulders relaxed. "Well then, there's nothing to talk about."

"She's going to date. She's a teenager," Brad added, baiting his brother the only way he knew how.

"Not for a while. A long while." Mason glared, his stare flickering between Brad and his teenage niece.

"Sarah, are you interested in a boy?" Brad asked.

"I'm not answering that question," Sarah moaned, not looking up, but the blush on her cheeks answered for her.

"You are. Aren't you?" Brad placed down his fork and rested his elbows on the table. "Come on, now. We're family. There's nothing to be embarrassed about."

All eyes were on Sarah now.

Her eyebrows squeezed together. "Uh ..." Her voice trailed off as though she were debating on what to say. She peered down at her uneaten food, tightly squeezed her eyes shut, and then blurted, "Yes. I'm kind of talking to someone right now."

Brad leaned back on his chair, watching with too much amusement as Mason's eyes went wide.

Funny how everyone, even Becky and Charles, was perfectly calm, but Mason ... he paled.

"You're too young." His eyebrow twitched, and he stared at her as though she were a foreign object.

"I'll be thirteen in a few months."

"So?" Mason argued, dropping his fork, making it clatter against the china.

"All right. All right." Charles raised a hand, defusing the escalating situation. "How about we just calm down and eat dinner?" He stared at his firstborn, dropped his gaze, and then stared at her some more.

"She's talking to someone? What exactly does that mean?" Mason asked to no one in particular.

Oh boy, he was going to have issues with Sarah growing up. I bit my lip to hide my smile.

"Mason," Charles said, exasperated. "Talking means talking. Not dating."

The rest of dinner was uneventful, silent even. Not the

normal, boisterous laughter that was usually the norm at the Brisken dinner table. Even Mary was silent.

"Can I be excused?" Sarah asked when her dinner plate was empty.

"One second." Brad stood. "We have something we've got to announce. A surprise of sorts."

Everyone automatically looked at my left finger, and for a moment, the tiniest of moments, my stomach dropped. *Will he?*

But then he plucked the tickets to the show from his pocket, and the whole table, Charles and Becky included, exhaled.

It wasn't like I wasn't ready. But it had only been a few months, and, yes, I'd thought of forever with Brad. I was a forever type of girl. I liked monogamy. Still, we were fairly new. Going from hating his guts to not being able to live without him was life-changing.

"Because I'm the best uncle and Sonia is the best auntie, we have a just-because surprise for our favorite nieces." He grinned, loving every second of this.

"We're your only nieces," Mary said, making the table laugh.

"Sweet Mary, did you want me to give your Harry Potter ticket to Sarah's new boyfriend?"

Both of the girls jumped to their feet. Sarah rushed to Brad's side, and he lifted the tickets over his head.

"Are those for the Harry Potter play?" Sarah squealed, jumping to reach for the tickets. "They were sold out. Daddy said so."

"Wait. Hold on a second." Brad tipped his chin toward me, and I walked to the door, returning to the kitchen with the two gift bags full of goodies.

"Yes. We got tickets." I lifted the bags and shook them in front of me. "And presents!"

The girls squealed and hugged me and then Brad. The gift bags were dumped on the floor, and they sorted through all their belongings like stray dogs in a garbage can.

"You think they're excited?" Brad whispered, bringing me closer.

"No. What would give you that indication?" I teased, smiling as I drank up the girls' joy.

"I love just-because surprises." He slipped his arms around my waist, nuzzling my ear. "Do you want yours?"

I turned my head, staring up at mischievous brown eyes. "What?"

"Girls, it's time." Brad nodded toward the girls, and they scurried out of the room.

"Time for what?" My eyes widened as Becky came in with an oversize gift bag with a Harry Potter stuffed animal peeking through the top.

Then, the girls came in, holding two separate signs on blank white poster board.

I peered back at Brad, wondering what the heck was going on.

Mary turned over her sign that said ... *Will you ...*

I held my breath.

No freaking way.

It was too soon. Plus, his family was here, and it wasn't fair that mine wasn't.

Then, Sarah took three sidesteps away from Mary and flipped over her sign, which read, *Me?*

Will you ... me?

The world stood utterly still, and I stopped breathing altogether.

"Brad?" My eyes went wide as I watched him walk toward the end and grab another sign from Mason.

He stood directly in between Mary and Sarah.

Shit. Shit. Shit. This is it.

Mary stepped forward. *Will you ...*

Then, Brad flipped over his sign, which read, *Go to Harry Potter world with ...*

Then, Sarah stepped forward with her sign. *Me?*

A sharp and unexpected disappointment flooded my veins. A disappointment that I hadn't known existed before this moment. It took a moment to collect myself and force a smile on my face.

Then, Charles pulled a sign from his back. *And us?*

My hands flew to my mouth, and that instant disappointment was replaced with a giddiness.

Everyone was going.

"Of course! I've never been to The Wizarding World of Harry Potter"

The girls rushed toward me, squeezing me in between them in a human sandwich, and I basked in the love of my nieces.

I couldn't hide my excitement as I jumped up and down with Sarah and Mary, staring at the love of my life with adoration and thankfulness. We'd been planning on how to surprise the girls with the tickets to the play when, all along, he had been making arrangements to surprise me.

After opening my bag of goodies with my very own wand, I turned to Brad, who snuggled next to me.

"The whole family?" I asked. I didn't think Brad liked to share.

"Yeah, I hope that's okay." His hands wrapped around my waist. "I did go to Medieval Times with yours."

He had, but this was different. This was a trip—shared

hotel rooms and breakfasts, lunches, and dinners all together.

"Is it too soon?" I asked before I could hold it back.

"Too soon? No. It's too slow if you ask me. We've integrated our big families nicely together. There's just one last thing to do."

I lifted an eyebrow.

"What?" He laughed. "Don't look at me like that. I saw your face when the girls busted out the white boards. You thought I was going to ask you *the* question."

I covered his lips with my hand. "No, I didn't," I lied.

He gripped my hand and tenderly kissed the inside of my palm. "Don't worry. I've got plans for you and me, the forever-and-ever and death-till-we-part kind."

This was my life now.

Entirely happy.

Entirely blissful.

Entirely in love.

Brad had unlocked my heart and soul, and he was the only one who had a key.

This time, I couldn't hide a thing. My smile was blinding.

Did you love Brad and Sonia's journey to finding love? Keep reading to find out about my Amazon Bestselling Romance - MARRY ME FOR MONEY.

PROLOGUE
Marry Me for Money

The woman was beautiful. She looked like a supermodel ready to walk the runway. The blackest of black eyelashes swept upward, accenting the depths of her emerald eyes. Curls of mahogany sat on top of her head while the apple of her cheeks were highlighted with a slight pink as if the sun had kissed her.

I should have been excited. I should have been anxious.

But as my heartbeat thrashed in my ears, all I felt was dread.

I sat on the stool, staring at the girl in the mirror. I wondered who this girl was. I wondered where the old girl had gone and how I could get her back. The problem was I couldn't. The lie was so deep, the charade so long that there was nowhere else to go, but to move forward.

It was an out-of-body experience as the chaos of the circus around me was happening. I hardly noticed the woman in front of me as she swished her little brush of pink gloss on my pouty lips.

Everybody was getting ready for the big day.

My big day.

Four photographers were scattered around the room, catching every moment and every detail from the shoes to the invitation to the flowers.

Orchids.

Orchids didn't give off a scent like every other flower. Too much water would drown them. Not enough sunlight would kill them. They were useless and high maintenance.

So, when the florist had asked me what kind of flowers I would like for my bouquet, I'd said, "Orchids."

It was the flower I despised the most. It wasn't because of its lack of beauty or its uselessness, but I didn't want anything that I would pick for my real day.

The photographers moved to the king-sized bed, and they snapped pictures of the regal designer wedding gown. This was another thing I never would have picked for myself. I remembered my last fitting. I had barely squeezed into the strapless couture dress. I would never choose a dress that I couldn't walk, dance, or eat in. I hated it, and that was the reason I'd picked it.

My stomach growled from starvation. I had no appetite the night before, and today Kendy, my maid of honor, wouldn't allow me to eat. It was so unlike her. I guessed it was for my benefit because I could barely fit into my dress. Either way, my stomach was eating itself because it had nothing else to feed off of.

The time went by slowly as if it were dragging on purpose to punish me for living the biggest lie of my life. Everyone always said their wedding day had flown by. This day was killing me, killing me softly and slowly.

All I wanted was for it to be over, but the day had just begun.

I took a deep breath and closed my eyes. *If I can only get through this day...this one day...*

I just needed to get through today.

Pick up your copy of Marry Me For Money today!

You can find it at http://bit.ly/AMAZONMMFM

Click to the next page to find a sneak peak into Mason's story.

STAY IN TOUCH

Thank you so much for reading BOSS I LOVE TO HATE. There are a ton of books to read out there, but you have chosen to spend your time with mine.
And for that...I appreciate you.

Brad and Sonia will be stopping by in Mason's story. Stay tuned because big things are planned for my new favorite couple.

Sign up to receive my newsletter and a bonus scene from Mason's book. Click here to download —>http://bit.ly/2UsJNDH

Here's where you can find me. Join my reader group to stay in the loop about my most recent books.

JOIN MY READER GROUP
WEBPAGE
FACEBOOK

STAY IN TOUCH

TWITTER
INSTAGRAM
GOODREADS
AMAZON
BOOKBUB

ACKNOWLEDGMENTS

And so....

Another book is under my belt. Wooo hooo!

Thank you God for my vivid imagination and creative mind that allows me to produce these stories so that I can entertain.

Release month is hectic and as I sit here, at Starbucks I realize that I haven't seen my family all day. I left at five in the morning to go to my day job and straight to Starbucks to work on this release. So you know who is manning the house full of girls? The Hubs. So I should thank him, right? It's the wifely thing to do.

To the hubs—Thank you for dealing with my issues on a daily basis, packing my lunch everyday and loving me unconditionally even when I'm a brat. I swear, if I ever get rich and famous or win the lotto, I'm retiring him.

It takes a team to get this done and I want to thank everyone that has helped me make this book the best it can be.

To my writer friends who listen to me vent daily and

help me promote — To Michelle, Tracey, Danielle, Jaimie, Erica, Jenny and Kristy L. True loyal writer friends are hard to find. I only have a few and I'm keeping you close and never letting go.

To every DND author and Support! author that has answered my questions and let me pop in their group —thank you.

To my beta readers—To Michelle, Kristy, Alyssa, Megan, and Amy. Thank you for your honest feed back and helping me in strengthening the story. You guys spent the time out of your day to read, analyze and answer all my questions and I appreciate you. To Elizabeth and Norma, thank you for being my 'last look' before it went out to the world.

To my family at Do Not Disturb Book Club and Support!. Thanks for giving me a place to meet new readers, share my ARCs and answer all my questions. To Kate for doing my amazing teasers, I heart you.

To my PA—Elizabeth, you keep me organized and sane and happy. I appreciate everything you do for me.

To my developmental editor, Megan— I heart you so much. So much! Thank you for helping me flesh out these characters and for always being honest with me even when the truth hurts. And now that you've left me, I feel lost. You had to have another baby, didn't you? And she's beautiful just like her mama.

To my cover designer—Juliana, you've got talent and so much patience. Thank you for putting up with me and my stunning cover.

To Kate—Thank you for doing my teasers. They're perfect.

To the bloggers that have consistently supported me

from my very first book to now. I heart you! Thank you for following me on this journey.

Last but not least to my readers— From those who have followed me from my very first book and to the new readers, thank you! thank you! thank you! I write for you.

ALSO BY MIA KAYLA

The Torn Duet

Search Mia Kayla on Amazon to go to my author's page and find out more about my books.

Torn Between Two - Book 1

Choosing Forever - Book 2

The Forever After Series

Marry Me for Money - Forever After Book 1

Love After Marriage - Forever After Book 2

The Scheme - Brian's book - Forever After Book 3

Naughty Not Nice - Forever After Book 4

Stand Alone

Everything Has Changed

Unraveled